FORGOTTEN SINS

After Lizzie Caulder saves Richard Gregory from drowning, he falls in love with her and proposes marriage. Lizzie finds herself swept into the glamour of 1920s high society—and into the heart of the family who had rejected her parents years before. She meets Henry, her grandfather and comes to see Pentire, Henry's gracious home, as her own. Then the calm world of Pentire is rocked when Lizzie's life is endangered by 'accidents' and her cousin Caroline also appears under threat. Are they both the target of some malicious enemy of Henry's. Or could the truth be much closer to home ...?

FORGOTTEN SINS

by
Emma Quincey

Magna Large Print Books
Long Preston, North Yorkshire,
England.

British Library Cataloguing in Publication Data.

Quincey, Emma
   Forgotten sins.

A catalogue record for this book is
available from the British Library

ISBN 0-7505-1362-4

First published in Great Britain by Judy Piatkus (Publishers)
Ltd., 1997

Published in Large Print 1999 by arrangement with Piatkus
Books Ltd.

Magna Large Print is an imprint of
Library Magna Books Ltd.
Printed and bound in Great Britain by
T.J. International Ltd., Cornwall, PL28 8RW.

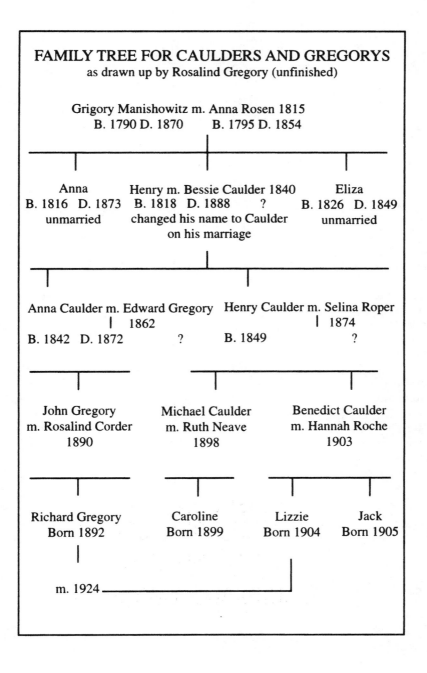

FAMILY TREE FOR CAULDERS AND GREGORYS
as drawn up by Rosalind Gregory (unfinished)

Grigory Manishowitz m. Anna Rosen 1815
B. 1790 D. 1870   B. 1795 D. 1854

Anna	Henry m. Bessie Caulder 1840	Eliza
B. 1816 D. 1873	B. 1818 D. 1888 ?	B. 1826 D. 1849
unmarried	changed his name to Caulder	unmarried
	on his marriage	

Anna Caulder m. Edward Gregory   Henry Caulder m. Selina Roper
| 1862 | 1874
B. 1842 D. 1872   ?   B. 1849   ?

John Gregory	Michael Caulder	Benedict Caulder
m. Rosalind Corder	m. Ruth Neave	m. Hannah Roche
1890	1898	1903

Richard Gregory	Caroline	Lizzie	Jack
Born 1892	Born 1899	Born 1904	Born 1905

m. 1924

Part One

WINSPEAR

Chapter 1

The rooks have come back to nest for the first time since it happened. Perhaps it is an omen, a sign—but whether of good or evil I cannot say. I know only that my life has for too long been overshadowed by a darkness that hovers at the edges of my mind like a creeping mist, ready to sweep in and engulf me.

Today, soon after it began to get light, I was wakened from a haunting dream by the sound of the birds outside my window; their raucous calls drew me from my bed just as they had the morning I first came to this house. Today, as then, I was caught by the view—the restless, ever-changing surface of the lake, sometimes silver, sometimes grey—and the woods.

Dark and dense, they have a brooding menace that can strike a chill into my soul even after all these months. Yet it was not always so. There was a time when I loved to walk in the dappled shade of those trees, when there were no shadows, no fears or bad memories, to set the shivers running down my spine.

Was what happened my fault? I have wondered ... blamed myself. If I had been less of an innocent, less naive ... but the tension and the hatred was already there, simmering beneath the surface. Perhaps it was inevitable that such intense passions would erupt one day.

9

And yet it might all have been different. When I remember, when I think of how it began, I cannot help wondering what would have happened if I had not stopped to watch the swans that afternoon ...

It had been hot coming home on the bus, which was stuffy and overcrowded with shoppers. My mind was still filled with the bustle and colour of Norwich market, so I was glad of a few minutes to stand by the river and watch as a family of mute swans glided by. There were two pure white adults and five fluffy, brownish-looking cygnets; the proud, protective parents hissed in passing as if to prevent me from approaching too close.

Smiling inwardly, I lifted my face to the sky, appreciating the kiss of the sun. It was peaceful on the grassy bank and cooler than it had been earlier, a breeze teasing strands of fine, light brown hair from my brow. I breathed deeply, conscious of a sense of tranquillity and wanting to prolong it for as long as possible. My throat was dry and I was more than ready for a cold drink, but even the thought of Maggie's delicious home-made lemon barley was not enough to make me turn away from the peace of the river. If my father was still in the same mood he had been in that morning ...

'Stop feeling sorry for yourself, Lizzie Caulder!' I chided myself aloud. I did not want to think about Ben or his moods just yet. Here by the river I was free, and there was no need to return to the house for a while.

My gaze wandered over the familiar scene,

10

alighting here and there like a butterfly seeking nectar. A little further down the river bank the ruins of an old water mill were besieged by a tangle of overgrown bushes; once prosperous, the mill had fallen into decay with the coming of the industrial age but despite the neglect it had a haunting beauty, and I thought that perhaps I would try to sketch it one day.

All at once, I caught sight of something moving amongst the bushes. The whole area had been fenced off because the river bank was dangerous just there. Surely no one had been foolish enough to clamber over the barrier? But there it was again, that flash of white.

It was a man. I could see him clearly now. He had climbed over the wire to get a better view of the mill and was taking photographs of the wheel, treading perilously close to the crumbling edge of the banks.

Suddenly I was overcome by a terrible sense of fear that caught at my throat, almost suffocating me; I'd experienced sensations like this twice in my life before and I knew that something bad was about to happen.

'Take care!' I cried. 'The mill pool is deep ...'

A child had fallen in a few years previously and been drowned. My head was whirling with pictures, unclear visions, and a premonition of tragedy. This man was going to die! Hot and cold shivers began to run down my spine.

'Be careful!'

The photographer could not hear my warning —or if he did chose to ignore it in pursuit of his pictures. The sensation of impending doom was so strong now that I could feel it in my throat; it was choking me ... unbearable. I dropped my shopping basket and started running as the man gave a cry and I saw the earth crumble away beneath his feet. He was falling, slipping, pitching into the murky waters of the pool; I saw him strike his head against the huge wheel before he went into the water. He was going to drown!

There was no time to think, no time to consider my own safety. I kicked off my shoes and dived straight into the black depths of the deep pool, something I should never have dreamed of doing normally despite being a strong swimmer and having had special lessons in life-saving at school—my mother had insisted on it because we lived so near to the river and both my brother and I had always been too adventurous for our own good.

The water was shockingly cold, making me gasp as I surfaced and drew breath. Where was he? Had he gone straight down? Could I find him in this deep, dark water?

I floundered about searching frantically for a sight of him. My dress clung about my legs, hampering my progress, but I hadn't had time to take it off, even if it had occurred to me to do so—which it hadn't. Like my mother before me, I was inclined to act on impulse, to leap first and think afterwards—just as well for the stranger since I'd always had a horror of the pool and the remembered tragedy of a child's cruel death.

Now I saw the man. He had been fortunate. His pale jacket had ballooned out around him, trapping air beneath it and acting like a float, saving him from sinking immediately. It would have been very much more difficult to find him had I been forced to dive beneath the surface of these murky waters.

He was unconscious, face downwards and beginning to sink, when I grabbed and turned him on his back, my hands beneath his chin as I had been taught. I knew I must get him to the bank quickly. I was making for a spot farther down, where there was a shallow edge often used by bathers and the slope flattened out, when he coughed and spluttered, coming round suddenly and trying to fight me in his panic. He struggled wildly, arms flailing, and for a moment it was impossible to swim with him and I could only tread water and hang on to him for all I was worth in an attempt to stop him from taking us both under.

'Oh, damn!' I cursed as I tried to remember what I had been taught. 'Don't be a fool! If you fight me we'll both drown ...'

My words were lost as his struggles became wilder and stronger, his legs kicking and jerking as he lashed out in blind instinct, still only half-conscious and caught in his terror. I used words that a lady should not know and pressed my arm against his throat hard, cutting off his air supply so that he went limp for long enough for me to beach him on the slope of the bank. Exhausted, I flopped down beside him, fighting for breath. Before I had recovered the man

13

made a convulsive movement and flung himself over on his side, belching out a rush of river water and foul-smelling bile that went all over my dress.

'Well done,' I muttered resentfully, then realized the dress was ruined anyway. It was my best—the raw silk which had once belonged to Lady Rouse and been given by her to the church jumble sale. I was not likely to find another like it for five shillings. 'Remind me to drag you out of the river again some day.'

'Sorry ...'

His voice sounded muffled, as if he were still only half-conscious, and I noticed that his eyes were closed. Glancing down at his face I saw that he was attractive, or might have been when not looking like a drowned rat. He had pale blond hair that clung in wet strands across his brow, a longish nose and a full, rather sensuous mouth—a very kissable mouth, I thought, and then wondered at my own forwardness. What on earth had made me think such a thing? He was a stranger, unknown to me, never seen before this moment ...

I felt a jolt, a sensation like hot wires running through my veins as he opened his eyes and gazed up at me. How blue his eyes were! So clear and penetrating.

'Are you in the habit of rescuing drowning men?' he asked. 'Or was I just lucky?'

'You were careless! Foolishly so.' He was attempting to joke about his brush with death but his manner made me angry, especially now it was becoming clear that he was very much

14

alive. Didn't he realize I had risked my own life for his? 'I shouted a warning. The bank isn't safe there—that's why there's a fence and a notice telling you it's private property. You're not supposed to go beyond the fence.'

'I was warned,' he admitted, and pushed himself up into a sitting position, putting one hand to his head as if it hurt him. 'Damn!' he exclaimed suddenly. 'The camera must have gone in, too. I don't suppose you got that, did you?'

'I wasn't exactly looking for it,' I muttered, annoyed by his apparent ingratitude. 'Foolishly, I thought you might be drowning and in need of help.'

He sensed my anger and a chuckle escaped him. 'You saved my life, didn't you? And I haven't thanked you. It's just that it was a particularly expensive camera—the latest thing from America.'

It was symptomatic of the Twenties, of course. Everything had to come from America, whether it be the latest Mary Pickford film, jazz music—or an expensive camera. The only thing that hadn't been imported since the end of the war was Prohibition. Had it been, my life might have been very much easier.

I was reminded of the grievances which had clouded my mood earlier and annoyance flared into anger. Men were always so selfish, taking everything one did for them as of right.

'Blow your camera!' I scrambled to my feet. 'I'm soaked to the skin, my dress is ruined—and I'm going home.'

I set off down the bank to where I had dropped my shopping, pausing to retrieve my shoes on the way. The stranger was calling to me to stop but I refused to look round; he came running after me, catching up with me as I bent to gather the scattered contents of my basket. I was relieved to see that the bottle of whisky I had purchased in town had not broken in the fall, because my father was sure to ask for it that evening and would be angry if it was not there when he needed it.

'Don't go off like that,' the man said, standing in front of me, blocking my path. 'I'm sorry if I upset you but it was a bit of a shock. I didn't think what I was saying. I've never been pulled out of the river before—especially by a pretty girl.'

I had over-reacted. He was in shock and it wasn't really him I was angry with at all.

'I didn't ask if you were feeling all right?' I said. 'It's not your fault about the dress; it wouldn't have been much good after the wetting anyway.'

'You ruined it for my sake so I'll buy you another.' His smile was fading and he looked a bit odd. 'And, no, I'm not all right. In fact, I feel bloody awful ...'

His legs buckled and he sank down into a squatting position. His colour alarmed me and I knelt beside him. He hadn't passed out this time but looked close to doing so.

'Is it your head? You hit it on the wheel as you fell. You were lucky your coat trapped the air for a few seconds. If you had gone straight

16

down I might never have found you—that pool is very deep.'

'Bit dizzy,' he muttered in a drunken-sounding drawl. 'Be all right in a moment. Bloody fool ...'

'I beg your pardon?' I went stiff as something was triggered in my mind. He sounded just like Ben when he'd been drinking.

'Not you ... me.'

'Should I fetch someone—a doctor?'

He opened his eyes and focused on my face with difficulty, taking his time before answering.

'It was just dizziness. Sorry if I swore at you. Bad habit I picked up in the army. I'm the fool, not you.'

'Are you going to be all right? Only I'd like to get home and out of these wet things.'

I was uncomfortable but reluctant to leave him, especially since his collapse, though his colour was returning little by little.

'Yes, of course you would—so should I.' He had risen slowly to his feet but was still groggy and shaken. 'I think I'd better go and lie down for a while. Would you mind if I leaned on your arm—just until my head clears?'

'Are you staying near here?'

He was not from Norfolk; I could tell that by his speech and his clothes which, despite their soaking, still had the expensive cut that could not mean anything but London-tailored.

'At that guest house across the green,' he replied, a flicker of amusement in his eyes. 'The one with the odd landlord—do you know it?'

17

'You mean Winspear House?' I bit on my bottom lip as he nodded. 'Yes, I know it. I'll walk with you—you can lean on me a bit harder if you need to. I'm very strong.'

After years of looking after my father, I was used to helping a man and perfectly capable of bearing his weight.

'Thanks.' He gripped my arm for a moment to steady himself and I noticed the distinctive ring on the middle finger of his left hand. It was fashioned out of a reddish gold and shaped like a tiger's head with open jaws and blood red rubies for eyes. Somehow I found it oddly repulsive, though I could not have said why. Nor could I have explained the sudden shudder that ran through me then. 'You're cold. I'm so sorry,' he apologized.

'It's nothing ... but I would like to get back.'

'I'll be fine if we take it slowly. You must be cursing me. I've been such an idiot, causing you so much trouble.'

I gazed up at him, mesmerized by the intensity of those blue eyes. He seemed nice enough now that he was beginning to talk sensibly, and I was inclined to be touchy sometimes, especially after Ben had had one of his drinking bouts, as he had the previous night. He had been in a foul temper when I'd left to go shopping earlier and, as I'd wandered round the ancient and beautiful streets of Norwich, I'd wondered why I didn't just keep on going—to London or even further. Perhaps America? My mother had once been offered the chance of acting on the Broadway stage.

'Why didn't you?' I'd asked years later, when she was ill and it was too late for such dreams. 'Why didn't you leave him—all of us—and just go?'

'Because I loved him,' Hannah had replied. 'Don't judge your father too harshly, Lizzie. He wasn't always this way.'

And he had been different ... before the accident ... before the drinking began to destroy him.

'Am I leaning on you too much?'

I recalled my wandering thoughts, looking up at the stranger with a flush in my cheeks. 'No, and you're no trouble. You've had a nasty bang on the head and a narrow escape from drowning. It was sheer chance that I saw you. Another few seconds and ...' Once again I shuddered violently.

'Lucky for me,' he agreed, and smiled. 'I haven't introduced myself, have I? Richard Gregory—freelance journalist and amateur photographer.'

'Oh ... you write then?' I felt my cheeks grow hot and could not look at him.

'After a fashion. I kept a diary in the trenches and bits of it were published. After the war, I sort of drifted into it.'

I nodded, suspecting that he came from a wealthy family and had little or no need to work. I recognized the type, having had years of experience of a father who lived mainly on the allowance his family granted him. My mother

19

had always hated it that the money came from the Caulders—but then, she had good reason for her resentment.

I realized Richard Gregory was looking at me, waiting for some response.

'I'm Lizzie—Lizzie Caulder,' I said as we crossed the green in the direction of the large, once beautiful but now slightly run-down house. 'My father is a writer too—or was before ...' I broke off as he started and looked at me in amazement. 'What's wrong?'

'Damn!' Richard smote his forehead with the palm of one hand. 'Of course! That's him, isn't it—Benedict Caulder? He's your father, the landlord of that guest house? I've put my foot right in it, haven't I? He mumbled his name when I took the room but I wasn't concentrating. I ought to have been, because I knew he lived somewhere down here.'

'You've read his work then?'

'All of it. He's brilliant. Wonderful stuff.'

'You don't find him too bitter?' I looked at him curiously. 'That's what his critics say—that he has become too bitter.'

'I don't suppose he appeals to everyone but I've read everything he ever wrote. This is the most amazing luck for me.

He had let go of my arm, seeming to have recovered completely from his dizzy spell. The colour was coming back into his face now and he was obviously feeling better.

'Ben doesn't like strangers much—that's probably why he was odd with you earlier. It was my idea to let a couple of rooms during the summer but he hates it. We do need the extra money, though, and he has to put up with it. His books don't sell that well and he hasn't written much since my mother died two years ago.'

'Your mother is dead? I'm sorry. I knew about your father's accident, of course, but not that Hannah had died ...'

'Why should you?' It was my turn to stare now. 'How do you know her name?'

'You haven't put two and two together? No, I suppose you wouldn't have been told ... after your father married he didn't have much to do with the family, did he?'

'With the Caulders?' I felt a prickle of hostility.

'Your father and mine were cousins,' Richard Gregory went on, seemingly unaware of my feelings. 'Father was years older than Benedict, though. I was told about Ben after the row with Grandfather Caulder. That's why I started to read his books, I suppose. I kept *A Man In His Own Time* with me all through the war. It was in tatters after four years in the trenches—rather like most of us.'

'That was the first of Ben's books,' I said, ignoring his remarks about the war. I knew from experience that most soldiers preferred not to be questioned about their time in the trenches, even now, when the war had been over for several years. 'I liked that one—it wasn't so harsh. I think they got worse after his accident.'

'It must be hard for any man to lose the use of his legs, and to do it falling from a ladder in

21

your own orchard must be particularly galling.' He gave me a sympathetic look. 'Takes it out on you, does he?'

'He made my mother's life a misery for years. He's not so bad with me because I stand up for myself. Most of the time it's all right ...' Except for the times when Ben drank himself into a stupor and woke up in a foul mood.

'Why do you stay here?' Richard asked, echoing the question that had been on my mind all the morning. 'A pretty girl like you ought to be thinking of getting married.'

I screwed up my mouth doubtfully. 'I'm not sure I want to marry. My mother would have been better off if she hadn't. She was an actress—a good one. She gave it up when she married Ben and started a family, but later when she was ill she told me that she had often regretted it. She wasn't bitter and still loved him, despite the way he treated her the last few years, but there were regrets.'

'Well, you don't *have* to marry these days. Not if you're brave enough to make a career for yourself.'

'I've thought about it,' I admitted. 'But I couldn't leave Ben. And then there's my brother Jack. He's still at college. He and Ben don't get on too well ...'

'Your father seems capable of managing alone,' Richard said. We had stopped outside the house and he was looking at me intently. I put a hand up to my hair, which had begun to fluff out and must be a terrible mess. 'Besides the family would help, if it's a question of money?'

'It isn't. And if you mean my grandfather, I would die first,' I said, feeling a rush of hot colour to my cheeks. 'After the way he treated my mother—calling her a cheap whore and refusing to meet her ...'

'That was a bit off,' Richard agreed as he sensed my anger. 'Things were different twenty odd years ago, you must realize that? Henry did relent afterwards; he would have made up the quarrel a long while ago—but your father wouldn't have anything to do with him. Though he ...' He hesitated, as if realizing he had gone too far.

'We took the allowance, that's what you mean, isn't it?' I held my head up, anger and pride making me fierce. 'My mother insisted on it after the accident. Ben was never going to earn much from his writing and we had nothing else. Besides, it was his by right. It was left to him in his mother's will. She always loved him. Things might have been different if she hadn't died when she did.'

'There's no need to look at me like that—as if you would like to hit me.' Something flickered in Richard's eyes. 'I wasn't suggesting that Ben shouldn't have taken the money. In my opinion the Caulders could have done more for him—for all of you.'

'We didn't need more.' I glared at him. 'We manage. And I don't see that this is any of your business.'

'You know, you have the most amazing eyes,' he said. 'I thought at first they were hazel, but when you're angry they're almost green.'

23

His words took my breath away and I was left with nothing to say. I turned away and walked into the house, leaving him staring after me. He followed me into the cool, dark hall; it had been cleared almost entirely of furniture to make it easier for Ben's wheelchair and had only a small table with the telephone and a wall mirror to brighten the gloom.

'I'm not Grandfather Caulder,' Richard said, and caught my arm to swing me round. I glared up at him, anger and resentment still simmering inside me. 'We don't have to be enemies, do we?'

A part of me cried out that we did, that I could never accept anyone from that family ... from the family that had hurt and despised my beloved mother ... but as I gazed up at Richard something changed. He was drying out, looking less like a drowned rat and more and more attractive. I felt a queer quivering sensation low in my belly and my mouth went dry. I shook my head as the anger began to fade. It was all so long ago and none of it had been Richard Gregory's fault. Besides, life in this little hamlet of ours was very dull; it might be fun to get to know my distant cousin.

'No, of course you're not,' I said, and gave him a rueful smile. 'I'm a bit touchy today. Perhaps I get it from my father?'

Richard laughed. He had a warm, infectious laugh and my heart lurched suddenly. I was twenty and other people said I was pretty; it wasn't the first time a man had smiled at me, but no one had made much of an impression

24

on me until now. Perhaps it was because of the way we had met ... it had lowered the barriers I usually kept between me and people I didn't know well.

'You're back then?' The woman's voice broke the pattern of my thoughts. 'We've got a guest staying. Your father put him in ...' Coming through from the kitchen with a tea towel in her hands, Maggie Green broke off in surprise as she saw us. 'Oh, you've met ... and you're both wet!'

I laughed as I saw the startled look in her eyes. 'Don't worry about it, Maggie. I'm going upstairs to change. I'll tell you about it later.'

'She saved my life,' Richard said. 'I stupidly fell in the mill pool and hit my head. I would have drowned if she hadn't pulled me out.'

'Well, I never.' Maggie's mouth dropped open. 'Fancy that ...'

'You're catching flies, dearest,' I said, and darted a kiss at her cheek. 'It was just me acting first and thinking after, the way you're always telling me not to.'

I laughed out loud as Maggie's plump, pleasant face tried to assume an expression of disapproval and failed, then ran up the stairs without looking back.

'It's ever so strange, isn't it?' Maggie paused with the small, sharp knife clasped loosely in her hand. 'You pulling him out of the river like that and him being a relative. Almost as if Fate had meant it to happen ...'

A shiver ran down my spine and I remembered

the suffocating fear that had gripped me as I stood on the edge of the river bank and watched Richard plunge to what would certainly have been his death if I had not been there.

'Yes, I suppose it is,' I said, somehow reluctant to think about the sensations I'd felt just before my impulsive dive into the river. 'He said he didn't know who Father was when he booked in, but ... well, it seems a little unlikely that he should ask to stay here by chance, don't you think?'

I couldn't help wondering if Richard's visit owed more to a deliberate decision to seek us out than to chance—but why should he pretend not to know my father was the landlord who had rented him a room at Winspear? Perhaps he had been embarrassed to discover I was Ben's daughter? People sometimes lied to cover an awkward moment without thinking of the consequences. One thing was quite certain, however. He hadn't chosen to fall in the river and risk death: that had to be Fate.

'His grandmother was Grandfather Caulder's elder sister,' I said, unravelling the intricate family history for Maggie's benefit. 'She married Edward Gregory and her son John was Richard's father. His mother visited us a couple of times just after the accident but I wasn't much more than six or seven at the time and I'd forgotten her name. I didn't know who Richard was until he mentioned the family and Ben probably didn't either. He might have refused to let him stay if he had realized the connection.'

'Your father doesn't think much of his relatives, does he?'

'No. He won't talk about them often—but he once told me his father always hated him, even when he was a child. Perhaps that's why he was such a rebel when he was young. I do remember an awful row between Ben and his elder brother Michael. I think it was something to do with the family business but I can't be sure. Father couldn't throw Michael out because he was in the wheelchair by then but he threw a brass oil lamp at him. It made a terrible mess everywhere and Hannah had to scrub the floor three times to get rid of the smell.'

'It was a good thing it wasn't lit at the time,' Maggie said, pulling a disapproving face. 'Might have set the house on fire ...'

'You mean the way he almost did last month?'

We looked at each other in concern. My father was never without a cigarette somewhere around, though he seldom took more than a couple of drags on it before putting it down, and there were small burn marks on most of the furniture in his room. A few weeks previously he'd left a cigarette burning on the edge of his desk then wheeled himself into his adjoining bedroom; the cigarette had fallen into a wastepaper basket and set the rubbish alight. If I hadn't happened to take a cup of tea into his study at that moment it could have been dangerous.

'That gave me nightmares,' Maggie said as I nodded. 'You ought to stop him smoking,

Lizzie. It isn't good for him. The doctor said ...'

'He doesn't care. You know that, Maggie. Sometimes I think he would rather be dead.'

'He can ruin his own health if he likes. But he shouldn't take risks with other people's. Supposing it had happened while you were asleep?'

Maggie was worried for me. Since Hannah died she had been almost like a mother to me and we were good friends. I saw the anxiety in her dark eyes and slipped an arm about her ample waist, giving her an affectionate squeeze.

'It didn't, and he *has* promised to be more careful.'

'That's as maybe.' Maggie smoothed a wisp of long brown hair into the bun she always wore at the nape of her neck. 'Why you put up with it all, I don't know. Working the way you do in this place and looking after him—and he with hardly a decent word to say to you.'

'He's my father. He isn't always this bad, you know he isn't. I expect he's in pain again. Besides, you stay—why shouldn't I?'

'I'm paid to work here and I go home to my family when I've finished.' She wiped her hands on her floral cotton apron. 'Anyway, I stay for your sake. I promised Hannah I would ... and I care about you.' She ended on a defiant note, her cheeks flushed. 'So that's that!'

'You were my mother's best friend.' I gave her another squeeze before moving the potatoes on to the old-fashioned cooking range. 'I don't

28

know what I should have done without you when she was so ill. And I couldn't manage this place without you.'

Maggie looked pleased but it was no more than the truth. Although we had paying guests for just a few weeks in the summer, the house was large and old, needing constant attention. I white-washed ceilings and papered walls as well as doing the routine cleaning and most of the gardening, though a local farmer cut the grass and looked after the orchard at the bottom of the long back garden. There was also an old cottage beyond the orchard which I had thought about letting, but it would need a lot of cleaning and I just hadn't the time to sort it out.

'It still isn't right,' Maggie said. 'When did you last go anywhere special or buy yourself a pretty dress? You ought to be courting at your age, not playing nursemaid to a cantankerous ...' She broke off as Ben's voice echoed through the house.

'Lizzie! Where are you, girl? Damn you—you know I can't get this wretched thing in there.'

Years ago most of the doorways had been enlarged to make access easier for his cumbersome chair, but Hannah had refused to have the kitchen door changed.

'I want somewhere I can escape to in peace sometimes,' she'd told us a little guiltily, and I felt much the same way. Besides, Benedict was prone to accidents and safer out of the kitchen.

I went through the hallway to my father's study. It was a large, sunny room at the back of the house and had a wide, gently sloping terrace outside so that he could wheel himself into the garden if he wished. Not that he did often, preferring to sit for hours at his desk, chain smoking, a whisky glass to hand as he scribbled endlessly, though most of what he wrote ended up in a wastepaper basket.

I paused in the doorway, a sinking sensation in my stomach as I realized his mood hadn't improved; if anything it was worse.

'I was helping Maggie with the dinner. What's wrong? You said you didn't want any tea so ...'

'What have you done with it?' he demanded, face flushed with temper. 'There was half a bottle of whisky on my dressing chest. You've hidden it again, damn you! How many times must I tell you, I won't be treated like a child?'

'You finished the bottle last night. I bought a new one in Norwich but don't you think you ought to go easy for a while? Doctor Marsh said it was killing you.'

'Damn Marsh!' Ben stared at me from angry, bloodshot eyes. He had once been a fine, good-looking man but pain and too much alcohol had taken their toll: his dark hair was now heavily streaked with grey and his face had gone puffy. He looked older than his forty-seven years. 'That man is a fool and I wish he would keep his opinions to himself.'

'Ben, please don't,' I begged, and sighed. 'He is concerned for you—as I am.'

'Well, don't be. The sooner I'm dead, the

sooner you'll be free of me. I'm not a fool, Liz. I'm a burden to you as I was to her. I killed her. I killed Hannah. You know that, don't you?'

'Stop it!' I pressed my hands to my ears, trying to shut out the words I had heard so often, those destructive, bitter words that tore us both apart. 'I'll get the whisky. Just don't start that again, I can't bear it.'

I ran from the study as tears pricked behind my eyes. Anything was better than listening to Ben tear himself into pieces over Hannah's death.

In my distress I didn't notice Richard coming down the stairs and we collided at the bottom with a bump. I might have fallen but he held on to me as I began to tremble, barely holding back my tears. He looked into my face with concern.

'Hang on, Liz,' he said. 'What's the matter? You're upset about something. What has Benedict been saying? He wasn't thrilled when I told him who I was after we got back—has he been taking it out on you?' He glanced towards the study as if prepared to do battle on my account.

'No, it wasn't that. You weren't mentioned.' I swallowed hard. 'Please don't call me Liz. Ben does it because he knows I don't like it, but I prefer Lizzie.'

Richard gazed down at me in silence, seeming to consider.

'I was looking for you. I'm going to a concert in Norwich this evening and wondered if you would like to come with me?'

31

'Thank you but I can't. I daren't leave Ben alone in the house—not while he's in one of his moods.'

'Couldn't you get someone in?'

'He wouldn't have anyone.'

'Then just leave him.'

'I can't.'

'Yes, you can,' Maggie's voice chimed in from the kitchen doorway. 'I'll pop home and tell Ann I'm staying for a few hours this evening. She can get the dinner for her father and brothers. I was thinking about bottling those gooseberries you picked anyway.'

'There you are.' Richard threw me a triumphant look. 'Maggie will stay so you have no excuse. I want to thank you for saving me this afternoon, and I'm moving on tomorrow. I should enjoy taking you out—to dinner and the concert.'

They had caught me nicely between them. I laughed as I saw Maggie's expression of satisfaction: she looked like a cat who had sneaked cream from the dairy.

'Thank you, Richard.' I gave in gracefully. 'I should very much like to go to the concert with you. Hannah loved music. We often went to concerts before she was ill.'

'That's settled then. I'm going for a drive but I shan't ask you to come. I'm sure you're much too busy.' He grinned at Maggie and I suspected collusion between them. 'Have her ready for me by seven, won't you?'

I glared at him but he winked at Maggie as he went out whistling.

I'm due back in London tomorrow evening.' He seemed regretful. 'It's Mama's birthday party so I can't get out of it.'

'You mustn't even think of it,' I said quickly, but my heart jerked because he obviously had. 'Your mother would be so upset. Anyway, you can come down again, if you want.'

'I should like that,' Richard said, and when I shot a glance at him he was smiling. 'Now—why don't you tell me all about yourself?'

'There isn't much to tell, other than what you already know.'

'I'm sure there is. What do you like to do in your spare time? You must have some time to yourself, surely?'

'Yes, sometimes.' I was silent for a moment, considering. 'I draw things ... not paintings. Just patterns, designs.'

'That sounds interesting.' He shot a quick look at me. 'What kind of designs?'

'Nothing really—just patterns. I suppose it's a waste of time. Ben thinks so and Maggie says I should draw people. I sometimes do quick sketches to amuse her but it isn't what I like doing best. Shapes fascinate me ... mosaics ... colour and pattern.' I gave a rueful laugh. 'You probably think it's a waste of time, too?'

'No, I don't. Perhaps you would show me some of your work one day?'

'Perhaps.'

Richard negotiated a bend in the road. 'Did you know that Grandfather Caulder made his fortune from jewellery? He was a working jeweller—a designer.'

'I had no idea.' I stared at him in surprise. 'Ben seldom mentions his family. I've only seen Michael once and that was as he was on his way out after Father threw something at him. I don't know anything about them.'

'Michael manages the shop in Bond Street,' Richard said, frowning slightly. I noticed a change in his tone and wondered if perhaps he did not get on too well with my uncle. 'The business has a reputation for dealing in particularly fine stones and your grandfather once made several important pieces for royalty—but the design side has stagnated since Michael took over.'

Grandfather Caulder a designer of important jewellery! Richard had certainly succeeded in catching my interest now.

'Do you think that's where I get it from—my scribbling? Ben has never mentioned it.' He might have told me!

'I should imagine it's very likely that you take after Henry.' Richard gave me an odd look that was tinged with triumph. 'Your father had that kind of talent himself. One of the reasons Benedict quarrelled with his father was over the business. I've seen drawings of various pieces he designed when he was still in school; they were good, very good—but he wasn't interested in following in his footsteps. He wanted to write and he did. He was as stubborn as Henry.'

'I think there was more to it than that. Ben and his father disliked each other. Ben can't stand his brother either.'

'I believe it's mutual,' Richard said. 'That's

why ...' He stopped speaking and shook his head. 'It doesn't matter. We don't want to talk about that old stuff, do we? Let's just relax and enjoy ourselves this evening.'

Chapter 2

I snipped a few heads of fresh mint then stopped, hand in mid-air, losing myself in dreams as I remembered something Richard had said the previous evening. It had been such a glorious evening!

The dinner he bought me had, after years of shortages and cooking for myself, been a delight, the deliciously light salmon mousse melting on my tongue—but perhaps listening to my companion talk of his life in London was what had given everything that extra sparkle. He had described the way it was before the war, the endless parties, told me about going to Ascot and Henley, strawberries at Wimbledon and country house weekends: he knew so many people, went to so many smart affairs—so many wonderful places—that it set my head whirling. I could scarcely imagine what it must be like to live that way.

'Everyone is trying to pretend nothing has changed,' Richard confided over brandy snaps with whipped cream and black cherries. 'Mama is carrying on regardless, as are some of her friends—but things can never be as they were.

They have changed and maybe it is for the better. Caroline says it's about time ...' He stopped and smiled to himself. 'I do a sort of gossip column for one of the papers. Under a pseudonym, of course. Recently I quoted something Caro said at a party about women's rights and she was furious. If she ever guessed who the spy was she would have my guts for garters.'

Ben had never pulled his punches where language was concerned so Richard's racy style didn't shock me. He was fun to be with and it was all so new and exciting, so different from the slow pace of our normal life. I laughed as he had intended and asked about the formidable Caroline.

'She's Michael Caulder's daughter, actually.' Richard's brow furrowed and there was a flicker of annoyance in his eyes. 'Caro is fine most of the time but she can be a bit of a bitch if she feels like it.'

'Oh.' I sipped my wine and digested the information. It was rather odd to be finding out about all these relations I hadn't known existed a few hours earlier. 'Are there anymore? I mean—does Caroline have brothers or sisters? Do you?'

'No, and no again.' I noticed a slight reserve in Richard's voice and wondered if my question had bothered him in some way. 'We're the only offspring of our revered parents. Your brother Jack is the only real Caulder left—after Michael and your father, of course.'

What was he implying? I sensed something.

40

been and yet somehow I didn't think it was me. For a few moments I struggled to recall her face. She had been so terrified ... so alone.

Throwing back the bedcovers, I went to look out of the window. I was in my own bedroom at Winspear and it looked down on the back garden which was bathed just then in the soft golden glow of the moon. I had forgotten to draw my curtains. Always, since early childhood, I had been prone to bad dreams if the moon was too bright.

I had woken to a room flooded with moonlight the night before my father had fallen from that ladder and damaged his spine—woken screaming, in pain and suffocating from a terrible tightness in my chest, a fear I could not explain. I had been dreaming then, too, or so my mother thought at the time.

'You tried to warn us, Lizzie,' she told me once, much later, when I was no longer a child. 'But I didn't understand you. I thought it was just a nightmare.'

'It couldn't have been anything else ... could it?'

Her look had frightened me and she'd sensed my fear. 'No, of course not, darling. But some people ... sometimes it may be possible to feel a premonition of danger to loved ones.'

I had dismissed the idea as nonsense then, but it had happened again the day before Hannah herself died, this time when I was awake. I had been in the garden when I became aware of terrible, agonizing fear ... just as I had when I knew Richard was going to fall into the river.

49

Now my dream was of a girl in danger.

'Lizzie Caulder, you're a fool,' I muttered and smiled. 'You shouldn't have eaten that cheese for supper.'

I turned away from the window, got into bed and drifted into a peaceful, dreamless sleep.

Norwich was such an impressive city, I thought, with its wealth of lovely churches, its maze of medieval streets and fine old buildings, some of which dated back to the time when the wool trade had made it such a prosperous area. Until the railways arrived in the nineteenth century the river had been the city's opening to the outside world, carrying its goods down to the sea, from where they were taken on by ship to Antwerp or Rotterdam.

After my foolish dream the previous evening I'd decided to get away from the house and go shopping in the market, and I had almost finished when I saw a poster advertising an exhibition of Roman art and jewellery, including some items which had recently been dug out of the earth at a site near Colchester. I glanced at my watch, frowning as I saw how late it was. If I stopped too long I would miss my bus and the next one would not get me home until nearly four that afternoon—but I would very much like to take a peep at that golden torc. Maggie wouldn't mind staying on for another couple of hours. She was always telling me to take more time off for myself.

I paid my shilling at the door and went inside the dark hall. It smelt musty, with an odd earthy odour that made me think of churchyards and old books, somehow reminding me of my dream once more—though why it should was beyond me.

The organizers could have made a little more effort to entertain, I thought as I wandered past the glass cases to stare at pieces of broken pots, brightly coloured mosaics, coins, part of a sword, some bits of leather that had once been a sandal, and then the necklace I had come to see.

It looked very heavy, as though it had belonged to a man rather than a woman. The tarnished gold had been cleaned enough to show a dull lustre and was twisted rather like a thick rope; there was a carved ball at either end of the open circle. I bent over the showcase to get a better look, at the workmanship then straightened up and took a step backwards. A muffled groan and something soft beneath my heel told me I had trodden on someone. I swung round in dismay, apologizing at once for my clumsiness.

'I'm so sorry! I didn't realize you were there.'

'It was an accident,' the man assured me. His voice was very deep and he had a slight foreign accent that I couldn't quite place. 'Please do not distress yourself.'

'Did I hurt you?' I was wearing court shoes and was rather afraid that my heel might have dug in hard. 'It's no excuse, of course, but I was so interested in the design that I didn't think to turn round and look before stepping back.'

'No broken bones, I think.' He smiled at me.

Until that moment I had thought him almost ugly, but the smile softened his features. He had a dark complexion and prominent cheekbones that gave his face rather a chiselled look, but his eyes had the warm brown shine of melting chocolate. 'It is an interesting piece, is it not? I had hoped to see more but the exhibition seems to be confined to the recent local find.'

'It was the torc I wanted to see, and the mosaics—though I must admit I have seen better.'

'Yes, so have I.' The man's eyes seemed to be laughing at me. 'But perhaps it was not a complete waste of time after all. May I take you for some tea? To make up for causing you so much anxiety.'

Until that moment I had been enjoying our chat but now I was suddenly aware of the dangers of taking tea with a complete stranger. The man was very tall, very masculine and well-built. At that moment he seemed intent on me ... somehow threatening. His look unsettled me and I took a step back, clutching my basket nervously to my chest.

Stories of abduction and worse flitted through my mind—and then I remembered my dream. Perhaps it had been a warning to me after all!

'I'm sorry. I must go. I have a bus to catch.'

I sounded nervous, flustered, and the stranger's smile vanished. For a moment I thought he was going to catch hold of my arm and prevent me from leaving, but he merely stood there, staring after me as I hurried away.

My heart was behaving very oddly. My knees felt like jelly; I was afraid I would fall—and I could not wait to get away. It was not for several minutes that I was sufficiently in control of my emotions to think clearly.

Why should the man have meant me any harm? I had been rude and foolish. The stranger had forgiven me for treading on his foot and offered me tea to make up for my distress at my own clumsiness—but something in his manner had unnerved me. With that build and those features he could have been a Roman legionary intent on conquering an inferior island race.

'What an imagination you have, Lizzie!'

I spoke aloud and laughed at myself. Of course the man had meant me no harm. Indeed, I had rather liked him until his eyes took on that hot glow, which was probably just because he had been pleased to meet someone who shared his love of ancient artefacts. For a moment I considered going back to apologize but there was no time.

I walked quickly towards the bus stop, wondering at my own behaviour. It was unlike me to behave so gauchely.

The bus was taking on passengers! I called out and began to run. If I missed this one I would have to stand and wait for ages.

One of the passengers saw me and asked the conductor to hold the bus. I scrambled on board to the cheers and laughter of the other passengers.

'Just made it, love,' said the woman who had

spotted me running. 'You'd have had a long wait otherwise.'

'Yes, I would,' I agreed. 'And I wanted to get home, because someone is coming this evening.'

'Your young man, is it?' the woman asked and I nodded, blushing. 'No wonder you were in a hurry.'

I smiled at her but said nothing, recovering my breath. It was silly of me to have panicked earlier. The man had probably been a holiday maker visiting the lovely old city, and lonely as people often were in a strange town.

Not that I'd wanted to have tea with him. I was glad I had caught the bus as I'd planned. It would give me more time to get ready for Richard.

Should I wear the dress he had sent me that evening or keep it for a special occasion? Perhaps that would be best, though I was longing to wear it.

My chance to wear the new dress came when Richard took me to a tea dance that Saturday afternoon. The dances were held in an exclusive hotel by the river in the centre of Norwich and were popular with both residents and visitors.

Richard had arrived very late on the Friday evening. So late that we only had time to take a little stroll in the garden before saying goodnight. But he had kissed me and this time didn't apologize afterwards.

'I've missed you so much,' he confessed

It couldn't matter one way or the other. He was a stranger passing through Norwich. I would never see him again.

'I think Henry Caulder might like to see some of these.'

'No!' My wandering thoughts were recalled abruptly as Richard spoke. 'No, I don't think so. I showed you because you asked, but I don't want anyone else to see them.'

'That's silly, darling,' he said in a persuasive tone. 'Wouldn't you like to see some of your designs made up in precious metals or stones?'

'No—not yet anyway. I'm not ready. Besides, these aren't good enough. I was just scribbling, amusing myself. If I wanted anyone to consider them seriously I would do something specific.'

'I still think Henry would be interested.' Richard shrugged as I set my mouth stubbornly. 'It was just an idea, darling, that's all.'

'I don't know Grandfather Caulder.' I tried to express my feelings in words but failed. How could I explain the resentment and anger Hannah had taught me to feel towards the Caulders over the years? 'It would seem as if I were asking for something ... expecting a favour. It's just a hobby, Richard. I should be embarrassed.'

'Then we shall forget about it,' he said, and reached out to brush a wisp of hair from my cheek. 'I was just thinking of you. I didn't want to upset you.'

'You haven't. I'm being silly, making too much of it.'

I couldn't explain why the idea of showing

63

my designs to Henry Caulder upset me: it was all tied up with the past, my mother and an odd premonition that warned me not to become involved with the family. And yet if I married Richard ...

'You will change your mind once you meet him,' Richard continued confidently. 'We won't talk about it for the moment if you don't want to, though it is a little silly when you so obviously have talent.'

'Am I going to meet Grandfather Caulder?'

'Of course. After we're married. It would seem churlish if you refused. I go down to Pentire often so ...'

'Pentire?' I experienced a sharp tingling sensation at the nape of my neck. 'Where or what is that?'

'Grandfather Caulder's estate, of course.' Richard frowned. 'It's in Sussex. Surely Benedict told you about Pentire? He must have done.'

'No.' I shook my head. 'I've never heard him mention it, and I don't particularly want to go there.'

'You're not going to keep up this silly feud forever, are you?'

It must seem silly to him, of course. He didn't know how much Grandfather Caulder's refusal to meet Hannah had hurt my mother; he didn't know of the years of hardship that had taken their toll of her; of the way her health had gradually worsened, leaving her tired and ill, her beauty gone. He hadn't seen the hurt in her eyes when my father became surly and unloving towards her ... he hadn't heard her sobbing late into the night, as I had.

'I suppose it would be silly,' I admitted reluctantly. 'It wouldn't be feasible after we're married, would it?'

'Henry isn't really so bad,' Richard said, reaching for my hand, his forefinger stroking the palm persuasively. 'I think he would like the chance to make amends, Liz.'

'I don't want anything from him. I'm not interested in his money. I've already told you that, Richard.'

'I didn't mean money. Just a chance to say he's sorry—a chance to show his better side. You're not too proud to deny him that, are you?'

'You seem very concerned about him.' I pulled my hand away in irritation. 'You call him Grandfather Caulder but he isn't your grandfather, is he?'

Richard's mouth tightened. 'I call him that because he likes it—and he has been very good to me. I've always thought of him as my grandfather.'

I sensed he was very annoyed with me but trying not to show it and felt a sudden flutter of panic. Our relationship was too new and much too precious to risk spoiling it over such a small thing.

'You're right. I am being silly,' I said. 'Of course I want to meet Grandfather Caulder—and when I've done something worthwhile perhaps we can show ...'

I was not allowed to finish. Richard drew me into his arms, silencing me with a kiss that sent thrills of pleasure running through me and drove everything else from my mind. What did old quarrels and old hatreds matter? Hannah would have been the first to say I must think of myself and my own happiness.

'I'm not sure how long I can wait,' he murmured huskily against my ear. 'Let's hope your father likes me enough to agree to an early wedding.'

'Richard ...' I breathed hard, gazing up into his eyes as I sensed a sudden urgency in him. 'Speak to him soon, please. I want to be with you always. I want to be your wife.'

His fingertips traced the line of my jaw, then moved down my throat. 'Perhaps after you've met Mama. We mustn't rush things, darling, no matter how impatient we both are. We don't want another feud in the family, do we?'

He was right, of course. If he had asked I would have run away with him at that moment but that was the impulsive side of my nature, the foolish, naive child in me who would have given herself in love and not thought twice. The sensible side of me knew it couldn't be that way; I needed Ben's permission to marry, not just because I was not quite twenty-one, but because I wanted his blessing. When I left home it would be necessary to employ someone to take my place, and that could only be done with his agreement. In the past he had angrily refused help from anyone other than me or Hannah, but that would have to change.

'Don't look so anxious,' Richard said, mis-interpreting my silence. 'My mother will adore you. She had almost given up hope of my ever marrying and will welcome you with open arms.'

'I am looking forward to meeting her—and your father.'

'Didn't I tell you?' Richard's expression became distant, slightly odd. 'My father died when I was a boy. I suppose that's why I've been so close to Grandfather Caulder. He has always been there in the background, keeping an eye on things. Mama never had much to do with Father's family—there are only a few cousins, I believe. After my father died she cut the connection completely.'

'I'm sorry. I didn't realize.'

'Don't be. I hardly remember my father. He was never there ... just a shadowy figure.'

Was there a note of bitterness in Richard's voice? I had a feeling that there was more, something he wasn't telling me, but I couldn't be sure. He wasn't as unmoved as his words implied; I could see a faint pulse flickering at his temple and sensed he was keeping a tight hold on himself. I was curious but didn't want to ask questions about something that so obviously disturbed him.

Richard smiled and squeezed my hand suddenly.

'What a serious pair we are,' he said. 'Let's talk about something more interesting, shall we?'

For the rest of the evening we did just that, discovering each other's preferences in literature and music.

I loved the novels of Jane Austen and Thomas Hardy, but Richard's taste was for the writing of men like James Joyce, D. H. Lawrence—and, of course, my father. However, we both had similar feelings about art and music.

'Walking, dancing and taking a boat on the river when I can manage it are my main interests,' Richard said. 'But I shall be happy to share yours, darling, whatever they are.'

'I like visiting museums and art galleries, but otherwise my interests are much the same as yours.'

'We shall entertain quite often. My friends will be envious when they meet you—but that won't happen until we're married. Someone might try to steal you away from me so I'll make sure my ring is on your finger first.'

I laughed, enjoying his teasing. He must know I was too deeply in love with him to look at anyone else, but it was lovely to hear him say the words that made me feel loved and cared for.

That night I lay awake long after we had parted, going over the things we had talked about, smiling, feeling a glow spread through my body as I remembered the feel of Richard's mouth on mine. How lucky I was that we had met. It was surely a perfect match. We were made for each other. I could hardly believe we had met only a few short days before.

Yet as I remembered the manner of our meeting I was suddenly cold, gripped by fear. Richard had almost died then. If I hadn't stopped to watch the swans ... if I hadn't acted so swiftly ... but Maggie was right. Fate must have planned it that way. For some reason that was beyond my understanding, I had been meant to save his life.

It was such a reassuring thought that the chill of fear melted away and I turned over, falling into a restful sleep. It was all happening so fast but if it was my destiny to marry Richard then there was no point in worrying about it.

On Sunday morning Richard and I walked to church together, enjoying the last of the current spell of warm weather. By the time we returned to Winspear it was beginning to cloud over and there were signs of a storm brewing.

He left for London at half-past three.

'I'll telephone this evening,' he said, 'and be down earlier next Friday, I promise.'

'I wish you didn't have to go—or else that I was coming with you.' I sighed, knowing it was impossible but reluctant to let him go.

'You will be with me all the time soon.' He kissed me again. 'Take care of yourself, darling.'

I waved until the car was out of sight then went into the house, intending to do some work on my designs, but hearing Ben call I paused, then entered the study.

'Has he gone?'

I nodded but didn't say anything. Ben was at his desk. He looked tired, his face etched with lines of strain, dark-shadowed by pain and suffering. My heart caught with pity; he had loved Hannah, despite all their quarrels and the bitter, cruel words he had heaped on her—and now he was grieving, grieving in a way that drained him of everything else.

'How are you? Is your back hurting?'

'The day it stops I shall be dead,' he replied harshly. His eyes stabbed at me, sharp and knowing. 'You're in love with him, aren't you? You're in love with Richard Gregory.'

'Yes. Yes, I think I am.' My nails curled into the palms of my hands. Now it was about to start, the taunts and the accusations. 'Do you mind?'

'He seems decent enough.' Ben's tone surprised me. He nodded to himself as if he had expected my answer. 'You should consider marrying him, Liz. There won't be much for you here when I'm gone. You'll share whatever this house fetches with your brother but there isn't much money. Hannah would have wanted to see you safely married. Richard turning up like that was providential. If he asks you, say yes. You're not likely to get a better offer the way things are—stuck here in this backwater with me.'

There was a hard lump in my throat and something about his manner made me uneasy. It was as though he were pushing me into marriage, pushing me away from him.

'If I did marry him ...' His eyelids flickered and my unease deepened. 'What about you? You've always hated having anyone else near you.'

'Maggie will look after things as usual. If I need a nurse, we'll get one. I want you to marry him if he asks.'

70

'He already has. We thought it was too soon to ask for permission to marry—that you would say we didn't know our own minds.'

'If it was anyone else I might be doubtful—but this is very suitable. Richard is old enough to know his own mind, and he's family.' Ben hesitated, then gave me another odd look. 'I want you to be safe if anything happens to me.'

'Father ... please don't.'

'I owe it to her, Liz. It's what she would want for you—marriage to a decent man and a good home of your own. Tell Richard to speak to me next time he's down. There's no point in waiting if you've made up your minds.'

'You sound as if you'll be pleased to see me go?' I was a little petulant, hurt that he had decided I was so easily replaced, and Ben laughed, the lines easing out of his face so that it was possible to see he must once have been a handsome man—a man capable of sweeping my mother off her feet.

'And you sound like Hannah! You look like her, too—before I killed the spirit in her.'

'Don't,' I begged. 'It wasn't your fault. She had a weak heart—that's what killed her.'

'Brought on by worry over me and too much work. I killed her, Liz. Nothing you or anyone else can say will change that. I promised her a wonderful life and I gave her years of misery—but you are going to have all I promised Hannah. I want that for you, all the things I could never give her. Marry Richard and be happy. She would have wanted that for you.'

I wasn't sure he was right. Hannah had learned not to be so impulsive as she grew older. She had regretted her own hasty marriage.

'Ben was in so much of a hurry. He insisted on marrying me first and telling his family afterwards. We should have waited—broken the news gently to his father,' she had said shortly before she died. She was propped up against the pillows, her hand in mine, eyes misty with regrets. 'If it hadn't been for that feud we might have had a chance ...'

Yes, I thought that Hannah might well have advised her daughter to wait.

'Love isn't always enough,' she had told me once. 'Be sure of what you want—and then don't let anyone stop you getting it.'

But I *was* sure of what I wanted. Falling in love with Richard was the best thing that had ever happened to me—and yet, at the same time I was aware of unease at the back of my mind.

'Perhaps you could live with us,' I suggested uncertainly. 'I could ask Richard ...'

'And ruin both your lives?' My father glared at me. 'I've never heard such maudlin rubbish! I may be an invalid but I'm not an imbecile, girl! I can look after myself, and what I can't manage, Maggie can do for me—or that ugly daughter of hers.'

'Oh, Ben,' I protested. 'Ann isn't ugly. She's a little plain, that's all.'

'Plain enough to be an old maid, and past thirty. She'll be glad of the work. Stop pulling a face, Liz. If you don't grab your chance, you

72

may end up in the same boat.'

'Thank you kindly. I take it you think I'm ugly, too?'

'You're beautiful—but so was Hannah until I crushed the life out of her.' He wheeled his chair to the window, his back towards me. 'Now get out and leave me alone.'

I stared at the back of his head. I was racked with pity but knew from past experience that nothing I could do or say would ease the grief inside him. No one could change the past: Ben *had* helped to hasten his wife's death. For years he had vented his fury at being tied to that chair on her, used her as his whipping boy, making her bear her share of his pain and frustration—now he could not forgive himself.

'Oh, Ben,' I whispered, and went from the room before I wept. Tears and sympathy only made him angry. 'I'm sorry ... so very sorry.'

Could I really marry Richard and leave my father alone? Perhaps if I talked to Richard when he came down—surely there was something we could do rather than simply abandon my father to his fate?

Richard would know. My heart lifted at the thought. I wasn't alone with my problems anymore. Richard would tell me what to do.

'I'm sure Benedict would never agree to live with us,' Richard said when I mentioned the idea to him that weekend. 'Don't worry, darling, we'll think of something for him—but not with us. It wouldn't work. Besides, my flat is small, nowhere near big enough for three and not at

73

all suitable for a wheelchair.'

'He would never agree to it anyway. I wondered if we ... perhaps we could live at Winspear?'

'Live in your father's house?' Richard shot an astonished glance at me and the car swerved into the side of the road. 'Not to be thought of! We can visit at weekends, of course, but we shall be living in London. My work, friends—everything is there. It just wouldn't do, Liz.'

'No, I suppose not.'

I smothered a sigh and glanced out of the window. Richard was driving us down to his mother's cottage and the scenery had changed from open fields on either side to narrow lanes with high hedges cutting off the view, though occasionally I caught sight of pebble-dashed walls and gardens that were a riot of tall, colourful hollyhocks, heavy round balls of hydrangeas and roses, roses, everywhere, filling the air with their heady scent. The windows were open wide, though the soft top was up on Richard's car because it had looked like rain when we started out and even now the sky was overcast and grey. Not the ideal day for a trip to the sea.

Of course I was going for the specific purpose of meeting Richard's mother. Why did I feel so nervous? He was adamant that she would love me—so why did I feel as if I were on trial?

Richard hadn't spoken to my father yet and I had an uneasy suspicion that I had first to be approved by Mrs Gregory.

was swept away on a tide of pleasure, bemused by the wonderful thing that had happened to me. All I cared for was Richard's happiness. I just wanted him to smile at me in the way that made my toes curl and set my heart racing.

I would have done or said anything to please him.

'We could arrange the wedding for early-September—what do you think?'

It was less than a month away but since we were both so sure of our love there seemed no point in waiting.

'That sounds wonderful,' I agreed. 'It will give us plenty of time to prepare everything.'

'I thought just a quiet affair. We don't need a crowd, do we? Your father, my mother and a couple of friends. We can do the rounds afterwards.'

I had expected him to want a lavish reception. I wasn't sure how I felt. I had several friends from school I could have asked but I wasn't close to them, so perhaps it didn't matter. I smothered vague feelings of disappointment.

'Maggie must come. She's almost family. And there's Jack ...'

'Of course.' Richard took my hand and kissed it. 'Whatever you want, darling. I was thinking of you—and Ben.'

He was right, my father wouldn't want a lot of fuss. A simple ceremony and a reception at the house were all that was necessary. Ben could slip away to his own rooms if he got tired.

'We'll go to Paris for a few days afterwards,' Richard was saying. 'You will love it, darling.

You needn't bother about clothes too much beforehand. We can buy you a new wardrobe there. I shall enjoy helping you choose. And we can visit the occasional gallery or museum, if you like?'

He was trying to please me, to make up for any disappointment I might have felt at not having a big wedding.

'It sounds wonderful.'

'It will be wonderful—just the two of us.'

The look in his eyes made me tremble with love. I was so lucky to have found a man who really cared—a man who wanted to make things perfect for us.

'We should be getting back.' He pressed my hand. 'Mama will think we've got lost.'

I gave him the smile he expected, though I knew Rosalind would not be worried. She had sent us off for the afternoon while she had her customary nap.

'My doctor says it is good for me,' she'd told me before going upstairs to lie down. 'I'm not an invalid but I tend to overdo things if I'm not careful. It's my nerves, you know.'

I imagined that she was the type of woman who worried over small things, that she could be fretful and demanding if she chose. I wondered if that was why Richard tried not to upset her—why he had waited for her approval before asking my father's permission to marry me.

He was so considerate, such a thoughtful man.

We had left her resting alone in her room, so it was a surprise on our return to find a large, expensive car parked in the driveway.

'It looks as if your mother has visitors,' I said as Richard drew his car in behind the first.

'Yes. Damn! Such a nuisance that *she* should arrive like this.'

His tone was so grim that I was surprised.

'You know who it is, don't you?'

'That car belongs to Caroline,' Richard said. 'Why did she have to come down this weekend? It's so typical ... no consideration for others ... it suits her so she must come.'

'What do you mean?'

'She hates the east coast and usually has to be dragged here—and yet today she turns up unexpectedly.'

'You are talking of Caroline Caulder? My cousin Caroline?' I felt a prickle of apprehension as I saw his expression. 'You didn't know your mother had invited her?'

'Caro wasn't invited for this weekend. She doesn't need to be invited.' His mouth thinned. 'She simply has an impulse and goes where it takes her. She must be curious about you. She has a way of finding things out, no matter how hard you try to keep them from her. I think she listens at doors ...'

'Surely not?' I was half amused, half disturbed by his manner.

'You don't know her. She likes to know other people's secrets. It gives her a feeling of power—and Caro always has to have her own way. She wants to know about you so she came down when she knew we would be here.'

'That sounds ominous. Should I be nervous?'

Richard looked at me, an odd expression in his eyes. 'Don't worry, Liz. She can be a bit of a bitch but don't let her upset you. I'll protect you if she tries to sharpen her claws on you.'

I was about to say I could stand up for myself when we heard the crunch of feet on gravel and turned to see two people come from the side of the house. The man was tall and dark and I was stunned as I recognized him: it was the one I had bumped into at the exhibition at Norwich the previous week! For a moment I was so shocked that I didn't notice the woman, then I became aware of her interest in me—an interest I fully returned.

So this was Caroline Caulder!

She was breathtakingly beautiful as she stood there, clinging to the arm of her companion. A slender, sophisticated, confident woman with a complexion like silk and roses, and green eyes—the greenest I had ever seen.

'Richard, darling!' she cried in a voice that had the silken burn of whisky and cream. 'You're back at last. We arrived ages ago and dearest Rosalind said you wouldn't be long. What do you mean by deserting us all? Anyone would think you had something to hide?'

Her eyes seemed to dwell on my face and I thought I saw a glimmer of amusement—as if she had summed me up in an instant and found me wanting. A poor little dab of a thing who could not possibly be a rival to her—and of course she was right. Very few women could compare favourably with Caroline Caulder.

'I took Liz to tea in Cromer,' Richard said,

a marked coolness in his manner. 'Mama knew that. I had no idea you were coming down—or that you were bringing a friend ...'

'Of course—you don't know Alexi, do you?' Now her eyes gleamed with mischief as she glanced at her companion. 'And you haven't introduced me to your little friend either.'

Her companion stepped forward, offering his hand to Richard. 'Alexi Paulinski,' he said. 'You are Richard Gregory, of course. Caroline has told me you write for a newspaper.'

'Pleased to meet you.'

They shook hands formally, polite but cold—at least on Richard's part.

'Alexi has taken the studio next to my house,' Caroline said, but her eyes were still on my face. 'He is a sculptor—bronzes and things. Richard, I'm still waiting.' She smiled at me suddenly. 'Forgive him, dear child. He is always like this. You must be Liz, of course. Ben's daughter ... Rosalind told me about you.'

'If you had given me half a chance, I should have introduced you,' Richard said, unsmiling. 'Liz—this is your cousin Caroline. Mr Paulinski, may I introduce my fiancée, Liz Caulder?'

Caroline's eyes narrowed as they fixed on the third finger of my left hand. 'Engaged already?' she cried. 'I don't see a ring. This must be something new. Rosalind didn't tell me you were engaged.'

'We decided this afternoon,' Richard said, 'but Mama was aware of my intentions.'

'I'm sure she was,' Caroline drawled sweetly. 'You were always so good to your mama.'

I sensed the tension between them and wished something would intervene. Caroline was obviously annoyed ... and Alexi Paulinski's dark eyes were making me uncomfortable.

It was so odd that we should meet in this way.

'I believe we have met previously, Miss Caulder?' he said, offering to shake my hand. 'At that exhibition in Norwich last week.'

'You didn't tell me you had met my cousin!' Caroline looked at him accusingly.

'I was not aware of the connection,' he replied. 'We merely exchanged a few words in passing—is that not so, Miss Caulder?'

They were all staring at me, waiting for my answer. I felt as if I were guilty of something, then my natural resilience bounced back and my head went up. I put my hand in his and he held it for a moment before releasing me. I was oddly comforted and knew he had meant me to be.

'If that is a polite way of saying I trod on your foot and then rushed off to catch my bus, then yes, we did meet briefly.' I met Caroline's curious gaze with a spurt of defiance. 'Richard has been telling me about you. Until recently I didn't know you existed.'

'How refreshingly honest,' she drawled. Her eyes narrowed to catlike slits and I sensed I was about to feel her claws. 'I've known about you for years—my little country cousin. Benedict's daughter. Now Richard has dragged you away from him. Are you sure you know what you're doing, Liz? Haven't you heard about the family curse?'

I had the distinct impression she was warning me off.

'I prefer Lizzie if you don't mind—and I have no idea what you mean by the family curse?'

'She's hinting that I'm not good enough for you,' Richard said, and laid a possessive hand on my arm. 'She's quite right, of course, but you must promise not to listen to a word she says—especially about the curse, which is nonsense.'

'Just a family joke—if you happen to find it funny.' Caroline gave an exaggerated shudder and for a moment I fancied I saw beneath the mask to the true woman. 'It's always so cold down here. I can't see why anyone should want to come to such an uncivilized spot. Do let's go in before we all freeze to death.'

'You will want to say goodbye to Mrs Gregory before we leave.' Alexi Paulinski took a firm hold on her arm. 'It was a pleasure meeting you. Mr Gregory—Miss Caulder.' His expression as he looked at me was unreadable but I sensed he was determined to have his way as he added, 'However, I'm afraid we must leave shortly.'

'Rosalind asked us to stay for dinner ...' Caroline protested. She seemed about to make a fuss but something in his eyes must have warned her because she suddenly laughed. 'Don't look at me like that, Alexi darling. I'll come quietly, I promise.'

We all moved into the house. A fire had been lit in the parlour, the fierce heat from fragrant pine logs taking the chill from the room. Caroline gave a cry of pleasure and rushed towards it, warming her hands in front of the flames.

I excused myself and went up to the room Rosalind had shown me earlier. I knew my fine hair had been blown and tangled by the wind and wanted to tidy myself before dinner.

It had been quite a shock to find Caroline and her friend waiting for us and I wasn't sure how I felt about it. Richard's manner towards my cousin was definitely hostile but I wasn't sure about Caroline—I thought she might be quite good at concealing her true emotions.

I wasn't surprised when the knock came at my door just as I had finished changing, nor that it was Caroline who asked if she might come in.

'Yes, of course. The door isn't locked.'

'Were you expecting me?'

'I thought you might come.'

'Yes, I thought you might.' She shivered. 'This is such a cold house. I can't understand why Rosalind is so attached to it. Give me the South of France any day.'

'I don't feel the cold. I suppose I'm used to it. Our house is old and full of draughts too. But then, I've never been to France so I can't make comparisons, can I?'

'You've got more spirit than I expected.' She eyed me thoughtfully. 'I think perhaps I shall like you after all.'

'Shall you?'

Caroline picked up a silver-backed hairbrush from the dressing chest and looked at the pattern of cherubs engraved into the handle.

'This is pretty. Is it yours?'

'It was my mother's. I use it now.'

'She was an actress, wasn't she? That's what all the fuss was about. Henry couldn't stomach the idea of his favourite son marrying someone so unsuitable ...'

'Henry. You mean, Grandfather Caulder?'

'I call him Henry. He's a darling really, a sweetie—if you know how to handle him.'

'And you do?'

'I've had years of practice.'

'I see.'

'I wonder if you do?' Caroline's face was alight with a Machiavellian mischief. 'Most of the time I can twist him around my little finger. He gives me anything I want. It drives Michael wild. They can't be in the same room for five minutes without jumping down each other's throats. Father is terrified Henry will leave all his money to me, and that makes him furious because he knows I shall just fritter it away.'

I could not help laughing at her. She was talking outrageously and I knew she was trying me out ... testing me.

'You say what you mean, don't you?'

'You don't, obviously. I have a viper's tongue.'

'Yes, I see you do.'

'Henry says I am a witch.'

'Does he know what you intend to do with his money?'

'He thinks I shall reform once I'm married.'

'And shall you?'

'Reform or marry?' Caroline's eyes sparkled with humour. 'Not that it matters. The answer is no in either case. One man wouldn't be enough for me. I collect lovers ... are you shocked?'

'No—did you want me to be?'

Caroline nodded, her mouth quirking at the corners.

'So you're not a little mouse then. I wonder if Richard realizes? I think he may be in for a shock one of these days.'

'What do you mean?'

I wasn't sure that I liked what she was saying.

'Don't ask me to explain. I say a great many foolish things and mean very few of them.' She tipped her head to one side, looking at me consideringly. 'Are we going to be friends, do you think?'

'Perhaps—when we get to know each other better.'

'Yes,' she agreed after a moment's thought. 'We must get to know each other ... whatever happens between you and Richard.'

'Whatever?' I guessed what she was hinting at. 'I'm going to marry him. Nothing will change that. We are in love.'

'Don't look at me like that!' Caroline cried. 'I'm not a rival. Richard asked me to marry him years ago but I turned him down. I told you, I'm not interested in marriage—and if I were it wouldn't be to Richard. We're too much alike.'

'What do you mean?'

'Do you really want to know?'

I was about to reply that I did when we both heard the sound of footsteps outside and then someone knocked at the door. Caroline put a finger to her lips as Richard spoke.

'Are you ready, Liz? Is Caroline there with you?'

'Yes. We're just coming,' she answered for me and opened the door wide. 'I suppose Alexi is getting impatient. I should never have brought him, then I could have stayed longer—not that you would care for that, darling Richard.' She shot a mischievous glance my way. 'Don't forget what I said—and expect me at the wedding.'

I stood with Richard, watching as she ran along the hall and disappeared down the stairs.

I was aware of his annoyance.

'I thought she must be with you. What was she saying to you?'

'Nothing very much. Just being herself, I think—trying to find out what I'm really like.'

'Oh, I see.' Was that a note of relief? I couldn't be sure but I did know he had been disturbed by her visit. 'We had better go down. Mama is waiting for us. She wants to discuss the wedding.'

I'd wondered if Richard's mother might think we were rushing things by fixing a date in early-September, but she wanted to arrange it all for us and seemed annoyed because we had not consulted her.

'Richard was telling me you were planning a quiet wedding. We might persuade Henry to hold it at Pentire—it's so beautiful there.' She frowned. 'Surely you would prefer a nice reception for your friends?'

She obviously liked Henry's estate and was

put out because she could not hold the wedding there and make it a grand affair.

'It might be better this way, for my father's sake. Richard suggested we should visit friends and family afterwards.'

'Well ... perhaps he knows best.' Her frown cleared. Richard could obviously do no wrong. 'But you must let me help you with your clothes. Could you come up to London one day? We could meet, have lunch and go shopping.'

'We're going to buy Liz a new wardrobe in Paris,' Richard said. 'Do stop fussing, Mama. You haven't told her how happy you are to have her as your future daughter-in-law.'

'But of course I have,' Rosalind said. 'I am looking forward to it so much. Once you've settled in London we shall see each other often, Liz. You will find it strange at first but I shall introduce you to everyone and ...'

'Mama will try to involve you in her card parties and her charity work,' Richard warned. 'You mustn't let her make too many demands, darling. I shall want you with me most of the time.'

'How selfish he is,' Rosalind said, but with a warm smile for her son. 'But then, all men are, aren't they? They never understand that we are not simply there for their pleasure.'

She was only teasing Richard. She clearly adored him and he was fond of her. Their banter flowed over me as Rosalind continued to talk about her friends and activities.

Caroline's visit had made a deep impression on me. Had Richard really asked her to marry him years ago? And what did she mean when she'd said she would never marry him because they were too much alike?

I tried hard to put the whole conversation out of my mind but it kept going round and round in my head, worrying at me, making me uneasy, so that when I went up to bed I was on edge.

I sat down at the dressing table and brushed my hair by the light of an oil lamp. It was a softer light than electricity and seemed to throw shadows into the corners of the rooms ... but perhaps the shadows were in my mind?

What had Caroline been trying to tell me? I had an odd feeling that she had wanted to warn me ... but about what?

It was always difficult to sleep in a strange bed and even more so when I had so much on my mind. I tossed and turned for a long time, falling asleep at last to dream of Alexi Paulinski.

'We have met before ...'

'You didn't tell me ...' Caroline's accusing tones made me cry out in my restless sleep, bringing me to a sudden, startled waking. 'Be careful, little cousin ... be careful of the curse of the Caulders.'

I sat up in bed, feeling odd. My cousin's accusing expression was fresh in my mind. Alexi Paulinski was obviously her current lover and I suspected that she was not quite as casual about her affairs as she'd pretended. Perhaps jealousy had prompted those disturbing remarks about Richard? She was warning me off Alexi. If so, they need never have been made. I had no interest in any man but Richard—and Mr Paulinski made me nervous.

Yet there was no reason why he should—no sensible reason!

I tried to dismiss Caroline's chatter as harmless but could not rid myself of the feeling that my cousin had been trying to warn me—yet why should she?

I shook my head, determined to put it all out of my mind and enjoy the rest of my visit, but Caroline had succeeded in casting a shadow over everything and I was not completely successful.

Richard glanced at me as we were driving home later that day.

'Something wrong? You've been quiet all day.'

'There's nothing wrong.'

'Women always say that but never mean it.'

'Nothing is wrong.'

He pulled the car over to the side of the road, parking in the gateway of a field where several horses were grazing, then turned to look at me, a serious expression in his eyes.

'Was it something my mother said? Or are you angry with me?'

'I'm not angry.' I twisted my white cotton gloves in my hands, then took a deep breath. 'Caroline told me you'd asked her to marry you and she turned you down.' I looked up at him, unable to hide my anxiety. 'Were—are you still in love with her?'

'I might have known it was Caro!' He cursed beneath his breath. 'Why didn't you tell me last night? Why torture yourself all this time?'

'I didn't want to say anything. I wouldn't have if you hadn't insisted.'

'As well I did.' Richard reached for my hands. 'My poor, silly love. What have you been imagining?'

'She is very beautiful ...'

'When I asked Caro to marry me, I was twenty-five and she was seventeen. There was a war on and I was afraid I might not come back. I suppose I thought it my duty to marry and perhaps leave a child behind me—to carry on the family name if I died. A young man's vanity—an unconscious desire for immortality.'

'Were you in love with her?'

I looked at him uncertainly, wanting to believe.

'She was pretty and I thought I might be. Fortunately for us both Caro knew better. She told me it was just panic and offered to go to bed with me if it would make me feel better.'

'Did you?'

'No, my darling, I did not. I was an idealistic young idiot then and her refusal hurt my pride. We quarrelled and it was a long time before either of us forgave the other.'

'Oh, I see.' I felt foolish. 'She did say she wasn't a rival but I couldn't help wondering if ...'

'If I'd asked you on the rebound?' Richard touched my cheek. 'I've never felt this way about anyone until now. Please believe me, Liz. It's you I want to marry.'

'I'm sorry for doubting you. Will you please forgive me?'

I felt wretched for having been suspicious.

'There is nothing to forgive. It was Caroline's fault. She said those things to hurt you—to cause trouble between us.'

I supposed she must have.

'But why? Why should she want to hurt me?'

'Who knows why Caro does the things she does? Sometimes I think she has a little demon inside her head. She can be a good friend and an amusing companion when she's in a good mood—but just watch out for those claws.'

'Yes, I will.' I was hesitant. I had liked her despite what she had said. 'She asked if we could be friends.'

'I would rather you didn't see too much of her.'

'That would be rather awkward, wouldn't it?'

'We can't stop her calling because she is family, but she is wild—a disturbing influence.'

That much was certainly true.

'She told me she collects lovers. I think she wanted to shock me.'

'I should imagine you were very shocked.'

'If I was, I didn't let her see it.'

'Good for you,' Richard murmured, a husky note in his voice. 'Just don't believe what she says—and don't listen to her ideas about women having the right to ... don't listen to her, Liz. Caro's trouble is that she has had too much of her own way. Her mother died when she was born and everyone spoiled her to make up for it.'

had promised to be with me as soon as he could—and to bring my engagement ring.

My frown cleared as I realized Caroline must have heard him telling his mother about the trip to Paris. He wouldn't have seen her when he got back to London the previous evening. It would have been far too late.

Besides, there was no reason why he should—was there?

Chapter 5

It was a week later that it happened. I had been shopping in the village and was very surprised when I came back to the house and found my cousin's car parked outside the house.

What was Caroline doing here?

As I went into the house I heard the sound of laughter coming from my father's study. The door was open and, as I approached, I could see her perched on the edge of Ben's desk, swinging her long, shapely legs and smoking a cigarette. He was laughing at something she had said to him, obviously enjoying her company.

'Ah, there you are, Lizzie,' he said as I entered. 'Caroline was just telling me about a party she went to the other night.'

'It was in a seedy night-club,' she explained. 'A friend of mine—Jiffy Harrington—is one of the true jazz aficionados. He has all the records

101

from America: the wonderful Louis Armstrong, Bix Beiderbecke, Mezz Mezzrow ... oh, you know. I could reel them off—but you would probably be bored.'

'I'm not in the least bored. Jack collects anything about Don Redman and Pee Wee Russell.'

'Well, you'll know what I mean by Harlem's Cotton Club then?' I nodded and she flicked back her hair. 'Jiffy insisted on taking us to this night-club. My dears!' Caroline rolled her eyes. 'It was awful. So boring and such a poor imitation of the real thing. I kept wishing we would be invaded by Al Capone and his gangsters—but no such luck.'

'I don't think I would care for an invasion by gangsters!'

'But you're not Caroline,' my father said, giving her legs an admiring glance. 'She is what the newspapers call a "Bright Young Thing"—have I got that right, Caro?'

'Spot on, darling,' she cried and fluttered her lashes at him flirtatiously. 'As I said to Saree, poor Jiffy was probably a bit squiffy to take us there in the first place, but it was certainly an experience.'

'Who is Saree?' I asked.

'One of my greatest friends,' Caroline said. 'Lady Sara, actually, though she hates to be called that. As it happens, she is the reason I am here.' Caroline glanced at Ben and then me. 'Saree has organized a charity dance for tomorrow evening and I wanted you to come. Do say you will, Lizzie? I've got a few spare and dark, rather haunted-looking, with a thin, pale face and grey eyes. Whatever he was saying seemed to upset Caroline because she walked away from him, her face set in an expression of anger. After that she started flirting heavily with Jiffy who looked as if he might already have had far too much champagne.

'Why so serious?' I turned as Lady Sara spoke. She was dressed in satin harem pants, a flowing tunic and jewelled turban. Her mouth was thick with dark red lipstick and a cigarette in an elegant holder dangled from between her fingers. 'You've met Alexi, haven't you? He has just arrived. I thought he had forgotten us.' Her smile was slightly accusing but indulgent. 'But I shall forgive him because he is here now.'

I had already seen him standing just behind her and my heart jolted as he smiled.

'Yes, we have met,' I said. 'Good evening, Mr Paulinski.'

'Please—I would prefer Alexi, if you could bear it?'

'Alexi then.'

'Why are you standing here alone? Has Caroline deserted you?'

'She introduced me to everyone.' I made excuses for my cousin. 'I have been dancing.'

'But you prefer not to, perhaps?'

'I like to watch sometimes.' I hesitated. 'This isn't really my sort of thing. Caroline wanted me to come, and it is for a good cause. Lady Sara was telling me about her mission. She is doing wonderful work.'

'Ah, yes, the mission. It is a worthwhile

cause, that is why I was talked into coming this evening.' He glanced after our hostess, who had walked off to talk with another of her guests. 'Saree was a little wild when she was young. She was married at seventeen to a man old enough to be her father and is now a widow—quite a rich one, I believe. They say she was one of the nudes Modigliani used for his Paris show of 1918 but it has never been confirmed, either by the artist or Saree.'

'I like her very much,' I said, watching as Lady Sara went to have a word with Lord Rupert before he left. 'I met her brother briefly. He looks very angry.'

'He is racked with guilt for being alive when so many of his comrades are not. It is a feeling shared by many, I believe.'

'It was a terrible time.'

'Rupert cannot forget. There are many others like him.'

'Yes, I suppose so—but surely it is time to forget?'

'If one can, yes.'

I suspected Alexi Paulinski could have said more on the subject if he had wished, but Caroline was coming purposefully towards us.

'Jiffy wants us all to go on to a night-club.'

'I do not think Miss Caulder wants to go,' Alexi said with a glance at my face. 'If you wish to go, I can take her back to your house, Caroline.'

'I shan't bother if you two aren't coming,' she replied with a yawn. 'It will probably turn

110

out to be one of Jiffy's mad ideas. We'll go home if you like, Lizzie. I've had enough anyway.'

For a moment her eyes seemed to range around the room as if searching for something— or someone.

'You are easily bored, Caro,' Alexi said with a smile. 'You should take up a good cause, like Saree.'

'Oh, not you too,' Caroline said, and pulled a face. 'Saree has been after me to help at the mission for ages. It just isn't my cup of tea, darling. I'll help with her charity affairs—but that's it.'

'I wouldn't mind helping, when we're in London,' I said.

'Saree will keep you to it if you offer,' Caroline warned. 'Let's go then. I shall fall asleep on my feet in a minute.'

'You drink too much champagne,' Alexi said. 'It isn't good for you.'

'What is?' she quipped. 'We live for but a passing hour ... and I intend to make the most of it.'

'But are you happy?'

'Happiness is an elusive thing,' she said. 'Don't ask silly questions at this hour, Alexi. I want to sleep and sleep and sleep.'

Caroline was still sleeping in the next room when I heard the phone ringing the next morning. I got up to answer it, hoping it wouldn't wake her.

'Hello ... may I help you?'

111

'Lizzie? Is that you?'

'Richard?' My heart raced at the sound of his voice.

'It is you!' He was annoyed. 'Mama told me she had heard you were staying with Caroline. I couldn't believe it, but when I rang your home Maggie told me you had come up for a charity dance. Why didn't you let me know?'

'I tried telephoning you, Richard. You were never there.'

'I've been busy. What on earth made you do it?'

'She came down and practically kidnapped me. I couldn't refuse—it would have seemed churlish.'

'Mama asked you to come up and you refused.'

'I refused Caroline once but she wouldn't take no for an answer. I'm sorry, Richard. I didn't think you would mind so very much.'

'I do mind. I think you should have consulted me first.'

'Everyone thought I should come. Ben and Maggie ...'

'They don't know Caroline as I do.'

'I'm sorry. I wish I hadn't.' I glanced up and saw Caroline yawning in the doorway. 'I wouldn't have if I'd realized it would make you angry. Please don't be angry, Richard.'

'I'm not angry. Just upset and disappointed. If you'd said you wanted to come up, we could have arranged something for you—something more suitable. Caroline's friends are not the sort of people I want you to know.'

'Lady Sara and her brother are very respectable.'

'But others are less so. Besides Saree was wild as a young woman. Her family despaired of her long ago. Now she is so wealthy she can ignore them.'

'I know. Alexi told me.'

'Paulinski? Was he there?'

'Yes.'

'That's exactly what I meant! He is a sculptor ... part of that whole Bohemian crowd.'

'Caroline told me his father was a Polish baron.'

'That is beside the point. He is mixed up with the wild set Caroline encourages, and I would rather you stayed clear of them.'

'I'm sorry, Richard.'

'Can you be ready in an hour? I'll pick you up and drive you home.'

I felt the sting of tears behind my eyes as I told him I would be ready.

'Was Richard getting at you?' Caroline asked when I replaced the receiver and followed her into the kitchen. 'Cup of tea—or do you prefer coffee?'

'Coffee, please.'

'Take no notice of him,' she advised. 'He doesn't own you. It isn't the way it used to be for women. We have the right to stick up for ourselves these days. Sometimes I get so angry with the way men treat us that I think of doing a Nancy Astor.'

'Go into politics?' I stared at her.

'Why not?' A smile flickered around her

mouth. 'Or perhaps not. My reputation is not so pure as it might be. Every decent citizen would be outraged; they would call me a wicked woman and throw mud at me in the streets!'

I laughed and took the cup she offered me. 'Surely it isn't that bad?'

'You'd be surprised.' She raised her eyebrows. 'Is Richard coming to fetch you?'

'Yes. It is rather rude of me to leave like this. I had promised to visit Lady Sara's mission.'

'I shall explain.' Caroline sipped her coffee. 'You are sure, aren't you, Lizzie—about Richard?'

'I love him.'

'Then I shall say no more about it, except to wish you every happiness.'

'Are you still coming to the wedding?'

'No, I don't think so. Alexi has asked me to go to Paris with him. He has an exhibition there.'

She was going to Paris with Alexi! That was just the kind of behaviour of which Richard was so disapproving.

'So you will be in Paris when we are there?'

'Oh, don't worry, we shan't intrude on you. If you see us you must just walk right by as if you didn't know us. Unless Richard isn't with you, of course.'

'Oh, Caroline!'

She laughed. 'We can still be friends,' she said. 'But I won't lead you into bad ways. You didn't enjoy yourself last night, did you?'

'Not very much.'

'Nor did I,' she said, and pulled a face. 'I'm

bored with the same old faces. I think I shall take up flying—if I can persuade Rupert to take me up.'

'Is that what you were talking about last night?'

Her eyes clouded. 'He refuses—says it's too dangerous. Too dangerous for me, but not for him. He thinks his life is worth nothing. He makes me so angry sometimes.'

'Alexi said he felt guilty for being alive when so many of his comrades died.'

'Alexi said that?' Caroline frowned. 'I think he might be right, though ...' She stopped abruptly, as if she had already confided too much. 'You'd better go and get ready. You don't want to keep Richard waiting.'

I wondered about Caroline as I followed her advice. What had brought that look of sadness to her eyes?

It was obviously something she wasn't prepared to share.

Richard didn't say much as he drove me home. His face was set in a tight, annoyed expression and I knew he was very angry with me. I turned to him as he stopped the car outside Winspear.

'Please don't be angry with me, Richard. I can't bear it.'

'I just wish you had told me, that's all. Mama was very upset to hear from someone else that you were in town. You could have telephoned her if you couldn't manage to contact me.'

'I didn't have her number.'

115

'You could have asked Caroline for it. Don't make weak excuses, Liz. It was hurtful for her—and me.'

'I'm sorry. It all happened so fast that I didn't have time to think.' I turned to leave the car, tears stinging my eyes.

Richard caught my arm. He made me stay in the car.

'Look at me, Liz.' I obeyed and he frowned as he saw my face. 'You can't go in looking like that.' He reached out to wipe a tear from my cheek. 'What a brute I am.'

I choked back a sob. 'I didn't mean to make you angry.'

'And I didn't mean to make you cry. Forgive me?'

'There's nothing to forgive—it was my fault.'

He leaned towards me, his lips brushing softly over mine.

'I'm sorry. I was upset—hurt because you had gone off with Caroline without letting me know.'

'I wish I hadn't.'

'No, no,' he said, his expression becoming contrite. 'There was no reason why you shouldn't. She is your cousin. I've been unfair to you, darling.'

'No, of course you haven't.'

I went into his arms as he kissed me again.

'I do love you, Richard.'

'And I love you.' He smiled and handed me an impressive leather ring box. 'I think this makes it official.'

I gasped with pleasure as I opened the box

and saw the beautiful emerald and diamond ring inside. The emerald was large, square and perfect—something that I knew was very rare. It must have cost a fortune!

'It's a family ring,' Richard said as I began to thank him. 'I believe it belonged to your grandmother. Henry insisted that I give it to you—but I could buy you something different if you don't like it? I couldn't afford anything of this quality, of course, and it does look good on your hand ...'

He had taken the ring from its box and slipped it on my finger as he spoke. I wished that I had the courage to ask for something simpler, less valuable—something he had bought for me himself—but after coming so close to a real quarrel, I was afraid to say what was in my heart.

'It's beautiful,' I whispered. 'Thank you so much, Richard.'

'I'm glad you're pleased.' He looked satisfied. 'Now wipe your face, darling, and we'll go in.'

That night, I looked at the beautiful ring Richard had given me as I slipped it from my finger and placed it safely in the impressive leather box on my dressing table. I noticed the inscription in gold lettering inside the lid: H. Caulder & Son. Makers of Fine Jewellery', and felt suddenly chilled.

It seemed to me that Henry Caulder had somehow cast a shadow over my life, and I sensed him hovering in the background, manipulating us all like some malevolent spider, enmeshing us in his web.

It was a beautiful ring, a valuable ring—but I wished that Richard had bought me something simpler, something I was not afraid to wear.

Perhaps I should have told him at once, but because we had come so close to quarrelling I had not dared.

Richard had been angry because I had let Caroline persuade me into visiting her in London.

'The Caulders are selfish, cold people,' Hannah had told me once. 'If I had not been as strong as I was they would have broken me against the rock of their pride—a pride that is based solely upon money.'

And I was about to become deeply involved with that family.

Chapter 6

The time was passing so quickly; it was September and the day of my wedding was coming closer and closer. I was anticipating it with mixed feelings. When I was with Richard I was sure that I loved him and was impatient to be his wife—but when I was alone at nights the doubts sometimes came to plague me.

I pictured Henry Caulder in my mind, seeing him as a harsh cold man—a man of whom I must be wary.

Surely he had not pushed his poor wife down the stairs?

No, no, that was nonsense.

I wished that Caroline had not put that idea into my mind.

Perhaps it was because I did not want to think too deeply about the future that I took up Ned Jenkins' cause.

Maggie told me about the tragedy one morning as we were working in the kitchen together, bottling the last of the raspberries.

'Ned's boss isn't so bad as they go. He has given them longer than he need have done,' she said. 'But once Ned lost his arm in that accident, it was certain he would have to go. The cottage is tied to the job and Ned won't be much use on the land now. He and his family will be on the dole—and goodness knows what kind of a place they'll be able to find for what they can afford. Twenty-nine shillings and three pence won't go far—and them used to cheap milk and eggs from the farm.'

The family's plight had preyed on my mind despite the fact that I had my own problems. At the end of the week I should be Richard's wife, a prospect that, while I longed for it, set the butterflies fluttering in my stomach.

That particular morning I had decided to take the Jenkins family a basket of food from the well-stocked shelves of the pantry at Winspear.

'You're that kind,' Mrs Jenkins said, accepting the gift gratefully. 'We shall all miss you when you go, Miss Caulder.'

'I shall visit sometimes.' I glanced round the

small kitchen. It was clean and neat, but there was no running water in the sink and the walls were showing signs of damp, which wasn't surprising given that the cottage had stood for more than two hundred years. 'You must say if it doesn't appeal to you, Mrs Jenkins, but I've spoken to my father and he has agreed to let you have the cottage at the bottom of our orchard. It hasn't been used in years and you'll need to get someone in to do a few repairs, but we shall only charge you a peppercorn rent of a shilling a year, and I think ...'

'Oh, miss! How can we ever thank you?'

'There's no need.'

But Sally Jenkins burst into tears, pouring out all her troubles in a rush of emotion and relief at being offered a way out of her predicament, and it was a while before she had calmed down sufficiently for me to leave her.

I was thoughtful as I walked home. It was disgusting that anyone should have to live in such poverty and it made me angry.

The cottage I had offered Sally had once been used by the gardener and his family, but that was long before Ben bought the house. The inside was in a neglected state, but the roof was sound and there was a well in the yard with a pump that still worked. Maggie had promised that her husband and two sons would help to make it fit for habitation, and, after seeing the conditions the Jenkinses were living in, I thought it might be an improvement.

'What did she say then?' Maggie asked as I walked in. 'Was she pleased with the preserves?'

'Yes, very. I told her you were going to help her get the cottage straight but I'm not sure she heard me. She was crying ... sobbing her heart out.'

'I'm not surprised! They were due to be out on the street next week.'

'I know.' I dumped my empty basket on the floor of the pantry. 'Has Jack arrived?'

'No, but there are a couple of parcels for you. I took one upstairs and put it on your bed—the other is over there.'

'Thank you. They must be wedding gifts.'

Maggie looked a bit dubious. 'I didn't take this one up because it smells odd.'

'Smells odd? What do you mean?'

'Nasty—strange.'

I looked at the square parcel Maggie had put on a stool near the back door.

'I can't smell anything.'

'Let me open it.' Maggie's face was grim as she cut the string and revealed a brown cardboard box. 'Can you smell it now?'

'I'm not sure ...' There was a faint odour coming from the box. 'Yes, I think so. Whatever can it be?'

'Let me open it for you?' I nodded and she took the lid off, screwed up her face and shut it again before I could see the contents. 'I thought as much. It's nasty, Lizzie. You don't want to look, believe me.'

I felt cold all over as I saw her expression.

'What is it?'

'A dead rat ... been dead for a while by the smell of it.'

121

Maggie picked up the box and ran outside to the rubbish bins. She washed her hands at the sink when she came back, then turned to look at me.

'There was just something odd about it when it came,' she said. 'The writing—it wasn't properly addressed. Big, scrawly letters, like a child's hand.'

'Who on earth could have sent it?'

'If I knew they'd soon wish they hadn't!'

'It must be someone's idea of a joke.'

'Some joke! With all the wedding presents arriving ... someone wanted to upset you.'

The coldness spread all over me.

'But why—why would someone do a thing like that?'

'There's a lot of weird folk about,' Maggie said with a dark look. 'Someone is jealous because you're marrying Mr Gregory.'

'But no one knows him.'

'No one round here.'

'What are you implying?'

'That Caroline ... she likes her own way. I wouldn't put it past her to do something like this, if she had reason.'

'Caroline?' I shook my head. 'She wouldn't. No, Maggie. I'm sure you're wrong—why should she?'

'I don't know, but she's a troublemaker. You watch out for her, Lizzie. She's a jealous madam, you mark my words.'

'I'm sure she wouldn't ...'

And yet I had felt all along that Caroline didn't want me to marry Richard.

'Do you want me to open your other parcel, just in case?'

'I'm sure it's all right. Whoever sent the rat wouldn't do it again—would they?'

'It looked all right,' Maggie said. 'But it was addressed to you personally, same as that.' She jerked her head towards the back door. 'Not the same writing, though.'

'It must be a wedding gift.'

We had already received several gifts from local people, but they had all been addressed to both Richard and me. Now two parcels for me had arrived on the same day.

'The postmark is London.'

'It's probably from Richard. Don't worry, Maggie. I'm sure it isn't another dead rat.'

I hurried upstairs. Richard had been too busy to come down the previous weekend but he telephoned often and had arranged for a local florist to deliver flowers twice a week. When I saw the large square package on my bed I thought he had probably sent me something pretty to wear.

I removed the string and wrappings, then hesitated before lifting the lid of the box inside. Supposing it was something nasty again? I needn't have worried. The exquisite lingerie packed in layers of tissue paper made me gasp with delight; there were saucy French knickers, camisoles and a nightgown, all made of crepe-de-chîne in a pretty flesh tone, as were the silk stockings. Very expensive!

I picked up the card and read it.

'Dear Lizzie ...' The lettering was bold and

123

well-formed. 'These are for your honeymoon with my good wishes. Good luck for the wedding—and the future! Be happy, Caroline.'

I re-read the message several times, then as I turned it over, I found a postscript.

'I chose these because I refuse to give Richard anything.'

What did she mean by that? Once again I was aware of a subtle warning.

I touched the delicate lingerie with reverent fingers. I had already bought myself a few pretty things, but nothing as fine as these. Caroline had been very generous in her choice of a wedding present.

We had been very lucky, receiving many useful gifts from people I knew locally, just towels and embroidered pillowcases, things like that, but Rosalind was giving us fifty pounds and a porcelain tea service. Ben had promised a similar amount and a silver teapot that had been Hannah's pride and joy.

Caroline's present to me must have cost her a great deal. I picked up her card again, wondering just what she was trying to tell me.

I was still puzzling over it when I heard a knock at my bedroom door and then a male voice asking if he could come in.

'Jack!' I whirled round in delight as my brother opened the door. 'You're home at last. I was afraid you wouldn't get here.'

'Not come to your wedding, Lizzie?' He pulled a face of mock reproach. 'Neither hell nor high water could keep me away.

I threw myself into his arms. It was so good to

have him home! I'd begged him to come when his college term ended but he'd made excuses about staying with friends and I'd almost given up hope of seeing him.

'Have you spoken to Ben?'

'Not yet.' Jack grimaced. 'He isn't going to be pleased when I tell him I've joined up.'

'Oh, Jack!' I stared at him in dismay. 'He wanted you to finish your degree at college and then go into the law.'

'It isn't what I want,' my brother said. 'I can't do something I'd hate, Lizzie. He shouldn't expect me to—he didn't do what his father wanted either.'

'No,' I had to agree though I still felt doubtful about what he had done. 'I suppose it's the same thing—though their quarrel was over the way Grandfather Caulder refused to meet Mother.'

'But he apologized later,' Jack said. 'He tried to make amends but they wouldn't let him—kept the feud going long after he'd relented.' His face was a little pink as he went on, 'Henry has written to me, explaining how sorry he feels about the rift between us and asking me to go and stay at Pentire for a few days.'

'Shall you go?'

'Yes, I think I shall. It was wrong of him to behave the way he did but I don't see the point of carrying this silly quarrel on indefinitely. If he wants to make some sort of amends ...'

'Do you mean money?'

'Why not?' Jack's colour deepened as I stared at him. 'I dare say he's got more than he knows what to do with. I shan't refuse if he wants to

125

give me some of it—why should I?'

'Oh, Jack!' I was half amused, half shocked. 'I keep thinking it might have made a difference to Hannah if he'd helped her when she needed it.'

'She was too proud to accept,' Jack said. 'Grandfather offered to pay for the best hospital treatment available when she was ill but she refused.'

'How do you know that?'

'Ben told me. He would have taken the money for her sake but she wouldn't let him. She said it was too late; it wouldn't have made any difference and she wanted to die at home.'

'He has never told me that.'

Jack shrugged. 'I got upset once when she was ill and yelled at him, asked him why the hell he didn't do something to help her—that's why he told me.'

'I see.' I was thoughtful. 'I think that might make a difference to the way I feel towards Grandfather Caulder but I'm not sure. It doesn't alter the fact that he caused a lot of unhappiness.'

'Well, I'm going to stay with him,' Jack said, 'and you shouldn't be too hard on him, Lizzie. He's getting on a bit and if he wants to make up for the past, maybe we should let him.'

'I'll think about what you've said. Richard is going to take me for a visit when we get back from Paris.' I smiled at my brother, linking my arm through his. 'Let's go and tell Ben you're here.'

It was my wedding day and the post had brought a pile of letters and cards from people who wished us well, but nothing had prepared me for Henry Caulder's gift. I read his letter, which spoke of an account opened in my name and a bank draft of six hundred pounds. It was a fortune. Far too much! I couldn't possibly accept it ... yet it would be rude to return such a generous gift.

I had been taught to dislike and distrust the Caulder family, in particular my grandfather. I thought of Henry as a stern, hard man who ruled with a rod of iron, uncaring of the feelings of others—and yet his letter to me was kind and seemed sincere, almost pleading.

What ought I to do? It would seem disloyal to Hannah if I let myself be swayed and yet ... I would ask Richard what I should do later, I decided, slipping the letter into my bag.

Maggie's voice was calling to me from outside my door.

'Are you decent, love?'

'Yes, of course. Come in.'

I had already slipped into my wedding gown. It was a simple cream lace dress with a square neckline, a dropped waist and long sleeves. Richard's beautiful emerald and diamond ring sparkled on my finger and I was wearing a pair of matching earrings he had sent me as a wedding gift.

More family heirlooms, perhaps? I wasn't sure.

In my hair was a band of seed pearls, which

held the veiling Hannah had worn at her own wedding.

'You look beautiful,' Maggie declared, and blinked away emotional tears. 'I've brought you this to wear ... something blue.' She held out the frilly garter. 'Something new, something old.'

'Thank you.' I kissed her cheek. 'Ann lent me a lace handkerchief so I've got everything I need for luck.'

'You deserve to be happy,' Maggie said. 'Your father was asking for you. He wants to talk to you before we leave for the church. And the flowers have arrived.'

'I'll come down now.'

I glanced round the room. Soon I would be leaving childhood behind forever and there was sadness mixed with my anticipation. Despite the pain and the tears of the past few years, I had been happy in this house.

Maggie sensed my hesitation. 'It's not far from London by train these days,' she said. 'We'll take good care of him.'

'Yes, I know you will.'

I dismissed my odd sense of unease. It wasn't as if I was marrying against Ben's wishes. He was pleased about it. He wanted me to marry. I knew he had been in considerable pain these past few days but he hadn't drunk too much, or not enough to bring on one of his sullen rages. It was almost as if he were biding his time ... waiting for something. For me to be gone from the house?

I shook my head, dismissing my fears as nonsense. Everything was going to be fine. I would visit as often as I could and there was nothing I could do for my father that Ann or Maggie couldn't.

Ben was sitting in his chair, staring out of the window. It was a shock to see him in his smart grey suit. The last time he'd worn a suit was for Hannah's funeral.

He turned as I entered, giving me a long, thoughtful look before smiling at me.

'You look lovely,' he said. 'Are you happy, Liz? I know I said there was no point in waiting but if you're in any doubt ...'

'I am quite sure I love Richard,' I said. 'Marriage is always a gamble, isn't it?'

'Did we teach you that?' He looked sad.

'I suppose you did, but you taught me other things too—like decency, honesty and courage.'

'You make me feel very humble.'

'I didn't mean to. I suppose I just wanted to say I loved you and Hannah.'

'You'll be all right, Lizzie. You are like Hannah. Whatever happens, you'll cope.'

'Yes, of course. Are you going to be all right?'

'Me?' Ben glared. 'What do you think you can do for me that Maggie's daughter can't?'

'Nothing. I'm being silly. Nerves, I expect.' I heard voices in the hallway. 'It sounds as if the cars have arrived.'

'I loved her,' Ben said, the words coming out in a choked whisper. 'Despite everything I never stopped loving her—and I love you.'

'I know. I love you, Dad. I always shall.'

'Be happy, Lizzie. That's all I want.'

129

I wanted to hug him but Jack came in to tell us the cars were waiting and the moment was lost. Ben was going in the first one with Maggie and Ann so that they could help with his chair. Jack and I were to follow in the next one. Lady Rouse's five-year-old niece was my only bridesmaid and she would come straight to church from her aunt's house.

Tears stung my eyes as I watched my father wheel his chair outside. Jack looked at me in concern but I shook my head, fighting my emotion.

'Are you all right?'

'Yes.' I blinked hard. 'It's just nerves.'

But it wasn't. Ben had called me Lizzie and told me he loved me. It wasn't like him and for a moment I wished I had waited. It was too soon! I hardly knew Richard. I couldn't desert my father ...

'Are you ready?' Jack asked. 'We should be leaving.'

How foolish I was! Ben didn't need me. He would be well cared for by Ann and Maggie—and I was in love with Richard.

'I'm ready,' I said, and took my brother's arm.

A small crowd had gathered outside the church and most of the pews were filled with local people: there were smiles and waves as I arrived, and stood for a moment in the sunshine, the breeze lifting my veil, ruffling the front of my hair so that a few fine tendrils escaped to curl about my face.

I took a deep breath, my hand trembling a little on Jack's arm as he walked me down the aisle to stand beside the tall, handsome man who would soon be my husband. Ben's chair was already in position and it would be he who would answer when the vicar asked, 'Who gives this woman to this man?'

Richard turned to look at me as I reached him. The smile he gave me settled the butterflies in my stomach. He loved me and I loved him—there was nothing to be nervous about. We were going to be so happy together.

I smiled in return, then fixed my eyes on the altar, watching the sunbeams turning the brass cross to a glittering gold. I thought I would remember this moment forever and was aware of an inner serenity, a happiness that flowed out from me to all those I loved.

The ceremony was soon over. We signed our names in the registry and then we were out in the warm summer air with the bells pealing and people throwing confetti. Someone gave me a lucky horseshoe tied up with a blue ribbon. A little girl in her best party frock, one white sock up to her knee and the other dangling round her ankle, offered flowers from her mother's garden. I bent to kiss her and got a rather sticky hug in return.

After the presentations we all paused for photographs to be taken by Jack and Maggie, and then we were back in the special hired car, which had been decorated with ribbons on the bonnet.

Richard leaned towards me, looking into my

eyes before he kissed me on the lips. 'Happy, darling?'

'Very,' I said, and I was. My foolish doubts had dissolved in the sun like morning mist. 'Very happy.'

'Good. I hope you always will be happy.'

It was only a short drive to the house. Maggie and Ann had got there before us and were waiting with trays of food and glasses of champagne to hand to the guests.

Richard's mother had brought a friend to the wedding. Like Rosalind she was a widow of many years and I vaguely remembered her being mentioned when I was at Cromer.

'I was sure you wouldn't mind,' Rosalind said. 'Marion drives and I don't care to because of my nerves. It was so much easier than the train.'

'You are both very welcome, of course,' I said, and kissed each of them in turn.

Richard had brought two male friends, one of whom had been his best man. He introduced them as Peter Ross and John Barton. They were both pleasant, well-dressed and good-mannered, but neither of them made as much of an impression on me as my most unexpected guest.

I had sent invitations to both Caroline and her father but I had not thought Michael Caulder would come without his daughter.

'Caroline was sorry not to be here,' he said, handing me a box wrapped in pretty paper. 'I hope you don't mind that I came alone?'

'No, of course not.' I offered my cheek for his rather tentative kiss. 'It is nice to meet you at last. You are very welcome.'

Remembering the last time Michael had been at Winspear, I was anxious as I watched the meeting between Ben and his brother. It was not particularly warm on either side but to my relief they shook hands and spoke to one another for several minutes in a civilized manner.

'I'm surprised Michael came,' I whispered to Richard later when we had a moment alone. 'I only invited him because Caroline said she wanted to come.'

'It's less surprising than you think,' Richard replied. 'He wanted a sight of the opposition.'

'What do you mean?'

'Nothing much.' He shook his head. 'I'll explain later, darling. This isn't the time.'

I felt a coldness at the base of my spine. What was Richard hinting at? He couldn't mean that Michael saw me as a rival for Grandfather Caulder's money, could he?

But in my heart I knew that was exactly what he did mean and I was afraid he was right. I had caught Michael looking at me in a considering way more than once.

How horrible it all was! That my uncle could think of such a thing on my wedding day.

I found the idea distressing and tried to put it out of my mind, concentrating instead on the congratulations of my friends. I had asked a few of my own acquaintances after all and now I was glad; it would have been an awkward little gathering otherwise: Michael, Rosalind and her friend, Richard and I—and my father.

We were a family group and yet we were so

far apart, divided by the feud that had split the Caulders so many years ago and perhaps by other things ... secrets that I could not even begin to guess at. I sensed them, simmering beneath the surface, hidden but not forgotten.

I was very aware of those simmering passions as I looked up from cutting the cake with Richard. I had been laughing, but as I saw the expression in Michael's eyes my laughter died.

Why was he looking at me like that? Did he really believe that I was scheming to gain a share of Henry's fortune for my own?

I was soon to discover that Jack agreed with Richard about the reason for our uncle's presence at my wedding. He laughed about it when we had a moment alone, catching me at the bottom of the stairs as I was about to go up and change out of my wedding gown.

'You've set the cat amongst the pigeons, Lizzie,' he said, highly amused by the whole thing. 'Our dear uncle has looked as if he were eating sour grapes all afternoon. He obviously thinks there will be less for him to inherit now that you've married into the family ... in a manner of speaking.'

'My marriage to Richard has nothing to do with it,' I said. 'I was a Caulder, now I'm a Gregory. I can't see why that should bother Michael. I'm not interested in the money anyway.'

'If you can't see it, I can.' Jack's brows arched mockingly. 'You should have seen his face when I told him Henry had invited me to stay! He looked green.' Jack chuckled, devilment in his brown eyes. 'He and Caroline have had it all their own way until now. I bet Michael thought he was going to get the lion's share.'

'Don't!' I begged. 'I can't bear all this talk of money and who's going to get what. I married Richard because I loved him, not because I was interested in Grandfather Caulder's fortune.'

'You may not be interested but Richard certainly is. I'd bet my last shilling on that.'

'What do you mean?' I asked, sickness swirling in my stomach. 'Are you suggesting that he married me because of ...'

'No, no, of course not,' Jack said hastily 'He loves you, Lizzie. I just think Richard wouldn't be averse to getting his hands on some of it—and why not? I shall accept whatever the old boy offers me and be grateful for it.'

'Oh, Jack.'

I couldn't blame him for wanting more out of life but I had Hannah's strict sense of morality. Money itself was a useful thing to have but you had to earn it and you had to use it wisely, otherwise it could provoke greed and then it might lead to evil.

'What?' Jack was defensive.

'You won't ask Grandfather Caulder for money, will you?'

'What do you think I am?' he asked indignantly. 'I said I would take it if he offered. I've never asked for a favour in my life and I'm not about to start now.'

Relief flooded through me. Jack was still the same quick-tempered, honest person I had always loved.

Perhaps his attitude was the right one. Perhaps the evils of great wealth lay in jealous, simmering greed—an unspoken envy of another's good fortune—not in an honest desire to share the benefits money can often bring.

'I'm sorry,' I said, and hugged my brother. 'Forgive me?'

'Of course.' He grinned. 'Forget what I said about Richard. I'm probably wrong. Just be happy, Lizzie, you're all I really care about.'

'And Ben,' I said quickly. 'You will visit him sometimes, won't you? Even if he is grumpy.'

Jack looked stubborn and I sighed. He and my father were so alike in every way. Too alike for their own good.

'Jack ... for me?'

'For you, Lizzie?' He nodded. 'Yes, I'll do it for you. Don't worry, nothing will happen to him. He'll probably be around to plague us for years. Only the good die young.'

'Oh, Jack.' I kissed my brother and ran upstairs.

Ben would be fine. Maggie and Ann would look after him, and I would visit on my return from Paris.

Why was I worrying?

I could not rid myself of the idea that Henry Caulder's influence had begun to cast a dark shadow over us all, that an irresistible force had begun to shape and move our lives, as though we were pawns on the chessboard of Fate.

I was letting Jack's fancies play on my mind. This was my wedding day!

I was determined to put it all from my mind. This business of Richard being a little too interested in Grandfather Caulder's money was just Jack's imagination.

Chapter 7

I stared at the reflection of my pale, tear-stained face in dismay. I had just had the most terrible quarrel with Richard. It was my wedding night and instead of spending it in his arms, I was sitting alone, weeping.

How could it have happened? One minute we were happily sharing a bottle of champagne in our hotel room, the next we were almost shouting at each other.

It had begun when I showed Richard the letter from Henry Caulder. He had read it carefully, nodded and handed it back to me.

'I'd thought he might be a little more generous,' he remarked, 'but perhaps he is waiting until you meet. He is a crusty old thing at times but Caroline certainly knows how to get round him. I've heard him swear he will never settle another of her bills when she overspends her allowance, but he always does. You'll have to ask her how she manages it.'

'I wouldn't dream of it!' I was shocked, stunned. How could he say such a thing! 'I thought this gift was too much. I was going to ask you if I should just return it or wait until we meet and then explain it is more than I can accept.'

'Not accept?' Richard stared at me in disbelief 'Are you out of your mind? He would be deeply offended. Anyway, you will need it to buy yourself some decent clothes in Paris. You can hardly wear your usual stuff once we're settled in London, and I'm afraid what I earn barely pays the rent. I was hoping Henry would settle the same allowance on you as he has on Caroline.'

'I shan't accept it if he does.'

'You'll change your mind when you've thought it over.'

'No, I shan't, Richard. So don't ask it of me.'

'I've just told you, I don't earn much and I have expensive tastes. You won't enjoy living on what I can give you.'

'I'll manage—or I'll find work.'

I was answering instinctively, out of stubborn pride. Richard's bluntness had shocked me so much that I didn't know what I was saying, let alone how I truly felt about all this.

'What kind of work? I couldn't permit you to do anything demeaning. But if you wanted to design for Henry's workshops, that would be a different matter.'

'I told you, my designs were just a hobby.'

'Don't be silly, Liz. Henry is looking forward to seeing them. He will soon put you on the right track. Your ideas are sound, all you need is some practical help. As I said to him ...'

'You told him about my designs? You

discussed them with him—when I told you I didn't want him to see them?'

'He was interested and ...'

'You had no right to do that! How dare you?' I was suddenly furious. 'When did you speak to him?'

'Soon after we first met. We had lunch together and I told him that you had saved my life. He was most impressed. He wanted to know all about you so naturally I told him.'

'How cosy,' I cried. I felt angry, betrayed. Jack's insinuations were fresh in my mind. 'Was that why you married me—so that you could ingratiate yourself with him?'

Something in Richard's face told me that I wasn't far from the truth and a terrible bitterness welled up inside me. Jack had been right: Richard was more than a little interested in the Caulder inheritance.

Without thinking, I struck him once across the face. He stared at me for a moment, the crackle of ice in his eyes. For several long, terrifying moments neither of us spoke, then Richard turned towards the door. He glanced back, his hand on the knob.

'If that's the way you feel, there's no more to be said.'

He went out before I could answer, shutting the door after him with a little snap.

'Richard ...' I whispered, my throat closing with emotion. 'Please ... please ... don't.'

I stared at my reflection in the wall mirror. Was that woman with the wide, frightened eyes really me?

'Please don't.'

I wasn't sure what I was asking. Was it for him to return so that I could apologize—or to turn back the clock, to unsay all those terrible things we had said to each other?

I walked over to the bedroom window, looking out at the muted lights of the harbour. Tomorrow we were supposed to be taking a steam ship for France, but now ... what had I done?

Why had I said those wicked, wicked things? Was it because of Jack's hints just before I went up to change my dress? Had they festered in my mind—or had the doubts been there all the time, hiding in a tiny corner of my subconscious?

Hadn't I suspected Richard's feelings about the money right from the start? Suspected, but dismissed the disloyal thoughts because I didn't want to face the truth?

No! I loved him. Damn Henry Caulder and his money. I hated him and the way his shadow had fallen over my life.

I couldn't bear it that I had quarrelled with Richard over such a silly thing. What could the money matter when we loved each other? I loved Richard and he loved me ... didn't he?

'Don't be too proud, Lizzie.' I could hear my mother's voice whispering the words she had said to me the day before she died. 'I've always been too proud for my own good.'

Had Hannah been trying to tell me she regretted the feud with her husband's family?

'Oh, Hannah,' I choked, my eyes misty with tears. 'What have I done? I love him so.'

It was my fault. I had listened to Jack's barbed hints and let them prey on my mind. And now I was being stubborn over the gift from Grandfather Caulder. Henry was a very rich man. Six hundred pounds was nothing special to him. I realized it would be ungracious of me to return it.

I must apologize to Richard before it was too late. I took two steps towards the door, only to see it flung open before I could reach it.

'Lizzie ... I'm sorry.' He looked distraught. 'Forgive me. Please. Henry always wants to know everything. I told him because he has been like a father to me ... the only father I ever knew.'

I flew across the space between us and into his arms. 'I'm the one who should apologize,' I cried, the tears flowing as he held me. 'Forgive me, Richard. It was something Jack said—and Michael's coming to the wedding like that. I love you. If we need the money, I'll work ...'

'We'll manage,' he said in a hushed, contrite tone. 'Don't cry, my darling. I did warn you I wasn't perfect. I do try to live within my means but I'm not as good at it as I ought to be. I suppose Mama and Henry have both spoiled me in their different ways. I shouldn't have said what I did just now—but I want you to have the best. Henry won't even know he has given you that six hundred.'

'I know.' I accepted his handkerchief to wipe my wet cheeks. 'Even Hannah said I was too proud. We'll take the money, Richard. I want

141

you to think I look nice and I do need more new clothes.'

'You always look beautiful to me, whatever you wear.' He looked at me so intently that it set my pulses racing wildly. 'And I imagine you are even more lovely without any clothes at all.'

'Richard ...' My mouth quivered. It was such a dizzying, tumultuous ride I was on, my emotions veering from joyous anticipation to extreme misery and now tentative happiness, leaving me limp and bewildered. 'I was so awful to you just now—and I do love you so very much.'

'Not as much as I love you,' he vowed, and swept me up in his arms. 'You mustn't doubt that, my darling, even though I can never be good enough for you.'

I surrendered to his kiss and the pounding of my own heart, squashing any lingering doubts as the passion mounted between us. I went to him in innocence and love, letting him do as he would with me and lying passively in his arms, too humble and nervous to do more than accept the sweetness of his love-making.

Richard was so gentle with me that first time. His hands were caressing, his mouth persuasive rather than demanding as he led me carefully into the pleasures of intimacy, teaching me what he expected with such tender patience that I was scarcely aware of the slight pain as he entered me, thrusting deep inside the silken moistness of my inner self.

It was all over suddenly and more quickly

than I had expected, though afterwards Richard continued to hold me, his hands smoothing the arch of my back as though he understood I needed something more.

I lay with my face pressed against his damp skin, letting the stroking hands quiet my still throbbing senses. I was vaguely aware of disappointment, though I was uncertain what I had expected to feel. Until now I had known very little about the act of intimacy between a man and a woman. No one had told me anything, though Maggie had dropped a few awkward hints.

'If Ann was getting married I should tell her to be willing and patient,' she'd said, her cheeks pink with embarrassment. 'Wedding nights are seldom what they're cracked up to be—but it gets better in time if you really care about each other.'

I did love Richard very much. So I hid my disappointment when he said he was going to wash and dress and go down to the bar to find out a little more about what time we needed to board in the morning.

'If I were you I should stay here and get some sleep,' he advised. 'It will be quite a while on the boat and then there will be another long train journey when we get to France. Get what rest you can, Liz.'

I would rather have gone with him but sensed that he wanted to be alone. Perhaps he was hiding his disappointment from me—perhaps it was my fault that I felt like this, empty and deflated. It must be. Richard was not a fumbling innocent. He was twelve years my senior and I would be a fool to imagine I was the first woman he had ever made love to, so it must be my fault.

I smiled and feigned sleepiness as he went into the bathroom. By the time he left I was almost asleep. It was better to sleep than lie there and worry, wondering what had gone wrong.

A long, long time afterwards I was disturbed by someone knocking against the side of the bed. I moaned as I attempted to open my eyes, feeling as if I were surfacing from a drugged sleep. Where was I? What was happening?

'Are you awake?' Richard's voice murmured against my ear. 'Come on, Liz. Don't sulk. You're my wife and I want you.'

I was suddenly awake, very aware of the heat of his body against my naked flesh. He had been drinking! I could smell the whisky on his breath and it sent a shudder of revulsion through me. I turned my head away as he tried to kiss me.

'No, Richard,' I protested as he grabbed at me clumsily. 'What's the matter—are you drunk?'

He swore and lunged at me, trying to trap me with the weight of his body. Instinctively, I rolled away from him and jumped out of bed. He was drunk!

Revulsion swirled in me, making me feel disgust and shock. What was he doing? Surely he must know that the one thing I couldn't stand in a man was drunken, abusive behaviour?

'I need to go to the bathroom,' I said, and made a dash for it, locking the door behind me.

'Lizzie! Get out here. I want you ...' he called in a thick, slurred voice that made me shudder. 'Lizzie ...'

I relieved myself, then ran a bath and sat in it. I was shaking, though I wasn't sure whether it was from fright or anger. How could he get drunk on our wedding night?

How could he do this to me?

He knew how much Ben's drinking upset me. I could hardly believe that he would behave so badly. I had never known Richard to drink more than a couple of glasses of wine at dinner. He had merely sipped his champagne at the reception—so what had driven him to this?

It must be my fault. I hugged my knees as the tears slipped down my cheeks. I had disappointed him so deeply that he'd drunk to forget ... which made me the guilty one.

Surely he understood that I was willing to be an equal partner in our loving? It was only that I was naive and ignorant of the finer pleasures of sexual love. I would learn if he was willing to teach me.

The water had gone cold. I hadn't heard anything for ages. I towelled myself dry and cautiously unlocked the door. A gentle snore told me that Richard was sleeping.

Pulling on one of my pretty new nightgowns, I walked softly to the bed. Richard looked so peaceful lying there that my heart twisted. He hadn't meant to frighten me. It wasn't his fault that he had married a foolish child. If I had disappointed him, I must make it up to him.

'Richard ... are you asleep?'

There was no answer. I drew back the covers and slipped in beside him. I lay looking at his face in the shaded light. He had warned me that he wasn't perfect but I had still married him. I had been shocked, disappointed and hurt that evening—but it hadn't stopped me loving him. Perhaps it was just part of leaving childhood behind, becoming a woman.

Hannah had gone on loving Ben after much worse.

I kissed Richard's shoulder. He stirred and moaned but did not waken. I stroked my hand across his chest, moving my fingers in the sprinkling of fine hair. How soft his skin was, and how much I loved him. I suddenly wanted him to wake up and make love to me, but another tiny snore told me it wasn't going to happen.

All at once I realized it was funny. Richard had come to bed lusting after me and I'd run away in fright. Now I was lying here in frustration while he slept.

'I'm sorry,' I whispered against his ear. 'I couldn't help being a silly little virgin, Richard, but I'll try not to disappoint you again.'

Richard was abject in his apologies. He woke me with the tray of tea the waiter had brought up, looking very much like a puppy caught in the act of wetting the carpet.

'Do you hate me very much, Liz?' he asked. 'I don't know what made me do it. I never drink spirits—they don't suit me. I only remember having a couple ...'

146

His expression made me want to laugh. I reached out and touched his face as he sat beside me on the bed.

'It doesn't matter,' I said, 'but I would prefer you not to do it again. You know how I feel about what strong drink did to my father. It changed him, Richard, made him a monster.'

'I can't apologize enough. I've no idea what I said to you when I came up.' A look of horror came to his face. 'I didn't hurt you, did I? I didn't force ...'

'You wanted to but I locked myself in the bathroom.' I laughed as I remembered the way I had lusted after him when he was sleeping. 'But when I came out you were asleep—and you looked so adorable lying there that I wanted to ravish you.'

He stared at me for a speechless moment.

'Is that too shocking? Shouldn't I have said it?'

'If it's what you thought then of course you must say it,' he replied. Amusement was slowly dawning in his eyes. 'You're such a terrific girl, Liz. I don't deserve that you should be so understanding.'

'I love you.'

'Yes,' he said, and reached for my hand, turning it over to kiss the palm. 'I'll try to deserve it, Liz. What happened last night—it will never happen again, I promise.'

'Let's forget it and start again,' I said, holding his hand to my cheek. 'What time is it?'

'Time for you to get up,' he replied, relaxed and at ease once more. 'We shall soon be boarding. We'd better hurry or we shall be late.'

'I can't wait to see Paris,' I said, and threw back the bedcovers. 'That's where we'll begin our honeymoon, Richard. Last night never happened. We'll have our wedding night in Paris.'

For me Paris was instantly a place of enchantment. Here there could be no disappointment. I was captivated by its elegance, its charm and its noise, from the first time I walked in the Jardins des Tuileries, clinging to Richard's arm, sheer excitement making me pause to exclaim in delight over buildings or places I had previously seen only in illustrations or photographs.

It was wonderful, more than I had ever dreamed or anticipated. I insisted on dragging Richard the whole of the three hundred and eighty-six steps to the top of Nôtre Dame's North Tower so that we could gaze out at the wonderful views over the Seine and really feel the medieval atmosphere of the beautiful cathedral.

I gave Richard little lectures on the history of the city.

'Did you know that it was Henry IV who ordered the construction of the Marais?' I asked him over a leisurely lunch at one of the many open-air restaurants with which the city abounded. 'He was the king who said, *"Paris vaut bien une messe."* Paris is worth a mass. He was laying siege to the city and they wouldn't

148

have him because he wasn't a Catholic, so he had to convert.'

'I should imagine it was worth any amount,' Richard replied with a wry twist of his mouth. 'Personally, I wonder why he waited so long to convert when all this was within his grasp.'

The inference was clear: Richard thought principles were easily swept aside for material gain.

'He thought he could take it by force,' I said. 'But the people were too strong for him. They preferred to starve and die rather than give in. Some people are like that.'

Hannah had been like those people. She had refused to forgive or forget, keeping up the quarrel with Henry Caulder when it might have been ended.

'You're enjoying all this, aren't you?' Richard toyed with the stem of his wine glass. I sensed he was bored. 'Are you too tired to go shopping?'

'No, of course not.'

My cheeks felt warm and I could not look at him. Paris was full of wonderful palaces and museums. I could have spent every moment of my day exploring but Richard had had enough of history. He preferred shopping or dining out at exclusive restaurants and night-clubs. We had already been to Maxim's and the Moulin Rouge, and Richard had half suggested one of the more risqué cabaret concerts but I'd pulled a face and he hadn't insisted.

He was on his best behaviour, going out of his way to please me since we'd arrived at the small but comfortable hotel in one of the quieter areas around Montmartre, which had once been a favourite haunt of poets, writers, famous artists and their models. More recently, the artistic community had migrated towards Montparnasse, away from the village atmosphere to that of the cafés and the wilder, more frenetic gaiety that seemed to have taken over the city since the end of the war.

Montmartre had a gentle, faded elegance, with its vineyard and the gardens Renoir had made famous with his paintings, and I knew Richard had chosen it to please me when he might well have preferred somewhere smarter. He was desperately trying to make up for his lapse on our wedding night and I was determined to be happy. Not that it was difficult when he made love to me so beautifully every night and morning; he had filled our room with flowers bought from street sellers and walked miles with me, visiting all the places I had longed to see.

Now it was my turn to please him.

'Yes, let's go shopping,' I said. 'Perhaps we could go to the Folies Bergères this evening or to a night-club again?'

'We'll buy you lots of pretty clothes,' Richard said, summoning the waiter with renewed enthusiasm. 'It's time we spent some of that money Henry gave you. He will want to know what you've done with it when we see him.'

I nodded in agreement, making no comment. He was so obviously bored with all the sight seeing. Since he wanted to buy me yet more new clothes, I might as well let him.

Our room was strewn with the results of two days of hectic shopping. I had never owned so many lovely things. I had been shocked at how much money we were spending on my wardrobe and had insisted that Richard should buy himself some of the exquisite silk cravats we had seen in an exclusive men's shop. He purchased half a dozen but declined shirts, saying he could buy better in London.

'Paris for your wardrobe,' he told me. 'London for mine.'

But he did allow me to buy him a beautifully engraved Art Nouveau glass bowl from a shop in one of the fashionable Grands Boulevards.

'It's René Lalique,' he said as he unwrapped it reverently in our room later. 'I've always thought him the best of the Art Nouveau designers for jewellery as well as glass. You should study his work, Liz.'

'I have—or as much of it as I could, which I admit wasn't very much. I think he excels in human forms, particularly women, don't you?'

Richard nodded. 'Thank you for the bowl, darling. It will go very well with my collection.'

He looked pleased as he turned away to set the bowl on a chest and study it from a distance. I was beginning to realize that Richard had meant it when he'd said he had expensive tastes and found it difficult to live within his means. Everything he wore came from the best tailors, the best shops; his shoes were handmade, crafted to fit exactly; his underwear was either silk or the finest lawn, as were his shirts. Even

151

his luggage was a matching set of leather bags with his initials on the silver clasps. His watch came from Asprey, his hats and gloves from the most exclusive makers—and he had a small but growing collection of beautiful things at his London home.

'One day we shall have a large house in the country as well as the London apartment,' he had told me as we lay in bed whispering together after we had made love. 'I shall fill it with beautiful things, Liz. Rare, priceless treasures.'

I didn't ask where he intended to get the money to finance his dream. I knew now that he lived on a small allowance from Henry Caulder plus what he managed to earn as a journalist. It was enough for most people to live comfortably on but would not provide the kind of luxury Richard seemed to need.

Perhaps he expected to inherit money from Henry or his mother's family? I refrained from inquiring. If it was only a dream it belonged to Richard and he was entitled to keep it.

I liked beautiful things, too, but was content just to look at them in museums or the windows of exclusive shops as I had when window shopping with Hannah years before. I did not need to own everything I admired—but I was beginning to think that I might like to design jewellery and actually see it made up in precious materials.

Paris had opened my eyes with its wealth of treasures. Several times I had longed for my sketch pad and the time to sit and stare, but Richard was always in a hurry.

'What are you thinking about?' he asked me once when I had been silent for a while. 'Are you happy, Liz?'

'Yes, of course.'

I smiled at him. Of course I was happy. This was my honeymoon. I was in the most wonderful city in the world and with the man I loved. How could I not be happy?

If there were moments of unease ... moments when I felt a little uncertain of the future ... then I kept them to myself.

It was our last day in Paris. We had spent the morning shopping and now we were having a very expensive lunch at the Ritz as a special treat. I desperately wanted to visit the Louvre again but I also wanted to please Richard and knew he had already been to enough museums and galleries to last him a lifetime.

'What shall we do this afternoon?' I asked.

'I have some business,' he replied, playing with his wine glass. 'Could you amuse yourself for a few hours, darling?'

'Yes, I expect so.' I was surprised at his request. 'I've been wanting to spend some time at the Louvre. I could make a few sketches, things like that.'

'That's settled then!' He summoned the waiter with alacrity, hurrying me out of the restaurant and into the sunlit street. 'I'll see you at the hotel at about six this evening and we'll go somewhere special. You can find your own way from here, can't you?'

'Yes.' I watched him rush to the kerb as a

153

taxi appeared. He muttered something to the driver, opened the door and got in without a backward glance. 'I shall have to, shan't I?'

I could not help feeling a little annoyed at his desertion. Whatever his business was, he was in a tearing hurry to get there. I had thought he would want to make the most of our last day in Paris and was aware of a sharp stab of disappointment. Something was obviously far more important to Richard than spending the afternoon with me.

It seemed that as far as he was concerned our honeymoon was over.

Chapter 8

How was I ever going to get all these extra clothes into my suitcases? I surveyed the chaos of our room with amusement. We hadn't thought about packing up when we bought all this stuff. I glanced at my watch: it was almost five o'clock. Perhaps I ought to pop out and buy another bag to pack it all in? Richard wouldn't return for another hour ...

I heard something outside the room and half turned, not sure what to expect. Had Richard come back early? I was walking towards the door as someone knocked. I ran to open it, a smile of welcome on my lips.

'Rich— Caroline!' I cried, surprise mingling with my disappointment. 'I thought it must

154

be ...' Something in my cousin's face made me falter. I felt suddenly cold. 'What's wrong? It isn't Richard, is it? He hasn't had an accident?'

'Isn't he with you?' Caroline gave a cry of exasperation. 'Trust Richard to be missing when he's most needed.' She looked me in the eyes. 'I'm sorry. I can't make this easy for you. Henry sent me a telegram. Your father is very ill ... he's dying, Lizzie. You have to go at once. I've made arrangements for you to fly this evening in a private plane.'

'Fly ... this evening?' I was stunned, too shocked to take in what she was saying. 'Ben, dying? What happened?'

'There was an accident. I don't know the details. All Henry said was that I had to get you home at once—the sooner the better.'

I felt ill. The room seemed to be going round and round. I gasped and clutched at Caroline's arm to steady myself.

'I was afraid of something like this,' I whispered, feeling dizzy with shock. 'I should never ... never have left him.' I choked, then took a deep, shuddering breath. 'Richard had some business. He won't be here for another hour or so.'

'The plane won't wait,' Caroline said. 'I've been taking flying lessons with Bob Morrison. He runs a small freight business and has to leave on schedule. He has already delayed his flight for me, so you have to leave now. If you want to see Ben alive, there's no time to waste.'

'Fly now—without Richard?' I was bewildered.

This was the stuff of nightmares and I felt as if I were suffocating, out of breath and floundering like a fish left behind by the tide. 'Leave now ...'

'Wake up, Liz! It's your father. You want to see him, don't you?'

'Yes.'

'Then do as I say. Alexi is waiting downstairs. He will take you to the airfield. Leave this end to me. I'll pack your things and I'll tell Richard what has happened. Don't worry, Lizzie. Just go!'

Her calm, practical manner had got through to me. I must do as Caroline said. I had no choice if my father was dying. Richard would understand.

'Tell him I'm sorry,' I said, reaching for the thin jacket I had worn earlier. There was no time to change, no time for anything but my instinctive need to follow Caroline's instructions and fly to Ben's side. 'And, thank you.'

'Go!' she commanded. 'Don't worry about anything. You haven't much time. I've been trying to reach you all afternoon.'

After visiting the Louvre I had spent an hour or so walking, enjoying the sunshine. I had been enjoying myself while Ben was dying. I felt a rush of guilt and grief that almost choked me.

'Alexi will look after you,' Caroline called as I rushed from the room. 'You can trust him, Lizzie.'

I ran along the landing and down the stairs. Panic was beginning to grip me. My father was dying! It was my fault for leaving him. I had known ... sensed that something would happen. It was my fault ... my fault ...

I was in such a state that I almost went past Alexi; he grabbed my arm, holding me still. I glanced up at him, tears welling as I saw the sympathy in his face.

'Richard isn't with you?'

'No. Caroline said my father ...' I choked on a sob of grief. 'I can't wait. I have to get home ... I have to see him!'

'Calm down,' Alexi said, his grip tightening. 'You won't change things by having hysterics. We'll get you home as quickly as we can. Caro's friend is waiting to fly you back to England and I'll take you to the hospital myself.'

'You—you're coming with me?'

Caroline hadn't mentioned that!

'You're in no fit state to go alone.'

'Thank you.' I took a deep breath and tried to stop shaking as he led me outside to a waiting car. 'I—I'm sorry. It was such a shock. I'll be all right in a moment,' I promised, and burst into tears.

'Here.'

Alexi offered me a large white handkerchief, saying nothing as I sobbed into it while we sped through the city traffic. I knew I was being foolish but I couldn't help it. I felt so guilty—guilty for having been enjoying myself while Ben was ...

My instincts had warned me something like this might happen. Why hadn't I listened to that inner voice? I had sensed that he was biding his time, waiting for me to be gone from the house.

157

What had happened? Had he got drunk and ... It was useless to speculate. I would have to wait until I was home, but it was such a long, long way and I wanted to be with my father now.

If only I hadn't left him alone.

Afterwards, I couldn't remember much of that nightmare journey home. I was numbed, dazed, aware of Alexi's kindness and the concern of Caroline's friend but of little else.

'Bob Morrison,' the pilot said as he greeted us in the dimly lit cargo office of the tiny airfield. 'You won't find it very comfortable back there, I'm afraid.' He helped me into the plane. 'I told Caro this kite was for freight, but you know her. When she makes up her mind to do something there's no changing her.'

'Caroline has recently taken up flying,' Alexi said as he joined me in the cargo hold. 'She twisted Bob's arm for you. It took a bit of doing to persuade him to come out of his way—but she is hard to resist.'

I nodded, trying to smile as I looked round me. There were no seats, only piles of old sacking and a few empty crates, which made the confined space a bit cramped. It all smelled of leather hides and some sort of disinfectant; I felt a little sick as the plane lurched into the air, throwing me against Alexi. He steadied me, smiling encouragingly.

'There's nothing to be afraid of. I've flown like this many times. After I left Poland, I joined the RFC as a navigator and then, when so many of them were being killed and needed to be replaced, a pilot—now those kites we flew were *really* scary. Sometimes they were tied together with string and a prayer, but this plane is different. More modern and airworthy. We'll be all right with Bob. He won't put us down in the sea.'

'I'm not frightened,' I said, my teeth chattering. 'Just cold.'

Alexi was wearing a thick jacket over his shirt. He took it off and put it around my shoulders, ignoring my protests that he would freeze without it.

'I'll huddle up in those sacks if I get cold,' he promised. 'This is a bit crazy but Caroline thought it was the one way you might just get there in time. She thought you would try anything for the chance of seeing your father alive.'

There were daily scheduled flights between London and Paris but they left at set times in the middle of the day and it wouldn't have been easy to get seats at short notice. By twisting her friend's arm to make a detour from his planned route, Caroline had not only avoided all the formalities, she had cut out several hours of waiting time—time that might prove vital if I were to see Ben alive.

'It was so good of her.' I felt the sting of tears but controlled them this time. 'To do all this ...'

And, like Maggie, I had wondered for a while if she had sent me that dead rat. I felt ashamed of myself for having doubted her. Whoever had played that nasty trick on me, it wasn't Caroline.

'She's like that,' Alexi said. 'She can be a bit of a monster at times but don't be fooled by that mask she wears, Lizzie. Underneath she is a very different person.'

'You must be very fond of her?'

'Yes, I am,' he said. 'We are good friends.'

Friends? I had thought they were lovers. But lovers could also be friends. That must be the best of all relationships; the kind I hoped to have with Richard one day.

I smiled at Alexi. I was getting used to him. He wasn't at all frightening once you were accustomed to his harsh features; in fact I was comforted now by the size and strength of him. Somehow I felt that Alexi Paulinski would never let a friend down, and I did desperately need someone to cling to at that moment.

'Your husband wasn't with you when Caro arrived?'

'No. He—he had some business.'

I felt as if I ought to make excuses for Richard.

Would he be angry because I had come back alone, without waiting for him? Surely he would understand that I'd had no choice? It wasn't like the party in London. He had been angry then but this was different.

And what did it matter if Richard was angry? All I cared about was my father. I should never have left him ...

'You mustn't blame yourself,' Alexi said as if he had read my thoughts. 'It could have

160

happened if you had been there.'

'Do you know what kind of an accident it was?' I looked at him fearfully. 'Was it a fire? Ben was always leaving his cigarettes about. Maggie said it was dangerous. She told me I should stop him smoking ...' Of course he couldn't know who Maggie was; must think me foolish to babble on like this—but he wasn't looking at me as if he thought me stupid. His eyes were warm and full of understanding.

'Your grandfather's telegram didn't give any details. Just that you should come home as quickly as possible.'

I nodded, silent now and apprehensive. Why had Henry Caulder been the one to send a message—and why to Caroline? Why hadn't my brother contacted me himself?

Oh, God, not Jack too! My skin crawled with fear. If there had been a fire while everyone was sleeping ...

'My brother—was anything said about my brother?'

'No. Just your father. Stop worrying, Lizzie. It won't be long now.'

It seemed like forever!

The torturing thoughts went round and round in my head throughout the flight and the long drive afterwards. I was so grateful that Alexi was with me. It would have been unbearable travelling alone, waiting for trains or buses instead of being driven directly to the hospital in a car borrowed from Bob. Alexi had become my friend somewhere over the Channel. It was only his quiet, comforting presence that had

161

prevented me from giving in to despair.

At times I thought we would never get there but at last Alexi stopped the car outside the hospital. I was exhausted, drained, and almost stumbled as I got out of the car. Alexi took my arm, supporting me as we walked into the entrance hall together. He didn't say anything to comfort me. We both knew that words were useless.

'Mr Caulder is in a private room,' a nurse told me in reception. 'Just down the corridor—the first door on your left. Mr Henry Caulder is with him.'

'How is my father?' I asked, my heart catching as I saw her grave expression. 'What happened?'

'Mr Henry Caulder will explain,' she said, seeming awkward. 'I'm afraid it is only a matter of time, Mrs Gregory.'

I caught back a sob of despair, throwing an agonized look at Alexi. Despite what I'd been told I had been praying it wasn't as bad as everyone thought, but now I realized there was to be no miracle. My father was dying.

'Go on,' Alexi urged gently. 'I'll be here if you need me.'

'Thank you,' I whispered and turned away, my heart giving a sickening lurch. Why would no one tell me what had happened?

I paused outside the door of the private room, then took a deep, steadying breath and went in. The lights were shaded but I could see Ben lying in a narrow bed. His face and head were covered in bandages. I had expected to see some evidence of treatment

162

but there was nothing—only the silence and the all-pervading hospital smell of disinfectant. He had been brought here and left to die in peace.

'Oh, Ben,' I murmured, moving towards the bed as the emotion rose in my throat, threatening to choke me. 'Daddy ...' I was a child again, remembering him as he had been before the accident: a tall strong man who had carried me, laughing on his shoulders. Oh, the bitter, bitter years when we had lost each other! 'No ... no ...'

A man had been sitting by the bed. I had not noticed him at first. He rose stiffly as I approached, offering me his chair. Tall and thin, with soft grey hair, he had deep lines at the corners of his eyes. Our eyes met and I was aware of a sense of pity and a deep, overwhelming grief.

Was this Henry Caulder? This old, sad, rather weary looking man? Where was the monster I had conjured up in my head?

'They say he doesn't know anything,' Henry whispered, his voice hoarse with grief. 'They say he can't hear. But I've been talking to him, telling him you would soon be here ...'

'Has he responded?' I asked, a last flickering hope dying as he shook his head. I took the seat he had vacated, reaching for Ben's hand. It was smooth and cool in mine. 'I'm here, Ben. I'm with you. I love you.'

His eyelids were visible in a slit between the layers of padding and bandages that swathed

163

his head but there was no movement, no flickering, nothing to indicate that he had heard me.

'What happened to him?' I asked, and looked up when Henry didn't answer. 'You must tell me. What kind of an accident? Was it a fire?'

'No.' Henry was reluctant to continue but I wanted to know. 'He was cleaning a gun and it must have been loaded. It went off and ... the bullet lodged in his head, damaging his brain but not killing him immediately.' He sighed heavily. 'They tell me he would be little more than a vegetable if he came through this.'

'No!' The possibility horrified me. 'No, not that. Not after all he has been through. That's too unfair.'

'I told them he should be allowed to die with dignity. They can't do much for him so there wasn't much point in messing him around. It's only a matter of hours.'

'Cleaning a gun?' I was puzzled. 'Why should he be cleaning a gun?'

I hadn't even known he owned one. I had never seen it, never heard him mention such a thing—let alone clean it. Something was wrong. Henry wasn't telling me everything. A nerve was flickering in his cheek. He was hiding the truth from me! He was afraid to tell me what had really happened. Coldness was seeping through me as I turned back to look at my father.

'He shot himself deliberately,' I said. 'I know

164

he was tired of living without her. He blamed himself for her death. And the pain in his back had been getting so much worse. He must have bought the gun to kill himself. That's why he wanted me to get married. He waited for me to leave and then ...'

'No!' Henry cried. 'I won't have you thinking that, girl. I won't have you burdened with such guilt. It was an accident. He was cleaning the gun and it went off ... that's what happened, Lizzie. It was an accident. The police agree with me. There is no doubt whatsoever.'

'Yes, of course.'

He had seen to everything, squashing any hint of scandal before it could be seized upon by the newspapers. That was why he'd sent his telegram to Caroline—why he was here himself. Nothing must be allowed to besmirch the Caulder name.

For a moment I tasted the bitterness in my mouth and was shaken by silent, mirthless laughter. I must not be fooled by appearances. Henry Caulder might be an old man but he was still the stern, harsh dictator he had always been.

I didn't look at him as I asked, 'Has Jack been told?'

'He was here earlier but had to leave. He said there was no point in sitting waiting for his father to die.'

'I shall stay with Ben. If you don't mind, I should like to be alone with him.'

'Of course. I shall be here when you need me.'

I didn't look round as he went out. I didn't want him here. I wanted Ben. I wanted him to open his eyes and glare at me ... I wanted him to be as he was on the morning of my wedding.

I bent my head to kiss his hand as the bitter tears began to fall. It was all so sad, so terribly sad. I couldn't wish for my father to go on living in these circumstances. A peaceful, quick death was best for him now. He had wanted to die. He had waited to make sure I was safe, then he had killed himself—except that he had made a mess of it and instead of dying instantly and cleanly, he was lying here with the life draining slowly out of him.

'Oh, Ben,' I whispered chokily. 'Oh, Ben ... you would be so angry with yourself if you knew. So angry ...'

'Messed up things again, haven't I, Lizzie?' I could hear him saying the words in my head. 'Always was good at making a sow's car out of a silk purse. Messed it up just the way I did for her ...'

I kissed his hand again, salty tears running down my cheeks as the pain twisted inside me. It was all so useless, so senseless. For a moment I thought his fingers moved in mine as if he were trying to reach me, but then I knew it was impossible. He was dead. He had stopped breathing as I wept for his years of suffering and his bitter, bitter death.

He was at peace and in my heart I was glad.

166

Part Two

PENTIRE

Chapter 9

Henry insisted on taking me back to Pentire with him that afternoon. There was no point in staying on at the hospital now and Grandfather would not hear of my going back to Winspear alone.

'If Richard had been here it might have been different,' he said when I made a mild protest. 'Benedict will be buried with Hannah as he would have wanted. You can trust me to arrange everything, Lizzie. But I cannot let you stay by yourself.'

'Richard will come as soon as he can.'

'Confound the man!' Henry growled testily. 'What did he mean going off like that—on your honeymoon? What was he playing at?'

'It was business,' I said, too numbed by my grief to defy him when he insisted on taking me to Pentire; Henry had taken over and I wasn't prepared to fight him—yet—but nor was I willing to let him speak ill of Richard. 'He couldn't know this would happen. He wouldn't have gone if he'd known I would need him.'

'Maybe not.' Henry glared down at me, reminding me so strongly of my father that I felt a sharp pain in my breast. 'But he should have been with you. Haven't quarrelled, have you?'

'Of course not.' My chin went up, anger

taking over temporarily from the grief. 'You have no right to say such a thing!'

'Just asking. No need to bite my head off, girl. I've sent Paulinski back to London. It was good of him to bring you home but I'll look after you now.'

There was something odd in his manner then, slightly defensive, I thought.

I didn't argue. In a way I was relieved that he had insisted on taking me down to Pentire. I didn't want to go back to Winspear. I wasn't sure I would ever want to set foot in the house again after what had happened. Even if Richard had been with me, I would have gone to a hotel.

I wanted to talk to Maggie, of course. There were so many things I needed to ask, but that could wait until after the funeral. I was too upset to think about anything at the moment. I just wanted to be alone with my grief.

'Alexi and Caroline were wonderful,' I said. 'I must thank them both properly ... when this is over.'

'I knew I could rely on Caroline,' my grandfather said. 'She is an enterprising young woman. The two of you should get on well.'

He sounded pleased by the idea, as if it were all part of some scheme or design of his own that we had been brought together. I had thought there was real grief in his eyes in that first moment at Ben's bedside but there was no sign of it now. He was in control of the situation, his emotions hidden, private.

I wondered about the man behind the mask.

In my dreams I had seen him as a monster but he was not that—no, there was obviously much more to Henry Caulder than the brutish tyrant I had imagined.

His driver picked us up from the hospital and drove us down to Sussex in a sumptuous Rolls-Royce town car, which was so comfortable that I fell asleep. I was exhausted, worn out by the frantic journey of the previous night and an excess of grief. When I woke at last my head was on Henry's shoulder and he had placed a wool rug over my legs.

I sat up and shook my head to clear it.

'I'm sorry. I was very tired.'

'Of course you were,' he said gruffly. 'This has all been very distressing for you. A pity it had to happen the way it did, but you're made of strong stuff, Lizzie. You remind me of Grigory. He would have approved of you, my dear.'

'Grigory?' I was puzzled. 'I don't know ...'

'You don't know about your great-great-grandfather?' Henry frowned his displeasure. 'His name was Grigory Manishowitz. He was a Russian peasant and brought his wife and family out of terrible poverty to England—quite an achievement in those days, believe me. He could have been put to death just for leaving his master.'

'Ben never mentioned that to me.'

'That was early in Queen Victoria's reign, of course. The family travelled on a stinking, rat-infested ship that almost sank in a storm, and when they got here Grigory had no money

171

... no way of earning a living.'

'What did he do?' I was fascinated by this insight into the past.

'He swept a crossing in the streets so that rich men didn't have to get their fine shoes dirty. If he was lucky they tossed him a penny into the gutter.'

'He sounds very interesting.'

'He was more than that. Remind me to tell you the whole story one day. We're just coming to Pentire now. See—there are the gates up ahead ...'

I looked out of the window, feeling sudden excitement.

'Richard says it's a fine house.'

'It suits me.' Henry gave me a sharp look. 'From now on Pentire is your home. Whenever you feel the need, you will be welcome here.'

'Thank you. I ...' Whatever I had been going to say was forgotten as I got my first glimpse of the house. Pentire took my breath away. It was magnificent.

I do not know what I had been expecting but certainly nothing as beautiful as this gracious Georgian house with its acres of parkland, its sparkling lake and extensive rose gardens.

The evening sun was slanting across immaculate lawns as the car drew up outside the house, turning the faded rose of old brick to glowing ruby and making the windows sparkle like brilliant diamonds.

'It's lovely,' I breathed reverently 'Quite, quite lovely—perfect.'

'I've always thought so,' Henry said. 'Not bad

for the grandson of a penniless immigrant.' His harsh expression softened as he looked at me. 'The view from my study is very special. I'm glad you like the place.'

I could tell that Pentire meant a great deal to him.

I smiled uncertainly. I still wasn't sure how I felt about this man. He had been kind to me in his way, taking charge of all the arrangements at the hospital, saving me from any unpleasantness with the authorities, but it was too soon to let down the barriers. I could never forget that he had refused to meet my mother. In time I might be able to forgive but there were too many memories ... painful memories.

'Come in,' he said. 'There's plenty of time, Lizzie. Don't feel as if you have to rush anything. We'll talk one of these days, when you're ready. Meanwhile Mrs Barker will see you comfortably settled in your room. She will bring a tray up to you—you won't want to come down for dinner this evening.'

I nodded, grateful for his thoughtfulness as I followed the housekeeper upstairs. I did need to be alone for a while. I needed to relax, let my grief flow in private.

Henry understood that. Perhaps he too wanted time alone?

I wondered about Richard. Where was he now? Caroline would have told him I had flown home to be with my father. He wouldn't be angry because I had come to Pentire without him, would he? I knew he had been looking forward to bringing me—introducing me to

Henry—but surely he would understand?

It was the loud calling of the birds that woke me at first light. I heard the sound of their raucous cries and went to the window to investigate. I could see a tall tree, its branches beginning to shed their leaves as autumn approached. Several rooks were circling above it and I thought it was probably their nesting site; the season was over, of course, but in the spring they would come back.

I knew that rooks often nested in the same place year after year. They were noisy, gregarious birds and some people considered it a nuisance to have them nesting nearby, but I rather liked them. I felt that they were welcoming me to Pentire.

It was a wonderful view from my window. I could see all the way across the gentle slope of parkland to the lake, which shimmered and danced in the early-morning light. And to the right was a wood—it looked rather dense and mysterious and I thought I would like to explore it one day.

I yawned, feeling heavy-eyed. It was well into the late hours before I had finally fallen asleep the previous night. I had been restless, unable to think of anything but my father and his tragic death, only sleeping at last out of sheer exhaustion.

How desperately unhappy Ben must have been to have planned his own death.

I must stop thinking about it or I would cry again.

Moving away from the window, I glanced at myself in the long cheval mirror which was part of the solid, good-quality but slightly old-fashioned furnishings of the room. I was wearing a softly pleated emerald green wool dress that belonged to Caroline; it set off my colouring and I realized that my cousin and I were very similar in size. I did not have her wonderful hair, of course, or her perfect complexion, but we could quite easily exchange clothes. Not that Caroline would care for any of mine; she was far more daring and fashionable than I could ever be.

It was fortunate for me that my cousin kept some of her clothes at Pentire. Henry had suggested that I should borrow from Caroline's wardrobe until my own clothes arrived, and the housekeeper had brought me a few of her things.

I knew Caroline would not mind my wearing her dress. She had tried to give me loads of things when I stayed with her in London, and only my pride had prevented me from accepting.

I wondered if my cousin was still in Paris—and what Richard had said to her when she told him where I'd gone.

I hoped he would not be angry.

There was no point in sitting in my room, worrying. It was a fine day, though I suspected the breeze might be cold out. I remembered seeing some coats hanging on a hallstand downstairs and decided I would borrow one and go for a walk.

I was right. It was chilly out, much cooler than it had been when Richard and I had left for our honeymoon. I thought with sadness of our happy time in Paris—so soon over and now shadowed by tragedy.

I set out towards the lake, wanting to explore as much as I could, hoping to block out the niggling worries that plagued me. Would Richard be annoyed because I had travelled back to England with Alexi Paulinski? I recalled his angry remarks after that disastrous trip to London with Caroline and felt dismay. In my haste I had disregarded all the normal conventions and these things meant something to Richard. He might well think I should have waited for him. Yet if I had I should have been too late to see my father alive.

Those few moments alone with Ben before he died had been painful but somehow restorative. I would always be grateful to the friends who had made it possible—but would my husband see it that way?

I walked swiftly, enjoying the exercise and a feeling of being at home. It was odd but I had felt it from the moment we arrived the previous evening; it was as if I had always known the house was there, waiting for me.

I stood for several minutes by the lake shore. A clump of willows clustered about the edge, their long, fine fronds kissing the water's surface as it was rippled by the breeze, and two swans glided majestically in the distance. For a moment I was reminded of another time, a moment when I had stopped to watch some swans, and I wondered ...

Shivering, I plunged my hands into the pockets of the old mackintosh I had borrowed and my fingers touched a packet of some kind. I drew it out and frowned as I saw it was a label torn from a packet ... of rat poison.

'Danger—Use with Care!'

I frowned, remembering the dead rat that had been sent to me a few days before my wedding.

Whose coat had I borrowed and what was the label doing in the pocket?

'Lizzie Caulder.' I chided myself aloud. 'You have a vivid imagination!'

It was a coincidence, of course. Someone had bought an arsenic compound to kill rats ... someone who visited or lived at Pentire. But that didn't necessarily mean that that person had sent me one of the victims.

Why should anyone have wanted to send me such a horrible thing? Maggie said there were a lot of weird people around, but I felt I must have aroused feelings of hatred or jealousy in someone who knew me.

'Stop being silly, Lizzie Caulder.'

I caught myself up. I was no longer Lizzie Caulder. I was Richard's wife. My name was Gregory now. Was it significant that I still thought of myself as Caulder?

I looked towards the other side of the lake as I tried to quash feelings of unease. There was an intriguing summer house just beyond the far shore and I decided to see if I could reach it by way of the woods that seemed to hug one bank.

It was colder in the trees, the dense foliage blotting out even the pale sun and making me pull up my coat collar. After a few minutes' walking I changed my mind about trying to reach the summer house, suddenly thinking that Richard might telephone while I was out. He could even had arrived by now.

I stopped in my tracks then swung round, but as I did so my eye was caught by a patch of bright crimson on the ground. What was that? Roses ... a bunch of dead roses lying between the spreading roots of an oak tree. Who on earth would bring roses to a wood?

How strange it was to see them lying there ... and creepy somehow. My heart started thumping and I was aware of an unpleasant tightness in my chest, almost as if I were suffocating. The feeling lasted for several seconds as I stood there, staring at the roses with morbid fascination. It was as if someone had put flowers on a grave ...

It was so cold here in the woods! I had a chilling sense of menace ... as if someone were watching me ... resenting me.

I shook my head at my own foolish thoughts. I was preoccupied with death, that's why I had thought the roses looked as if they had been placed on a grave. No one was buried there, unless perhaps it was a beloved dog or some other pet. Would anyone put flowers on a dog's grave?

It wasn't a grave. Of course it wasn't!

Suddenly, I could not wait to be back in the warmth and comfort of the house. I walked briskly, the wind tugging at my hair, stinging my cheeks and the end of my nose.

Mrs Barker greeted me as I entered the house by a small side door.

'I saw you coming, Mrs Gregory,' she said, helping me off with my coat. 'Fancy you wearing this old thing. It was Mr Henry's but I think everyone has used it from time to time.'

'It was there. I didn't think anyone would mind.'

'Of course they wouldn't,' she said. 'Before I forget, madam, there was a telephone call for you.'

'Was it from my husband?'

'No, Mrs Gregory—a Mr Paulinski. He rang to inquire how you were and said he would telephone again later.'

Her dark button black eyes were bright with curiosity.

'That was kind of him,' I said, hesitating before asking, 'Do you know where Mr Caulder is at the moment?'

'In his study. He said I was to show you the way if you asked.'

'Thank you. I shall need a little help to find my way. It is rather a large house.'

'Confusing at first,' the housekeeper agreed. 'I'll be glad to take you round and show you everything one day, madam. And you'll be welcome in the kitchen anytime, if you care to visit.'

I smiled, following her through the wide, airy hall with its shining wood floors and delicate antique furniture, which smelt faintly of lavender polish. I hadn't taken much notice

179

of my surroundings on our arrival but now I saw that it was a beautiful interior with many fine things, including lots of paintings and good porcelain.

The housekeeper paused outside large double doors with square panelling.

'Shall I announce you, Mrs Gregory?'

'I'll just knock and go in,' I said. I waited for a moment as she disappeared the way we had come, then knocked, opened the door and peeped round. 'May I come in, Grandfather? I can come back if it isn't convenient.'

'Come in, Lizzie.' He was seated at his desk but got up and walked towards me. 'Sit here by the fire. You've been out and it's chilly this morning.'

His windows over looked the lake. He must have seen me walking. I held my hands to the fire, rubbing them together to get the blood flowing. Pine logs crackled and spat, throwing out an intriguing fragrance along with a fierce heat, which soon warmed me.

'It isn't really cold,' I said, 'but it was much warmer in Paris. I suppose that's why I'm feeling it a bit.'

'I expect so. I like a good bite to the air myself Never been one for the heat. Caroline loves it, of course. She runs off to the Riviera whenever she can manage it. She telephoned me earlier to say she's in London but will be down tomorrow.'

'Then I shall be able to thank her properly. I was in too much of a state to do so at the time.' I walked to the long French windows and looked out. 'It is a lovely view from here.'

I glanced back, trying to seem casual. 'Richard didn't phone, I suppose?'

'I dare say he is already on his way.' Henry picked up a silver coffee pot and tapped the side to test for heat. 'Mrs Barker brought this a moment ago. It's still hot. I asked for two cups, in case you decided to join me.'

I was looking at the picture of a young woman. She was pretty with soft fair hair and blue eyes, but her mouth had a slightly sullen droop and I thought she looked a little weak.

'That's Selina,' Henry said gruffly, coming to stand just behind me. 'Your grandmother— painted just after we were married.'

'She was pretty.'

I glanced round at him. His face had gone hard.

'Pretty enough. I suppose,' he said. 'I could ring for tea, if you prefer?'

I had the distinct feeling that he was trying to change the subject, that he did not want to talk about the woman he had married. Was that grief in his eyes—or guilt?

'Coffee is fine. Shall I pour?'

'Yes, my dear, if you will. I take mine black, one sugar.'

I poured the coffee into two dainty porcelain cups, adding sugar to both and cream to my own. Henry's eyes were intent under their hooded lids as I handed him his cup.

'Are you feeling better this morning?'

'Resigned, I think. If Ben had made up his mind to do it ... No, Grandfather, don't lie to me! I know it wasn't an accident. I shan't say

181

so to anyone else, but let us at least be honest with each other. You don't really believe it was an accident, do you?'

His eyes met mine for a moment then he turned away, gazing into the fire.

'I'm not sure,' he said in a voice harsh with emotion. 'It could have been, and yet ...'

'He must have known the gun was loaded.'

'Perhaps. I wanted you to believe it was an accident ... to save you pain. You mustn't blame yourself, Lizzie.'

'It might not have happened if I had been there,' I said, 'but it wasn't my fault. Ben made his own decisions. He was very unhappy and had been in pain for a long time. At least now there is no more pain for him.'

'You are very strong. I think that must come from your mother.'

'It does.' He was looking at me now. 'You were wrong not to receive her. I'm not sure I can forgive you for that. You hurt her badly. She could never forget that you didn't think her good enough to be your son's wife.'

'I was wrong,' he admitted. 'I realized that long ago. I made a mistake and wanted to make amends but ... your mother refused to let me. Benedict agreed with her, of course. He was always stubborn, even as a small boy. But I think he might have forgiven me if she had ...'

'Ben told me he thought you hated him from the beginning.'

A flicker of grief passed over Henry's face. 'If he believed that, he was mistaken. I always loved

182

him. We were much alike—stubborn and proud, too proud to say sorry. Perhaps he mistook sternness for hatred.'

Or perhaps Ben had found it easier to believe in his father's hatred after the quarrel? It would have absolved him of the guilt he might otherwise have felt.

I thought about it as we drank our coffee. Whatever the truth of the past, I sensed that Henry's pride had cost him dearly. He had regretted the rift between him and his son—and he had grieved for Ben, even if he was not showing it now.

'I think I can accept what happened,' I said at last. 'You were at fault but so were they. I think Hannah regretted not making her peace with you at the end.'

'Thank you, my dear. You are very generous.' He put down his cup. 'I've told Jack I intend to make him an allowance each quarter. I should prefer him to come into the business but I shall not insist. He must make his own decisions. You see, I have learned ...' Henry paused for a moment. 'Richard tells me you draw things. Would you consider showing me your work one day?'

'I think you would be disappointed. What I have done so far was just scribbling but I do have some ideas. When I've done something worthwhile.'

'Perhaps you would like to visit our workshops? Once you are settled in London, I could come up and take you myself. It would help you to see the way things are done—though we can usually take an idea and interpret it in our own way.'

'I should like that very ...' I stopped speaking as someone knocked at the door, which was then thrust open. 'Richard! Oh, Richard!'

I jumped to my feet and ran across the polished wooden floor. Richard opened his arms to me, holding me crushed against him as I buried my face in his shoulder.

'Forgive me,' he said. 'I should have been with you. I'm so sorry ... so very sorry about your father.'

'I wanted you with me,' I said, my voice catching. 'It was so awful. Seeing him lying there ... knowing he was dying and that I couldn't help him.'

'I should have been with you,' Richard said again. 'When Caroline told me, I was devastated. I feel as if I've let you down.'

'No, of course you haven't.' I gazed up at him, forgetting that I had felt that way a few times during the terrible journey home. 'You couldn't have known it would happen.'

'It was an article I'd promised to write,' he said. 'I went to the races to report on the fashions the women were wearing, and the Parisian gossip. I didn't take you because I thought you would be bored. I feel awful about having been at something so frivolous when you needed me.'

Why did I feel there was something almost stage managed about his confession ... as if it were more for Henry's benefit than mine?

'Your duty was to Lizzie.' Henry glared at

him from across the room. 'The scribbling you do for that rag of a paper is hardly work, Richard. If you want something more substantial, I might be able to find you a position at the workshops.'

'Thank you, Henry. I'll give it some consideration,' Richard replied equably. 'But I do have an obligation to the paper.'

'Please yourself.' Henry's feathers were obviously ruffled.

'Richard will think about it,' I promised, wanting to keep the peace. 'Now, if you will please excuse us, we should like to go upstairs and talk.' I clung to my husband's hand, leading him from the room.

In my bedroom we kissed properly. Richard's fingers caressed my cheek in a gesture of warmth and affection.

'I do love you, Liz. I'm so sorry you had to go through all that alone. It was typical of Caro, packing you off like that. If I'd been there I should have forbidden it. Flying is much too dangerous—and to send you off with that pilot friend of hers ... Besides, there wasn't much point. Ben never recovered consciousness, did he?'

'No, he didn't.' I felt a sinking sensation inside me. I had hoped he would understand but he obviously didn't. 'But he was alive when I got there. That meant a lot to me—to be able to say goodbye, to hold his hand. I am very grateful to Caroline for what she did.'

'Then that's all that matters. So long as you're not blaming yourself, Liz. It would probably have happened even if you'd been there. Guns are dangerous things. They should never be left loaded; it's asking for trouble.'

Richard clearly believed it had been an accident. Someone had obviously told him all about it, perhaps the housekeeper—or Caroline? I considered telling him what I thought was the truth, then decided against it. Perhaps it was best if everyone believed Henry's version. It would do no good to keep insisting that I thought otherwise. Nothing could bring my father back.

'It was a terrible shock,' I said, hiding my emotion. 'I wasn't sure what to do, Richard. I hated deserting you like that but Caroline said she would explain and ...'

'You did as she told you. You were in a state of shock and she is very hard to resist when she makes up her mind about something.'

'That's what Alexi said.' I faltered as I saw Richard's frown of annoyance. 'He drove me to the airfield and then all the way to the hospital when we got here—wasn't that kind of him? I would have found it so much harder travelling alone.'

'Paulinski? He was with you all the time—in the aeroplane?'

'I was in such a state. He insisted and I was too upset to think clearly. He is Caroline's friend, Richard. She told me I could trust him—and he was very kind to me.'

'Caroline's latest lover, you mean.' Richard's mouth tightened. He was very annoyed but trying not to show it. 'You were safe enough,

186

I suppose. He wouldn't dare to attempt a seduction in case you told her—and I doubt if your type would appeal to him anyway. If he's attracted to Caro, you would seem virginal by comparison.'

'I'm hardly that now.' His careless words had hurt me. They seemed to dismiss me as unattractive compared to my cousin. I remembered the way he had left me, to get drunk on our wedding night, and once again I was sure I had disappointed him.

'No, of course not,' he said hastily. 'It wasn't meant the way you think, Liz. I prefer my wife to seem unobtainable to other men.'

'Well, of course I am! I wouldn't dream of anything else.'

'I should hope not.' Richard's smile was teasing now as he attempted to smooth over my bruised feelings. 'We'll forget all about it, darling.' He touched the tip of my nose with his finger, rather as if I were a child to be humoured. 'How do you like old Henry then? A bit crusty but all right, wouldn't you say?'

'I think I may like him in time. I've hardly spoken to him yet.'

'Do you want to stay here a few days—until it's all over? Or shall we go up to town this afternoon?'

'Whatever you want, Richard.'

In my heart I felt I could have stayed at Pentire for the rest of my life, but I was determined to please him—to make up for having left Paris without him. We had not

187

had the best of starts to our marriage and I wanted it to succeed.

'Well, I may have to go up to town one day, but I can come back the same evening. If you're happy here, darling, we may as well stay. It will give you a chance to get to know Henry, and we shall be in town most of the time once we're settled.' He looked at me thoughtfully. 'I suppose there will be some sorting out to do over your father's affairs? Jack is only nineteen. We can hardly leave it all to him.'

'I think he is coming down this evening. There isn't much to sort out, apart from the house. Ben left it between us.'

'Are you certain of that?'

'He told me it was all to be shared between us.'

'Jack won't want to live there. You'll have to sell.'

'Or let Maggie and her family run it as a guest house.'

'You wouldn't get much out of that. I'm sure Jack will want to sell. It wouldn't be fair to expect otherwise. He's young. He'll want his share of the money.'

'Whatever Jack wants to do.' I shrugged. Why must Richard bring it up now? The last thing on my mind was selling Winspear. 'I'll just leave it all to Jack—and you. Would you sort it out for me, Richard?'

'Of course, darling. There's no need for you to bother about anything. That's what husbands are for.'

'And I thought they were for something quite

188

different.' I gazed up at him teasingly. 'I missed you last night, Richard. It was so lonely in that big bed without you.'

He laughed, reaching out for me. 'Then I shall have to make up for it, shan't I?' He drew me closer then bent his head and kissed me, his lips brushing mine with a tenderness that made my heart leap. 'I do love you, Liz. You believe that, don't you? Even though I may not always be what you want me to be.'

'But you are,' I cried, clinging to him with an odd desperation that I could not explain even to myself. 'You are exactly what I want, Richard. We are going to be happy together, I know we are.'

I wanted it to be that way, yet even as I said the words I was fighting my growing sense of unease ... the feeling deep down inside me that things were not as they ought to be.

Chapter 10

'I have something to show you,' Henry said to me that evening after dinner. He glanced at Richard across the gleaming surface of the impressive, two-pillared mahogany dining table, which was set with silver, good crystal and a Sèvres dessert service, including a large épergne that spilled over in a luscious display of fruits, nuts and sweets. 'Would you mind if I had Lizzie to myself for an hour or so?'

'Of course not. I have some business to discuss with Jack.' Richard glanced at my brother. 'Shall we give the port a miss and have a game of billiards instead?'

'Why not?' Jack looked at me. 'I'll see you later, Lizzie. We'll talk before you go up, shall we?'

'Yes.' I smiled at him, met Richard's eyes for a moment, then followed Henry from the room. He led me to his study, which I had already gathered was his favourite place. 'Was there something important you wanted to talk to me about?' I asked once we were alone.

'I wanted to show you these.' Henry spread out some faded pages from a sketch pad on his desk top. 'Ben did these when he was at school. This is a design for a diamond tiara—these are matching bracelets, earrings and the necklace, which is of course the most important part of the suite. The work was remarkable for a young boy, don't you think?'

I was studying the detail, which showed various angles, precise settings and written explanations of how the diamonds should be cut.

'Very good, I would say. I couldn't produce anything like this. I don't have the practical knowledge. My designs are only ideas—shapes and colours that I find pleasing.'

I was even more convinced that Henry would be disappointed if I showed him my scribbling.

'That is all I would expect for the moment. The art of cutting a precious stone is an exact skill. You could not be expected to know without first studying the whole process and even then it takes years to achieve the skill to cut something like this.' He took a black velvet box from his desk drawer and opened it. I gasped as I saw the necklace inside, and Henry nodded. 'It is beautiful, isn't it?'

'Magnificent,' I agreed. 'I've never seen anything like it. Hannah used to take me to London for a treat sometimes and we spent ages looking into the windows of various shops, some of them expensive jewellers—but there was never anything on display to compare with this. I suppose this sort of thing is kept inside to be shown in private to special clients?' I touched the large, pear-shaped pendant reverently. 'This is such a wonderful colour. Is it perfect? I read somewhere that it was very rare to find a stone this large without a flaw.'

'Very rare. It would have been even larger before it was cut, of course,' Henry said. 'And I have not been able to find any inclusions or faults. Sometimes you can see tiny black specks or lines under a magnifying glass, but this has none.

'Surely it must be worth a great deal of money?'

'A small fortune,' Henry agreed. 'That's why I have not shown it to anyone. You and I are the only ones who know it is here.'

'Then I am honoured to have seen it.' I glanced towards the door, thinking I heard something. 'Perhaps you should lock it away again. though? Such a priceless treasure must be a temptation for others.'

Henry hesitated, then very deliberately went

over to the painting of Selina, on the wall opposite his desk, and lifted it down, revealing the safe behind. He took a key from the pocket of his waistcoat and unlocked the safe, put the necklace inside and relocked, slipping the key back into his pocket.

'It will stay there for the moment,' he said, 'but I thought you might like to see it.'

'Thank you. Whoever made that must have been an exceptional craftsman.'

'Thank you, my dear. I'm glad you approve of my work.'

'You made that?'

'Many years ago. Alas, I should not be capable of it now.' He held out his hands, which shook a little. 'These are not steady enough, and my memory is not what it was. I forget small things ... little details.'

'We all do from time to time—at least, that's what Maggie says.'

'Maggie is your friend?'

'Yes. She was also my mother's friend. She helped me to nurse Hannah when she ...' I bit my lip. 'Jack said you offered to pay for special hospital treatment but she refused?'

'I wanted to help,' he said with what I was sure was genuine regret. 'I was sorry when I was told she was so ill. I knew when she died but I didn't tell the family. Rosalind would have insisted on going to the funeral and Ben would have hated that. I was there at the back of the church but I slipped away before anyone noticed me.'

'You were there?' I was surprised. 'Richard

said no one knew anything about it.'

'I don't tell Richard everything.'

I was silent as I absorbed what I sensed was a hint of criticism.

'Would you really give him a job?' I asked at last.

'If he wants one.' Henry poured himself a brandy. He offered the same to me but I shook my head. 'I find it helps my digestion. You're too young to be bothered with that, of course.'

I felt that he was conscious of the gap between us—that he regretted all the wasted years.

'I drink very little.'

'Too much is dangerous, of course. Ben drank too much sometimes, didn't he?'

Was there nothing he did not know about us?

I remembered my fanciful thoughts, when I had imagined him as a brooding presence throwing a shadow over our lives. If he was not the menacing figure I had conjured up in my mind, he was certainly a powerful force, though whether for good or otherwise I had not yet decided.

'I would like to give you an allowance, Lizzie.'

I blushed, remembering. 'I don't believe I have thanked you for my wedding present yet? It was very generous. I'm afraid we spent a lot of it in Paris buying new clothes.'

'That was very sensible of you. Caroline receives a similar amount each quarter. I would like you to ...'

'Please,' I said quickly. 'I would rather you didn't. Perhaps I could work for you, as a clerk or something? I'm quite good with figures.'

'Want to work for me, do you?' Henry's thick brows lowered. 'Design me something like this then.' He took a small box from the top of his desk. 'This came from Italy. I want a similar range to sell in the shop—medium price, which means gold or silver with semi-precious stones.'

I opened the box. Inside was a green enamel flower brooch set with two cabochon amethysts in silver gilt. I recognized it as being in the Art Nouveau style, but it wasn't one of the best examples I'd seen so I thought it had probably been designed and made just after the turn of the century rather than earlier.

'It is very pretty,' I said, 'but not to be compared with the necklace, of course.'

'Very few people could afford to buy that necklace,' Henry said with a grunt of satisfaction. 'But trinkets like this are bought every day of the week as a birthday gift for a mother or a sweetheart. Michael is against it but I think it's the trade of the future. A lot of the very ornate stuff is old hat these days. Women wore it to court and at exclusive balls, but things are changing. Money is tighter. We can't expect to sell the important pieces as often as we once did—but this will sell over and over again if we get it right.'

'I think I could come up with ideas for a similar brooch.' I felt a flicker of excitement as I faced the challenge he had set me.

'Design a whole range,' Henry said, his eyes bright. 'Not a copy—something similar but with a look of its own.'

'May I keep this for the moment?' I asked, closing the box. 'And could I borrow Ben's drawings for a while?'

'The brooch is yours,' Henry said. 'A trinket to seal the bargain. The drawings are rather special but you may have them for a while. They may help to inspire you, but please take great care of them.'

I promised I would.

'And you won't expect me to accept that allowance? You will let me earn my keep?'

'I wouldn't expect anything less of Hannah Caulder's daughter,' Henry said. 'She was a fine woman, Lizzie. My only regret is that I was too damned stupid to know it at the start.'

Jack was waiting for me when I left the study. I saw him standing at the far end of the hall, staring out of the window. It was too dark for him to see anything; the sky was a blanket of black velvet with hardly a star visible. Something about the set of his shoulders told me that he was very tense.

'Are you all right?' He turned as I touched his arm and I looked anxiously at his face. There were shadows beneath his eyes, as though he had not slept well. 'Will the army let you have time off for the funeral?'

'Henry sorted it out for me.' Jack's face creased with emotion. 'I'm feeling guilty. Maybe

195

if I'd been the son he wanted, Ben wouldn't have done it.'

'Don't!' I sensed his suffering and touched my fingers to his lips. 'Please don't, Jack. Neither of us is to blame. He did what he wanted. We can grieve but we mustn't ...' I broke off as he started to cry. 'Oh, my dearest, don't punish yourself so.'

We moved into each other's arms, tears streaming down our faces. It was a moment or two before Jack gave me a little push away from him. He fumbled for his handkerchief and blew his nose hard.

'What a pair we are,' he said. 'I'll be staying here for a while. I've been given compassionate leave. Grandfather made sure of that. He wants to get me into Sandhurst but I'm not sure I'm officer material. I would rather try life in the ranks for a start, see how I go on.'

'Do you think you will like it?'

'We'll see.' He shrugged but I thought I caught a flicker of doubt in his eyes. 'Richard says you want to sell the house. It's all right by me. I wouldn't want to live there again.'

'No, nor me.' I wondered about the alternative but Jack went on before I could tell him what was in my mind.

'Henry is buying me a Bentley,' he said. 'I can use it to come down for visits—and I might have a go at racing it at Brooklands when I get the chance.'

'Surely that's dangerous? Can you drive?'

'I've had a few lessons from a friend at college. Besides, Richard has promised to show me the ropes.' Jack hesitated for a moment. 'He's all right, you know. I wasn't sure about him at the wedding but I like him now I'm getting to know him.'

'I'm glad you two get on.' I felt a surge of affection for my brother. 'What do you think of Grandfather?'

'He's a good sort,' Jack said. 'No, I really like him, Lizzie. It isn't because of the car—though he has been very generous.'

'I like him too,' I admitted. 'I didn't want to because of Mother—but I can't help myself. I'm going to work for him—or I might, if he likes my designs.'

'Oh, yes, Richard said something about that. Did you know your scribblings were any good?'

'Not really.' I smiled inwardly. Jack obviously hadn't seen them as anything special. 'I might not be able to do it but I'm willing to try.'

'You'll do it. Once you set your mind to it, you can do anything. You're like Mother. You look as if a puff of wind would blow you away but you've got a rod of steel in your back.'

'I shall take that as a compliment—I think!' I was laughing inside. Jack was young despite his nineteen years, full of enthusiasm and very outspoken. I loved him very much.

'It was meant as one.' He grinned at me. 'Richard is in the drawing room. We've got new arrivals—cousin Caroline and some foreign chap called Paulinski.'

'Alexi and Caroline?' I was surprised. 'Caroline said she was coming tomorrow. I didn't know Alexi was coming with her.'

197

'He's her lover—or so Richard says. Looks a bit like a Polish bear to me. Do you imagine she leads him around on a chain?'

'Jack!' I laughed and shook my head at him. Alexi was undeniably fearsome at first glance because of his size and harsh looks, but I had good reason to know how gentle he was. 'If he is a bear, he's a very good-natured one. He was so kind to me the other night. I don't know what I would have done without him—or Caroline. She arranged it all.'

'Caro is a very emancipated woman,' my brother said. 'I think she would be fun to know. Did she tell you she had taken up flying? I mean, actually piloting the kite herself? She was explaining all about the number of flying hours she has to put in before she can get her licence—and she offered to take me up with her once she's passed all her tests and things.'

He sounded a little dazzled by Caroline and I felt a twinge of apprehension. Jack was only nineteen and was being swept up into a new and exciting world.

'You won't lose your head over all this, will you?'

'What do you mean?' He looked offended. 'I'm not a complete fool, Lizzie.'

'I didn't mean that.' How could I explain my sudden feeling of unease? 'This is all very different for both of us, Jack. It's just that I don't want to lose you, too.'

'You worry too much.' His equilibrium was restored. 'I'm not going to die on you, Lizzie. Scout's honour!'

'No, of course not. I'm being silly.'

Jack was excited by all the new possibilities that were opening up for him. I mustn't spoil things with my silly fears. I mustn't let Ben's terrible death—or the unfounded sense of being swept along by an unseen force—prey on my mind.

It was like that moment in the wood, when I had felt that someone was spying on me ... resenting the fact that I had come to this house.

But why should anyone feel that way?

We had reached the drawing room. As we paused outside, Caroline's voice could plainly be heard. She was talking about Alexi's work being shown at a well-known gallery in Paris.

'It was a great success,' I heard her say as we went in. 'One of the leading firms has offered to buy the copyright of Alexi's sculpture "A Nude Reclining"—that's in inverted commas, darlings! They want to turn it into bases for electric table lamps. Isn't that so, Alexi?' She went into a peal of delighted laughter, looking directly at me. 'Have you heard that Alexi will soon be as successful as Raoul Larche or More-au-Vauthier?' Seeing my frown, she arched her fine brows. 'You must have heard of them, surely?'

'Why should she?' Alexi asked. 'Not everyone is interested in bronzes or their creators.'

'But Henry has that wonderful clock in his study. Cast by Daubrée, it has semi-clothed figures from models by Moreau-Vauthier. You must have noticed it, Lizzie?'

199

'Your cousin has only just come to this house,' Alexi reminded her. 'And perhaps she is not in the mood for admiring clocks—or for our chatter.'

'Oh, of course,' Caroline said, and flushed. 'I wasn't thinking. I'm sorry, Lizzie. Here I am laughing and ...'

'Don't be sorry. It was nice to hear you laughing—and I am interested in Alexi's success. But why were you laughing? I thought the only way most sculptors made any real money was by having their work bought by manufacturers who cast copies over and over again, then sell to people who would otherwise not be able to afford a work of art—so why is this so amusing?'

Caroline glanced at Alexi again, eyes leaping with mischief. 'Shall we tell them?'

'That must be your decision, Caro.'

'It is a model of me!' she cried, and laughed again. 'Isn't it too deliciously funny? I shall be bringing light to the homes of hundreds of people all over France—and perhaps England, too, if they are imported here.'

Alexi had modelled Caroline in the nude! Yet why should that surprise me? She was beautiful and his lover. It was natural that he should use her as his model—and yet it was still a little shocking.

I could see that Richard was very shocked— even angry.

'I haven't agreed to it yet,' Alexi said, but clearly he was as amused by the idea as Caroline.

200

'Oh, but you must,' she insisted. 'It will make your fortune, Alexi. Who knows what comes next? They may want to turn me into inkwells and sweet dishes ...'

'You had better not let Henry hear of this,' Richard said, his mouth tight. 'I doubt he would see the funny side especially if it should become known outside the family.'

'Oh, don't be such a prude,' Caroline said, and pouted at him. 'Alexi modelled it on me but it doesn't look exactly like me—not the face anyway.'

Richard shrugged and looked at me. 'Shall we go up? You look a little tired, darling.'

'I am a little,' I agreed, sensing his annoyance. Caroline's behaviour had made him very angry. It was a little daring, of course, but I did not see why he was so upset. I looked at her and saw an odd expression in her eyes. 'Shall we see you tomorrow, Caro?'

'Of course. I intend to stay for the next few days and so does Alexi. He wants me to pose on a horse next. Shall I do a Lady Godiva and ride naked through the park?'

She was looking directly at Richard as she spoke, deliberately taunting him. I saw real anger in his eyes and another emotion I thought might be jealousy. I felt hurt. He had sworn to me that he did not love Caroline, but I suspected he did feel something for her. And why not? She was lovely. It wasn't surprising that someone wanted to buy the copyright of the model Alexi had made of her. It would appeal to many people as a thing of beauty, and bronze

201

figures of that type were very popular.

'Good night then.' I said. 'Caroline, Jack—Alexi. I am rather tired.'

I had not felt it until that moment but now I was developing a headache—and a pain somewhere in the region of my heart. I was beginning to suspect that Richard had not been entirely truthful with me. I suspected he was still more than a little in love with Caroline—and that that was why he had felt disappointment on our wedding night.

I was second best because he could not have Caroline! She had turned him down and so Richard had married me ... a naive, ignorant girl he thought would make a comfortable wife.

No wonder he had found our wedding night so disappointing!

I wasn't going to cry. Somehow I must hide my hurt from everyone. Richard must not guess I had discovered his secret. If our marriage was to survive I had to come to terms with my suspicions as quickly as possible, but for now I must pretend that nothing was wrong.

'I really am tired,' I said when we were alone in our room. 'I know I said I missed you last night, Richard, but I have the most terrible headache.'

'Poor Liz,' he said, and kissed my forehead. 'There's a bed in the dressing room. Would you prefer it if I slept there tonight?'

'Would you mind awfully?'

'Not if you're feeling wretched—and you are, aren't you?'

'I'm so sorry, Richard.'

'Don't worry, darling. I am a little tired myself.' He smiled at me and walked to the door of the dressing room. 'Good night, Lizzie. I hope you sleep well.'

I stared at the door as he closed it behind him, and felt empty. I wanted to call him back, to tell him my headache wasn't that bad and that I wanted him to make love to me, but I couldn't. I couldn't forget that look in his eyes as he'd watched Caroline laughing at Alexi: it was the look of a hungry man, a jealous, angry man.

No, I wouldn't call Richard back. Not this evening. The wound was too fresh, too raw, for me to let him close to me, because I couldn't bear him to know he had hurt me.

I undressed and crawled into bed, resisting the urge to weep. I was tired and my head had really begun to throb. I couldn't think about all this now. I would think about it in the morning.

I felt much better when I woke the next day. My headache had gone and I was feeling foolish; I had let my imagination run away with me the previous evening. Richard wasn't in love with Caroline, of course he wasn't! He had been shocked by her outrageous suggestion about riding naked through the park, that's all. It wasn't love but anger I had seen in his eyes.

I checked the dressing room but it was empty. He must have gone down to breakfast already. I was about to dress and go down myself when Mrs Barker brought in a tray of tea, freshly buttered toast and pots of her own preserves.

'Oh, I was about to come down. You're spoiling me.'

'You're no trouble, Mrs Gregory. Mr Caulder said we were to look after you and I've nothing else in particular to do.'

She must have a hundred and one other duties, but it was nice being spoilt.

'Thank you, but you mustn't do it again. Tomorrow I shall go down for breakfast with everyone else.'

'Just as you wish, madam.'

I ate a leisurely breakfast, then bathed and dressed, wondering where Richard was. Perhaps he had gone for a walk? It was what I intended to do, though later I wanted to start work on my designs. I had several ideas I thought might be suitable but I wouldn't know for sure until I had a pencil in my hand. It was rather exciting and had helped to dull the intense grief of Ben's tragic death—which was, of course, why my grandfather had suggested it. I hadn't and would not forget, but now I had something else to think about and it was easier.

I took the old coat from the hall-stand and went out, thrusting my hands into the pockets. The torn scrap of label had gone. Someone had emptied the pockets. I wondered who had done that, and why?

Mrs Barker had hung the coat up for me. But why should she have removed that label from the pocket? Perhaps it didn't matter; it meant nothing, just that someone had used poison to get rid of some rats.

The wind was colder and sharper that

morning, heralding a definite change in the weather. It was autumn now and the leaves had begun to turn to wonderful oranges, reds and copper. Soon they would start to fall in earnest and then it would be winter—winter in London ...

'Are you looking for Richard?' A man's deep voice broke the pattern of my thoughts and I swung round to face Alexi. 'I believe he went down to the stables. He was looking for Caroline. She took her horse out earlier but I saw her ride back to the stables a few minutes ago. You will probably find them both there.'

'I was going for a walk,' I said, waiting as he came up to me. 'You didn't go riding with her then?'

'She prefers to ride alone in the mornings—to get rid of the cobwebs as she says. I enjoy a leisurely walk.' His brows rose inquiringly. 'Do you ride?'

'There was never any opportunity for me to learn.'

'Your life has been very different from Caroline's, I believe?'

'Yes.'

I turned away from his probing gaze, feeling that those dark eyes of his saw too much. The rooks were making a terrible noise in the branches of a tree that looked forlorn and leafless, rather as if it were dying, and a shaggy dog was racing towards the woods, barking loudly. For some reason I remembered the roses and felt chilled.

'It's much colder today, isn't it?'

'You wish to walk and I am delaying you. Forgive me.'

'Please.' I touched his arm as he was about to turn away. 'Will you walk to the lake with me? I wanted to thank you for what you did the other night. I was in such a state, I don't think I said much ... but I was very grateful. I don't know what I should have done without you.'

'It was no more than anyone would have done in the circumstances,' he said, his harsh, almost ugly features softening with a gentleness that transformed them, 'but I should very much like to walk with you. You were very brave that night. I wanted to tell you that.'

'You asked about my life just now,' I said as we began to stroll in the direction of the lake. 'We may not have had the advantages of money but Jack and I were happy enough as children. Until my father's accident I think my parents were as happy as most, but after that he was always in pain. He became frustrated because he was tied to his chair and that made him cruel to my mother at times. She still loved him, even when she died—but he had not made her life easy. And he never forgave himself for her death. He felt he had ruined her life and brought on her illness.'

'Life is so often unfair,' Alexi agreed. 'My mother died when I was born and my father never forgave me for it, even after he took a beautiful mistress and brought her to live with us. She had a son and he doted on Crispin. When I was sixteen he sent me to the Military Academy, where I was enrolled in the cadets—and so when the war began, I was one of the first to fight. I was wounded and taken prisoner but escaped. I made my way home—then found that my father and all his household had been killed, the house burned to the ground.'

'How terrible for you!' I cried. 'What did you do then?'

'I walked and walked. It was winter and the snow was thick. Often I was hungry, and always cold and tired. I was taken prisoner again, and escaped again; eventually I reached the sea and took passage on a ship for England, working my way as a cook.'

'Can you cook?' I asked. He was a fascinating man and I found his story compelling. I laughed as he put on a woeful face and shook his head. 'And then you joined the Royal Flying Corps? What an eventful life you have had!'

'I did not join the RFC immediately. Because I had an English governess for some years, I was able to speak the language well—but I could also speak Polish, German and a little Russian. I worked for British Intelligence as an interpreter for a while—and then because I was interested, I learned to fly.'

'And after the war you became a sculptor?' I said, filled with admiration for this man. How wrong I had been to judge him by his looks, which would never flatter him. He was cultured, very clever and so interesting. 'What made you do something like that?'

'I wanted to create beautiful things because I had seen so much that was fine and good destroyed,' he replied, his eyes taking on a dark, brooding expression. 'It is strange the way Fate shapes our lives, is it not? If my father had not sent me away, I should probably have died with him. Instead, I am here in this peaceful English garden with a beautiful young woman.

'And if I had not seen Richard fall into the river that afternoon, I might never have met any of you.'

'But we were destined to meet in quite another way,' he reminded me with a rueful smile. 'Don't you remember?'

'Of course,' I cried. 'I trod on your foot and then ran away because you ...'

'Because I frightened you?'

I blushed. 'That was silly of me, wasn't it? If I had stayed I should have discovered that you were not at all frightening.'

'I made the mistake of rushing you,' he said. 'I was afraid you would go and wanted to stop you—but I should have remembered that young English ladies are not in the habit of accepting invitations to tea from strange men.'

Especially large, foreign men with eyes that seem to see right into your soul, I might have said but didn't, because it would have been rude and revealing.

The waters of the lake were a dark, stormy grey, the surface disturbed by gusts of wind that sent out larger and larger circles, and there were a few spots of rain in the air—but it was not the threat of rain that made me say what I did.

'I think we should turn back now. I'm glad we met again and that we've become friends.'

'It is good that we are friends.' For a moment Alexi's eyes met mine and I felt something, a sense of loss, of regret perhaps. 'Lizzie, I have no right to say this but ...'

Whatever he meant to say was lost as we heard someone call out. We turned towards the house and saw Caroline waving at us.

'I believe she is calling to us.'

'Yes. We'll walk to meet her, shall we?'

Caroline came halfway to meet us. Her hair was blown by the wind and her eyes were glowing. She looked beautiful as she tucked her arm through mine, encompassing us both with her brilliant. slightly wicked smile.

'I always feel so good after I've been for a gallop,' she said. 'You should ride with me one morning, Lizzie.'

'I've never been on a horse, but I should very much like to learn.'

'I'll teach you,' she offered. 'We're about the same size. You can borrow some of my things and come out with me after lunch today, if you like. Alexi wants to make some sketches for one of his bronzes so he can draw bits of both of us.' She laughed joyously, eyes bright with mischief. 'No, dearest Lizzie, I'm not suggesting you should do a Lady Godiva. Your husband would never forgive me.'

'Where is Richard? Have you seen him this morning?'

'He came down to the stables to give me a lecture,' she said, 'then I think he went off to see Henry. You will probably find them both in the study.'

'Then I think I shall join them,' I said. 'If you will both excuse me now?' I smiled at Alexi and let go of my cousin's arm. 'I shall look forward to my riding lesson this afternoon.'

I left them and walked quickly across the immaculate lawns to the house, pausing to glance over my shoulder before I went in. Caroline was standing with her arms about Alexi, smiling up at him, then she reached up and kissed him on the mouth.

I went inside, sniffing the air as I caught a familiar perfume. What was that—lavender polish or hair oil? I was not sure why that intimate scene between Caroline and Alexi had disturbed me. Or why I had felt an odd sense of loss when Alexi spoke of our first meeting. Life was so strange. Supposing I had accepted his invitation to tea?

What a peculiar thought to have come into my head! I was just back from my honeymoon and very much in love with my husband. It could have made no difference to my life whatsoever.

I hurried towards the study, then paused outside the open door as I heard voices raised in anger. I should not be listening to this and was about to turn away when Henry said something that kept me rooted to the spot.

'Did you imagine I would not know my own pistol, Michael? I am not blind nor am I a damned fool! Ben used my pistol to kill himself—and I want to know how it got there?'

'He phoned me.' Michael's voice was laced

with guilt as he answered his father. 'He asked me if I could get him a gun—said he'd heard prowlers at night and was worried about being stuck in that damned chair, unable to protect himself.'

'You are to blame for this ...'

'That's not fair!' Michael protested. 'I swear I never thought he intended to kill himself. It wasn't loaded when I gave it to him, I give you my word. I was as shocked as ...'

I turned away from the study, feeling sick. I had wondered where the gun came from and now I knew. I couldn't face Michael or anyone else for the moment. All I wanted was to be alone.

Chapter 11

I hid myself away in the small back parlour no one else seemed to use; it was cold and smelled a bit musty, as though the windows hadn't been opened in a while, but at least I could be alone.

I had fetched my sketch pad from my bedroom but couldn't find the inspiration I needed to do more than a few meaningless squiggles. All I could think about was my father.

If Michael hadn't given Ben that pistol ... I felt angry, and the pain of my father's death churned inside me again. Of course my uncle couldn't have known what would happen, it wasn't fair to blame him the way Henry had, but nevertheless I couldn't help feeling that it *was* his fault. He ought to have known how accident-prone Ben had always been.

No, that was silly. Michael had merely done what his brother asked of him. He couldn't have known what would happen. No one could.

My nose had begun to run from the cold and I wiped it furiously. Why was everything so hard? Why had Ben decided to kill himself? But I knew the answer: he'd had nothing left to live for after I'd married. And he had suffered too much pain for too long ... at least he wasn't suffering now.

When the gong in the hall announced lunch I was sufficiently in command of myself to join the others for the meal, which was being served in the large dining room because Richard's mother had arrived at some time during the morning and that meant the whole family was present.

'My dear Lizzie,' Rosalind said, and kissed my cheek when we met in the drawing room for a pre-lunch sherry. 'Such a dreadful, dreadful accident. I am more sorry that I can possibly say.'

I gave a murmur of appreciation, though I was beginning to feel a little overwhelmed by all these new arrivals. I wished it could have stayed as it was on the day of my arrival, just Henry and me ... and Richard, of course.

'You look awful,' my husband whispered as we went into lunch. 'So tired and pale. You were sleeping this morning so I decided to let

212

Jack take my car out for a spin. You didn't mind I wasn't around, did you?'

'No, of course not.'

I had been glad to be by myself after hearing the argument between Henry and Michael.

I forced a smile but found it difficult to behave normally and spoke very little during lunch. Afterwards, I would have preferred to hide myself away again but Caroline reminded me about the riding lesson.

'You'll find some breeches and kit on your bed,' she said, dropping her voice to a whisper. 'It will get you away from this lot. Talk about the vultures gathering ...'

I smothered a laugh. Caroline had sensed my discomfiture. They had all had good intentions in coming down but it made me feel as if I were being smothered and I was glad to escape with my cousin.

'This is a terrible strain for you,' she said as we walked down to the stables a little later. 'Shall I take Alexi and go back to London?'

'Please don't!' I begged. 'You and Alexi are the only ones who don't make me want to run away and hide ... apart from Richard, of course.'

What I really meant was that I didn't want to be left alone with either Michael or Richard's mother, and I had a feeling that Caroline understood perfectly.

'All right, I'll stay and protect you,' she promised, amused. 'Now—let's see how you shape up with the horses. I'm going to put you on a decent mount, no point in giving

213

you some old dobbin.'

The horse Caroline had chosen was a handsome black gelding, well-trained but mettlesome and high-spirited. I had thought I might be nervous but found I felt an immediate affinity with the horse and was proud of the way I was able to make contact with the beautiful creature, which snickered gently as I stroked its head.

'You are a beauty,' I said. 'I'm going to enjoy getting to know you, my lovely one.'

It was a very successful afternoon. Caroline was an excellent teacher, giving her instructions in a clear precise manner that was easy to follow. I discovered I had a natural ability and needed to be shown only once or twice how to sit and hold the reins.

'You'll do,' Caroline told me as we walked back to the house together afterwards. She offered me a rather sticky black-and-white-striped humbug from a packet in her pocket and took one herself. 'A few more lessons like that and you'll be able to go out alone—that's if you are still interested?'

'I enjoyed myself very much. You've made me feel better. Thank you, Caro.'

'My pleasure. I thought when we first met we could be friends, and I was right.' Caroline hesitated, then pulled a wry face. 'Don't let the family get you down. Rosalind is a fusspot but all right underneath. As for my father—his problem is that he wants to be thought well of by Henry but can never quite manage it. He is more to be pitied than feared.'

'Yes, I think I see that.'

'We get on well most of the time, though I do provoke the poor darling at times. He's very fond of me, of course. Wants me to settle down and have a family but ...' There was a catch in Caroline's voice. 'He doesn't understand how impossible that is.'

'Don't you want to get married—ever?'

'You can't always have what you want.' Her smile was a little too bright. 'But I manage most things. Don't look so worried, Lizzie. I'm just spoilt. Ask anyone.'

Was Caroline hiding a secret sorrow? I would have liked to ask but something in her eyes warned me not to.

I thought about what she'd said concerning her father. Henry was rather fearsome and I could understand that his son might feel inferior to such a man—especially after I had heard them arguing over the gun Michael had given my father.

I had decided not to tell anyone what I'd overheard. My uncle had given the gun to Ben in good faith. When you thought about it, he was no more to blame than anyone else.

'Jack told me you've actually piloted a plane yourself?' I said to change the subject. 'I think that's awfully brave of you, Caro.'

'Not really. It is the most amazing feeling, being up there in that vast sky—alone, in complete control.'

'You mean, you've actually flown alone?'

'I've done one hour solo. To get my licence I have to have eight hours flying with my tutor and to complete three hours of solo flying, then

215

I take a simple examination and that's it.'

'How wonderful!'

'You ought to try it, Lizzie.'

'I don't think Richard would like that somehow—he didn't like me flying home with your friend.'

'No, I suppose he wouldn't,' Caroline said thoughtfully. 'Rupert said it was too dangerous for me at first—then he introduced me to Bob, but only because he knew I would just go off and join a flying club if he hadn't. They're popping up all over the place now that Avro have begun to produce more light aircraft suitable for private flying. It's *the* fashionable thing to do, darling. So, of course, I must do it.'

Caroline arched her brows at me and I laughed.

'So you're friends with Lord Hadden again then?'

'I suppose you could say that.' A shadow passed across her face. 'We had a bit of a thing going once but ...' She shrugged her shoulders.

'Oh, I see.'

'Do you? I doubt it.'

I felt she had snubbed me and was silent for a moment. Obviously I was treading on dangerous ground. Caroline clearly didn't want to talk about her relationship with Rupert Hadden ... whatever that was or had been.

We walked without speaking for several minutes.

'I think it was rotten luck, the accident

happening the way it did,' Caroline suddenly said, as if deciding the silence had gone on long enough. 'If there's anything I can do to help, just say.'

'You've done a great deal already. You and Alexi.'

She nodded, looking at me thoughtfully. I felt she wanted to say something important but whatever it was remained unspoken as Richard came out of the house to meet us.

'Everyone is having tea in the drawing room,' he said. 'We were all wondering where you two had disappeared to.'

'I don't think I'll bother with tea.' Caroline pulled a face. 'I'm going to have a nice bath. What about you, Lizzie?'

I would have preferred to follow her example but even as I hesitated, Richard took a firm grip on my arm.

'I must smell of horses.'

'No one will mind. Come and have a cup of tea. Mama was worried about you at lunchtime. She thought you looked unwell. I want her to see you now, with the roses in your cheeks.'

'Does that mean I look better?' I was still smarting from being compared unfavourably to my cousin.

I allowed him to steer me inside the house. Once we were alone he smiled down at me, flicking a strand of fair hair from my cheek.

'You were looking tired but the fresh air has done you good. I should have thought all that exercise would have made you hungry? Mama noticed you ate hardly anything earlier.'

'Now you mention it ...' My spirits lifted. He was smiling at me in that special way—the way he had when we first fell in love. Perhaps I had been foolish to imagine he was regretting our marriage. 'I might eat a little something.'

Somehow having tea was easier than lunch had been. The atmosphere was more relaxed and Richard seemed determined to make a fuss of me. He brought me a plate of delicious little sandwiches and passed the tea his mother had dispensed from a large silver pot.

Rosalind came and sat next to me on the comfortable sofa, nodding in satisfaction as I ate three of the sandwiches and drank my tea.

'I was concerned for you,' she said. 'You were so pale earlier, I thought you must be sickening for something, Lizzie dear, but now your lovely colour has come back. It was kind of Caroline to put herself out for you. She doesn't often do so—unless she really likes someone. I'm glad you two are going to be friends. It might have been so different, and that could have been awkward.'

'Why?' I furrowed my brow. 'Why shouldn't we be friends? There's no reason, is there?'

'No, of course not.' Rosalind shot a nervous glance at Richard, obviously embarrassed. 'It was just my silly tongue running away with me. No, my dear, no reason at all.'

I knew she was covering up but before I could question her further we were interrupted by the arrival of Caroline's father.

'Have one of these cakes, Lizzie. Mrs Barker made them fresh today—ginger, you know.

She's very good with ginger.'

Michael sounded awkward as he offered me the dish of ginger slices. I thought I saw guilt and distress in his eyes and felt a surge of compassion for him. He must be feeling terrible about what had happened and it wasn't really his fault, even though Henry obviously blamed him for giving Ben the pistol.

'Thank you,' I said, taking the slice of cake nearest to me. 'I like this sort. Ginger cake has always been one of my favourites, especially when it's soft and gooey like this.'

'Good.' Michael's strained expression eased slightly. 'It was a terrible thing,' he said gruffly. 'If there's anything I can do ...'

'You are very kind.' I bit into the cake. 'Oh, this is delicious.'

'I've always been partial myself. No one else in the family cares for it much. Mrs Barker always makes it for me.' He demolished a large slice in two bites, smiled at me and moved away.

Perhaps I had misjudged him at the wedding— or perhaps Ben's death had shocked him, made him realize there were more important things than money. Anyway, he was trying to be kind and that was all that really mattered.

The feud that had split the family was over. We were all united in our grief and that was how it should be.

I was dreadfully sick about an hour later. I had gone upstairs to bathe and change for the evening when I began to feel queasy, then all of a sudden I had to dash to the bathroom where I vomited violently several times. I came out of the bathroom, white-faced and dizzy, tottering towards the bed before collapsing on it.

Richard found me there ten minutes before dinner. I was lying with my eyes closed, wearing only my silk underslip.

'What's wrong?' he asked. 'Aren't you coming down to dinner? You're not sulking, are you?'

For a moment I felt too ill to answer. I tried to sit up but the room started going round and round and I fell back with a moan.

'Are you ill?' Richard was anxious now. 'What is the matter? Are you in pain?'

'I've been sick and I feel dizzy. I'm sorry, Richard. I can't face dinner this evening.'

'Shall I send for the doctor? Why are you sick? Has this ever happened before?'

'No—not that I can remember.' I closed my eyes, holding back a sigh. All I wanted was to be left in peace. Why must Richard make so much fuss?

'I'm going to speak to Henry,' he said. 'I think we should have the doctor.'

I tried to protest but he was already leaving the room, not listening to me. It was so silly to make a fuss. I would be all right in a few minutes—if only the room would stay still for a little while! My eyes closed again. I really did feel awful ...

'What's wrong?' Caroline poked her head round the door. 'God! You look wretched. Was it something I said?' The joke fell flat and her expression changed as she approached the bed. 'You were fine earlier.'

'I've been sick and I feel dizzy,' I said. 'I think I must have eaten something that disagreed with me.'

'Mrs Barker isn't usually that bad a cook.' Caroline frowned. 'Henry is sending for the doctor. I'll go away and leave you in peace, shall I?'

She went without waiting for an answer. I closed my eyes again. My head was throbbing now and I couldn't remember ever having felt this ill in my life. What on earth could have brought it on?

It was nearly half an hour before the doctor arrived. He took my pulse, tested my heart and then shook his head over me.

'What have you been doing to yourself, Mrs Gregory?'

'Nothing. Why?'

'It's a bilious attack,' he said. 'You may have eaten something that didn't suit you but more likely it's the result of excess emotion. You've worn yourself out with grief. This sometimes happens after an unhappy incident. Rest this evening and tomorrow. I am sure you will feel better by then, but call me out if this happens again.'

I closed my eyes, feeling too ill to answer him. It was true that I had been under a great deal of strain, but I wasn't the type to suffer with my nerves. It must be something I had eaten either at lunch or tea.

Richard came back after the doctor had gone. He sat on the edge of the bed and held my hand.

I could see he was upset.

'That man is a fool,' he said. 'You've obviously got a touch of food poisoning. The thing is—no one else has. You didn't eat anything when you were out this afternoon, did you? Any berries ... anything at all?'

'No—at least, Caro gave me a mint humbug when we were walking back from the stables, but that couldn't have made me sick. Besides, she ate one herself and she isn't ill, is she?' He shook his head. 'There you are then.'

'It was fresh salmon in some of those sandwiches. Perhaps there was something wrong with yours ... Fish can be a bit dodgy sometimes.' Richard sounded worried. 'I don't believe it's nerves, Liz, and I've told Henry so.'

I wasn't sure what he was getting at. My headache was beginning to ease but I still felt unwell.

'The sandwiches I ate were mostly cucumber,' I said. 'And I had a piece of the ginger cake Michael brought me, that's all.'

'*Michael* brought you?' Richard's face went hard. 'It isn't like him to wait on people. Did it taste all right? It wasn't bitter or peculiar in any way?'

'No, of course not. It tasted sweet and delicious. Why do you ask?'

'It's just odd, that's all. Odd that he should bother. He never does.'

I looked at him, wide-eyed and alarmed. 'Richard! You're not suggesting that Michael ... he wouldn't! He was trying to be nice to me, that's all. You surely can't think he would try to make me sick?'

'I'm not sure what I'm suggesting,' he replied, tight and thin-lipped. 'I only know that Michael was always very jealous of your father. He must fear that Henry will favour you above Caroline, if only because the old man needs to make amends for the past. I wouldn't rule out something like this ... as a means of upsetting you, frightening you away from Pentire.'

'Oh, Richard!'

What he was suggesting was horrible. I couldn't believe anyone would do such a thing.

I pushed myself up against the pillows. I was beginning to feel a little better. Richard was wrong. He *had* to be wrong. My uncle would never deliberately make me ill.

'Michael ate a slice of the cake himself.'

Richard shrugged. 'I'm not suggesting that anyone was trying to kill you—just to make you feel ill and unsettle you.' He saw I was agitated, and frowned. 'Perhaps it was just strain—but if I were you, I wouldn't trust Michael too much. Or Caroline either, for that matter.'

'Don't,' I begged. 'I can't believe that either of them would deliberately set out to make me ill. Not just because of Grandfather's money. I've already told him I don't want an allowance. I would much rather earn my keep by working for him.'

'He told me,' Richard said. 'He's delighted with the idea of you designing for him. But don't you see? That is exactly what Michael

223

must fear. If Henry thinks you take after him, he's bound to favour you—and then he might be less generous towards the others.'

I closed my eyes, remembering what Caroline had told me about Michael's desperately wanting his father's good opinion and never quite managing to please Henry however hard he tried. It was just possible that he might be jealous of me.

It was then that the thought flashed into my mind—such a terrible, wicked thought that it made me cry out. Supposing Ben's death hadn't been an accident or suicide—supposing someone had put a gun to his head and deliberately shot him?

'No ... no ...' I muttered. 'Please, no ...'

'Are you feeling worse, Liz?'

Richard was bending over me. He looked so shocked and frightened that I reached for his hand, squeezing it to reassure him.

'It's all right,' I said. 'It's just all this suspicion and distrust. It upsets me.'

'I shouldn't have said anything. But it was such a shock to find you like that.' He looked at me anxiously. 'Are you sure you don't want the doctor again? You're not in pain, are you?'

'No, I'm all right. In fact, I feel a little better. I'm just tired, that's all.'

'I'll leave you to rest then.' He bent to kiss my forehead. 'I'll look in later but I shan't disturb you, darling. I'll sleep in the dressing room tonight.'

'Thank you. You are so thoughtful, Richard.'

I closed my eyes again after he had gone.

Surely he was wrong? No one was trying to harm me ... and yet someone had sent me that dead rat. Had that been a warning?

I had felt someone was watching me in the woods ... watching and resenting me ... but that was merely fancy.

I had eaten something that didn't suit me but it wasn't an attempt to poison me. It couldn't be. No one in the family hated me that much, did they?

I lay awake for a long time, thinking, going over the events of the day in my mind. Mrs Barker had brought me breakfast in bed; Caroline had given me a boiled sweet; Michael had given me cake ... and Richard had passed me a cup of tea.

Any one of them could have ... No! I wasn't even going to consider it.

If I let such thoughts fester in my mind I would go mad. It was all nonsense and I refused to let it worry me anymore.

Having made up my mind, I turned over and went to sleep.

I felt a little lethargic in the morning so I did as both Richard and the doctor wanted and stayed in bed.

Mrs Barker brought me a tray with some fruit, buttered muffins, and tea in a silver pot; she had also picked a rosebud from the garden and set it all on a dainty tray cloth with the best linen napkins.

'I'm sure I don't know what made you ill last night, Mrs Gregory,' she said, sounding upset. 'I'm always most particular with food. Mr Caulder was asking if the salmon was fresh and I told him Mr Barker finished them sandwiches off later and he's as right as rain.'

'Please don't worry, Mrs Barker,' I said. 'I'm perfectly sure it wasn't your fault. Perhaps I have been overdoing things recently.'

'It might have been a germ you picked up in Paris,' the housekeeper said. 'I told Mr Caulder that's probably what it was. You've been looking peaky ever since you arrived.'

'Yes, perhaps it was,' I agreed to comfort her. 'I'm better today but I think I shall stay in bed this morning.'

'That's right. Mrs Gregory. If you need anything, you just ring and someone will be up in two ticks.'

'I should like my sketching things, please. I left them in the back parlour yesterday.'

'You never sat in there without a fire?' She was horrified. 'Damp that room is! No one ever uses it—not since the mistress died. You've took a chill, madam, that's what you've done.'

'The mistress—do you mean my grandmother?'

'That's right, madam. She always liked that room, said she felt comfortable there.'

'Were you here when she died?'

'Not on the day she died, madam. I had gone to visit my sister—but it was me what found her when I got back ... lying there at the bottom of the stairs. It was the back stairs. I'm sure I don't know what she was doing there. If she'd wanted one of the maids, she only had to ring.

It wasn't her habit to come down to the kitchen. Not since her illness ...'

I noticed a gleam in Mrs Barker's eyes. She was enjoying a little gossip. Obviously she still thought there was something a little odd about the way my grandmother had died.

'She had been ill for a while, I believe?'

'She started having sickness and dizzy spells.' Mrs Barker frowned as if something had occurred to her. 'But not like you, Mrs Gregory. She had pains in her stomach. The doctors said it was women's trouble ... to do with her having children, but ...' She paused and shook her head. 'If you ask me, they don't know what they're talking about half the time.'

'No, perhaps not.'

'I'll see a fire is lit in the back parlour today, Mrs Gregory. You may depend on it, that's what brought on your trouble—damp that room is. Not fit for anyone to sit in.'

She went off with a satisfied nod, clearly convinced that the mystery of my sudden illness was solved.

Perhaps she was right. I had got very cold sitting there without a fire. It was odd that of all the rooms in the house I had chosen the one Selina Caulder had used before she became too ill ... and even stranger that I too should succumb to sickness and a dizzy spell.

A case of history repeating itself?

Now I was letting my imagination run away with me!

I was alone for most of the morning. I spent it drawing designs for various brooches, some of them similar to the one Henry had given me and others of my own creation. I drew them over and over again, changing the patterns and form slightly until I finally settled on two I felt satisfied with—two very different styles.

The first was a flower rather like a pansy. I had decided that it should be made of silver with enamelling in two shades of blue, and that there should be a tiny gold bumblebee on one of the petals.

'Eyes to be tiny sapphires,' I wrote in my notes. 'The second brooch is gold with insets of lapis lazuli and onyx.'

The second brooch was very different from the one Henry had given me as an example. It was a simple design of interlocking triangles, bolder and stronger than the flower shape. At least I thought so, but perhaps Henry would hate it. I almost decided to screw the paper into a ball and discard it, then changed my mind. Why not show it to him first? He could only say no.

I picked up my pencil and began to work on a design for a matching pendant. Someone knocked at the door and a moment later Caroline walked in, carrying a tray of food.

'Mrs Barker let me bring lunch up. I thought we could share a tray. It's only cold ham and potato salad. Could you eat a little?'

'Yes, I'm sure I could,' I said, clearing my things away so that she could put the tray on the bed and perch beside me. 'Are you sure you wouldn't rather have yours downstairs with the others?'

Caroline pulled a face. 'Heavens, no!' she said. 'You could cut the atmosphere with a knife down there. Alexi sent his best wishes. He left this morning. He has to work, poor dear, but he'll come for the funeral and I'll go back to town with him afterwards. Besides, Richard has practically accused the whole family of having tried to poison you and Alexi thought it best to leave in the circumstances.'

'Richard has ... surely not?' I looked at her in dismay. 'It is too bad of him. He is being very silly over this.' I patted the bed. 'Sit with me and we'll pick at what we want, shall we?'

'Obviously you don't share his paranoia,' Caroline said as I helped myself to the dish of creamy potato salad. 'As if any of us would be stupid enough! If we wanted to kill you there are less obvious ways—not that we do, of course.'

'Of course not. I think Mrs Barker was probably the closest to solving it this morning. I haven't felt really well since I came home. It must have been a germ. Anyway, it's gone. I'm much better now.'

'Then you can come riding with me again this afternoon, can't you?'

I sensed it was important to her. She needed me to show everyone that I didn't believe she or her father had tried to harm me.

'Yes, of course I can,' I said. 'It was all a lot of fuss over nothing. Richard is making too much of it.'

'That's what I told him. Henry was quite upset—and my poor father thinks everyone

229

suspects him because he brought you that ginger cake.'

'But he ate some of it too, and I could have chosen any slice from the dish. Everyone is being very silly. No one tried to harm me, Caro. It was a germ—a bilious attack.'

She looked thoughtful. 'It's because of Selina, I suppose.'

'Yes, Mrs Barker said something. She was the one who found her at the bottom of the back stairs ...'

Caroline nodded. 'I think that is what upset Henry so much. We wouldn't want another accident, would we?'

'You think there was something odd about Selina's fall, don't you?'

'I always have,' Caroline admitted. 'I don't think Henry pushed her but ...' She gave an exaggerated shudder. 'I just know there's something ... some secret they don't want us to know.'

'They?'

'Who knows?' Caroline laughed. 'I'm being melodramatic. It's just that I clearly remember the hushed whispers and long faces. I couldn't have been more than three or four at the time.'

'Things often seem worse to a child.'

'Yes, I suppose they do—but there is something. Henry always clams up whenever I mention Selina and so does my father. Rosalind is the only one who will talk about her and she insists that Selina was very ill.' She laughed at herself again. 'Anyway, are you coming out with me this afternoon?'

'Yes, I shall. And we'll both have tea in the drawing room afterwards, shall we?'

Caroline's eyes gleamed appreciatively. 'Thanks, Lizzie. I owe you a favour for this. I shan't forget.'

'You don't owe me anything. We're friends, aren't we?'

'Alexi was right about you.'

'What did he say?'

Caroline went into a peal of delighted laughter. 'He says we are more alike than anyone realizes. That anyone who thinks you are a meek little mouse is in for a rude awakening.'

I smiled. 'Yes, perhaps we are alike in some ways.' I dug my fork into the salad. 'Don't think you're getting more than your fair share of this, Caro. It's delicious.'

'Oh, Lizzie,' she cried. 'I do like you! If anyone wants to kill you they can do it over my dead body.'

'Don't!' I felt a chill at the base of my neck and for a moment I could hardly breathe. 'I don't want either of us to die. We've both got far too much to live for, haven't we?'

Caroline hesitated briefly, then an odd smile slanted across her mouth, giving her the look of a tragic clown.

'Yes,' she said. 'I suppose we have ...'

It was the next morning that Rosalind sought me out as I was returning from my usual walk in the park. She met me in the hall and I sensed that she had been waiting for me.

'You look better today,' she said. 'You

231

are feeling better, aren't you, Lizzie? You've completely recovered from that germ ... or whatever it was.'

'I'm fine. I've just been for a lovely long walk.'

'You like to walk, don't you, Lizzie? I've seen you sometimes ... coming from the woods.'

'It's so beautiful here,' I replied. 'Don't you think so?'

'Pentire is beautiful,' she said, and there was something in her voice that made me look at her more intently than before. 'I've always loved coming down here. I lived here for a while, you know—when Selina was ill.' Tears glistened on her lashes. 'I wanted to show you something, Lizzie dear, if you can spare me a few minutes?'

'Of course I can.' I said, following her into the house and down the hall to a small room I had not noticed before. I glanced around it curiously. 'I don't think I've been in here.'

'No one comes here very much,' she said. 'We just store things. She went over to a tall cabinet and pulled open the cupboard at the bottom. 'This is what I want to show you. It isn't finished yet, because I haven't got all the birth dates in place ...'

She brought a large, vellum covered book to the centre table and opened it. I saw that someone had been attempting to draw up a family tree for the Caulders and Gregorys.

'This is my work,' she told me with pride. 'I did it for Henry because the family means so much to him. Look, this is where it all began. Do you see?'

'Grigory Manishowitz,' I read. 'Married Anna Rosen in 1815 ...' I ran my finger down the drawings. 'They had three children, Henry and two girls called Anna and Eliza who died unmarried—so there have been two Henrys in the family. Both Grandfather and his own father were called Henry, and altogether there have been three Annas. Isn't it odd how people use the same names over and over again?' I glanced up at her. 'It certainly makes it all very complicated. I should never have understood all this if you hadn't written it down, Rosalind.' I studied the drawing carefully. 'Grandfather's father married Bessie Caulder and changed his name to hers ... I see ... and Henry's sister Anna married Edward Gregory and you married their son John, who was Richard's father of course. And Caroline's mother's name was Ruth. How interesting ... it is fascinating to see all this, Rosalind.'

'Here is your name, Lizzie,' she said. 'And there is Richard's. See how I've linked you together. Do you see how right it is—how perfectly it all fits?'

There was something odd about her manner then; it was more than pride in her work, almost gloating, as though she felt my marriage to Richard was a part of some grand design or plan of her own.

'Yes, it's very ... nice, Rosalind.'

'I always try to make Henry happy,' she said. 'Because he has been so very good to me.

You do think he will like what I've done, don't you?'

'I am sure he will. And I'm sure appreciates you. In fact, I know he does.'

'Do you think so?' She gave me an eager look, almost as if she needed to be reassured. 'What a sweet girl you are, Lizzie. I am so pleased Richard married you.'

'Thank you,' I kissed her cheek. 'And thank you for showing me your work, Rosalind.'

'I wanted you to see it,' she said with a satisfied smile. 'Because I thought you should see how right it is that you are married to Richard ...'

'Yes. Yes, of course,' I said. 'You must excuse me now, Rosalind—Henry is waiting for me.'

'Then you must go to him,' she said. 'Run along, my dear. Henry doesn't like to be kept waiting ...'

She was still looking at the book as I went out. I was thoughtful as I made my way to Henry's study. I hadn't realized before how important his good opinion was to her.

Chapter 12

It was two days later. Michael had gone back to London, because he had to get back to the shop, and Richard travelled up with him.

'I'm sorry, darling,' he apologized before he left. 'It's work again. I wish I didn't have to

234

leave you, but you are feeling better now, aren't you?'

I assured him I was.

'Just come back soon,' I said. 'I shall miss you.'

'Take care of yourself while I'm gone.'

'Of course. Don't worry, Richard. Nothing is going to happen to me. It was a germ—something I picked up in Paris.'

'Perhaps.' He looked anxious. 'I do care about you, Liz.'

Once again I assured him that I was better and told him not to worry. He was fussing over the whole thing far too much.

After he had gone I went for a walk as far as the lake. One day I would try to find my way to the other side, but for now I had other things on my mind. I had decided to have another little chat with Mrs Barker.

Her domain was in the basement of the house, but I knew there was a sunken garden at the rear and that the kitchen windows looked out on an old courtyard with a disused well, a crumbling stone sun dial, worn flags with grass thrusting between the cracks—and a herb garden in which she grew much that was needed for her recipes and cordials.

It was here that I found her, gathering bits and pieces in a flat basket. She looked up as I approached, an odd expression in her eyes. Was that guilt? No, she was smiling at me in welcome. My imagination was beginning to run away with me.

'So you've come to visit me,' she said. 'Come

into the kitchen, madam, and I'll make you a nice hot drink.'

I stopped to smell some rosemary and then reached out towards a soft, furry-leafed plant I hadn't seen before.

'I wouldn't touch that if I were you, Mrs Gregory,' she said. 'If you was to get some of the milk from that plant on your hands you might find yourself being sick again. I'm always very careful about washing my hands after I've been in my herb garden. Some of these plants can be dangerous, unless you know what you're doing.'

'Do you know a lot about herbs?'

'I've learned over the years—there's good and bad uses for all of them. You just have to be careful, that's all.'

I nodded and followed her into the kitchen, which was huge and old-fashioned, its floors laid with red quarry tiles that had worn smooth beneath countless feet. The dressers were filled with blue and white Dutch earthenware and stretched the entire length of one wall. Mrs Barker saw me looking at them and nodded her satisfaction.

'Them's my pride and joy, madam,' she said. 'And them stoves there. I've been offered new fangled stoves but I prefer to use my wood-burning ovens. You don't get near as good results with these modern things.'

'Maggie would agree with you.'

'That would be a friend of yours, madam?'

I sat down at the well-scrubbed pine table and watched as she busied herself with making the tea—after having first given her hands a good wash at the deep stone sinks.

'It's good to have someone to talk to,' she said as she poured steaming hot tea from a large brown pot. 'It's a pleasure for me to have you here, Mrs Gregory.'

'I thought I would like to have a little chat. You have been with my grandfather so long. You must know the house and family so well?' I sipped my tea, smiling inwardly as I saw the gleam in her eyes. Mrs Barker obviously enjoyed nothing more than a good gossip.

'Well, it's funny you should mention that, because only this morning I was saying to Barker that someone has had her nose put out since you arrived ...'

'Aunt Mabel.' Mrs Barker was cut off in mid-flow by the arrival of a young woman I had never seen before. 'You'll never guess what Lily saw in the woods! It's started again ...' She broke off, her cheeks going red as she saw me. 'Oh, I beg your pardon. I didn't know anyone was here.'

'This is my niece Sarah,' Mrs Barker said a little awkwardly. 'She lives in the village with her husband Ted and daughter Lily. Sarah visits me sometimes. As I was just saying, it's nice to have someone to talk to now and then ...'

'Hello, Sarah.' I smiled at her. 'I'm Lizzie Gregory.'

Her smile was rather fixed as she nodded at me and I sensed her hostility.

'It's nice to meet you, Mrs Gregory. My aunt

237

told me you were staying. I'm sorry to have intruded. I'll go ...'

'There's no need.' I finished my tea. 'I was just going. Please, stay and talk to your aunt.'

I got up and walked back to the garden door.

'Don't forget what I said about them plants, madam,' Mrs Barker called after me. 'It's best not to touch anything you don't recognize unless you're wearing gloves.'

I thanked her and went out. Mrs Barker was obviously concerned for my health. I felt that she was trying to warn me of some threat—that she might have told me something important if her niece had not arrived at that moment.

Was it possible that she had changed her mind about the cause of my sickness?

But that would mean someone had tried to make me ill, and I didn't want to believe that. It would have to be someone in the house, a member of the family.

I remembered the look in Mrs Barker's eyes when she had spoken of my grandmother's illness. She had thought of something then, but had dismissed it instantly. Had she been putting two and two together since?

Wasn't that what I was doing? And making five!

I laughed at myself and went into the house. It was odd how the imagination could play tricks on you once something had been put into your mind.

It was because of Ben's tragic death, of course, and the shadow of grief and uncertainty which would be in all our minds until the funeral was over.

Would it never be over? I shivered as the deep, dank cold of the church seeped into my bones and made my nose run. I wiped at it with my already damp handkerchief and took a deep breath, trying to blot out the terrible sense of grief and loss I was feeling.

Outside, the wind was gusting across the open fields behind the church and the rain had begun to beat against the windows, making the atmosphere even more dismal and forbidding. The necessary formalities had seemed to drag on forever but now, suddenly, the waiting was nearly finished.

The official verdict had been accidental death and the family was allowed to hold the small, private funeral I knew my father would have wanted.

My eyes were blinded by tears as I listened to the vicar's oration but most of my weeping had been done in the seclusion of my own room these past few days. By the time we had seen Ben's coffin lowered into its final resting place I was in control of my emotions once more. I turned to walk to the waiting cars.

It was Friday and both Richard and I were returning to Pentire for the weekend. We would leave after lunch on Sunday and drive up to town in Richard's car.

'It will give you longer to finish those designs for Henry,' Richard had said when he came back from town the previous evening. 'Once we're settled in London, we shan't want to come down again for a while.'

I'd agreed, though I was strangely reluctant to leave Pentire for the flat in London. I knew it was silly and wrong of me. Richard's home was in London. He had made it very clear where his interest lay before we were married.

In a way I was eager to be alone with him, to do all the things that were expected of a new wife, but these past few days at Pentire had made me restless.

I was perfectly well again. The violent sickness had not returned and I was inclined to think that it must have been a germ I had picked up while travelling—so why didn't I want to leave the protection of my grandfather's house?

'We're coming down to Pentire for the weekend,' Caroline said as I paused at the church gate. 'Perhaps we can go riding together? I hear you've been getting on well since I left?'

She had returned to town a couple of days after I recovered from my bilious attack, leaving me alone at Pentire with Henry and Rosalind, who had insisted on staying to keep me company.

'I thought I should stay with you, Lizzie dear,' my mother-in-law had said. 'And there will be things to do. Writing letters ... Henry always relies on me in these matters. I've always done all the things poor Selina never could. She was such a delicate woman—but we were all so very fond of her.' Tears filled her eyes. 'And I've always tried to please Henry.'

She had obviously thought the world of

Selina. I murmured something and escaped as soon as I could. Rosalind was well-meaning, of course, but I found her company a little irksome.

'I went riding to escape from ...' I began as Caroline looked at me expectantly, then I saw Maggie hovering just beyond the church gate. 'Oh, excuse me, Caro. We'll talk later. I must speak to Maggie.'

'Maggie ... please wait!'

She hesitated, looking uncomfortable, as if she would have preferred to slip off without seeing me.

'You're not going to leave without saying goodbye?' I felt hurt. 'Is something wrong? Have I offended you?'

'No, of course not.' Maggie hesitated, clearly uneasy. 'We feel as if we've let you down—Ann and me. You trusted us to look after your father and we ...'

'Oh, Maggie,' I cried as I saw the grief and shame in her face. 'It was an accident. You were not to blame. It could have happened if I was there. Please, you mustn't blame yourself.'

She nodded. 'Nasty things, guns. I thought it was dangerous when I first saw it but I never expected ...'

'You'd seen the gun before it happened?' I was surprised. When had she seen it? Surely Michael had given it to him? 'I didn't know he had it.'

'Nor did I until I saw it—that was on the day of your wedding,' she replied, an odd look in her eyes. 'You'd gone up to change for the

241

honeymoon trip and I went out into the hall. I heard something in the study so I went in ... the top drawer of Mr Caulder's desk was open and the gun was lying there in full view. It gave me the shivers to see it.'

'Was anyone in the room?' Michael must have put the gun there, of course, but it seemed odd that he should have left the drawer open. Surely it should have been properly locked?

'The French windows were open but I couldn't see anyone so I pushed the drawer shut and went back to the parlour. Your father was there, talking to Mr Michael ...'

'To my uncle?'

Maggie nodded. 'It's been on my mind. It struck me as odd that the drawer should have been left open. I'd never seen your father with a gun either.'

'Apparently he asked my uncle to get it for him—for protection,' I said. 'He thought he'd heard prowlers, and being tied to that chair, I suppose he felt a bit vulnerable.'

Maggie looked relieved. 'Yes, I can see why he might want it,' she said. 'He was right about the prowlers—there was a break in at Lady Rouse's house just last week. They stole some valuable silver and hit the butler over the head.'

'How dreadful! How is the poor man?'

'All right, but he might not have been.' Maggie's awkwardness had gone. 'That gun being there like that had bothered me, but if Mr Caulder asked his brother to get it for him ... it must have been an accident like they said.'

'Yes, of course it was.'

242

'Still, it was strange ... leaving the drawer open like that.'

'Yes, that was odd.' I thought about it. 'Unless someone else had been in the room and you disturbed them?'

'But why would anyone interfere with your father's things?'

'Curiosity, perhaps—because he was a famous writer.'

'Yes, maybe.' I could see she was not convinced. 'I keep thinking I should have said something.'

'I doubt if it would have made any difference. You know how careless my father was. Whatever happened, it wasn't your fault, Maggie.'

'No.' Once again her face was clouded by doubt. 'I hear you're thinking of selling the house?'

'It's for the best. Neither Jack nor I would want to live there again.'

'No, I don't suppose so.' Maggie's eyes veered away, avoiding mine. 'We shan't be seeing you much in future.'

'I shan't come down as often as I'd planned, of course, but we'll keep in touch. I'll write, Maggie. And I will visit sometimes, I promise.'

'I hope so ...' She broke off as Richard came up to us. 'Mr Gregory.'

'How are you, Maggie?'

'Well, thank you, sir.'

'We had better go, darling.' Richard touched my arm. 'It's nice to see you again, Maggie.'

'Could have been in better circumstances.'

I kissed her cheek. 'Take care of yourself. I

shan't forget you. Believe me.'

Maggie nodded but I could see she thought I would forget my old friends now that I had a new family.

'Believe me, Maggie.'

'Come along, darling.'

Richard steered me towards his car. He opened the door for me, then got in himself

'Well, that's over,' he said as he started the engine. 'This has been an unhappy time for you, darling, but there's no need for you to come down here ever again.'

I felt chilled. It had been cold standing talking to Maggie but this icy feeling came from inside me. Richard didn't seem to understand that I wanted to continue old friendships. I didn't want to turn my back on Maggie and all the years of my childhood.

'There are a few things I need from the house.'

'Henry says you can store anything you want at Pentire. He has asked if he can have your father's books. I thought you wouldn't want them so I agreed. He will add them to the library at Pentire so they will always be there if you do want them.'

'I can't think of a better place for them. Once our personal things have been cleared, the rest of the furniture can be sold with the house.'

'About the cottage ...' Richard paused and frowned. 'Apparently your father let it for a peppercorn rent. I don't know whether we could persuade the tenants to get out?'

'No!' I was shocked. 'It was my idea to let

them have it. The family has nowhere to go. If anything we should give them the cottage, sign it over to them legally.'

'I doubt we could get them out anyway,' he said, 'but you may as well hang on to it. Not that it will make much difference to the price of the property as things stand.'

'I would never allow the family to be turned out, Richard. We shan't sell the cottage with the house.' I could not conceal my annoyance and he seemed to sense there was no point in continuing the discussion.

'As I said, the lease is watertight so it doesn't make much difference. We'll get what we can for the house without it.'

I stared out of the car window without answering. The past few weeks had seen a marked change in the weather. It was damp and miserable, which might account for my mood—yet I didn't think so. Why did Richard always attach so much importance to money? Couldn't he see there were many more important things?

I was overcome with a feeling of sadness and regret. Saying goodbye to Maggie had upset me. It seemed that all the ties with my old life had gone and I wasn't sure I was going to be as happy in my new one as I had first thought.

At tea-time I made an excuse about having a headache and went upstairs to lie down, but I was too restless to stay in my room and, after a few minutes, went back down, letting myself out of the back parlour to avoid meeting anyone else. My sense of loneliness had not gone away and I felt a brisk walk might drive out the nagging ache that had settled around my heart—an ache that was not just because of Ben's death.

It was my marriage that was the cause of my present uneasiness. I had made love with my husband only once since my return from Paris and it had not been particularly successful.

Richard had left me afterwards to sleep in the dressing room. Why? And why had I felt so empty afterwards? Empty and vaguely guilty. It was not what I had expected of my marriage and I was beginning to wonder what was the matter with me.

I ought to be happy—so why was I restless and full of self-doubt?

Was I the kind of woman who should never marry? And yet when Richard had first kissed me, I had longed to be in his arms—now I almost dreaded it. He was just as patient, kind and gentle as before but now I felt he was merely going through a performance, that he did not really want me.

It was cold out that afternoon. I had wrapped up well and was determined to try and find my way through the woods to the other side of the lake and the intriguing summer house, which I had not yet visited.

I was walking towards the woods when I was startled to see a huge dog go hurtling past me, barking its head off. Almost immediately, I saw a child some distance ahead of me, a little girl of perhaps five or six years old. She screamed as she saw the dog and started to run into the trees, the dog bounding after her, still barking fiercely.

I was alarmed. Was the child being attacked? I began to run, fearing that the dog would savage the child before I could reach them. It was the first time I had seen a child in the grounds, though I had glimpsed the dog before and believed it belonged to one of the gardeners. It was a large shaggy animal and could easily overpower a child.

Images of a terrible tragedy filled my mind and I ran as fast as I could. It was only a few minutes before I caught up with the child and in an instant my anxiety was relieved as I saw that she was kneeling on the ground with her arms wrapped about the dog lovingly. She was hugging and kissing it. Her screams had been the natural exuberance of a child with a much-loved pet and she had never been in danger.

I smiled as I fought to recover my breath. Thank goodness. I had been afraid she would be hurt.

The girl had noticed me now. She looked at me with interest.

'Hello,' I said. 'I haven't see you before. What is your name?'

'Lily,' she said. 'And this is Wolfie ... quiet, Wolfie!' She stroked the dog's head as it growled low in its throat, obviously considering me a threat to her. 'I've seen you. I saw you in the woods one day but you didn't see me. I know who you are—you're the new favourite ...'

'What do you mean?'

'That's what my ma said ... you're the new favourite and Madam has had her nose put out because of you.' Lily looked at me curiously. 'Did you put her nose out on purpose?'

'No, I didn't.'

'Ma said you did. She don't tell lies.'

I saw the hostility in the child's eyes. Why was she looking at me like that? Obviously she had heard gossip ... in Mrs Barker's kitchen! I suddenly remembered something the niece had said about her daughter Lily seeing something in the woods.

'Do you often come to the woods, Lily?'

'You won't tell her, will you?' The child looked frightened. 'She said she would beat me if she caught me here again.'

The dog caught her fear and growled, its hair standing up as if it thought I meant to harm her.

'Who said that, Lily?'

She glanced round, clearly nervous. 'I don't like her. She frightens me ... and Ma said I would be in trouble if ...'

'Lily ... Lily, where are you? Come here at once! If you hide from me I'll give you a thrashing when I get ... Oh!'

I turned as I heard the sharp voice, recognizing the rather pretty woman who was standing just behind the child and the dog. I had suspected Lily was the daughter of Mrs Barker's niece and now I saw the likeness between them; they had the same dark brown hair and grey eyes.

'Lily!' she said crossly. 'Why did you run off

like that? You know we've got to get back for your father's tea.' She glanced at me. 'I'm sorry, Mrs Gregory. Lily knows she isn't allowed in the woods but she will run off if I turn my back for five minutes.'

'She wasn't doing any harm. I came after her because I thought the dog might harm her, but she was in no danger.'

'That stupid great dog loves her,' Sarah said. 'She would like to take it home but her dad wouldn't have it in the house. Besides, it isn't ours. I keep telling her to leave it alone but she won't listen.'

'I don't suppose anyone minds her being here. I certainly don't. I love children.'

'That's all right then—but I would be grateful if you didn't say anything about it up at the house. There's some who don't feel as you do, Mrs Gregory. It's best you don't mention you've seen us at all.'

'Then I won't, though I can't see what harm Lily could possibly do here, Mrs ...'

'Sarah Jones,' she said, a hint of pride in her face now. 'My husband is a saddler and has his own business in the village. He would be cross if he knew Lily had been running in these woods—thinks I don't keep a strict enough eye on her.'

'I'm sure she is safe enough with that dog to protect her.'

'Yes.' There was an odd expression in Sarah Jones' eyes. 'Well, it was nice talking to you, Mrs Gregory. We must go now. Come along, Lily.'

'Please don't scold her. I'm sure no one really minds her playing here.'

But Lily's mother made no reply, simply seizing her daughter by the hand and dragging her off. I watched them go, then walked further into the woods, watched by the shaggy dog with what I fancied was a baleful eye.

Why should Sarah Jones think anyone would mind her daughter playing with the gardener's dog in the woods? What possible harm could she do?

My thoughts were centred on the child and her mother so when I saw the patch of bright colour lying on the ground just ahead of me I wasn't expecting it. More flowers! Lying in exactly the same spot as before. The dead roses had been replaced by a bunch of bright salmon pink dahlias, the colour so unexpected and shocking that I was stopped in my tracks. They were very fresh, as if they had been placed there only a few minutes earlier.

Who could have brought them here? Perhaps even more importantly, why? Why would anyone bring fresh flowers to a wood?

Once again I experienced that sudden icy chill. It was most odd—rather unpleasant. Surely it wasn't possible ...

No, it was only a morbid trick of my imagination. No one was buried here!

Could Sarah Jones have placed the flowers there? Was that her reason for visiting her aunt?

It was all very mysterious. I wondered about it as I walked on, determined to reach the other side of the lake this time. Of course it wasn't a grave, but perhaps some tragedy had happened in the woods? Someone might have fallen from a tree and been badly injured or killed and the flowers were put there as a memorial.

I might ask Caroline about it. She seemed to know most of what went on at Pentire. Yes, I would ask her what she thought—but I wouldn't mention the child with the dog. Sarah Jones had been most insistent that I shouldn't tell anyone Lily had been here.

I wondered why.

'Where have you been?' Richard demanded as I walked into my bedroom almost two hours later. 'We've all been worrying about you, thinking something terrible must have happened.'

'Have you? I'm sorry,' I apologized at once. 'I didn't think anyone would even notice I was gone. I went for a walk to the other side of the lake and it took longer than I thought. I wanted to take a closer look at the summer house but when I got there it was locked.'

'For heavens sake!' Richard exclaimed. 'I could have told you if you'd asked. Why go on an afternoon like this? You'll probably catch pneumonia. It was a ridiculous thing to do.'

'I don't see why. I am not particularly prone to colds and chills. Please don't make such a fuss, Richard. I'm perfectly all right.'

'You're going to be late for dinner. You could have told someone where you were going so that we didn't worry. It was very thoughtless of you.'

251

'I'm sorry. I didn't realize it would take so long to walk there and back. I shall be very quick changing, Richard. Please apologize for me if anyone was really worried.'

He went out without answering and I sighed. Richard was turning out to be rather a touchy person and not as easy to get on with as I had expected, but perhaps it was my fault. I ought not to have gone without telling him, and if I had disappointed him in some way I could not really blame him for being out of temper with me—though it was hurtful all the same.

Where had all the bright promise of a few weeks earlier gone? I had expected to be so happy and now ... now all I felt was a peculiar, aching emptiness.

Chapter 13

'I'm sorry if you were worried,' I said to Henry when we were alone in his study that evening. 'I didn't mean to upset anyone. I just went for a walk and it took longer than I thought.'

'I told Richard he was making a fuss,' he said gruffly. 'But Rosalind was upset, too, and I don't like to see her like that. She can be rather a tiresome woman, I know, but she means well and I've always been quite fond of her. She's a part of the place.'

'She told me she has always helped you where she can—writing letters, small things—the little tasks Grandmother would have done if she were alive.'

'Yes, Rosalind has always made herself useful,' he said, his eyes straying towards the picture of his wife. 'Especially after she lost her own husband. She was grateful to me for taking care of everything—of her financial affairs and Richard's schooling. She nursed Selina, you know. Devoted herself to her for months when she was ill. I don't think she has ever forgiven herself for not being here when it happened. Selina fell down the stairs.'

I nodded. 'Yes, I know.'

'I thought you would.'

'Was my grandmother completely alone at the time she fell?'

'Barker was attending to his duties somewhere in the house, and we had a couple of live-in maids then. Nowadays Barker and Mrs Barker manage between them, though I believe a woman comes in from the village daily to do the rough work. While Selina was alive, Rosalind spent most of her time here but when my wife died she began to live more and more at her own house in London.'

'But on the day Grandmother fell, Rosalind had gone out?'

'She had popped down to the village for a short time. When she came back it was too late. Selina had been having dizzy fits for a while and ...' A deep sadness came into Henry's face as he paused. 'I don't think any of us realized how ill she was. We were used to her being an invalid.' He sighed. 'After Ben was born, she was advised not to have another child and our marriage almost ceased to exist. We were like two strangers, polite but distant. That was my fault, of course. Our relationship was never as happy as it might have been. I ought not to have married her.'

'Didn't you love her?'

'She was very pretty,' he said. 'And she came from the right background. The family had money and position—and I needed both.' Henry gave me a direct look. 'I am being frank with you, Lizzie.'

'Yes, I understand that. Thank you.' I wanted to know, to understand what had shaped this man. 'Please go on. I've been told so little about the family and I would like to know everything. You told me that Grigory came here as a penniless immigrant but what happened then?'

'My father married Bessie Caulder, the daughter of a butcher who owned a shop in the East End of London. He took his wife's name and, as he became more prosperous, he asked me what I wanted to do in life. He was surprised when I chose to become a working jeweller.'

'Why did you?'

'It was pure chance. I found a gold ring in the street once and was fascinated with the engraving on the shank. When I discovered that it was worth what seemed a lot of money to the grandson of a penniless immigrant, I decided I was going to make my fortune as a jeweller.'

'And you did.'

'Yes, I did, with Selina's help.' Henry sighed. 'I already had one foot on the ladder by the time I met her but it wouldn't have been as easy without her. It was through Selina that I met the right people, became accepted into her world. I would have made money without her but I could never have achieved all this.' He glanced round the room, his eyes moving over the valuable furniture and paintings. 'I would never have been able to buy Pentire.'

'How did you meet?'

'At the wedding of a customer who rather liked me and asked me to be one of his ushers. It was quite an honour. I was in business for myself then, but it was only a small workshop.' His voice drifted away as he remembered the past and there were shadows in his eyes, sadness.

'And you knew at once that you wanted to marry her?'

'Selina was dressed in pink and wore a large hat with lots of veiling and roses.' Henry looked rueful, slightly ashamed. 'I was quite the young dandy then, different from the men she had met before. She fell in love with me instantly and it showed. I suppose that's why I asked her to marry me. I thought I could make her happy—but she was too soft, too easily hurt. I am not always an easy man to live with, as you may have noticed. After she died so suddenly, I realized that I had cared more than I'd thought but it was too late by then. She had got out of bed for some reason, turned dizzy and fallen to her death.'

'You were away. You must have been shocked when you heard the news?'

'I was in London. I was still working then. Selina always said I cared more for the business than her, and when she needed me I wasn't here. I have always regretted that ... regretted that we did not make up our foolish quarrel.'

I thought I understood. Henry had married a woman out of his class. He had devoted himself to the pursuit of wealth, forcing his way up the ladder of social acceptance, becoming a part of the world his wife had been born to, but always knowing that he was an intruder—the grandson of an immigrant. A Russian peasant. *'Not quite the thing, my dear.'* He had money but that could not buy him the thing he wanted most. How that must have stung a man of his pride, driving him on to acquire more and more wealth.

I understood now why the idea of his favourite son marrying an actress had been such a terrible blow. He had worked so hard to put his humble beginnings behind him, to reach the status of a gentleman with a large country house, and then his favourite son had let him down. It must have seemed that all his striving, all his scheming had been for nothing.

'I'm so sorry.'

'It's in the past now. I've made so many mistakes. So many mistakes.' He hesitated, then looked at me. 'I can't change what happened to my wife—but I would like to make up for what I did to your parents, Lizzie. I would like to think that you could forgive me?'

I looked at him long and hard. He wasn't a monster after all, just a human being with human failings, much like everyone else.

'I think I already have.' I went to kiss his cheek. 'Good night, Grandfather.'

'Good night, my dear. I am very happy to have had you here these past few days. I hope you know that?'

I assured him I did, then left him and went up to bed.

I had intended to ask him about the flowers in the woods, but once he'd started to talk about Selina I'd realized I couldn't. He had been speaking from his heart and it was a sad story, as sad in its way as Ben's and Hannah's.

Were all the Caulders fated to be unhappy in their marriages? It seemed that perhaps Caroline was right when she said the family was cursed.

I was awake early the next morning. Richard's side of the bed was already cold. He must have left me to go and sleep in the dressing room again. Unless he had gone off somewhere? He sometimes did disappear for hours at a time without telling me, which made it a little irritating that he should expect me to report my every move.

I threw back the bedcovers and went to gaze out of the window. It had rained hard in the night but the sky was clear now and it looked like being a nice day. The sun was shining, bringing a welcome warmth to the air. Perhaps we were in for an Indian summer!

I decided I would go for a ride before breakfast. It would clear the cobwebs from my head and shake off my mood of growing unease.

As I pulled on the riding clothes Caroline had lent me, I was trying not to remember the way Richard had turned from me the previous night. I had snuggled up to him as he lay beside me, expecting, hoping he would make love to me, but instead he had given me a brief kiss, wished me sweet dreams and turned on his side to sleep. I had been too hurt to protest or ask what was wrong. Besides, in my heart I believed I knew what was upsetting him.

I had noticed the way he'd watched Caroline with Alexi at dinner and again in the drawing room afterwards. It was his manner that had driven me into following Henry to the study —because I couldn't bear to see the jealousy in my husband's face.

I could no longer pretend to myself that Richard was unaffected by my cousin. He was a different person when she was staying at Pentire: on edge, ready to snap at me and moody. It was obvious to me that he had never fully recovered from his disappointment at being refused by Caroline. Perhaps he did love me in his own way but his feelings for Caroline were stronger.

Could I live with the suspicion that my husband was still in love with my cousin? I would have to, unless I wanted to end the marriage before it had hardly begun.

I couldn't bear to think about such a thing. I

was still in love with him, despite everything.

I could see that Richard was far from perfect. He was extravagant, often thoughtless and sometimes selfish. If I had waited for a while, if I had known him better, would I have married him?

Of course I would!

I crushed my doubts as I let myself out of the house and began to walk towards the stables. At least I had no need to be jealous of my cousin. Caroline had made it clear she wasn't interested in Richard. I did not think she liked him very much.

Was the strong feeling I sensed in Richard merely antagonism? Was his vanity hurt because Caroline had rejected him? Hatred and love were both very strong emotions could I have confused one with the other?

Yet if Richard's feelings for Caroline were not those of a lover, why had he turned away from me in our bed?

I made a determined effort to put my doubts out of my mind as I reached the stables.

'I think I'll take Avenger out on my own this morning, Tom,' I said to the groom who usually accompanied me on my rides. 'Has Caroline gone out yet?'

'Yes, Mrs Gregory, about twenty minutes ago.' He looked at me uncertainly. 'Are you sure you don't want me to come with you?'

'It's time I had confidence enough to ride alone,' I said. 'Don't worry. I shan't go for a mad gallop. Just a nice trot around the park.'

'You'll manage that,' the groom replied,

responding with a smile. 'You're coming along very well, Mrs Gregory.'

I accepted his help in mounting, then set off at a sedate walk, gradually increasing the pace to a steady canter. After nearly two weeks of riding regularly once a day, I felt confident of controlling Avenger at this speed. I wasn't yet ready to ride hell for leather the way Caroline did, but this gentle pace was a pleasant way to spend an hour or so and I would miss the exercise when we were in London.

Pentire was such a lovely place to be; the soft shimmering of the lake and the woods clustering at its banks, open parkland and the gracious old house slumbering in the pale sunshine, all combined to give me a feeling of peace.

It was silly of me to let my imagination run away with me. Richard had told me he loved me so many times. I ought not to doubt him. If he hadn't loved me he wouldn't have married me; there was no reason why he should ...

I suppose I was dreaming, not really noticing what was going on around me, lulled by the tranquillity into a false security. When the shots came I was completely unprepared for them—and for Avenger's reaction.

He pricked his ears, his head shot up and then he bolted. I was too shocked to react properly. My horse had been frightened by several loud bangs, which seemed very close to us, and was out of control. I tried vainly to steady him, pulling frantically on the reins and calling to him to stop, but there was no halting his mad flight.

It was all so sudden, so terrifyingly swift. I think I screamed as I fought for control, but I never had a chance. For a while I managed to hang on, but I was too inexperienced, too shocked, to master the terrified horse and suddenly I felt myself falling ...

I must have hit my head as I fell for I was not aware of what happened next. I did not see the horse careering riderless across the park, nor did I hear Alexi's cry of alarm. I learned later that he had been down at the stables sketching and was on his way back to the house when he heard the shots and saw me fall.

I came to myself to find him bending over me. He was touching me, his hands sure and gentle as he examined me for broken bones.

'Lizzie?' he said. 'Lizzie ... can you hear me?'

I moaned, my eyelids fluttering as I tried to focus on his face.

'My poor little one.'

'Alexi ...'

'It's all right,' he said, touching my face with his fingertips. 'I don't think you've broken anything. Can you feel my fingers?'

'Yes ...'

'I'm going to move your head a little. Tell me if it hurts.' He was so gentle, so steady. 'Your neck is all right. I don't think you've damaged your back. Try to move your legs now ... carefully ... and your arms ... that's it.'

A horse and rider came galloping up and Caroline jumped down, coming to stand over us and watch as Alexi finished his examination.

'How is she? I heard shots and then I saw Avenger bolting.'

'She hit her head and passed out for a few minutes,' Alexi said, 'but she seems all right.' He broke off as I groaned. 'Where does it hurt, Lizzie?'

'All over,' I said and sat up. 'Oh ... I feel dizzy.'

'Don't try to get up. I shall carry you.'

'I can walk ... so silly ...'

'You will be if you don't do what Alexi says,' Caroline retorted. 'Let him carry you, Lizzie. We'll get the doctor.'

I was too weak and shocked to protest.

'Thank you,' I whispered as he bent to lift me gently in his arms. 'I feel so stupid. I was riding well and then ...'

'Don't talk,' he instructed. His face was grim as he looked across at Caroline. 'Your horse was frightened, Lizzie. It wasn't your fault. Some fool fired a gun near you.'

I saw the look that passed between my cousin and Alexi. They both thought someone had fired that gun deliberately.

I closed my eyes, leaning my head against his shoulder. It felt so good to be in his arms, so safe. I was close to tears.

Surely no one hated me so much that they would fire a gun with the intention of making my horse bolt?

I could have been killed.

Alexi was carrying me towards the house. My head was going round and round and I felt so ill. I heard voices ... Richard's voice and my grandfather's.

'What's happened?'

'Is she all right?'

'Get the doctor. Her horse bolted and she had a fall.'

'My God!' Richard cried. 'Give her to me.'

'No,' I whimpered, and burrowed into Alexi's shoulder. 'No ... don't ... please.'

'I'll carry her up,' Alexi said in a tone of command. 'For God's sake, Richard! Didn't you hear what I said? Your wife has been hurt—get the doctor, man!'

Alexi was striding past them, ignoring Richard's protests. He carried me up the stairs. Mrs Barker was fussing round us, calling instructions, showing him the way, and then we were in my room. Mrs Barker had pulled back the covers on the bed.

Alexi laid me down. I whimpered as he let me go, not wanting to leave the security of his arms. He smiled down at me and I was comforted by the warmth of that look.

'It's all right, Lizzie,' he said. 'You're safe now.'

'I'll see to her now, sir.'

Mrs Barker was there, waiting to undress me and cosset me. I looked beyond her to Alexi as he moved away, his eyes lingering on me as if he was as reluctant to go as I was to have him leave me.

'Alexi ... thank you.'

He smiled, nodded and then he was gone. I felt bereft, lonely, close to tears of self-pity.

'I'll help you get comfortable, madam,' Mrs Barker said. 'You just leave everything to me.'

'I fell,' I said, closing my eyes as the dizziness swept over me. 'I heard shots and Avenger bolted ... and then I fell.'

'It's a mercy you weren't killed,' she said, making little clucking noises as she pulled off my boots. 'Wicked things, horses. That's what I always say.'

I felt too dizzy and ill to answer her. All I knew was that I had felt safe in Alexi's arms and now ... now I just wanted to cry.

Everyone agreed that I had been lucky to escape so lightly. I had bruises and a nasty bump on the back of my head, which gave me a thumping headache for several hours, but otherwise I was unhurt.

Richard visited me later that morning, after the doctor had gone.

'Henry is furious,' he told me. 'He wants to know who fired those shots—and so do I.'

'It must have been one of the gardeners, surely?'

'He has spoken to all of them and they deny it.'

'Then who could it have been?'

'It could have been anyone,' Richard said, looking angry. 'The whole family is capable of handling a gun, with the exception of your brother. And he wasn't here anyway.'

'Oh, Richard, you don't think ...'

'Michael is the only one who takes a gun out

regularly,' he said. 'I saw him the last time he was down.'

'Please ... please don't!'

He looked at me. 'Does your head still hurt?' I nodded and he bent to kiss me. 'Poor Liz. I'll leave you to sleep in peace, shall I?'

'Yes, please.'

I did sleep for a while after he left, but I was too restless to stay in bed. I had thought the family feud was over, that we had all been brought together by Ben's death, but it seemed I was wrong. I couldn't let all the quarrels start again over what must have been an accident.

No one in the family had fired those shots. I refused to believe it.

My head was still aching but I got up and dressed. I would go down for tea and put a stop to all this nonsense before it went too far.

The quarrel had already started before I got there.

'Don't look at me like that.' I heard Michael's voice first, loud and angry. 'Why should I want to shoot Lizzie? I like the girl.'

'I'm not accusing anyone of trying to kill her,' Henry muttered. 'It was obviously an accident—but damnable carelessness on the part of whoever fired the damned thing.'

'But was it?' Richard put in. 'Lizzie isn't a very confident rider. Everyone knew that. Those shots may not have been aimed at her but I think they were meant to make her fall.'

'Richard!' I saw the shocked look on Rosalind's face as I walked into the drawing room. 'That is a terrible thing to say. No one in this house would dream of harming Lizzie.'

'No, of course they wouldn't,' I said, and they all turned to look at me. 'Please stop this at once. It was an accident.'

They were all too angry to listen.

'I'm not so sure. I haven't forgotten that certain people in this room weren't particularly happy when they heard I was going to marry Liz ...'

'You are ridiculous, Richard,' Caroline said furiously. 'If anyone thinks that either Michael or I resent Lizzie being here they are wrong. I am as upset as anyone that she was hurt.'

'Well, someone fired that gun,' Henry said. 'I've checked and one of my sporting guns has been fired recently.'

'I'm damned if I'm going to stay here to be insulted,' Michael said, banging his cup down so hard that it cracked. 'You all think I did it—I can see it in your faces.' He got up and walked from the room, his shoulders stiff with indignation.

Caroline looked at me. 'Sorry, Lizzie,' she said, and hurried after him.

'We all know it couldn't have been anyone else,' Richard said as the door closed behind them. 'Michael is the only one who takes a gun out these days.'

'Where were you?' My grandfather glared at him. 'Why are you never around when she needs you?'

'I had just got back from taking Jack to the station to catch his train. He had to be back in camp by noon.'

'Are you sure one of your guns had been fired?' Rosalind asked. 'Couldn't it have been used last time Michael was down? He did go after a few pigeons then, I saw him.'

'Perhaps.' Henry frowned. 'But both Alexi and Caroline heard the shots, and something spooked the horse. I've ridden Avenger for years and he doesn't play up for nothing.'

'Could it have been a car engine backfiring?' Rosalind asked. 'Sometimes they make a terrible noise. I've been frightened myself. Surely no one would have done such a thing on purpose? I can't believe anyone would deliberately harm her.'

'No, of course they wouldn't,' I said. 'Please ... please stop all this. Someone did fire a gun before Avenger bolted, but whoever it was couldn't have seen me. It was an accident, that's all. Please don't quarrel over it, I can't bear it.'

'You shouldn't be up,' Richard said, looking at me in concern as I sat down and put a hand to my head. 'You look dreadful. Does your head still ache?'

'Yes, a little,' I admitted, 'but not as much as it did.' I glanced round the room, looking for someone I could not see. 'Where is Alexi? I wanted to thank him for helping me. I was so confused when he brought me back.'

'He caught the next train to town as soon as the doctor said you were only bruised,' Henry said gruffly. 'I dare say he felt he was in the way.'

'Oh.' I was aware of a sudden sharp

267

disappointment. I had wanted to see Alexi, to talk to him, thank him. 'I must telephone him later. Caroline will have his number.'

'A formal note should be sufficient.' Richard looked and sounded annoyed. 'It was ridiculous of him to behave as he did—ordering everyone around as if you were his wife.'

'I suppose he thought it was easier for him to carry me up,' I said. 'Alexi is so much stronger than most people—and he was already holding me.'

I closed my eyes for a moment as I remembered my own reaction to his refusal to release me to Richard's care: it had been one of relief. I had not wanted Alexi to leave me at all.

'What's wrong?' Henry's anxious tones cut through my thoughts. 'Not feeling worse are you? You should have stayed in bed, girl.'

I opened my eyes and gave him a straight look.

'Please stop fussing, all of you. I've had enough of being treated as though I were an invalid. What happened was an accident. No one was to blame. I'm bruised but otherwise perfectly all right. I shall go riding with Caroline in the morning, and I'm going to tell her so now.'

'Well, that told me,' Henry said and there was a gleam of satisfaction in his eyes.

I heard him chuckle as I turned and left the room.

'That wife of yours has a mind of her own, Richard.'

268

I closed the door before I heard his reply.

I met Caroline coming from the little room that led off from a hall at the back of the library. It was the room that housed Henry's gun collection as well as various other bits and pieces like shooting sticks, boots and fishing tackle. Henry had shown me the room himself and I knew that his sporting guns were kept in a locked glass case, and the key was in Henry's desk. The family knew that, of course, and so must the staff.

I had expected to find my cousin here. She would have come to check the guns as I should in her place.

'Shouldn't you be lying down?' she asked, a faint air of guilt mixed with her concern. 'You had a nasty fall, you know. When Alexi found you, you were unconscious and we were both very worried about you.'

'I was lucky,' I admitted. 'My head still aches a bit but I'm all right. Honestly, Caro. Please wait for me tomorrow morning. I should like to ride with you.'

'It's always best to get back on as soon as possible after a fall,' she agreed, eyeing me approvingly. 'Good for you, Lizzie. I'm glad this hasn't put you off riding.'

'It wasn't Avenger's fault or mine.' I hesitated. 'I wondered if we could talk? Shall we go into the library? We shan't be disturbed, because they are all having tea still—except for Michael.'

'He went off in a huff, but I'm willing to talk. We ought to get this out in the open.' She led

269

the way into the long, comfortable room with its shelves full of leatherbound books, an important table in the middle of the room, several sets of mahogany steps and a sofa at either end, then turned to me expectantly. 'What's on your mind?'

I hesitated. I wasn't really sure what was bothering me but I had to start somewhere—and Caroline was the only one I could talk to about this.

'When we first met, you said if ever you married it wouldn't be to Richard—that you and he were too much alike. What did you mean?'

'Oh ...' She let out a sigh of relief and I knew she thought I had been going to say something quite different. 'Just that we're both too extravagant and selfish. We both want our own way too much to agree for long. Anyway ...' Her cheeks went slightly pink. 'There's someone else I rather like.'

She must be speaking of Alexi, of course. I was aware of a curious tightness in my chest, which I tried to ignore.

'Are you going to marry him?'

Caroline's answer was a long time in coming. 'Yes, if he asks me, which he probably won't.' Her smile was a little fixed. 'Why did you ask about Richard?'

I breathed raggedly, half sighing. 'I just wondered, that's all. I wondered if you thought there was something I should know?'

'Richard and I don't always get on, as I'm sure you've noticed.' Caroline frowned, seeming uncertain herself 'I was probably annoyed with

270

him over something when I said that to you—I shouldn't have done. He has his good points as well as the bad and he is obviously very much in love with you.

'Is he?' The words just popped out. 'I've wondered lately if he really does.' I faltered and blushed.

'He was making enough fuss over your fall earlier.' Caroline's brows arched. 'It isn't my business if you've quarrelled, but it isn't surprising. It was bound to happen sometime. Richard can be moody and selfish but he's all right in most ways. Except ... no, I have no right to say it.'

'Please do,' I said. 'I want you to tell me what you think. I shan't be offended.'

'Richard seems weak to me.' Caroline was thoughtful for a moment. 'Henry told me Richard's grandfather went to pieces when his wife died and he had to raise John Gregory himself. Apparently, the boy turned out to be a bit of a rogue. Henry had to settle lots of bills for him and there were arguments ... I think Richard must take after the Gregorys. Rosalind isn't weak, for all her fussing.'

'No, she isn't.' Rosalind didn't always show what she was thinking, but I had sensed something hidden beneath the surface.

'Have you quarrelled with Richard? It isn't my business, of course, but I'd noticed you were a bit quiet even before the fall.'

'No, we haven't quarrelled.' I pulled a wry face. 'I think it's probably called adjusting to married life.'

She nodded sympathetically. 'You haven't exactly had it easy, have you? Your father dying like that, and all the rest of it.'

'Ben was always accident-prone. Perhaps I take after him?'

'You believe your fall was an accident?'

'What else could it have been? Someone was probably after a rabbit—a poacher perhaps. If the shots had been meant for me, I should be dead, shouldn't I?'

'Unless someone just wanted to frighten you.'

'If someone thought that a fall from a horse would scare me away from Pentire they don't know me.'

'No, they don't, do they?' Caroline laughed. The shadows lifted from her face and her relief was obvious. 'It gave me a fright, Lizzie. When I saw Avenger bolting like that, I was afraid you might be badly injured or even dead.'

'You'll have to give me some more lessons, then I shan't come off so easily next time.'

'No one could have controlled a terrified horse who was bolting like that,' Caroline said. 'Not even me. If I had been where you were, I might have fallen just as you did.'

'Then that proves no one did it deliberately,' I said. 'I didn't see who did it so whoever it was must have been in the trees.'

'What are you getting at?' She looked puzzled.

'All they could have seen was a woman on a horse—and I was wearing your clothes. From a distance I could have been mistaken for you.'

272

'Yes, you could. I hadn't thought of that,' she said, her eyes narrowing to tigerish slits. 'That *is* a comforting thought—those shots could have been meant for me not you!'

'I'm sure it was a poacher,' I said. 'There's no reason why anyone would want to harm either of us.' I remembered something I had been meaning to ask her and frowned. 'Has there ever been a tragedy in our woods, Caro? Someone killed or badly hurt?'

'Not to my knowledge. Why?'

I explained about the flowers.

Caroline stared. 'That's rather odd, isn't it? Why should anyone take flowers to a wood and leave them there?'

'I don't know. You have no ideas then?'

'I've never heard anyone mention anything that could account for it. I could ask Henry, he would know. It might be something that happened years ago.'

'But someone still remembers.'

'Yes.' Caroline gave an exaggerated shiver. 'Someone just walked over my grave. I'm goose pimples all over.' She opened her eyes wide. 'You don't think it's ...?'

'It might be someone's pet,' I said. 'I expect that's all it is. One of the gardener's children or something.'

'I'll ask Henry about it,' Caroline said. 'I expect it's nothing but it is rather strange ...'

'Yes, I thought so too.'

'I'm glad you're all right and that you don't think one of us was trying to harm you. I must admit it gave me a shock but now I think you're right. It was probably a poacher.'

Our outing with the horses the next morning passed without incident. I was a little sore but determined not to show it, or any sign of the nervousness I felt inside. I patted Avenger as he nuzzled at me affectionately, as if trying to apologize for what had happened the previous day.

'It's all right, old fellow,' I whispered, feeding him a slice of apple I'd popped into my pocket for him. 'It wasn't your fault.'

After our ride Caroline and I had breakfast together, then she left for London.

'You will come and see me one day?' she asked before she went. 'Alexi's studio is next door. I think you would like to see some of his work. He is brilliant, though he's finding it difficult to get commissions yet.'

'Yes, of course I shall visit. I must thank him for helping me, and I should love to see his work. Perhaps he will show me the model he did of you?'

'He was very concerned about you. He rang me last night, did I mention it?' I shook my head and she smiled. 'Richard was lucky he saw you first.' She laughed as I looked puzzled. 'See you soon, Lizzie.'

I was still staring after her, wondering what she had meant by that last remark, when Richard came out of the house to find me.

'Henry wants to talk to you,' he said. 'Caroline has gone, then? I blame her for your fall. If she hadn't encouraged you to ride it would never have happened.'

'I enjoy riding. No one was to blame, Richard. I'm perfectly all right—as I told you last night.' He had insisted on sleeping in the dressing room in case he disturbed me, behaving as though I were some sort of invalid.

'Is something wrong?' He looked at me as if sensing my mood. 'Have I said something to upset you?'

'Why should anything be wrong? Excuse me, please, Richard. I must see what Grandfather wants.'

I walked away from him, my head high. Tears were stinging behind my eyes but I refused to let him see I was hurt. I had begged him to stay with me but he had insisted I would rest easier alone. I couldn't pretend to myself any longer: Richard wasn't in love with me. He already regretted our marriage.

Henry was in his study when I walked in. I had my emotions under control by then, but my heart lurched as I saw my designs spread over his desk top.

'Are they hopeless?' I asked, bracing myself for his reply, which I knew would not spare me. I must not be too crushed if he was brutal about my work. 'I did warn you I know very little about jewellery and nothing about the practical side of production.'

'You've done very well for a first effort,' he said. 'The bumblebee is distinctive, though it makes the range more expensive than it might have been.'

'Yes, I suppose it does. The design would probably work without some details. I could try if you like?'

'I like these,' Henry said, tapping the flower designs with his finger, 'but not as much as this other stuff. Now *they* have something exciting and new about them.'

'Do you really like my own ideas?' My feeling of disappointment evaporated as I saw the gleam in his eyes. 'I almost didn't show you those.'

'That would have been a pity. I gave you that brooch to get you started, but I shall let you have a free hand in future. Design what you like and come to me for practical advice if you need it.'

'Thank you, I shall.' I breathed a sigh of relief. 'You won't forget about showing me the workshops?'

'I'll come up in a couple of weeks or so,' he promised. 'You'll want a little time to get settled into your new home.'

'Yes, I suppose so.'

My reluctance must have shown because Henry's eyes narrowed with sudden suspicion. 'You don't sound too happy about it. Haven't fallen out with Richard, have you?'

'Of course not.' I wandered over to the window, not wanting him to see my face, which I knew would reveal too much of my thoughts. 'I shall miss this view. Pentire is so beautiful.'

'It's your home whenever you need it.' His voice had a rough edge to it as he went on,

'I shall miss you, Lizzie. Visit me again soon, won't you?'

'Richard expects to be in town for a while, but we'll come when we can.'

There was silence between us for a moment and I listened to the ticking of the lovely bronze mantle clock, thinking how regular and peaceful it sounded. Outside the wind sighed and moaned in the trees and far away a dog was barking, reminding me of the child Lily and her mother.

I want to stay here always. The words were in my head and heart but remained unspoken.

'I've asked Mrs Barker for an early lunch,' Henry said. 'You'll want to be off as soon as it's over.'

His words broke the spell. Still I did not turn. What was wrong with me? Why was I so reluctant to leave? It couldn't be just that I felt so at home in this lovely place?

'Yes. I should make sure everything is packed. Excuse me, please.'

'Lizzie—you are all right?' Henry's anxious look stopped me as I reached the door. 'You've been a bit quiet lately but I haven't asked. You've had enough to cope with without my interference.'

'I've been grieving,' I said. 'Don't worry, Grandfather. I'm not ill. I shall be fine once I've had time to sort myself out.'

I would settle once we were in London, I thought as I walked upstairs. Perhaps then Richard would be more like he had been on our honeymoon.

Part Three

LONDON

Chapter 14

Richard's flat was small but exquisitely furnished and decorated. I was surprised at the number and quality of the antiques he had acquired. He obviously had excellent taste; although the individual pieces of furniture were necessarily smaller, what he had was the equal of anything I had seen at Pentire.

'Well, what do you think, darling?' he asked, a note of pride in his voice as I stood in the sitting room and looked around. 'Shall you be happy here?'

'I could be happy anywhere with you,' I said, but a little voice in my heart added, if only you really loved me.

'Can you see your bowl?' He pointed to a swan-necked bookcase; the glass-fronted shelves at the top were filled not with books but with pieces of overlay glass that I guessed had been made by someone like Emil Galle or the Daum brothers, two of the finest makers of such things. 'I told you I had a place for it, didn't I?'

'These things ...'

I touched a Derby figure with the tips of my fingers. 'They must be worth a great deal of money, Richard?'

'All my collection is genuine and the best I could afford,' he said. 'I never buy anything less than perfect.'

Where does the money come from? The question was in my mind but remained unspoken.

Richard saw the look in my eyes. 'I told you I was extravagant. Sometimes I win money, at the races or cards. When I do, I buy something like this.' He opened a silver-gilt box so that I could see the singing bird inside. 'I won this in a card game. It's pretty, isn't it?'

'Yes.' I felt a chill at the base of my neck. 'Do you often gamble, Richard?'

'Don't worry, Liz. I'm very lucky and seldom lose.' He went over to the sideboard and poured himself a drink. 'Care for a sherry, darling?'

'No, thank you.' I watched as he drained his whisky and poured another one. 'You must lose sometimes? Everyone does.'

'Now and then.' He pulled a face. 'You might as well know—I borrowed some money from Caro to pay a gambling debt a few weeks before we were married, but I've paid her back.'

'How much?' I was shocked by his casual revelation.

'Five hundred.' He took a cigarette from a gold case and tapped the end against it. 'Don't look like that, Liz. I told you, I paid her back. We're not in debt to anyone.'

'That's hardly the point. I didn't think you could afford to gamble like that—it's a lot of money, Richard.'

'It might seem to be,' he agreed, looking annoyed. 'But as I said, I win more often than I lose. Did Henry pay you for those designs, by the way?'

'He's going to pay me once a quarter.'

'So it's more or less an allowance? Well, that's a relief. I've been paid for a couple of articles about Paris so we shan't starve in the meantime, but it will be easier knowing we can rely on his money. The marvellous thing is, he has so much of it.'

And that's what matters to you, isn't it?

I almost spoke the words aloud but managed to stop myself. I stared at Richard as he lit his cigarette and it was as if I were seeing him for the first time. How utterly thoughtless and selfish he was! I hadn't realized until now, at least not the full extent of his narcissism. To stand there openly gloating because my grandfather was going to pay a quarterly retainer for my work!

He had married me for the money, of course. I saw it clearly now. He had expected a generous settlement on our marriage and was probably hoping Henry would leave me a substantial amount in his will. He thought of Henry as his own grandfather but he wasn't. Richard was the grandson of Henry's sister Anna and Edward Gregory. It wasn't likely that he would be a main beneficiary but I might—especially now that I was working for my grandfather, following him in the trade he loved—and Henry had an urgent need to make up for his mistakes of the past.

Richard had thought it all out before he married me, perhaps even before he came to Norfolk to look me over. Because, of course, he had. It had been a lie when he pretended not to know who Ben was. Of course he had known—there weren't likely to be two Benedict Caulders tied to a wheelchair and living in Norfolk. Richard had deliberately lied to me over and over again. He had planned everything except his tumble into the river and even that had turned out to be lucky for him.

He wasn't really in love with me at all.

The pain swept over me with dizzying swiftness. What a fool I had been ... naive, easily persuadable, eager to believe whatever he told me.

Richard was looking at me oddly. 'Is something wrong?' he asked when I continued to be silent. 'Are you feeling unwell?'

'I do have a headache,' I replied, my throat so tight that I could hardly get the words out. 'If you don't mind, I think I shall have a bath and then lie down for a while.'

'Very sensible,' he said. 'You won't mind if I go out this evening, will you? If I'm late back, I'll sleep in my own room. I thought we would each have our own room, darling. It isn't done to intrude on each other's privacy too much, and I've never been very much inclined to that side of things.'

'Of course. I understand,' I said, swallowing hard. 'I shall probably be asleep when you come in anyway.'

I walked into the bathroom and locked the door, turning on the taps to drown the sound of my sobs.

I was dreaming. I knew I was dreaming and yet it was not like a dream.

I watched the woman get out of bed. She had been sick and was feeling very ill, very unhappy. It was as if I were inside her head and yet it was not me.

She had been calling for help for a long time but no one had answered her cries. In desperation she had got out of bed to find someone ... anyone. Where had they all gone? Why had she been left alone?

She walked slowly, as if she were half asleep, her hand touching the wall, fearing to fall and hurt herself. The dizziness was much worse again and she could hardly see where she was going.

I tried to call out, to warn her. She should have stayed in bed. I knew that she was in terrible danger and wanted to save her but I could not speak. I could see her. I could sense her fear and her pain but I could not move. I could not reach her.

She had paused at the top of the stairs. She hesitated, then looked back as if she had heard something. I saw her face clearly then and there was fear in her eyes ... fear and something else.

'No! Don't ...' I cried aloud, and woke up. 'Please don't!'

I was trembling as I reached for the light switch. The dream had been so strange ... so real.

I was in my own bed at the London flat, but I knew the dream had been of Pentire—and the woman I had seen was my grandmother. Not pretty and pink like her portrait but pale and

285

ill, her hair streaked with grey.

It was such an odd feeling. Almost as if I had been there, a witness to those last moments before Selina fell to her death.

But she hadn't fallen. She had been pushed.

How could I know that? My dream had ended as Selina looked back. I hadn't seen her fall. What had disturbed me was the expression in her eyes ... fear and recognition. Yes, I had seen recognition in her eyes. She had known the person who stood in the shadows behind her.

It was a dream! Only a dream. It meant nothing, and yet I felt it was a warning.

I got out of bed and went to the bathroom. I was being foolish, letting things prey on my mind. Imagining there was something sinister about my grandmother's death.

Richard had not come home yet, although it was past midnight. I was alone in the flat and my nerves were on edge. It was all foolishness. A lively imagination working too hard.

Someone had sent me a dead rat; I had found a label from a packet of rat poison in the pocket of an old coat; I had been sick and dizzy ... all these things were meaningless incidents by themselves, but there were also the shots that had caused me to fall from my horse.

Who hated me enough to want to frighten or harm me?

I believed that Richard regretted our marriage —was that reason enough to want me dead?

I felt chilled. Surely Richard wouldn't ... besides, the dead rat had been sent to me before we were married. No, he might still be in love with Caroline, but he had married me for other reasons. He would gain nothing by my death.

Who would? Caroline ... Michael ... even Jack?

I could not believe any of them wished me harm. My brother certainly didn't. I thought Caroline was my friend ... Michael then?

No, I would not believe it. It was all too horrible. I'd had an unpleasant dream. There was no more to it than that. My bilious attack had been caused by a germ and the fall was an accident.

I was overwrought. My father's tragic death had been almost too much to bear and now the discovery that my marriage had been a mistake was pressing down on me.

It wasn't surprising that I'd had a bad dream.

'Are you sure you want to come?' Caroline said as I joined her outside the flat the next afternoon. It was cold and our breath made little white clouds on the frosty air. 'Saree has been on at me to visit the mission for ages and I remembered you saying you wanted to see it, so ...'

'I'm glad you rang me,' I told her. 'Richard said he would be late this evening and there's really very little for me to do at the flat. I was always so busy at Winspear.'

'Feeling a bit lost?' Caroline asked as I settled in the car beside her. I nodded. 'Well, I'm quite sure Saree will find plenty for us to do when we get there.'

'I was going to work on some designs,' I said, 'but there's no reason why I shouldn't play truant for a while.'

'None at all,' she agreed, and drew away from the kerb. 'To tell you the truth, I've been putting this off for ages.'

'Why?'

'I suppose it makes me feel guilty. I spend as much on one dress as Saree needs to keep the mission going for a month.'

'You're not responsible for all the poor people of London,' I said. 'Besides, you help to raise money for the mission, don't you?'

'I've been arranging a masked ball,' she said. 'There were masses of envelopes to write and I've persuaded Noel Coward to put on a little play for us, so that should help. I'm badgering all my friends for five guineas a ticket. Henry says he'll buy several.'

The streets were becoming dirtier and meaner. The people looked poor, their clothes shapeless and worn. Men hung around in groups in the doorways of boarded-up shops as if they had nothing better to do, and children played in the gutters amongst the filth that had accumulated from markets and debris blown by the wind.

'What we really need is for the Government to do something about all this unemployment,' Caroline said. 'Saree is helping but ...' She glanced out of the window. 'Why did she have to choose such an awful area to set up her mission?'

It wasn't easy to find the right place. We had to stop several times to ask the way, and some of the men looked at us with sullen, hostile eyes. When we finally found the mission, Caroline had to park her car on a patch of waste ground at the end of the street because it was too narrow to turn round and she didn't want to have to back all the way up when she left.

'It makes me wonder if it's safe to leave the car here,' she said, looking round her uneasily as she locked the door.

'Why don't you ask him to look after it for you?'

Caroline looked at the young lad I had pointed out. He was dressed in torn trousers, a shabby jacket and greasy cap, and his feet were bare. He was obviously fascinated by the car and came running eagerly when she beckoned, grinning at us and wiping his nose on the sleeve of his disreputable jacket.

'Wot yer want, missus?'

'Will you watch my car until I come back if I give you five shillings?'

'I'll die fer yer fer a crown, missus!'

Caroline smiled. 'Here.' She handed him half a crown. 'I'll give you the rest when I come back. Don't let anyone touch my car, will you?'

'Cross me 'eart and hope to die!' He made a movement across his throat and grinned at Caroline, sticking his hands in his trouser pockets and whistling as we walked away. I glanced back and saw him strutting up and down by the car, as proud as a puppy dog with two tails.

'How can he be so cheerful?' Caroline said.

'He smells as if he hasn't washed in months, his face is covered in sores and he looks half-starved.'

'Yet there was an unquenchable spirit in his eyes—didn't you think so?' I asked. 'And you've undoubtedly made his day by giving him the responsibility of looking after your car.'

'Look at this mud,' Caroline grumbled, picking her way between the potholes. 'What on earth made Saree choose such a godforsaken place as this?'

'It was probably cheap.'

The mission looked like a disused warehouse and must be hundreds of years old. From somewhere at the rear came the sounds of the river—water lapping against the banks and a faint chugging as a long boat fought against the tide. And the smell! Indescribable.

'I don't know how anyone could bear to live in a stinking hole like this. Saree must be mad ...'

Caroline stopped mid-sentence as she opened the mission door and we heard the cheerful buzz of voices and laughter. She looked at me in surprise, as if wondering whether we had found the right place. Saree had described the plight of the women and children whose men were out of work as desperate and Caroline had obviously expected them to look miserable and worn down with poverty, to find an atmosphere of depression and overwhelming despair.

'I think we've walked into a party,' she whispered to me as some children shrieked with glee as they chased each other round the hall. 'This isn't what I expected at all.'

The children were playing a game of tag, their mothers gossiping contentedly as they sorted through clothes hanging neatly on rails or dipped into boxes filled with woollen socks and shoes.

At one end of the huge room there was a long table loaded with plates of food and a large metal urn from which Saree was dispensing steaming soup for the women and children. She was dressed in a pair of old slacks, a long flowing tunic and had a silk scarf knotted round her head turban-style. She looked up and smiled as she saw us.

'It's good of you both to come,' she said. 'We always need extra hands. Caroline, if you wouldn't mind filling some of those mugs with orange juice for the children? The midday rush is about to start any moment. Lizzie, you can fill the water jugs from the kitchen behind me?'

'Yes, all right,' I said, and smiled at Caroline. Neither of us was really dressed for the part, but it didn't matter.

'When you've filled those mugs you could go through the new intake of clothes,' Saree said. 'They need sorting. Some will be useless except to sell for pennies as rags. Some will have to be washed, but the good things can go straight out on the rails. We seem to be getting more and more visitors every day. I'm not sure we can cope unless we get more helpers—and more funds.'

I picked up the jug and took it through to the back. Two women were buttering slices of

291

bread and filling them with generous amounts of cheese and pickles. I wasn't surprised that the mission was popular if this was the fare provided. Some of the women and children out there looked as if they could do with a decent meal and this was probably better than they were used to even when their men were in work.

I was glad Caroline had asked me to come. It was a worthwhile way of spending the morning and it saved me from thinking about my own problems.

'It makes you realize, doesn't it?' Caroline said as she parked her car, which had been jealousy guarded and protected by her faithful urchin, outside her own house. 'Just how lucky we are.'

'Yes, it does,' I agreed. 'I shall certainly help Saree out as often as I can ... and with any fund-raising schemes.'

'Saree does what she can but it is a much bigger problem than one person can tackle, Lizzie. I think someone should do something to attack the root causes and not just the symptoms.'

'Yes, I suppose you are right,' I said as I followed her into the house. 'But what can be done?'

Caroline was standing in her hallway; she appeared to be sniffing the air, as if she didn't like what she could smell.

'What's the matter?'

'That perfume ... rather sweet and cloying.'

She looked at me. 'Can you smell it?'

I breathed deeply. 'Yes, I can, faintly. What is it?'

'I don't know.' Caroline frowned. 'It's not my perfume. I would never use anything that sickly.'

'Have you had any visitors?'

'No, not today or yesterday. Besides, this is quite strong. As if someone has been here recently.'

'Perhaps it came in with us from the garden?' I suggested. 'It might be a winter-flowering shrub.'

'Perhaps.' Caroline gave a little shrug. 'It's just that I've had the oddest feeling a couple of times recently ... as though someone was in the house.'

'Don't!' I shivered, feeling an icy chill trickle down my spine. 'I'm having nightmares as it is.'

'Are you?' Caroline looked at me sharply. 'What about?'

'It was silly but I dreamed about Selina last night. About her falling down the stairs. Only in my dream she was pushed.'

'That's my fault for putting it in your head,' Caroline said with a rueful smile. 'I'll put the kettle on and ...' She walked into the kitchen and then stopped. 'Look!'

A bunch of large, white, heavily scented lilies was lying on her sink drainer. Caroline had gone pale and I thought for a moment she was really scared.

'That's the source of the smell,' I said. 'Didn't

you know they were there? Does anyone have a key?'

'My treasure ... that's Mrs Beale. She comes in twice a week to do for me, as she says, but she wouldn't bring me flowers.' Caroline picked the flowers up and took them to the back door, throwing them outside into the garden. 'I hate these flowers. Lilies always make me think of churchyards.'

'And graves,'

Caroline turned to look at me. 'I asked Henry about the flowers in the woods. He pretended he didn't know anything about them but I think he did ... he just didn't want to tell me.'

'You don't think it could be a grave, do you?'

'I told you, I've always thought it odd the way no one ever says what Richard's father actually died of.'

'Caroline! You can't mean ...' I stared at her in horror. 'That would mean Henry or one of the family ... you can't think that!'

She frowned, then shrugged her shoulders. 'No, I don't suppose I do, but it is a bit weird, isn't it?'

'Yes, it is, and those flowers ... just as if someone was visiting a grave.' I watched as she made coffee. 'Someone sent me a dead rat in the post just before I married Richard. Maggie thought it was a nasty joke but ...'

'Oh, Lizzie, that's horrible,' she said. 'I don't like to sound melodramatic but it does seem as if someone wants to upset us both, doesn't it?'

'Those shots could have been meant for either of us ...'

Caroline was thoughtful. 'I did wonder if it might have been Michael. I knew he had taken a gun out. But I tackled him about it and he swore to me that he only fired one shot and that was right over at the other side of the lake. I believe him, Lizzie. He was quite annoyed with me for suspecting him, but I'm sure he told me the truth.'

'He wouldn't have fired at you, anyway.'

'Who would want to harm either of us?'

'I wish I knew.' I sighed. 'Perhaps we're getting a bit paranoid over all this? The flowers could have been sent by an admirer. Your Mrs Beale could have taken them in for you.'

'Yes, I suppose she could.' Caroline laughed. 'It's just that I've never made any secret of the fact that I don't like lilies.'

Richard brought me flowers when he came in that evening: sweet-scented, very expensive hot-house roses. He kissed my cheek and asked me what I had been doing all day. I told him I had been to Saree's mission with Caroline and he frowned.

'I'm not sure that I like the idea of your spending time in a place like that,' he said. 'You might pick up all sorts of things.'

'Richard! That's not a very nice thing to say. Saree's mission is very necessary.'

'Of course it is, darling, and I'm sure you can help her in lots of ways, without actually going there.'

'I really think I should make my own decisions about things like that, Richard.'

'Well, you won't be able to go tomorrow because Mama has asked you for lunch. I said you would go. You don't have anything more important to do, do you?'

'No, of course I don't.'

I was annoyed. It wasn't that I had any objection to having lunch with Rosalind, but I was beginning to resent the way she and Richard seemed to want to order my life.

'Stop sulking then, darling,' he said. 'I've got tickets for the theatre tonight, to make up for neglecting you last night.'

'Oh, Richard ...'

'I thought you would be pleased?'

'I am—of course I am.'

He could be thoughtful when he chose, and there were times when he smiled at me and I almost believed he loved me—but a coldness had started to form about my heart and I was not sure that I really cared what he felt anymore.

I stood looking at the two houses at the end of the square after I had paid my cab fare. One was Caroline's and the other Alexi's. I'd been in London now for nearly a week and hadn't yet spoken to him. I wasn't sure why. After he'd left Pentire I'd been desperate to see him, but now I was uncertain.

I wanted to see him and yet I didn't.

I walked towards Caroline's house, wondering whether I would find her in. I ought to have telephoned but Rosalind had phoned after breakfast and talked for so long that in the end I had just picked up my things and left the house in a rush.

'You will come to my card party tomorrow, Lizzie dear?' Rosalind was so persuasive and it was difficult to refuse without offending her. 'And that charity meeting next Thursday—you haven't forgotten?'

'I can't manage that,' I had apologized with a feeling of relief. 'Henry will be in town and has promised to take me to the workshops. He will only be here for a couple of days so I must keep my time free for him.'

'Yes, of course. I wouldn't dream of interfering with your plans, dear—but it is so nice for me to have you as a friend. I was so pleased when Richard brought you to see me that day in Cromer. I thought after ... well, it seemed that he would never marry ... but when he found you! I hope you know just how happy you've made us both? Richard adores you, of course, and I'm so very fond ...'

She had gone on and on in the same vein for so long that I hadn't got round to phoning Caroline as I'd promised. If she wasn't in I would go for a walk in the park and then take another taxi home. I could probably catch a bus but I wasn't used to London yet; I didn't know my way around and was a little apprehensive of getting lost.

I rang Caroline's bell and waited. Nothing happened so I rang again, waiting for several minutes. Still no answer. I was about to turn away when the upstairs window next door opened and Alexi put his head out.

'Caro went shopping. Come round the back, Lizzie. My door is open. Let yourself in and come up.'

He closed the window before I could reply. It would be rude to walk away and ignore the invitation. Besides, I wanted to thank him for helping me after my fall.

My heart was behaving a little oddly as I made my way down the little side path and let myself through the gate, noticing that it connected both back gardens. Alexi's door was unlocked and I went in, finding myself in a large, untidy kitchen which was south-facing and must be warm in summer. There was a bowl of unwashed crockery in the sink, newspapers piled on chairs, clothes and all kinds of bits and pieces on the pine dresser and table, but the floor and windows were clean and it wasn't unpleasant to see the clutter. I went through the hall and up the stairs.

'I'm in the studio,' he called. 'Come in, Lizzie. I've almost finished.'

The whole of the top floor at the back of the house had been opened out to make one huge room with large windows and a skylight to maximize the light. It was furnished with a sofa, a table littered with pens, pencils, knives, chisels, brushes and tools of his trade that I didn't recognize; there were several easels, a couple of chairs—and Alexi's workbench.

He was standing at the bench with his back towards me, and as I approached I saw that he had been working on a clay model of a rearing horse.

He turned to me, wiping the clay from his hands on a cloth smeared with paints and plaster.

'It was at a tricky stage. Once this stuff gets too dry you can't do anything with it—but I've finished with this for the moment. We can have a cup of tea if you like?'

'Are you sure I'm not taking you from your work? I could make the tea and bring it up if you want to carry on?'

'This is only a first attempt. I shan't make a cast of it—the head isn't quite right and the position of that leg ...' He shook his head ruefully. 'Completely wrong.'

I had thought it wonderful but he was obviously a perfectionist. And of course it was expensive to make a plaster cast, especially when you didn't have money to waste.

'Will Caroline be long, do you think?' I asked as I followed Alexi downstairs. He had taken off his stained working coat and was wearing a rather frayed shirt that stretched tautly over his broad shoulders, hinting at the strength of the muscles beneath. He really was a powerful man, I thought, and smiled as I remembered how gentle he had been when I fell from the horse.

He washed his hands at the sink before looking at me. 'With Caro one never knows. She comes and goes as it suits her.' He shrugged. 'Has she forgotten an appointment?'

'No. I told her I would telephone if I was

coming—but I was delayed and forgot ...'

I couldn't explain the desperation that had made me want to escape from the flat after Rosalind's phone call or the increasing frustration and unease that had built inside me over the past few days.

Alexi's dark eyes seemed to linger on my face. I felt a sense of panic, as if my soul were laid bare to him, as if he could read all my thoughts, then he moved away to put a kettle on the stove.

'You've recovered from your fall?' he asked without turning round. 'I hope there have been no more accidents?'

'No, none at all. I am very well, thank you.'

I had never felt better physically but I was so very unhappy. Tears stung my eyes and to my horror I began to cry.

'I'm sorry,' I gulped as he swung round. 'I didn't mean ... I'll go ... I mustn't ...'

Alexi caught my arm as I started towards the door. I gazed up at him and there must have been an unconscious appeal for help in my eyes. For a moment he hesitated, then he drew me into his arms and kissed my mouth, his fingers moving over my face with a kind of reverence. It was such a soft, tender, comforting kiss that I made no attempt to pull away. I let him kiss me, then rested my head against his shoulder and sobbed out all the pain and disillusionment that had lain over my heart like a dark cloud since the first night in Richard's flat, when I had cried myself to sleep and wished I could go back to the day I had dived in to pull a stranger out of the river—that I could save my foolish heart the pain of loving unwisely.

'You are very sad,' Alexi said, stroking my hair. His face was grim as he gazed down at me. 'It is more than your father's death, I think?'

'Richard doesn't love me,' I said as my tears dried. 'I'm not sure why he married me—perhaps for Henry's money, or the hope of getting some of it. He—I think he wants someone else. He was disappointed on our wedding night because I was a silly little virgin ...' I gasped and blushed. 'I shouldn't have said that.'

'Richard is the fool, not you,' Alexi said, and let me go. I had stopped crying and he smoothed the tears from my cheeks with his fingers. 'A woman can give such a precious gift to only one man—that man should not take it lightly nor dismiss it as of no importance.'

'I—I tried to make it up to him, to be what he wanted.' I dried my face with his handkerchief, which had a few paint stains but was otherwise clean. 'I seem to be collecting these. I keep crying all over you. You must think I am a very foolish woman.'

'I have very broad shoulders, as you may have noticed.' He teased me gently. 'They are always at your service—and I don't think you in the least foolish.'

'You are so kind to me. I should have had tea with you that day in Norwich.'

'If you had I might have spirited you off to my lair,' he said, a wicked gleam in his eyes. 'Caro tells me I look like a barbarian—untamed

301

and dangerous. Sometimes I think she is right. If I were not forced to behave in a civilized way I should carry you upstairs to my bed and never let you return to that fool you married.'

His statement took my breath away. I stared at him in bewilderment, not certain whether he meant what he was saying or if it was just his way of making me feel better about myself. I had opened my heart to him on impulse and perhaps he was teasing me because he felt awkward at knowing my secrets. My cheeks burned and I dropped my gaze before his intense look. Could he really see into my soul or was that just my vivid imagination?

'I never say what I don't mean, Lizzie.'

'Alexi ...'

I wasn't sure what I was going to say to him but it didn't matter anyway, because before I could say anything the door was thrown open and Caroline came in. She stopped in surprise as she saw us and frowned.

'Lizzie—what are you doing here?'

My heart took a frightening somersault. I had almost done something I would surely have regretted. Alexi was Caroline's lover. She wanted to marry him. How could I have thought for one moment that he had meant those teasing words? No one could prefer me to Caroline; she was so beautiful, so sensual. He was just being kind to me. Shame and embarrassment washed over me and I avoided looking at him as I answered Caroline.

'I came to visit you but you were out. Alexi kindly asked me to wait—but I was about to leave anyway.' I glanced at my watch. 'Is that the time? I must rush. Richard will be back soon and we're going to a party.' I darted at Caroline and kissed her cheek. 'I'll telephone you another day. 'Bye, dearest Caro.' I risked a fleeing glance at Alexi. He seemed annoyed. 'Bye, Alexi—see you both soon.'

Then I was leaving the house and out on the street, waving to a passing cab. It was true we were going to one of the endless parties Richard seemed to enjoy so much that evening, but not for hours yet. I simply had to get away before either Caroline or Alexi guessed what was on my mind.

I could hardly believe it myself but if Caroline had not come at that precise moment I had been on the verge of asking Alexi to make love to me!

I felt hot all over as I admitted the shaming truth to myself. It was so wicked of me! And it wouldn't have been fair to either Caroline or Alexi himself, because I wasn't in love with him—of course I wasn't. How could I be? Only a few weeks previously I had believed myself madly in love with Richard.

I still loved him, of course I did. Our marriage hadn't turned out quite as I'd hoped but it wasn't so very bad. Richard was always considerate towards me and we hadn't quarrelled, not really quarrelled, since our wedding night. It was just that I knew he didn't love me—or not as I had wanted to be loved.

If I had let Alexi make love to me just to restore my hurt pride it would have been a terrible betrayal. Richard didn't deserve that.

I had been keeping a distance between us since that first night at the flat, but this evening I would invite him into my bed. I was at fault and it was up to me to make our marriage work.

Chapter 15

'I've told you how much Henry relies on me, haven't I, Lizzie dear?' Rosalind said, the sparkle of tears in her eyes. 'Because, of course, I did so much for him when poor Selina was so ill. He really wouldn't have been able to manage without me.'

'You must have been very fond of her?'

'Oh, yes, I was.' She wiped her tears, then looked at me in concern. 'You've been very quiet all afternoon. You're not ill, are you? I've not had the best of health myself these past few years. I hope you won't be sickly. Poor Richard can't cope with illness—unless, of course, you were in a delicate situation? You know what I mean ...'

'No, of course I'm not having a baby.' I blushed, my heart sinking as Rosalind continued to look at me intently. Did my unhappiness show that much? 'We were up rather late last night, that's all.'

We were alone in her neat parlour after the other guests had gone and I had been trying to hide my feelings, but Richard's mother had obviously noticed something.

'Richard was abrupt with me this morning when I telephoned,' she went on. She had a faintly accusing air, as if she suspected that her son's ill humour was my fault. 'You haven't quarrelled with him, I hope?'

It was far, far worse than a quarrel but I couldn't tell Richard's mother that or what had kept me awake the previous night. Long after he had gone to his own room I had lain staring into the darkness, listening to a clock ticking and the branch of a tree scratching against my window, my heart aching as I felt the bitter sting of regret.

'No, we haven't quarrelled,' I said, avoiding her penetrating look. 'I'm sorry if Richard was short with you when you rang earlier. I think he had a headache and was late for an appointment—not that that excuses his rudeness to you, of course.'

'Oh, well.' Rosalind's feathers were smoothed by my apology. 'As long as you are both happy. Richard means everything to me, Lizzie dear. He is all I have in the world since his father ...'

I was tempted to ask her just what had happened to Richard's father but, seeing the odd, half angry, half wistful expression on her face, I knew I could not probe what was obviously still an open wound. I could not help feeling sympathy for her. She had been a widow for a long time and perhaps she was lonely, despite all her friends and her charity meetings.

I kissed her cool, papery-soft cheek, catching a breath of her sweet, cloying perfume. 'Richard is lucky to have you for his mother,' I said. 'I am sure he knows that—even if he sometimes forgets to show it.'

'What a sweet girl you are,' she murmured, tears in her eyes. 'I never like to demand too much of him. He has his own life and I know he must think I'm a nuisance at times.' I shook my head and she smiled bravely. 'How like you to deny it. I am so glad he married you and not that ...' She faltered, as if afraid of hurting my feelings. 'You did know that Richard foolishly thought himself in love with that selfish Madam once, didn't you?'

'You mean Caroline, I suppose?' I frowned, trying to remember where I had heard that term 'Madam' recently. 'But that was a long time ago—wasn't it?'

'Several years,' she agreed. They had a bit of a fling when he first came home from the war. He was decorated for bravery, you know, and Caroline couldn't do enough for him at first. She seemed nice enough when she was young but ...' Rosalind's mouth screwed up in disapproval. 'It's her father's fault for not remarrying after his wife died. She needed a mother—just as my poor, dear boy needed a father. But he had Henry, of course.' She seemed almost to purr with satisfaction at the memory rather like a well-bred cat. 'Henry has been so very good to me and my son. Pentire has been a second home to us—even though *Madam* does think she owns the place at times.'

I remembered what the child Lily had said about Madam having had her nose put out. Had it upset Caroline because Henry had told me to regard Pentire as my home? She admitted freely that she was spoiled, and that she knew how to twist him around her finger.

'Pentire is very beautiful,' I said, ignoring Rosalind's comments about my cousin. 'I should be quite content to live there myself.'

'And perhaps you will one day—you and Richard,' she said with an odd, satisfied smile. 'You mustn't let anything Caroline says upset you. She was Henry's favourite before you came along and she's bound to feel that you've usurped her place.'

'Surely not?' These insinuations were making me uncomfortable. 'There's no reason why she should. I don't want to take anything away from her.'

Rosalind's eyes darted to a spot somewhere behind me. She went to run her finger over the mantelpiece, shaking her head as she collected a speck of dust.

'I must speak to my housekeeper about the daily woman. If I don't check all the time she skimps on her work. Now, as I was saying ... since Richard broke off his relationship with Caroline she has lost no chance of turning people against him. It really is very naughty of her.'

'I'm sure she doesn't mean to,' I began, then remembered my first meeting with Caroline. 'At least, she doesn't mean any harm. She says things without thinking sometimes, that's all.'

'So long as she doesn't try to come between you and Richard. I am so very fond of you both and should be upset if either of you was unhappy.'

'We are very happy,' I lied. 'I ought to go now. I want to collect something for Richard on the way home and he will be back soon. He is taking me to dinner with some friends this evening.' I hesitated, but knew it had to be said. 'You must come to dinner with us soon.'

'That would be lovely,' Rosalind agreed, the sparkle of tears in her eyes again. 'Thank you, dearest Lizzie. You are such a thoughtful girl. I shall look forward to it.'

I kissed her goodbye. As I left her house to walk home through the gathering dusk I was trying to conquer a feeling of being trapped between Richard and his mother. It was wrong of me, of course. Rosalind was just trying to be kind—it wasn't her fault that I felt smothered by her constant demands for my company. No, it wasn't really Rosalind who was making me so restless, it was Richard himself.

Why had I rushed into a marriage I now believed to be a mistake? Why hadn't I waited until I knew him better?

If I hadn't begun to realize it before, Richard's behaviour at the party the previous evening would have opened my eyes.

The evening had begun badly. He had not been in the best of moods when he came home to change. The newspaper he wrote for had rejected a piece he had submitted, and then

308

the shirt he had wanted to wear was discovered at the bottom of the dirty linen basket in the bathroom.

'I asked you to have it washed for this evening,' he'd said with a look of annoyance. 'You know it's my favourite.'

He had not mentioned it particularly so far as I could recall, but I was already feeling guilty because of the way I had let Alexi kiss me and accepted the blame without comment.

'I'm sorry, Richard. I'll do it myself to-morrow.'

'It's raw silk. It needs special attention. I've told you where to take my things. Surely you can manage to do small things like that?'

'I'll take it in in the morning.'

'But I wanted to wear it this evening.'

I could hear a clock ticking. It was so loud that it felt as if it were inside my head.

'Can't you wear one of your others? You have so many shirts, Richard.'

'This is the shirt I prefer.' He scowled at me. 'If you can't be trusted to do simple tasks, I shall have to ask Mama to do them for me.'

'As you wish.'

His eyes narrowed in annoyance but he didn't say anything more. I wondered if he had expected me to beg him to give me another chance, and smiled inwardly; I wasn't quite as responsive to Richard's whims as I had been at the start. Some twenty minutes later he had emerged from his room wearing an almost identical shirt.

He had been distant with me as he drove

to the party, which was being held in a large house in Mayfair. However, when we arrived he switched on the charm, introducing me to everyone as if he were the loving husband I had once expected him to be.

I was greeted warmly by his friends. Several of the women promised to call on me and asked me to visit them, seeming very willing to admit me to their circle.

I relaxed and began to enjoy the party, despite Richard's moodiness earlier. It was a lovely house, furnished with beautiful antiques, lots of important pictures and silver—the kind of house I knew Richard coveted. The food and wine were both plentiful and delicious, the conversation interesting, even if a lot of it was about people and places I didn't know.

It was not until much later in the evening that I realized I hadn't seen Richard for quite a long time. Excusing myself to a woman who had been chattering on for the past twenty minutes or so about the morals of young women who smoked in public, I went in search of my husband.

I found him in our host's library playing cards with three other men, two of whom I recognized as being the particular friends he had invited to our wedding.

Richard glanced up with a frown of annoyance as I entered, obviously not pleased at being distracted from his game.

'Did you want something, darling? I am rather busy at the moment.'

'He means he's on a winning streak and

doesn't want to be disturbed,' Peter Ross said, and grinned at me.

'I was wondering if we might go home?'

'You go if you're tired,' Richard muttered. He was watching the cards the fourth man was laying on the table, a feverish gleam in his eyes.

He obviously wasn't bothered whether I stayed or went.

I turned away. I knew the fourth player was a wealthy American and from the expression on Richard's face guessed that he was expecting to win quite a bit of money from him.

I felt physically sick and knew I could not stay a moment longer.

I made a vague excuse to my host about feeling unwell and his manservant called a taxi for me.

I was too angry to cry. Richard's behaviour was so disgusting that I would not allow myself to be hurt by it. My own feelings of guilt had vanished. I had intended to try and bridge the gap between us, but now I knew there was no point. If he could be so rude to me, he could not really care for me at all. He had married me as a way of gaining Henry's favour and now clearly intended to live his own life, much as he had before we were married.

When I got back to the flat I went into my own room and locked the door. It was very late when Richard at last came home. He rattled the handle, calling my names several times before giving up and going to his own room. I suspected he had been drinking heavily.

311

It seemed that the only times he wanted to make love to me were when he was angry or under the influence of alcohol.

I had gone beyond tears and lay sleepless all night, staring into the darkness and regretting my hasty marriage. What a silly, gullible fool I had been to believe that Richard loved me!

In the morning he had been subdued and heavy-eyed. He had hardly spoken to me—and when Rosalind telephoned he had been abrupt with her.

I hoped his mood would have improved when he came home that evening, but if it hadn't I could cope. The pain was passing now and the anger had set in.

Richard brought me an armful of expensive hot-house flowers when he came in about six that evening.

'Do you hate me?' he asked with the smile that had once made my knees turn to water. 'I deserve it if you do. I am a moody devil and I don't deserve to have you, Lizzie darling.'

He could remember I preferred to be called Lizzie when he wanted to get round me!

'Your shirt is hanging in your wardrobe,' I said. 'I asked for it to be done quickly and it was ready this afternoon. I hope it meets with your approval.'

'Don't be angry with me,' he said. 'I am sorry for being such a bear yesterday. I was worried because the paper turned down that article and I needed the money, but it's all right now. I've sold something else—and I won a hundred guineas last night. So this evening we'll go out and celebrate.'

It was on the tip of my tongue to say I didn't want to go out, but the alternative was not particularly attractive. If we had a quiet evening at home Richard might want to make love to me and at that moment I did not feel I could bear him to touch me.

'As you wish,' I said. 'I've asked Rosalind for dinner one evening next week. Perhaps you will let me know which will suit you best?'

'What a bore,' he said, pulling a wry face, 'but I suppose she pushed you into asking her. Let me telephone her myself and arrange it.' He unfastened his tie. 'We could ask Henry at the same time—take them both to a decent hotel instead of having them stuck here for ages. Mama never knows when it's time to leave. Besides, your cooking isn't up to a top chef's, is it, darling? All right for when we're not hungry but not for guests.'

I made no comment, watching in silence as he turned and went into his own room. The feeling of panic clutched at me once more. What was I going to do? I felt so unhappy. How could I stand being married to a man I was learning to dislike more and more?

Yet how could I walk away from a marriage that had only just begun? Everyone would blame me. They would think I was a spoiled child who wanted things all my own way. It was impossible. I was trapped by convention.

I couldn't leave Richard. I would just have

to accept things for what they were and make the best of my life.

That night I dreamed again of Pentire, but this time it was of the woods. A woman was running in terror, screaming as the branches clawed at her face and hair, hampering her progress, preventing her from escaping the evil that was pursuing her.

It was similar to the dream I'd had at Winspear before I was married, and yet it was different in some way. When I woke I could not remember why it was different, and yet the feeling of horror remained with me throughout the morning.

I was wandering aimlessly around the flat, trying to shake off my feeling of unease, when the telephone rang. I snatched it up, breathless, hoping it might be Caroline asking me to go shopping with her.

'It's me,' Henry said. 'Haven't caught you at a bad moment, have I? You sound a bit out of breath?'

'Oh ... I was in the other room,' I said. 'No, of course it isn't a bad time.'

'I rang because there's an exhibition in town this week I thought you might like to see. I understand there will be a good display of old jewellery. A lot of it will probably be Victorian but some is earlier. You might see something that will give you a few ideas.'

'Yes, that sounds interesting,' I said. 'I was feeling at a bit of a loss this morning, wondering what to do with myself. I should love to go—and

I'm looking forward to visiting the workshops when you come up.'

'I wish I could manage it sooner but there you are. Perhaps you and Richard could come down the following weekend?'

'I'll ask him,' I promised. ' 'Bye now, and thank you for ringing.'

As I replaced the receiver I heard the letterbox and went out into the hall to pick up a handful of envelopes. Most of them were for Richard, but the last was addressed to me. A cold chill ran down my spine as I saw the writing. Large and ill-formed ... like that of a child ... the same as on the parcel Maggie had opened for me.

I took the letter back into the parlour, turning it over in my hand, reluctant to open it. I knew even before I did so that what it contained would be unpleasant.

'The wicked shall be punished,' I read. *'And the harlot was stoned to death and it was justice.'*

I felt sick as I read the words. Who would send such a letter?

I could no longer pretend to myself. Someone was trying to frighten me. But who? And why?

I had to get out! I couldn't stand being in this flat another moment.

I grabbed my coat and purse and fled, leaving the letter lying on the floor where it had dropped from my hand. Who hated me enough to do something like that?

Once I was out of the flat I felt better. The streets were filled with people and the shops were just beginning to dress their windows with Christmas displays, though the weather was wet

315

and dirty, not in the least seasonable. I would soon have to start sorting out Richard's card list; he seemed to have so many acquaintances and I wasn't sure whether he sent them all cards or not.

The exhibition hall was almost empty when I arrived, which was a shame because Henry had been right about there being a good display. I walked round the brightly lit glass cases, finding them fascinating and pausing to study some Northern Greek snake bracelets that dated from the sixth century BC. There were also pieces of gold repoussé work from Rhodes, which dated from a similar period.

I lingered by the cases showing Greek and Roman jewellery for some time, remembering the tarnished gold torc I had seen that day in Norwich when I had accidentally trodden on Alexi's foot. I looked up, glancing round the hall as if expecting to see him. Of course he wasn't there—why should he be?

A small display of Anglo-Saxon pieces interested me. I liked the bold, clear shapes and would definitely draw on some of these ideas for designs in the future. I made some notes in a little book I carried in my purse for just such a purpose.

I studied a collection of sixteenth-century gold and enamel pendants, many of which were set with curious baroque pearls that had been used in imaginative ways to enhance their natural form. Some were Italian, others German or Spanish, but all were fascinating because of their boldness and originality. This was the kind of thing I wanted to achieve, but less ornate, something more in keeping with modern taste—the feeling for simplicity that I was beginning to notice in many forms of design.

I moved along the cases, lingering by a collection of jewelled crosses, pendant scent flasks in silver-gilt, and wonderful enamelled and jewelled necklaces. There was so much to see and I could never hope to take it all in in one visit.

I glanced round the hall once more and sighed. I had some shopping I ought to do before I went back to the flat—and it had been ridiculous to hope that I might bump into Alexi. Of course I wouldn't, and it was wrong of me even to have thought about it.

I was reluctant to go home but of course I had to, I was loaded down with shopping. I had so much that I had to juggle with my parcels as I hunted for my door key and was not at first aware of someone waving at me.

'So I've caught you at last,' Caroline said, grabbing a parcel as it was about to fall. 'Have you been out for ages or don't you answer your phone?'

She was looking particularly lovely that morning, her red hair tucked beneath a little fur-trimmed hat and a fox stole thrown casually over her tailored suit. I felt untidy beside her and knew that my fine hair must have blown all over the place in the wind.

'I have been out longer than usual,' I said

as I succeeded in opening the door and leading the way inside. I dumped some of my parcels on a hall chair. 'I went to a jewellery exhibition. Henry rang me earlier and told me about it.' I noticed that Caroline was wearing a fresh, light perfume that reminded me of flowers in a spring meadow. What was that other smell? I'd thought I could smell something when I came in but now I wasn't sure. 'Did you ring about nine this morning? I heard it but was in the bathroom and didn't bother to answer. I thought it might be Rosalind again.'

Caro laughed. 'I know exactly what you mean! Once she starts talking you can't get away.'

We smiled at each other and went into the sitting room. Caroline was obviously at home in Richard's flat. She walked about the room, inspecting bits and pieces as I took the food into the kitchen and then came back to join her.

'I see Richard is still acquiring things,' she said, picking up a silver rose bowl. 'This wasn't here a few months ago.'

'He buys something whenever he has the money.' I was looking for something—the letter I had left lying on the floor. 'Did you pick up a letter, Caro?'

'Letter?' She arched her brows, a naughty smile on her lips. 'What kind of letter, Lizzie? Was it from your lover?' Her smile faded as she saw my face. 'Obviously not. Where was it?'

'On the floor—there.' I pointed to an empty

spot on the carpet. 'I dropped it before I went out and ... now it has gone.' An icy chill went down my spine. 'I know it was there.'

'What kind of a letter?'

'Rather unpleasant,' I said. 'The handwriting was odd ... and the message was like a bit out of the bible.'

'What did it say exactly?'

'Something about the harlot being stoned ...' I shuddered. 'I don't remember exactly. I just dropped it and ran.'

'I'm not surprised,' Caroline said. 'Rather unpleasant, as you said—like the lilies in my kitchen.'

'Did you discover how they got there?'

'Mrs Beale denies all knowledge of them, I'm thinking of having my locks changed.'

'I should if I were you.' I glanced round the room again. 'It couldn't have walked away by itself.'

'Perhaps Richard came back and picked it up?'

'Perhaps.'

Caroline looked at me thoughtfully.

'Is something wrong, Lizzie? Apart from the letter?'

'No, of course not.' I forced a smile. 'Shall I make tea or would you prefer coffee?'

'Either.' Caroline frowned. 'If I've come at a bad time, I can go. I was going to sell you some tickets for Saree's ball but ...'

'Yes, of course I'll buy some. How much are they?'

'Five guineas each. I know it's a lot but it is for a good cause.'

I took a silver box from the mantelpiece and opened it, thrusting my fingers inside although I could see it was empty.

'What's wrong?'

'I thought there was fifty pounds here,' I said. 'I must have mislaid it. Sorry, Caro. I don't have enough in my purse.'

'Oh, don't worry about the money,' she said. 'You can pay me later. Henry says he wants some tickets so he'll probably stump up for all of us.'

'The money must be somewhere. When I find it, I shall pay you for our tickets.'

'If you want to hide money from Richard, you'll have to think of somewhere safer than that,' she said. 'He has probably borrowed it. He'll pay you back when he's ready, of course.'

'As he did you?'

'So he told you then?'

I nodded. 'I just wish he'd told me he wanted that fifty pounds. It was supposed to be for emergencies.'

'Don't let it worry you,' Caroline said with a shrug. 'Just be a bit more careful in future. He is a compulsive gambler, Lizzie—and that kind can never be trusted with money: it's like a fever in their blood. They can't be content with an occasional flutter, they need the constant excitement. Henry refused to settle any more gambling debts for him ages ago, that's why he came to me. If you are short I can lend you ...'

'No, no, it's all right,' I said quickly. 'We buy everything on account and settle quarterly. I've enough for taxi fares—and Richard will give me money if I ask him.'

'Sorry. I shan't say another word.' Caroline sat down and slipped off her shoes, curling up on the sofa as if she had done it many times before. 'Let's talk about something else, shall we? I'm going away tomorrow and I shan't be back until just before the ball.'

'Are you going anywhere exciting?'

'Rupert is driving me down to the airfield for my last few lessons before I put in for my pilot's licence. We thought we might as well stay over for a couple of days rather than come back and then go all the way back for my exams.' Her eyes sparkled and I sensed she was very excited. 'Once I've got my licence, I'll take you up, Lizzie. I've already promised Jack a trip over to France.'

'He told me. I think my brother is halfway to being in love with you, Caro.'

'How delightful,' she cried, and gurgled with laughter. 'Don't worry, darling, I shan't gobble him up, gorgeous though he is. I might have been tempted once—but I'm in love. It's for real this time.'

'With Alexi?' I avoided her eyes as guilt stabbed me. 'I'll make the tea.'

'Alexi?' Caroline seemed surprised. 'No—it's Rupert, of course. I've been in love with him for ages but I thought there was no hope.'

I trembled inside. 'Rupert?' I echoed. 'Rupert

321

Hadden? Saree's brother?'

'I thought you must have guessed?' Caroline's eyes were shadowed. 'The war affected him badly. The thing is ... we probably shan't be able to have children. Rupert thought it wouldn't be fair to marry me so he kept me at arm's length. But we've talked things over and now ...' Her voice cracked. 'I think ... I really think it might work out.'

'That's wonderful,' I said. 'But I thought ... I mean you and Alexi are lovers ...'

'Everyone thinks that and I've let them,' she said. 'It doesn't bother me but it isn't true. It never has been. I love Rupert.' She stopped speaking and stared at me. 'You've gone pale. Are you all right?'

'Yes, fine. I'll make the tea.'

My heart was racing wildly as I jumped up and went into the kitchen. Caroline wasn't in love with Alexi! They were not and never had been lovers!

'Alexi was saying he would like to use you as a model for one of his bronzes.' Caroline's voice floated through from the sitting room. 'He doesn't mean in the nude, of course. He wouldn't expect that. But probably in something soft and flowing ...'

I almost dropped the tray as I carried it back into the sitting room. I felt confused, excited and guilty all at the same time. Was this his way of inviting me back to his studio?

'Did he ask you to ask me?'

'He sort of mentioned it hopefully when I told him I was coming to see you before I left. Why

322

don't you go round this weekend?'

'I'm not sure,' I said. 'It depends on Richard—what he wants to do.'

'You should do what you want sometimes, Lizzie.' A wicked smile lurked in Caroline's eyes. 'It was simply a suggestion, but I think you may find Richard is busy this weekend.'

'What do you mean?'

'Oh, it was just something I heard—I may be wrong.'

'Is there an important race meeting or something?'

'Or something,' she replied with a lift of her brows. 'My lips are sealed. I shan't say another word. But remember, you were warned.'

'You think Richard will lie about it, don't you?'

'Perhaps. If he does you will know, won't you?'

If he lied to me again that would be the end.

'So Henry is taking you to the workshops next week,' she changed the subject. 'He tells me you have some wonderful ideas. I think it is very exciting. I can't wait to see them made up.'

She had clearly decided to say no more about Alexi or Richard. I was relieved. I wasn't ready to open my heart to my cousin just yet.

The rift between Richard and me was growing wider and wider—but was it wide enough to justify leaving him?

And what would I do if I did?

323

Chapter 16

In the event I did nothing, even though Caroline was proved right. It was as we were having dinner that evening that Richard told me he was going to Bristol at the weekend on business.

'You wouldn't want to come with me, darling,' he said, and refilled his wine glass. 'It's just covering a conference for the paper and you would be bored. It will mostly be work and maybe a few of us will go out for drinks, you know the sort of thing.'

I knew he was lying to me. I guessed he was going to a house party where there would be gambling for high stakes. I was angry but also relieved that he hadn't asked me to go with him.

'Next weekend I'll take you somewhere nice,' he said in a soft, persuasive tone. He stood up as I began to collect some plates and came round the table to try and take me in his arms. 'You're not cross with me, are you?'

'Would it matter if I was?'

I moved away from him and he frowned.

'I thought we might have an early night,' he said. 'You've seemed to avoid me recently, Liz. Nothing seriously wrong, is there?'

I was annoyed that he assumed he could just turn the charm off and on and expect me to come running. Didn't he realize how much his

324

careless behaviour had hurt me?

'I'm afraid it's that time of the month again,' I lied. 'I'm sorry, Richard. I shall go to bed early but alone.'

'In that case, I think I shall go out for a couple of hours.'

'Please do,' I said. 'If I'm asleep when you leave in the morning, I'll see you when you get back from ... your business trip.'

He seemed taken aback by my coolness. He gave me an odd, uncertain glance, then nodded. 'You look washed out, darling. Perhaps you've been working too hard on your designs? I'll tell Henry he's expecting too much of you. Mama told me she thought you seemed tired recently.'

'That's nonsense! Please say nothing of the kind to Henry. I am perfectly able to cope.' I turned away abruptly, then hesitated as I remembered something. 'Richard—did you come back to the flat this morning while I was out?'

'No, why?' He sounded surprised.

'It was just ... I thought I'd left a letter in the sitting room and when I came back it wasn't there.'

'Didn't you tell me Caroline was with you when you came in?'

'Yes, but I don't see ...' I frowned at him. 'She wouldn't have taken it. Besides, I asked her and she said she hadn't seen it.'

'Caroline often lies. If she had picked it up she would hardly have admitted it, would she?'

'I'm sure she didn't take it.'

'Then you must have put it somewhere else.'

'Yes, I suppose so.'

I went into the kitchen and washed the dishes. By the time I had finished Richard had gone. I sighed, feeling restless and uneasy. The letter and its subsequent disappearance had unsettled me.

It meant—must surely mean—that either Caroline or Richard was lying to me. One of them had to have picked it up and was pretending not to know anything about it. Why? And who had sent me that letter?

The flat felt empty and I was restless and uneasy. I tried reading but couldn't concentrate on the words. After a warm bath I got into bed, hoping to sleep, but it was ages before I did. The disturbing thoughts just kept going round and round in my head. Who could I talk to about all this? Who could I trust?

I ought to have been able to go to Richard with my fears, but we were too far apart. I wasn't sure how I felt about him anymore. Could I have fallen out of love with him? Had it ever really been love at all?

I had been so naive when we first met, so ignorant. Richard was the first man to kiss me. I had taken that breathless excitement for love, but now I saw that it was the first awakening of womanhood.

Richard had swept me off my feet, but I had been deceived in him; the man I loved did not exist. Now I was trapped in marriage with a man who did not love me—a man I was actually beginning to dislike.

I felt hurt and bewildered. What was happening to me?

I was tempted to go to Alexi. He had always been so kind to me, so gentle, and I needed a friend. But wouldn't that make me as bad as Richard? I would be using Alexi to soothe my hurt pride, because I wasn't in love with him. Or was I?

I had felt something when he kissed me—but was it love?

I was afraid to trust my own instincts. It would be terrible if I rushed from one unhappy situation to another and then discovered I had made yet another mistake. Besides, how could I just walk out of my marriage after a few weeks? It wasn't as if Richard had done anything wicked. We hadn't quarrelled violently; he hadn't hit me or made threats against me ... so far as I knew.

Of course he hadn't sent me that letter! It was wicked of me even to think it for a moment. He was thoughtless and selfish but he wouldn't do anything as devious and malicious as that, of course he wouldn't.

But someone had. Someone wanted to frighten or hurt me—why?

None of it made sense. Perhaps I had imagined the letter? Was I beginning to imagine things ... like those dreams that were not dreams? Was there something wrong with me—with my mind?

No, no, no! I was confused and unhappy, but I had seen that letter and I had left it lying on the sitting-room floor. Which meant that someone had taken it.

In the morning, after Richard had gone, I was tempted to call a taxi and go round to Alexi's house. I was still uneasy, still restless, and needed to talk to someone. And yet if I went to Alexi, I knew he would take me in his arms, he would kiss me ... and this time Caroline would not come to interrupt us. If Alexi took me to his bed, I would not deny him.

It was wrong of me even to think of betraying my marriage vows. In my mind I could hear Hannah's voice telling me to think carefully.

'You're too like me,' she warned. 'If you go to this man your marriage will be over, because afterwards you could never return to Richard.'

Hannah had put up with all the pain and bitterness for years, but she had loved Ben and he had loved her despite everything. Surely I was entitled to expect more than I had found in this loveless marriage?

I waged war on my own conscience. Why shouldn't I go to Alexi's studio? Why shouldn't I turn to a friend for comfort?

My hand reached towards the telephone, hovered over it as I tried to reconcile my conscience—and then the bell shrilled.

I picked it up, my heart thudding guiltily. Was it ... could it possibly be Alexi ringing me?

'Hello.'

'Lizzie?' Henry's voice boomed at me. 'I'm in town unexpectedly, came up last night. I can't take you to the workshops because they close

328

on Saturdays. I'm actually on my way back to Pentire. I wondered if you and Richard would like to come down for the weekend?'

'Richard is away on business,' I said. 'But I would love to come, if that's all right with you?'

'You know it is,' he said huskily. 'Can't think of anything that would suit me better. Can you be ready in half an hour?'

'I'm ready now,' I said. 'I left some clothes in my room at Pentire. I'll be waiting for you when you get here.'

I wasn't sure whether I was relieved or disappointed as I replaced the phone. The prospect of spending the weekend at Pentire was pleasurable but I had only postponed a decision I was going to have to make sooner or later.

Before long we were driving down to Pentire, just Henry, me and his chauffeur. It felt good and I was aware of my own anticipation—a feeling of warm satisfaction. I was going back to a place I loved.

'It will be just you and me for once,' my grandfather said after we had been driving for a while. 'I hope you won't be bored?'

'I could never be bored at Pentire.' I laughed. 'Nor with you, Grandfather. I shall probably bore you with all the questions I want to ask.'

'No chance of that. I'm ready to listen whenever you're ready to start.'

I nodded, but my thoughts drifted away as I gazed out of the window. The lights and noise of London had been left behind long ago and a swirling mist shrouded the countryside from time to time, hiding fields, houses and trees beneath its damp, enveloping greyness. It was an unpleasant day for travelling but within the car I felt comfortable and safe.

'I was wondering,' I said, after a moment or two, 'how you would feel about a range of silver jewellery with semi-precious stones—things like cornelian, amethyst or amber, with a Celtic influence.'

'It could be interesting,' he said. 'Have you done any sketches yet?'

'No. I wanted to discuss it with you first.'

'Make a few drawings,' he suggested. 'We can talk it over in the morning. We shall have plenty of time this weekend.'

'Yes, plenty of time.' I was looking forward to it now. 'I hope the mist clears. I should like to go for a long walk tomorrow. I've always been used to walking and it isn't the same in London.'

'Pavements are too hard,' he agreed. 'I used to thrive on city life once but now I can't wait to get home—that's why I decided to come back today even though I'm coming up again next week, to take you to the workshops and attend that masked ball of Caroline's.'

'I'm glad you did. It is an unexpected treat for me.'

The lights of an oncoming vehicle were a blurred orange glow as the car swept up over the brow of a humped-back bridge that curved sharply to the left. Henry's driver honked the horn to warn of our approach and there was a slight screeching of brakes from the other car as we passed a little too closely for comfort, then the silence of the country road was once more broken only by the sound of the car engine and the hum of the tyres.

'Time was you wouldn't see another vehicle on this road unless it was a farm cart,' Henry muttered crossly, and rubbed at his chest. 'Damned fool!'

I looked at him in concern. His skin had gone grey and he seemed unwell, as if he were in pain. 'Are you all right?'

'Just a touch of indigestion,' he said, 'nothing to worry about, girl. So don't look at me like that. I'm as fit as a fiddle.'

I didn't say anymore but I was concerned. The slight incident with the car had upset him. His colour was coming back now—but I sensed that his health was not as good as he claimed.

His hand closed over mine as I continued to be silent. 'Don't worry about me, Lizzie. It's nothing much. I've been told I should be careful, but if I do as I'm told I could live for years.'

'That's good,' I said, and smiled at him. 'I don't want to lose you. We're only just getting to know each other.'

'That's why I shan't die,' he said. 'I've got too much to live for.'

The next morning was an unexpected treat, dawning not only fine and bright but with an unseasonable warmth that felt more like spring than a few weeks before Christmas.

I decided to make the most of it, leaving the house as soon as breakfast was over. I intended to walk down to the village, which was very small, just a cluster of pretty cottages, a shop that acted as a post office for the local people, a pub and a blacksmith. It had originally been built as part of the Pentire estate, though now there was talk of building new council houses to the west of it.

'It won't be the same,' Henry had told me as we sat talking by the fire in his study the previous evening, 'but you can't stop progress and people need somewhere to live. Still, it's a shame. You haven't been to the village yet, have you?'

'Only through it in the car,' I said. The fire was making me warm, relaxed and a little sleepy.

Outside I could heard the wind whispering in the trees; the last of the leaves, now crumbling and dry, had fallen, leaving the branches bare and stark against a sky streaked with the light of a crescent moon.

I got up and walked to the window, looking out at the lake and the dark, dense cluster of trees at its edge.

There was some mystery out there in the woods. I sensed it and it made me uneasy.

'You should see the village while it's at its best,' Henry advised. 'These places will eventually be swallowed up by the march of the twentieth century.'

'I'll walk down in the morning if it's fine.'

I turned back to him and smiled, smothering my unease.

When I saw it properly for the first time the next morning, I was surprised at the prettiness of the village; it was like something out of a nineteenth-century painting, with little thatched cottages, a tiny grey stone church, a working blacksmith's forge and the sixteenth-century inn by the green, complete with a contingent of noisy ducks who waddled expectantly across the green towards me.

'I'm sorry, I don't have anything to give you,' I said. 'I would have brought some bread if I'd known.' I looked towards the inn, wondering if I could perhaps buy a sandwich to feed the hungry mob. 'I'll come back.'

I walked into the public bar, glancing round at the small, square oak tables and basic wooden chairs. No attempt had been made towards attracting anyone other than regulars and there were no flowers or frills of any kind. Two old men sat in a corner by the window, pints of beer on the table in front of them. They seemed engrossed in a discussion of their own, taking little notice of me as I went up to the bar and inquired if I could buy a sandwich.

'Sorry, miss, we don't do food here,' the host told me. 'There's a place about ten miles further on. You take the main road and turn towards the ...'

'Thank you but I'm staying in the area,' I explained. 'I just wanted something to feed to the ducks.'

'Oh, aye, the ducks.' He nodded, plainly thinking I was another silly visitor passing through. 'Staying round here, you say?'

'At Pentire. Henry Caulder is my grandfather.'

'You'll be Mrs Gregory then.' His frown cleared like magic. 'You should have said; that's different. You wait there and I'll see what the missus has.'

I was left standing as he went through a little opening at the back of the bar. I was aware that the two old men in the corner were staring at me with interest now, and smiled, feeling a need to break the silence.

'It is a lovely village. I hadn't seen it properly until today.'

Another man had come in. He was tall and dark-haired with strong features, heavily built and dressed in worn cords and a rainproof jacket. He nodded to the two old timers and, after giving me no more than a glance, took his place at the bar a couple of feet down from me. In another moment the innkeeper's wife came bustling through from the back carrying half a loaf, her eyes bright with curiosity.

'Will this be all right, Mrs Gregory?' she asked. 'It's yesterday's and I was going to use it for toast but you're very welcome to it.' She offered her hand across the bar. 'I'm Enid Granger and my husband is Albert. He didn't know who you were until you said.'

'You are very kind,' I replied. 'I just wanted to feed the ducks and thought you might sell sandwiches, but the bread is ideal. How much do I owe you, please?'

'Nothing—it's a pleasure.'

'You must let me pay,' I said. She shook her head. 'Then perhaps I can buy a round of drinks for everyone?' I glanced towards the old men in the corner. 'Another pint for these gentleman and whatever you would like ...' My smile faded as I turned to the newcomer and saw his scowl.

'Thank you kindly, ma'am.' One of the old timers lifted his glass to me. 'I'll accept—so will me mate.'

'I don't drink,' Enid Granger said, 'but I'll have a lemonade with you.' She looked at their other customer. 'What about you, Ted? Will you have a drink with Mrs Gregory?'

'No.' He turned and strode out of the pub, still scowling.

'Well!' Enid looked shocked. 'I've never known Ted Jones to be so rude.'

'Nor to refuse a free drink,' her husband said. 'He must have got out of bed the wrong side this morning. Take no mind to him, Mrs Gregory. I'll have a half, if you like.'

I paid for the drinks, stood chatting about the prettiness of the village and the unusual warmth of the day for a few minutes, then left.

I lingered for several minutes on the green, feeding the greedy ducks who surrounded me, squabbling and grabbing the pieces of bread I broke off and threw to them. When I had no bread left they grabbed at my skirt and I was forced into a laughing retreat.

'They're hungry, poor things,' a voice said

behind me, and I swung round to see Sarah Jones standing there. She had a bruise on her cheek, which was turning dark purple. 'Doesn't matter how much you give them. Lily feeds them whenever we've got scraps but they always want more.'

'Yes, I expect so,' I said. 'Where is she today?'

'Playing somewhere,' Sarah replied. 'I saw you and thought I'd better apologize for my husband. He was rude to you in the pub just now.'

'Not really.' I frowned. I had no right to pry into her affairs but something made me ask, 'What happened to your face?'

'Ted hit me. We had a row.' Her eyes veered away as if she didn't want to meet mine. 'That's why he's in such a mood this morning. It's me he's mad at, not you.'

'I'm sorry.' I felt awkward, uncomfortable. I didn't know Sarah well enough to comment on her husband's behaviour and yet I felt I had to. 'Has—has it happened before?'

'No. Ted's good to me. I deserved this,' she said, her tone faintly hostile. 'I should have been straight with him from the start.' She took a small box from her pocket. 'Would you give this to Mr Gregory, please? Tell him Ted found it and said I had to give it back.'

I opened the box and looked at the small but good gold locket inside; it was obviously meant for a child.

'I don't understand?'

'Mr Gregory gave me that for Lily. It's her birthday soon.' She blushed, clearly embarrassed. 'It was just a kindness, Mrs Gregory, but Ted took it the wrong way. He made me bring it to you—said he would thrash me again if I didn't. I'm sorry ...'

My thoughts were whirling round like fallen leaves in a gale. All at once I knew exactly why Ted Jones had refused my offer of a drink—and why he had given his wife a black eye.

'Lily ... she's Richard's daughter, isn't she?'

'It was a long time ago.' Sarah made no attempt to deny it. I thought there was even a faint air of triumph about her then, as if she had wanted me to know.

'But he gave you the locket quite recently?' I needed to be sure about this.

'Yes.' She bit her lip. 'There's been nothing, not for years. I should have told Ted but he thought she was his. Now he's fit to kill me. Especially since he found that ...'

I nodded, surprised to find that my only feelings about her affair with Richard were ones of sympathy for her. I should have been angry or upset, but I wasn't.

'It must have been very difficult for you. Obviously there must be no more gifts. I'll tell my husband.' I paused. 'Richard does know that Lily is his?' Sarah nodded. 'But there was no question of marriage between you?'

'Not good enough for him, was I?' Now the hostility blazed out at me. 'Just a bit of

337

fun, that's all it was to him. He never cared tuppence for me—couldn't wait to dump me when he knew.'

'I'm sorry ...' I faltered as her eyes flashed. 'No, you don't want that, do you? I'll give the locket to Richard—make sure he doesn't bother you again.'

'Tell him to keep out of Ted's way. I think he might kill him if he got the chance.'

I stood watching as Sarah turned and ran across the green to a cottage on the other side, then slipped the small box into my pocket.

Walking home I felt oddly calm, as if none of it really mattered. For some reason it was not a surprise that Richard had an illegitimate child—and it certainly explained why Lily had been forbidden to play in the woods, and why Sarah had begged me not to mention finding her there. Richard had probably warned her to stay clear of me.

Only a few weeks ago I would have been shocked and hurt, but now I didn't particularly care.

Henry was in his study, about to pour himself a pre-lunch sherry, when I walked in. He looked at me sharply, as if he sensed that I was upset about something.

'It's turned colder,' I said as I went to the fire to warm my hands. 'When I went out it was lovely but as soon as the sun disappeared it got bitter.'

'Have a sherry to warm yourself up, girl.'

'No, thank you.' I hesitated. Then: 'I suppose

338

you don't have a telephone number for Caroline, do you?'

'She's away with that Hadden fellow,' he said. 'Taking some sort of exam ... getting her pilot's licence.'

'Yes, I know.' I avoided his curious gaze. 'It's just that I wanted to talk to her about something.'

'Important, is it?'

'Yes ... quite.'

'Don't fancy telling me?'

I was tempted but knew that he was far from well. If I told him about Lily he would be concerned for me, upset—and there was no need. I would not burden him with my problems.

'No, Grandfather. It's just something I want to talk to Caro about but it can wait until I see her. I keep wondering how she is getting on—but I expect she will pass, don't you?'

'Caroline usually does what she sets out to do.' His thick brows met in a frown. 'Has she said anything about Hadden to you? Mentioned her plans or how she feels about him?'

'Just that he's a friend,' I lied, knowing that Caroline wouldn't thank me for betraying a confidence. 'I do hope she's getting on well. If you will excuse me, I'll just pop upstairs. I did a couple of sketches last night and I want to show them to you.'

As I went out into the hall the telephone shrilled. I picked it up.

'Hello, this is Lizzie Gregory. May I help you?'

'Lizzie?' Rosalind's voice was sharp with surprise. 'Is that you? I've been ringing you and you weren't at home.'

'Grandfather came unexpectedly and carried me off with him,' I said. 'Richard was away and I just couldn't resist the chance to come down to Pentire. I've told you how much I like being here, haven't I?'

'Yes.' She sounded upset, almost angry. 'If I'd known you were going ... I should have liked to be asked to come with you, Lizzie. I should have thought you would have known that.'

'I'm sorry ...' I began, but the receiver was put down at the other end with a little bang.

I was frowning as I went upstairs. I knew Rosalind was fond of the place, but why she thought she had to be there every time I visited Henry I could not imagine.

I had the dream about the woods again that night. The woman was desperate as she ran through the trees; this time it was as if I were there, just as when I had watched Selina get out of bed and walk to the top of the stairs ... witnessing the last moments before her death.

I was there in the woods. I could smell the dampness of rain in the air, feel a cool breeze on my skin—and I could see it all. I could sense the woman's fear, feel her terror—but I could not speak. I could not stop what was going to happen.

I was sure that I was being warned. To

dream the same dream over and over again
... surely that was a warning, a premonition of
evil? I believed that something bad was going
to happen out there in the woods, and that
if I could only understand my dream I could
stop it.

What did it mean, and who was the woman
in the woods? Who was she afraid of?

'Where did this come from?' Richard came into
my bedroom at the flat as I was brushing
my hair the following evening. He had a
small jeweller's box in his hand. 'Who gave
it to you?'

'You must know,' I said, not turning round.
I had put the child's locket on his dressing
chest. 'You gave it to Mrs Jones for Lily,
didn't you?'

'The bitch!' Richard's face was reflected in
my mirror and I could see he was furious. 'I
suppose she told you?'

'That Lily is your daughter?' I put down my
hair brush and turned to look at him. 'Yes, she
told me everything. Her husband forced her to
give me the locket. He had found it and it
made him angry. Sarah had a black eye. She
had to tell me, Richard ... but I think I had
half guessed it anyway.'

'It was over years ago,' he muttered, looking
angry and ashamed. 'Is that why you've been
so odd with me recently?'

'No, it isn't. Sarah gave that to me only
yesterday. If I have been reserved it is your
own fault, Richard.' I stood up. 'I don't like

341

being lied to and I am not a fool.'

'What does that mean?'

'I know you were gambling this weekend.' I took a deep breath. 'And I know you don't love me.'

'That's ridiculous! Of course I love you.'

'Do you?' I looked into his eyes. There was anger and annoyance reflected there but no pain. 'No, I don't think so.'

'Lizzie ...' He took a step towards me. I held up my hands to ward him off.

'Please don't touch me, Richard.'

'Don't be silly. You're my wife.'

'If you try to kiss me, I shall walk out of this flat now and never come back.'

'You don't mean that?' He looked shocked. 'Just because of a foolish affair years ago?'

'It isn't because of Lily—though I would have respected you more if you had told me from the start that you had a child.'

'Sarah didn't want her husband to know.' He looked guilty and moved away. I could see he was uneasy. 'Besides, Henry ...'

'Henry wouldn't have approved if he'd known about Lily? No, I don't suppose he would, and that is important to you, isn't it?'

'Lizzie ...'

'Don't worry, I shan't tell him. Providing you don't try to touch me ever again.'

Richard stared at me in silence for a moment. 'I suppose I know why,' he said. 'Damn you, Lizzie. Damn you!'

He left the room, slamming the door after him.

Chapter 17

I had been looking forward to this visit to the workshops ever since Henry had suggested it. I knew already that he had six craftsmen working for him; they produced various ranges of jewellery, some of which were sold in his own shop, though much went to wholesalers and other jewellers these days.

In the front workshop three men sat at a long bench near a window that could be seen from the street in Hatton Garden. They were working on setting the stones into rings, brooches or necklaces that would be sold to other dealers. As he took me inside, Henry told me that the real business was carried on in a secure room at the back.

'Maurice has been concentrating on your designs,' he said, stopping at the head of the bench by a man with thinning grey hair and a wrinkled, pleasant face. 'Have you anything ready to show my granddaughter?'

'Yes, Mr Caulder.' The man got up and went to a huge, solid-looking iron safe at the back of the room, bringing back a large flat box. He placed it on the bench and looked at me. 'These pieces need a final polishing, Mrs Gregory, but you can see how the range is shaping up.'

He opened the case to reveal its contents and I felt a thrill of pleasure as I saw he had made up the flower brooch, necklace and bracelet. The bracelet was particularly pretty, because I'd designed it as flower, bee, flower, with a large gold bee as the clasp: each of the bees had tiny sapphire eyes and the colour combination of pale and dark blue enamelling had worked even better than I'd dared to hope.

'You've made them so beautifully,' I cried. 'I never imagined they would look this pretty.'

He glowed with pride at my praise. 'It was a pleasure to work with your designs, Mrs Gregory. I've started to think about the second range but there's nothing to see yet. Come back in two weeks and I may have something to show you.'

'How did they cost out?' Henry asked, picking up the brooch to examine the workmanship more closely.

'A third more than you originally wanted,' Maurice replied, 'but in my opinion it would be a shame to cheapen the range by removing the bee. That's what makes it so distinctive. I think we could sell it on to the wholesalers as it is if you wanted? I know of one or two who might be interested.'

'No, no,' Henry said. 'We are going to sell Lizzie's designs exclusively through the shop. When we have enough ready to make a collection, I'm going to launch the range through the quality magazines. I might throw a party and invite the press—so keep all this stuff out of sight if you get any dealers in, Maurice. I don't want anyone making a cheap copy.'

'I'll attend to it, sir.' Maurice closed the case

and carried it back to the safe.

'You didn't tell me what you were planning,' I said as Henry guided me towards a door at the back of the shop. I would probably never have dared to show him the designs if he had!

'Wasn't sure how they would turn out,' he said gruffly. 'Got any more for me to see yet? I shall need at least three or four ranges before I can launch you.'

'I'm working on something,' I replied. 'I'll show you when we go home. Where are you taking me now?'

'In the back. I want you to see my real craftsmen at work.' He buzzed twice and a little spyhole at the top of the door slid back. An eye peered at us suspiciously. 'It's me, Thomas, and my granddaughter.'

The door was unbolted from the other side and I followed him into the inner workshop. Immediately, I was aware of a different atmosphere, almost as if we had stepped into a place of worship. The carpet beneath my feet was so thick that I felt as if I would sink into it, and there was a hushed silence.

Besides the man who had let us in there were two others seated at individual tables. One was studying a piece of jewellery with a small magnifying glass held against his eye; another seemed to be sorting through something that to my untrained eye looked like odd shaped pebbles.

'Uncut diamonds,' Henry said, sensing my curiosity. 'We buy them from the Dutch merchants in parcels. We have to take a

345

parcel as it is; they won't allow us to pick and choose. Each parcel is graded according to its quality and it's up to us to sort out the stones after we've bought them.'

'May I see?' I asked, and picked up one of the larger stones. 'I would never have dreamed that a diamond would look like this in its rough state.'

'Perhaps that's why the first stones weren't recognized for what they were,' Henry said. 'India was the source of the first known diamonds, and it is from there that many of the finest stones have come. Of course, diamonds have been found in many countries now, but the most important is South Africa. They were discovered there in 1866 by a young Dutch farmer from Hopetown. He found a pretty pebble by the river and showed it to his mother. It weighed 21 carats and was eventually exhibited in Paris. It was later sold for five hundred pounds.'

'You know so much.' I was fascinated. 'Wasn't the Cullinan Diamond found in South Africa?'

'In 1905. It weighs a fabulous 968.9 carats—but even that was not as large as the Excelsior which weighed 995.2 carats and was also discovered in South Africa—in 1893, I believe.'

'How can you remember all this?' I asked, awed.

'The memory plays tricks,' he said. 'Some things stick, but unfortunately mine is not always so reliable these days.' He glanced at a parcel of cut diamonds on the table. 'These are what we call fine white—that means the colour and clarity is classed as 1-2 and they have few inclusions. There are finer stones than these but we keep those for very special pieces.'

'Like ...' I had been about to mention the necklace he had shown me in his study but remembered in time that it was a secret. 'Are there special names for the various cuts?'

'We mostly use what is called the brilliant cut these days,' he said. 'The trap or emerald cut does not show a diamond's fire as well, but is sometimes necessary for a special design or if the stone needs to be cut that way. A diamond is the hardest substance known but if you find the right angle the stone will break cleanly.'

'There is so much to learn.'

I felt humbled, knowing myself to be ignorant but wanting to learn, wanting to please both Henry and my own desire for excellence. I began to realize that this was no longer a hobby but something that would direct and change my whole life.

'The cleavage direction is important.' One of the craftsmen spoke directly to me, showing me an uncut stone he was preparing to work on. 'There are four directions of weakness along which the crystal will split and it is up to the cutter to determine the best one. If a stone is knocked accidentally along the cleavage line, it may develop flaws or even split.'

'But that doesn't happen here,' Henry said, and smiled at the man who had spoken. 'Johann is far too experienced. If you are ever concerned about how to use a stone to its best advantage, ask his advice.'

'May I?' I asked, feeling very humble. 'Could I come along one day and watch you working?'

'You will be very welcome,' he replied, and smiled. 'Now that we know you there will be no difficulty—but please do not bring a friend. We have to be very careful in this part of the workshop.'

'I shall always come alone,' I promised. 'Thank you so much for letting me see all this.'

'One day Johann will let you see some of our treasures,' Henry promised. 'But we keep them locked away in vaults until we need them.' He took my arm, steering me towards the door. 'I think that is enough work for today. Now I shall take you to lunch at the Savoy.'

Richard was on his best behaviour that evening. I think our little argument had shocked him and he was unsure of me. He didn't believe that I meant what I'd said, not yet, but he had realized that I was not quite the meek and mild innocent he had thought me.

He had arranged for us all to have dinner at a pleasant little Italian restaurant that had been recently opened and set out to entertain Henry and Rosalind. He was attentive to me, making so much fuss of me that I felt irritated and was driven to snap at him when he insisted on giving me his white silk scarf as we left the warmth of the restaurant for the chill of the night air.

'I don't need it,' I said. 'I'm quite warm

enough, thank you, Richard.'

'But you might catch a chill,' Rosalind said, giving me an odd look. 'Richard is right to be concerned, Lizzie dear.'

I withheld the words of scorn that rose to my lips. Richard was an attentive husband only when it suited him ... or when he wanted to make the right impression.

I knew that my grandfather was watchful but refused to meet his eyes. The unhappiness I had found in my marriage was my own fault and I was determined to work it out for myself.

The following afternoon I paid another visit to the jewellery exhibition. It was the last day and I wanted to have a look at the collection of Victorian pieces that I hadn't had a chance to see the first time.

There was a particularly fine display of turquoise jewellery. Lockets studded with the small blue stones, brooches with hanging pendants, earrings and a butterfly pendant I liked very much.

I moved on to a collection of garnets and pearls, then a selection of love hearts, some simple, others made of fine diamonds and opals. There were several memorial rings: the Victorians had been sentimental about these things and liked to wear them as a sign of mourning, but they didn't appeal to me particularly.

I lingered the longest by the final collection of Fabergé and the Art Nouveau designers, particularly admiring an opal, enamel and silver brooch by Liberty & Co and a mother of pearl pendant by a designer I hadn't known of called Otto Prutscher. But of course the Fabergé collection was outstanding. I was glued to a case containing several pretty flower-shaped brooches when a deep male voice behind me made me spin round in surprise and delight.

'Lizzie ...'

'Alexi!'

'I thought it was you,' he said, eyes moving over me with a warmth that set my cheeks on fire. 'I came to see the Roman collection. A little more interesting than the one we saw in Norwich, don't you think?'

'Oh, yes, much,' I agreed. My heart was beating madly and I was afraid he would guess how pleased I was to see him. 'This is my second visit—there was far too much to see all at once. I've learned such a lot from this exhibition.'

'And now you are leaving?' He sounded disappointed. 'To get ready for this masked ball Caro has organized, I suppose?'

'Are you coming this evening?'

'Of course. She would not allow any of us to escape.'

His laughter made me feel weak at the knees. I was aware of a tremor of excitement inside, and also of guilt.

'I suppose I ought to be going,' I said reluctantly. 'I've been out all day.'

'Unless ...' Alexi's eyes held a wicked sparkle 'you would care for some tea?'

'Yes ... oh, yes, I should,' I replied. I ought to

have refused, of course, but I wanted to spend a little more time with him. 'Why not? Yes, Alexi. I will have tea with you.' *Or fly to the ends of the earth if you want me to,* my unruly heart cried out. 'I should enjoy that. There's plenty of time to get ready for this evening.'

'And so you made a study of the great artists?' I said, listening in fascination to Alexi as he talked of his work. 'I have seen photographs of Vincenzo de Rosi's *Vulcan* in a magazine—his work shows such strength, such power.'

'Exactly, and that is why I sometimes despair,' Alexi replied. 'How can I ever achieve even a tenth of that greatness? There are so many wonderful artists ... Giovanni Francesco Susini, Mochi, Bandini, to name but a few. I could go on and on.'

'I'm sure you will achieve what you want in time.' My heart beat wildly as his dark eyes looked into mine. 'Tell me again about your brother Crispin?'

'I was telling you that he fell into the moat that day when the ice had just begun to melt?' I nodded and a shadow came over Alexi's face. 'I dived in after him but he was in there for several minutes before I got to him. He took a chill and, unfortunately, it turned into something far more serious.'

'And your father blamed you for his accident? That was unfair, Alexi.'

'I loved Crispin. Perhaps I ought to have been jealous because he took my place in my father's affections, but I loved my brother. When it seemed that he would die of a fever, I prayed that God would take my life and let him live in my stead.'

'Oh, Alexi,' I said, seeing the sadness in his eyes. 'And Crispin did live, only to be killed in the war. How you must have suffered!'

'It was a terrible time, but I survived and now I have so much to be thankful for.' He reached across the table to touch my hand. 'But we have talked too much of me. What is troubling you, Lizzie?'

My heart jolted, making me breathless and uncertain.

'I—I'm not ready to talk about it yet, Alexi. Will you be patient with me for a little while longer?'

'Yes, of course,' he said. His eyes seemed to hold and caress me. 'You must know that I would wait forever if need be.'

'This is such a bore,' Richard said as he looked at the costume I had laid out for him. 'Why you let Caro talk you into buying the tickets for this wretched ball, I don't know. I hate this kind of affair.'

'I told you about it and you said I should hire these,' I reminded him. 'I am going as Marie-Antoinette and you wanted to be the king.'

'It is a ridiculous costume, far too heavy to wear, and that wig is filthy,' Richard said, glaring at me. 'If we must go, I shall wear an evening suit.'

'As you wish.'

I turned away, refusing to let his sulkiness

spoil my feelings of anticipation. It had been an enjoyable day and the evening was going to be exciting. Richard might find masked balls boring but I'd never been to one and was looking forward to seeing everyone in costume. Especially Alexi, who had refused to tell me what he would be wearing because it was supposed to be a surprise.

'I don't suppose it matters. Grandfather won't be wearing a costume either but said he would have a mask and a silk domino.'

'I'll wear a mask if it will please you,' Richard muttered. 'Don't nag, Liz. I don't like women who complain all the time.'

I drew a deep breath and counted to ten before answering. He was in one of his difficult moods again and I'd had almost as much as I could stand, but was determined not to let him make me lose my temper. Besides, I was feeling guilty because I'd gone to tea with Alexi.

'Grandfather is going to take me to meet some friends of his in the trade tomorrow,' I said. 'I told you yesterday that they had made up my flower designs at the workshops, didn't I?' Richard muttered something. 'Well, tomorrow I'm going to see gold being cast into various mounts ... to help me understand the way it should be used.'

'Is Henry satisfied with your new designs?'

'Yes, I think so. I showed him two or three more and he took two of them with him.'

'Then he must have been pleased. Henry never pulls his punches, even with those he cares for most.' Richard had lost his look of petulance. 'You are doing well, darling. Stop scowling at me and get changed. We don't want to be late for the ball, do we?'

'Of course not.'

I walked into my bedroom and shut the door, closing my eyes for a moment. How could I have been so blind? Why had I not seen Richard's true nature at the start? The signs had been there but I had not heeded them. I had rushed into this marriage, which I now knew was a terrible mistake, but could see no way out of it; I was trapped by convention—by the rules of an unforgiving society.

The excitement I felt at the prospect of the ball had nothing to do with the fact that Alexi would be there. Of course it didn't ... it mustn't, because I could never leave Richard.

I glanced at my reflection in the mirror. My face was very pale and there were shadows beneath my eyes. I could not even think of asking him for a divorce, knowing all the scandal and upset it would cause. Or could I? Divorce wasn't easy but it might be possible ... if I was determined and brave enough.

The large ballroom was overflowing with people wearing exotic-looking costumes and masks that covered the top half of their faces. There were Romans in togas, sheikhs in flowing robes, Cavaliers and Roundheads, nymphs, shepherds, and slave masters with their captives on golden ropes.

Caroline was a magnificent Cleopatra and Alexi had come as a pirate. He was wearing a mask but I would have known him anywhere, even before he spoke to me.

'Marie-Antoinette,' he murmured when he approached me later in the evening. 'A fitting costume for a beautiful lady. May I beg the favour of a dance, Majesty?'

I laughed as I saw the wicked glint of his eyes behind the velvet mask. 'Will you promise not to spirit me aboard your ship and hold me to ransom?'

'I'm not sure I should make promises I cannot keep,' he replied. 'I might take you captive, my lady, but I shall not let you be ransomed at any price.'

'You are indeed a wicked pirate, sir,' I protested, but my heart beat wildly as his large hands curled about mine possessively and he drew me on to the dance floor, his arm immediately going around my waist. 'I'm not sure I ought to dance with you.'

'But you will,' he said, pressing me closer to him. 'You will because you feel it too, Lizzie—my sweet, precious Lizzie.'

I could not deny the feeling inside me as he held me so firmly and yet so gently against him. It was a heady, swooning sensation that I now understood was desire, a burning, wanting ache that threatened to overcome all my scruples. How wicked I was to feel such an urgent need for a man who was not my husband!

'It was no coincidence that I was at the exhibition this afternoon,' Alexi said, his voice a husky throb in my ear. 'I have haunted the wretched place every day in the hope that you might be there.'

'Oh, Alexi.' I gazed up into his dark eyes and saw my own need reflected and intensified. 'I don't know ... I don't know what to do ...'

'Come to the studio tomorrow,' he whispered, his lips moving like a caress against my hair. 'Come soon, Lizzie. We have to talk ... please?'

He was no longer teasing me. My heart took a huge, frightening leap as I heard the urgency in his voice. I knew what he was asking of me, just as I knew he would not be satisfied with an affair. He would expect me to leave Richard—to go away with him.

'Please,' I said, my gaze soft and pleading. 'Don't say anymore. Not yet, Alexi. I have to think about this. I need a little more time.'

'There is nothing to think about,' Alexi said, and his face was suddenly hard. 'Richard does not love you—you told me so. Come to me, Lizzie. I shall take you away. You can trust me to take care of you. Always.'

'You said you would wait?'

The music had stopped. Alexi was just standing there, staring down at me in a demanding, unyielding manner—the very picture of the barbarian Caroline had named him. He looked capable of throwing me over his shoulder and making off with me if I denied him. I felt that everyone must be watching us—reading what was in his mind—and started to walk away. He followed and caught my arm, turning me to face him.

'Lizzie, you know I love you?'

'Yes,' I whispered, my throat catching. 'Later, Alexi ... tomorrow ... please ... not now.'

I resisted his hold and he let me go. My heart was hammering against my ribs and my mouth felt dry; I was finding it difficult to breathe and knew I must escape for a few minutes. It was easy for him to tell me to leave but harder to make that decision. My marriage had been a terrible mistake, I was in no doubt of that—but could I simply walk away from it? Richard would be more annoyed than hurt but there were others to consider. Like Rosalind and Henry.

Would Grandfather be disappointed in me? His opinion mattered more than I would have thought possible a few weeks previously.

I decided to go in search of the powder room but as I was about to leave the ballroom a woman wearing a dress of the Victorian period caught hold of my sleeve.

'Lizzie—it is you, isn't it?'

I sighed inwardly as I recognized Rosalind's voice. 'Yes, it's me. I wasn't sure you were coming this evening.'

'Henry bought me a ticket—and this dress belonged to my mother.' She opened a feather fan and fluttered it. 'How warm it is in here. Have you seen Caroline? She's half-naked! I'm so relieved you didn't decide to flaunt yourself the way she has this evening.'

'I think she looks wonderful. So beautiful, and just as I imagine Queen Cleopatra must have looked all those centuries ago.'

'She's in a terrible mood,' Rosalind went on

as if I hadn't spoken. 'She was very short with me just now when I asked her if she was warm enough. I'm so glad Richard didn't marry her! I really could not have borne her tantrums. I'm surprised Henry doesn't put his foot down more. She needs some discipline. Her behaviour this evening is quite shameful ...'

I glanced across the room. My cousin was talking to Lady Sara and seemed agitated, as though something had upset her. It was in marked contrast to Caroline's mood the last time I'd seen her. The happiness had seemed to shine out of her then; now she looked as if she were on the verge of tears. What could be wrong?

'Excuse me,' I said. 'I must find the powder room.' I walked away from Rosalind before I was tempted to say something rude in defence of my cousin.

Why was Caroline so unhappy this evening? Her emotional state was clear just from glancing at her across the room, and it was unlike her to show her feelings so plainly. Something serious must have happened to upset her.

In the powder room I splashed my face with cold water. Richard had been right about the costumes being heavy. How could women have borne to wear them all the time? No wonder so many of them fainted! I would be glad to take mine off when I got home ...

Why was I fooling myself? It wasn't the costume that was bothering me, it was Alexi. He had asked me to go to him and I knew that he would demand an answer very soon.

358

Well, he would have to wait until I'd discovered what was upsetting Caroline. Something was troubling her and I wanted to know what it was. I decided to ask her as soon as I returned to the ballroom, but when I did Cleopatra had disappeared. I was thinking about going in search of her when Henry came up to me.

'Can you spare a dance for me?'

'Yes, of course. I was looking for Caroline but she seems to have vanished. Have you seen her recently?'

'I think she went somewhere with Michael,' he said. 'I don't suppose she will be long.'

Caroline had still not returned when my dance with Henry was over. I left him talking to Rosalind and went to look for her. Something momentous must have happened to make her look as unhappy as she did that evening.

In the hall I almost bumped into Michael. He was scowling, his face like thunder as he put out his hand to steady me.

'Have you seen Caroline?' I asked.

'She's in the library—and acting like a bear with a sore head. I'm damned if I know what's the matter with her but perhaps you can get some sense out of her. She won't talk to me.'

'Thank you. I'll go and find her.'

I went into the library. Caroline was sitting on a sofa, her head in her hands. She looked up as she heard me and I was startled by the deep anguish in her eyes.

'What's the matter?' I asked, starting towards her in concern. 'You look awful—and I've just

359

spoken to Michael. He was in a foul mood. Have you quarrelled with him?'

'Men ...' Caroline drawled, assuming her habitual expression. 'They are hell, aren't they? He is in a temper because I told him the truth about something.'

'That's not why you're upset,' I said, eyeing her thoughtfully. 'You've been on edge all evening. Rosalind told me you had snapped her head off earlier.'

'Damn Rosalind!' Caroline cried, wild defiance in her eyes. 'She's too interfering for her own good—as you'll discover if you stay with Richard long enough.'

'What do you mean—if I stay with him?' I stared at her. 'What are you saying?'

'You'll be a fool if you do,' Caroline said. 'You know what a selfish devil he is, Lizzie. He'll lie to you and cheat ...' She took a deep breath. 'He asked me to go to bed with him the night I waited for him in Paris. It was your honeymoon and he was prepared to cheat on you then—he would have done if I hadn't told him to go to hell.'

'Why are you telling me this?' The gorge rose in my throat. Caroline was in no mood to lie and I knew that this was true. Richard wanted Caroline. I'd seen it in his eyes—seen the jealousy and the longing when she was teasing Alexi. 'Why now, Caro?'

'Because I'm a spiteful bitch.' She laughed harshly, close to hysteria. 'Or because I care about you and don't want you to be as miserable as I am.'

'That's it, isn't it?' I said, and moved closer to her. 'I knew you were unhappy. What's wrong, Caro? Can't you tell me? I'm your friend, you know that. You must know it?'

'Yes.' The tears wouldn't be held back now. She sank back in the sofa and covered her face with her hands. 'I can't tell you, Lizzie. Not even you.'

I sat beside her, putting my arms around her and holding her as the bitter sobs racked her body.

'It's all right, Caro dearest,' I said, and kissed the top of her head. 'Let it all come out. I'm here. I'm with you. You don't have to tell me, I understand. We are close to each other and we know each other's hearts. You were right about Richard. He doesn't love me and I don't love him. I should never have married him. I didn't know him ... not really. He is shallow and selfish and ... I'm thinking of leaving him.'

'Do you mean that?' She looked at me. 'Why? Has something else happened?'

I told her about Sarah and her child.

'It wouldn't have mattered—it happened so long ago,' I said, my voice catching. 'Except that it is another lie. Richard has lied to me over and over again and I've realized I don't love him, Caro. I should never have married him. I ought to have waited until I knew him better.'

'I should have told you what he was.' She looked stricken. 'At one time I thought I might marry him. I was proud of what he'd done during the war and we seemed to get on well.

Then I found out about his gambling. One night he turned up at my house in a terrible panic because Henry was threatening to cut off his allowance if he didn't stop, and he had been drinking ...' Caroline took a deep breath. 'He wanted to make love to me and I refused. He got angry and tried to rape me. I fought him off but he hurt me and I couldn't forgive him. I broke off our engagement the next day ... told him that I would tell Henry what he had done if he ever tried anything like it again.'

'So that's why you tried to warn me against him?'

Now I understood all her mysterious remarks. Richard had told me she was spiteful and I had believed him, but in my heart I had known there was something she'd wanted to tell me.

'I liked you as soon as we met,' she said. 'I wanted to warn you, but you seemed to be so much in love with him and ...'

'I thought I was,' I said, 'but I didn't know him.'

'That ring he wears ... the tiger's head?' She hesitated, an odd expression in her eyes.

'Yes, I know. I've never liked it.'

'He told me he took it from the hand of a German officer he'd killed.' Caroline glanced nervously over her shoulder and then back at me. 'Sometimes Richard frightens me, Lizzie. I think he is two people ... the charming man everyone quite likes and someone rather more sinister.'

'What do you mean?' An icy chill ran through me.

'I'm not sure.' Caroline shivered. 'I can't explain ... but there are two different people inside him.'

'Do you think he ...'

'Do I think he could have fired those shots that made you fall from your horse?' Caroline's expression was grave. 'I don't know, Lizzie. I think he might be capable of anything to get his own way.'

She glanced towards the door again, as if she had heard something. Why was I not warned then? Why did I not get up and go to investigate? If I had—if I'd seen who stood there listening to our every word—it might all have been so different ...

Chapter 18

I spent a restless night, tossing sleeplessly in my bed. It seemed to me that Caroline was right: the Caulders were cursed, the whole family. There was a dark shadow hanging over us all.

Caroline had not told me what was making her so miserable, but I knew it must be something important to upset her the way it had; I thought perhaps she had quarrelled with Rupert Hadden again, but could not ask questions unless she wanted to tell me—anymore than she had been able to tell me her true feelings about my marriage to Richard.

'You should leave him,' she had said to me as

363

we sat in the library by the flickering flames of the fire. 'He doesn't deserve you, Lizzie. Don't worry about what other people say. Think of yourself, of your own happiness.'

Her words had preyed on my mind as I tossed restlessly half the night and I was still uneasy when I woke, my thoughts tumbling into confusion and uncertainty.

Was it my duty to stay with Richard or should I follow my heart and leave him?

I spent the whole of the morning turning it over and over in my mind, completely forgetting that I was supposed to meet Henry at the workshops.

My marriage was an empty sham and it was never going to get any better. Richard wasn't in love with me. He had married me because he wanted Henry's money. The awful truth made my stomach churn with sickness and I knew I could never bear him to touch me intimately again.

Caroline had told me things about Richard that had shocked me ... things I still found it difficult to believe. I might have suspected my cousin of speaking out of spite, except that I knew she was suffering too much herself to inflict a similar heartache on anyone else.

Why was Caroline so unhappy? I wished she had confided in me or that there was something I could do to help her. All I had been able to do was murmur useless words of comfort and offer to listen when she was ready to open her heart.

It took me a long time to make up my mind

to go to Alexi. A part of me knew that what I felt for him was love but it was difficult to accept that I was no longer in love with Richard.

Was I a shallow person, incapable of real or lasting emotions? No, that wasn't true! Perhaps I had never loved the real man, only the image of his fair good looks and charm.

Richard had seemed to be a prince to the unawakened girl I'd been when he came into my life. He had broken through the hedge of thorns to rouse me from a deep slumber—but in reality he was a cold, ruthless schemer who cared only for himself, his own needs, his own desires.

I could not go on living as his wife. Despite all the scandal and pain it would cause, I must leave him.

I came to the decision painfully and slowly, but once my mind was made up I would not change it. I packed my things and left the suitcases in my room for collection later. Richard would not be home until the evening and it would have looked presumptuous to turn up on Alexi's doorstep with all my belongings. He had told me he loved me but I needed to hear him say it again. If he asked me to go to him I would, but whatever happened I had made up my mind that I was leaving Richard. Our marriage was over.

Once the decision was reached I felt as if a dark cloud had lifted from me. I took a taxi to Alexi's home. The journey seemed endless and I was on thorns all the way, shocked at my own behaviour, nervous and uncertain, but at last we were there. I got out, paid my fare and went round to the back of the house as Alexi had asked me to the last time, planning to surprise him. My heart was racing wildly. It was such a shocking, desperate thing I was about to do but I believed Alexi really loved me.

It was as I approached the back door that I saw them through the window: Alexi was holding Caroline, kissing her, smiling down at her in that gentle, teasing manner of his.

I was stunned. How could he? How *could* he? After what he'd said to me the previous evening! Were all men faithless? I had thought Alexi was different but now it seemed that he too had lied to me ... the pain of this new betrayal twisted and burned inside me as I backed away, vomit rising in my throat and threatening to choke me.

I ran out into the street in an agony of confused emotions, too upset and shocked to think clearly, to realize that there might be an innocent reason for Caroline being in Alexi's arms.

I was tormented by the bitter doubt that gripped my mind. How could Alexi ask me to come to him if he was in love with Caroline? But Richard had married me while he still wanted her—wanted her so much that he had left our bed on his honeymoon to get drunk.

Lies, lies, lies and deception! Richard had lied to me for the sake of material gain and now it seemed that Alexi too had lied, but his was a far worse betrayal for he had known that I was vulnerable and unhappy. And Caroline? I had thought her my friend but now ...

A part of me hated my cousin when I saw her in Alexi's arms. For a while on that cold winter's afternoon I was filled with rage and a burning need to inflict pain myself; I understood then how jealousy and anger might drive a person to the brink of despair, but anger soon faded into hurt and confusion, my feelings so muddled and tangled that I hardly knew what I believed.

Alexi and Caroline ... could it be that they were lovers after all? Why should she lie to me about it ... unless it was all part of some devious scheme to destroy me?

My mind was so disordered that I spent hours wandering about the streets, consumed by the pain inside me and a growing feeling of despair. I had no idea where I went or what I did. If people stared at the wild-eyed creature I must have seemed, I was not aware of it.

What was happening to my life? Was there no one I could trust?

Caroline had told me she was in love with Rupert Hadden, that she had never been Alexi's lover. How could I believe her now that I had seen her in Alexi's arms? If she had lied to me about one thing, had she lied about others?

I was torn by doubts. Someone hated me. Someone had caused me to fall from my horse. Someone had sent me a letter that could only be interpreted as a threat.

Caroline had been waiting for me when I got back to the flat that day. She had been in the sitting room alone for a few minutes before I noticed the letter was missing. She'd had the time and the opportunity to pick it up—but why should she? Unless she was afraid it would incriminate her in some way.

Richard said she was capable of anything to get her own way. Caroline said Richard was selfish ... more than that, had hinted that he could be dangerous.

Who should I believe? Which of them was lying? And why?

Richard or Caroline ... Richard or Caroline ... or both of them? Had both of them been in it together from the start? Did they both want me out of the way?

If I were dead, Caroline would be Henry's favourite again.

The tortuous thoughts were going round and round in my head, driving me insane. Perhaps that was it ... perhaps I was going mad. Perhaps none of this was really happening. Yet I knew I hadn't imagined that scene at Alexi's house.

I felt so ill and miserable. If I had not possessed such a strong urge to survive I might have thought of ending my life in some desperate way—but I was Hannah Caulder's daughter.

At last I took a cab back to the flat. I didn't know what to do. I didn't want to stay with Richard, but where else could I go?

My grandfather was still in London. I was supposed to have met him at the workshops! He would be wondering where I'd got to, why I had not kept my appointment with him. I ought to telephone his hotel and leave a message but I couldn't face speaking to him at the moment.

If I told him I was leaving Richard he would take me down to Pentire but he would want to know everything and I wasn't ready to tell him. Not yet.

My emotions were in turmoil, my mind trapped in a maze of blind alleys and false hopes. I felt as if I were in some kind of waking nightmare—as if I would wake up in my own bed at Winspear and hear my father's voice calling to me.

'Oh, Ben,' I choked. 'I'm so confused. Why did I leave you? Why did I marry him?'

My father might still be alive if I hadn't left him alone. The thought filled me with a sense of guilt and hopelessness.

I walked up the stairs to the flat with reluctance. Then I saw it propped against the door: a wreath of white lilies. My heart jerked wildly as I saw the inscription in that odd, childlike scrawl.

In memory of Lizzie.

I shivered, feeling cold all over. It was horrible! Horrible! Who had put the wreath there? Who hated me so much that they wanted to torment me like this? I glanced over my shoulder. Was someone watching me?

Why were they doing this to me? Did they hope that I might be driven to some desperate act? Or was there an even more sinister reason for all this?

I was suddenly very frightened. Something truly evil was at work. I couldn't stay here another moment! I had to escape.

I unlocked the door with shaking hands,

went into the empty flat and snatched up a small suitcase, then paused to take twenty pounds—money Richard had replaced—from the silver box on the mantelpiece.

I had to get away. I had to leave before he came back and stopped me.

As I went out into the street I knew where I was going. I walked quickly, pulling up my coat collar against the cold wind that had sprung up. It was getting dark and a fine drizzle had begun to wet the pavements, turning them slippery where little piles of leaves had gathered and were slowly rotting into a pulp.

I saw a taxi passing and hailed it. The driver pulled up at the kerb and opened his window.

'Where to, miss?'

'Liverpool Street Station,' I said without hesitation.

'Going home to your folks?' he asked in a broad cockney accent.

'Something like that,' I replied. 'Visiting friends.'

'Thought so. It's going to be a rough old night—turning a lot colder, so they say.'

I nodded but didn't answer. My stomach was still churning with fright. Who had sent me that wreath? Was it meant as a threat against my life or only to scare me?

I settled into the back seat and closed my eyes. I would catch the first train to Norwich and then take a bus or a taxi home. I still had a key to Winspear and most of the furniture had been left where it was until the place was sold.

As yet, thankfully, Richard hadn't managed to find a buyer.

'The estate agents say there is some unease because of what happened,' he'd told me once. 'But don't worry, Liz. People soon forget. We'll find a buyer eventually.'

More than two months had passed since our wedding but it seemed much longer. I had been a naive child when I met Richard but at this moment I felt like an old woman, dried up and without hope.

It was dark when I let myself into the house and it felt bitterly cold—the kind of icy chill that eats into the bones, the cold of an empty, deserted house. Shivering, I reached for the light switch. Nothing happened and my heart sank as I realized the electricity had been disconnected.

I hadn't expected that, but then, I hadn't been thinking too clearly when I'd left London: I'd just needed a place to hide and sort out my feelings. For a moment I was assailed by panic. How could I stay here now? How could I bear to be alone in this cold, dark house?

In a moment of despair I considered abandoning my plans to stay there but then my courage returned. This was foolish and cowardly. Someone was trying to upset me but I wasn't going to let them win.

In London I had been vulnerable but this was my old home and I had always felt safe here; it was only since my involvement with the family that unpleasant things had begun to happen—and for the moment none of them knew where I was.

I calmed down and began to think. There were candles and oil lamps in the pantry. We had kept them for emergency use because the electricity went off without fail whenever there was a storm.

Dropping my case in the hall, I felt my way along the passage, cursing as I bumped into something hard and banged my knee.

'Damn ... damn and blast it!' I cried, rubbing at the sore place. Tears sprang to my eyes but I blinked them away. 'To hell with all of you!'

I wasn't quite sure who I was cursing: Richard, Alexi or Caroline. Perhaps all three of them. The pain in my knee made me angry and I was beginning to think again, to come out of the suffocating mist of raw emotion that had blocked out everything else on the journey down.

I found the kitchen. It was a bit easier to see where I was going here. The curtains were wide open and there was a certain amount of light from outside, enough for me to find the pantry door without further mishap.

I felt along the shelves to find the candles and matches, lit a stubby candle and then two fresh, new ones, carrying them back into the kitchen one at a time. It took me several minutes to get one of the oil lamps going but once I had it cast a warm glow over the room and I started to feel better. Now I could see what I was doing.

I opened the door of the kitchen range and discovered that it had been laid for a fire. The paper was a little damp so I broke one of the candles and pushed the pieces in amongst the wood. After a few minutes the fire caught and before long I felt the heat coming out to meet me, gradually warming the room and the hob. Soon I would be able to make a cup of tea.

I had found tea, sugar and tins of sticky condensed milk on the shelves of the pantry, also some preserved fruit and packets of porridge oats—so I could eat too if I felt hungry.

It would be warmer to sleep here on the old daybed against the wall than go upstairs, I thought, beginning to feel much better. In the morning I would start to open up the house, light more fires and air the beds ... I would go into Ben's study.

For a moment I pictured him sitting in his chair, the gun in his hand, and a shudder of horror went through me. All that blood and ...

'Don't be such a fool,' I told myself sternly. 'Ben never harmed you when he was alive and he's not likely to now.'

It wasn't my father I needed to fear, but a malicious mind that had set itself against me for some reason.

I went over to the sink and turned on the tap. Water gushed out of it. Thank goodness! No one had thought to turn it off at the mains. I wouldn't have wanted to start hunting for the stopcock at this time of night.

I'd written to Maggie and told her to clear the pantry shelves of anything she wanted but nothing had been touched. Remembering my friend's expression after the funeral, I knew that she had been hurt because Richard had hurried me away and had thought I would forget her.

My spirits lifted at the thought of my friend. There was at least one person I could trust. I would go and see her in the morning. I hadn't had time to work it all out yet but if I was going to live here I would need some sort of plan.

And I would have to phone Henry soon, let him know where I was. In my distress and anxiety to get away I had neglected to leave him a message; he would be very worried, but in the morning I would telephone Pentire and let him know I was all right.

I slept peacefully for several hours. I had thought I might dream or lie wakeful all night, but the kitchen was warm and the daybed surprisingly comfortable.

I was upstairs in my old bedroom the next morning when I heard a noise below. I'd been putting stone hot water bottles into the beds to air them; fortunately, the house hadn't been left empty too long but they were already a little damp.

The noise startled me, setting my nerves on edge again. I lifted my head to listen. There it was again ... someone moving about downstairs ... quiet, stealthy movements, as though whoever it was didn't want to be heard.

My spine tingled. Someone was in the house! I took a deep breath to steady myself. Had I left the door unlocked? I'd been in a daze when I'd arrived the previous evening. I must have left the front door on the latch, because someone was definitely down there! Perhaps a tramp looking for somewhere to stay during the cold spell—or was it those burglars Maggie had told me about? The house had been unoccupied for a while and although there wasn't much of value, whoever was downstairs couldn't know that.

Or was there something more sinister going on? I felt a tremor of fear. I had thought I would be safe here but now ...

There was no point in staying up here waiting for the intruder to come and find me. Better to confront them than have them creep up on me, I thought, and looked round for a weapon. My gaze fixed on a small black spelter vase and I picked it up, clasping it firmly in my right hand as I left the room and crept to the top of the stairs.

'Come out, whoever you are!' I cried, making my voice as harsh as I could. 'I know you're down there.'

There was silence for a moment, then someone came out into the hall. 'Is that you, Lizzie?' Maggie's relieved voice called out. 'It gave me such a fright when I saw the door was unlatched and heard someone moving about upstairs. Sally Jenkins told me she thought she'd seen a light here last night but I didn't believe her.'

'Maggie!' Relief swept over me. I laughed and ran down the stairs to greet her. 'Oh, Maggie—it's so good to see you!'

The emotion in my voice made her look at me sharply. 'Come here and give me a hug, love,' she said, opening her arms.

'I had to come,' I said, my voice catching. 'I

didn't know what else to do ...'

'Whatever it is, it will sound better by my fire,' she said after we had embraced each other fiercely. 'We'll go home, love, and talk this over. Ann has gone to the market in Norwich so we'll have the place to ourselves.'

'Yes.' A feeling of relief washed over me. Here was someone I could trust completely, someone I could talk to without reserve. 'Yes, I'll come with you, Maggie. And then I'll pop into the Post Office and make some phone calls. I shall want the electricity reconnected as soon as possible and I have to let my grandfather know where I am.'

'Yes, you must do that,' Maggie agreed. 'Lizzie, if this is some kind of a lover's tiff ...'

'It's much more than that,' I said sadly as I pulled on my coat and shut the front door behind us, locking it this time. 'It was a mistake, Maggie ... a terrible mistake. I should never have married him.'

'Are you sure?' she asked. 'I know sometimes it isn't easy for a young woman to adjust to married life. I expect quite a few feel like walking out in the first month or two.'

We were walking across the green towards the row of cottages where Maggie lived with her husband, daughter and two sons. Across the road the river looked grey and somehow threatening on this late-autumn day, a swirling mist lapping across the surface in thick drifts.

'Richard isn't in love with me,' I said on a strangled breath. 'And I don't love him. I'm not sure I ever did. It was infatuation or ignorance,

I'm not sure which. I thought it was love ... but I was wrong.' I took a deep breath. 'But it isn't just that—things keep happening, Maggie. Frightening things.'

I told her about the shots, the threatening letter and the wreath. She looked shocked and horrified.

'That's wicked!' she cried. 'I'm not surprised you were upset, Lizzie. It sounds to me as if this is a matter for the police.'

'I'm not sure what to do—that's why I came down here, to give myself time to think. Besides, Grandfather isn't well. I don't want to worry him.'

'Well, come in and get really warm. Winspear is freezing without all the fires going,' Maggie said, unlocking her back door. 'Isn't this a nuisance, when you can't go out without turning the key? We've all had to start locking up recently because of those burglaries. That's why it gave me a nasty turn when I thought someone had got in at the house. And when I think someone has been trying to harm you ...' She shook her head in distress.

'I'm not sure they want to harm me. It's more as if I'm being warned or punished for something.'

Inside Maggie's large, comfortable kitchen the chill around my heart began to melt. I had been going through the motions of putting Winspear to rights, still feeling numbed and strange, but now I was suddenly back to normal. I was not alone. I had friends.

'I'm sorry I gave you a fright. I was going to

come and see you this morning but I wanted to put water bottles in the beds ready for tonight.'

Maggie stared at me in concern. 'You're never going to sleep there alone? Not after what's been happening?'

'Why shouldn't I? I did last night.'

'I wouldn't have let you if I'd known,' she said. 'Not until you've got your electric and the telephone back on. That's if you're intending to stay?'

'I'm not sure how long I want to stay,' I said, and frowned. 'I may spend some time with Grandfather at Pentire. But I've been thinking. I don't want to sell the house, Maggie. Richard said Jack would want to sell his share but if he does I could probably borrow the money from Grandfather and pay him out. I was thinking of opening it up again—as a proper boarding house this time. I wondered if you and Ann would run it for me?'

'You'll certainly need someone to sleep there with you for the time being but I'm not sure about the rest,' Maggie said, though she looked interested, pleased. 'Ann might consider taking it on. She's not the nervous type and when it's up and running there will be guests most of the time—she would enjoy that.'

'Do you think she would consider it?' I asked. 'If I could keep it going, I would always have somewhere to come back to if I wanted ... it would still be my home.'

'You could always come to me in an emergency,' Maggie said, and laughed as she thought of her crowded house. 'We could find you a bed somewhere—even if it was on the sofa in the parlour.'

'Thank you, Maggie. You've made me feel so much better.'

'You look a bit peaky to me,' she observed, mouth pursed disapprovingly. 'What have you eaten this morning?'

'I had a cup of tea. I wasn't hungry ... I haven't had much since yesterday morning come to think of it.' As if to echo Maggie's point my stomach rumbled. 'I suppose I am a bit peckish.'

'You silly girl.' Maggie shook her head at me. 'I'm going to cook you a proper breakfast. After that we'll go to the Post Office and you can make those calls—then I'll help you to get the house decent. If you're set on sleeping there tonight, Ann will stay with you.'

'Oh, Maggie,' I cried with a choking laugh, 'I have missed you. Whatever happens in the future, we mustn't lose touch. Promise me we won't?'

'Such nonsense!' Maggie scolded. The trouble with you, my girl, is you're half starved. Now just sit down at that table and wait while I make you the best breakfast you've eaten in a month of Sundays ...'

The small shop was busy and I had to wait my turn to use the telephone. When I managed to get through to Pentire at last my grandfather had just that minute arrived, and after a brief wait came on the line, sounding annoyed and out of breath.

'Is that you, Lizzie? Where the hell have you been?' he demanded harshly. 'Running off without a word like that. I can't imagine what you were thinking of. You could have left a message for one of us. We've all been worried sick.'

'I'm sorry,' I apologized. He was obviously anxious and I felt awful for causing him distress. 'I was upset over something and didn't think. I rang earlier this morning but there was no answer.'

'Mrs Barker went shopping and Barker was probably in the cellar,' Henry said. 'We're all at sixes and sevens. Are you all right? That's the main thing—and where are you?'

'I'm at Winspear,' I said. 'I've decided I don't want to sell. Maggie and Ann are going to run it for me as a boarding house—at least, I have to talk to Jack about it, but I don't think he'll mind.'

'I've asked him to come down this weekend, as a matter of fact. I would like you to come too, Lizzie. I have something to say to the whole family—something I should have said weeks ago.'

'That sounds rather serious?'

'It's important.'

'I'll come if you want me to.' I hesitated, then took a deep breath. It had to be said and there was no point in delaying. 'I'm leaving Richard. I know we haven't been married long. You may think I haven't given it enough time, but I've made up my mind. It was all too rushed. I didn't really know him. Please don't try to talk

380

me out of it. I can't—I won't live with Richard again. It's over.'

Henry was silent for several seconds and I braced myself for his disapproval. He was sure to be angry or disappointed in me. A divorce in the family would reflect on his good name and I knew how much that meant to him.

'That's your business. I shan't tell you what to do—but I hope you're not going to cut yourself off from the rest of the family? You won't stay away from Pentire or me?'

His words brought me a sharp sense of relief I had not expected such understanding.

'No, of course not. And I want to go on designing for you. If you still want me to? I know it will cause a dreadful scandal if I leave Richard, and I'm sorry, but I can't stay with him.'

'To hell with what anyone else thinks,' Henry said gruffly. 'I've let convention rule my life too much in the past and I've paid for it—but no more. Most of my mistakes came about because I cared too much what other people thought of me; because I thought I had to be accepted in the right circles. I was a damned fool, Lizzie. It's what you think of yourself that counts—and that little gem has taken me a lifetime to learn! If you've made up your mind to a divorce, I'll stand by you no matter what. All I care about is your happiness, girl. Come down this weekend and we'll talk ... please?'

'Yes, yes, I will—thank you.' I blinked away a sudden rush of tears. 'I'm sorry if you were worried.'

'No matter, so long as you're safe.'

'My friend is helping me to open up the house and she will stay with me tonight. I'll come down tomorrow.'

'You ought to let Richard know you're all right, as a matter of courtesy.'

'Yes, I will. I have tried to telephone but he wasn't there.'

'I'll let Rosalind know,' Henry said. 'She was having hysterics last night. Best leave her to me, Lizzie. She's going to be very upset over this. She'll take Richard's side, of course. Bound to. She has always spoilt him and this will bring on the tears—but I can handle her. She'll come round when she's had time to adjust ... time to realize that it's all for the best. No sense in the two of you making each other unhappy.'

I agreed that I would leave him to tell Rosalind the news. I hadn't been looking forward to it, or to meeting my mother-in-law once she knew what was happening. Rosalind was going to be very upset about all this—unless Richard could be persuaded to tell his mother the truth, and somehow I doubted that.

I asked the postmaster to try Richard's number again, but when there was still no reply I paid for my calls and left. Perhaps I would try again later.

Maggie and Ann were already at the house when I got there. They had fires going everywhere and the sight of the roaring flames behind the wire guards was very cheering, as was the smell of fragrant pine logs. The cold, unwelcoming atmosphere of the previous night had gone and it was beginning to feel like home again.

'What do you want to do about your father's rooms?' Maggie asked as we enjoyed a cup of tea together. 'We left them until you got here. I wasn't sure if you would want them touched?'

'I've decided to move into them myself,' I said. 'Guests might feel uncomfortable if they knew what had happened there. Ann could have my old room and that will leave five bedrooms to let. We could convert Hannah's parlour into a sixth if we need it.'

I'd cleared my mother's wardrobe earlier, packing her clothes in scented tissue. I'd previously discussed it with Jack and he'd agreed I could send both Hannah's and Ben's clothes to Lady Sara's mission.

It was time to start afresh. The memories would never leave me but I was remembering the good things now—the times when we had all been happy together, before Ben's accident.

'Are you sure you want to use Mr Caulder's rooms?' Maggie asked, looking at me anxiously.

'Yes.' I was confident. 'His study will make a good studio for me, and I can put a spare bed in there in case Jack wants to stay sometimes.'

'Won't you be spending most of your time with your grandfather?'

'I'm not sure—but if I don't need the rooms you can always let them. I'm leaving it to you and Ann. You'll have complete control, even if I'm here.'

'I'm looking forward to it,' Ann said. 'It makes a change to meet new people. I like a chat now and then. It gets boring being at home all the time.'

When she smiled and looked interested as she did now, Ann wasn't really plain at all. I suspected that running the boarding house would change her life completely—a change she herself felt was for the better.

'I'm not sure why but I just want to hold on to the house,' I said. 'And it couldn't be in better hands.'

I felt a warm affection for them both. Here at Winspear with my friends I could think more clearly about what had been happening to me. I could decide what I ought to do about the future.

'Now I'm going to start moving my things into Ben's room.'

It had taken the three of us the best part of the day to get the house back to normal. The faint odour of mustiness had been vanquished by lavender-scented beeswax and the fires had taken the chill from the air, making it comfortable again.

I looked round my father's study with satisfaction. Most of his books had already been removed to the library at Pentire, and now that I'd brought a few bits and pieces down from my own and Hannah's rooms, it looked very different.

I'd known a moment's disquiet when first entering the study but it hadn't lasted long. I had been closer to my father in the last few days before my wedding and felt close to him here.

I believed that if he could, he would applaud what I was doing.

'You'll always cope, Liz.' His voice was clear and strong in my mind. 'You take after Hannah.'

Were they together now—Hannah and Benedict? I wasn't sure I believed in an afterlife but hoped the Bible teachings were true and that my parents were together and happy at last.

I turned as Ann tapped on the door then poked her head round. 'You've made this look a proper treat,' she said. 'If you don't mind, I'll bring a few bits and pieces from home tomorrow—just to make my room seem cosy.'

'Do whatever you want. It's your home as much as mine now.'

'I've always fancied a place of my own,' she replied, a note of satisfaction in her voice. 'It's so crowded at Ma's place, with the boys and Pa cluttering everything up as soon as you've tidied. I shall enjoy keeping this house nice.'

'I may not be here much,' I said. 'But I've realized I need somewhere of my own—somewhere to come if I want to be quiet.'

Ann nodded, understanding perfectly. 'We'll always be pleased to see you when you do come, Lizzie. I was about to make a cup of cocoa before I go up. Do you fancy one?'

'Yes, please. Why don't you bring yours in here so that we can sit and talk by the fire in comfort?'

Ann was pleased with the invitation. She went off to make our drink and I added more wood to the fire, poking it to send a shower of sparks up the chimney.

When Ann returned we sat in the deep, comfortable armchairs and talked local gossip.

'Did they ever catch the man who attacked Lady Rouse's butler?' I asked as she set down her empty cup.

'No, and there have been more burglaries since,' Ann replied as she gathered our cups. 'Don't let's talk about it or I shan't settle. Not that I'm nervous—it just makes me so cross. People didn't ought to do things like that. I know what I'd do to the rogues if I got my hands on them! Their heads would ache for a month of Sundays.'

I was still laughing as she went out to the kitchen. I could hear her moving about for a while, then she called goodnight as she went upstairs.

I wasn't particularly sleepy. It was warm and comfortable by the fire, much better than it had been in the kitchen the previous night though I had slept reasonably well even then. I settled down with my sketch pad on my knees, trying out a few designs for rings. One of the most distinctive I'd ever seen was the tiger's head Richard always wore.

It made me shudder as I remembered what Caroline had said about it. How could he wear something he had taken from the hand of a man he had killed?

Was Caroline right—was he really two people? The charming man I had fallen in love with, and someone quite different?

386

Who should I believe—Richard or Caroline? Richard or Caroline ... Richard or Caroline ...

I knew Richard had lied to me several times ... but perhaps Caroline had lied to me, too? I felt again the hurt I had experienced when I saw her in Alexi's arms. Were they lovers? If so, why had she lied? Why had he pretended to love me?

It was all so confusing. I could no longer be certain of anything.

Who had sent me that letter and the wreath?

A wreath for me and lilies for my cousin. Were we both in danger?

Someone had put those lilies in Caroline's kitchen. Though she could have done it herself, of course, to make me think we were both being threatened ...

Chapter 19

Abandoning my work just before the clock struck midnight, I went through to my bedroom and started to undress. I had just pulled on one of my old, warm nightgowns when I heard the noise. It sounded like breaking glass and had come from the back of the house.

For a moment I froze in fear, then gave myself a mental shake. I must have imagined it! It was talking to Ann about those burglaries—but no, there were noises coming from the direction of the kitchen. Someone was trying to get in and this time it wasn't Maggie.

Burglars, or someone trying to frighten me?
My stomach tautened with nerves. I was frightened but also determined to confront whoever it was. Picking up a heavy brass candlestick, I went out into the hall and paused as I saw Ann creeping down the stairs. She was armed with a cricket bat that belonged to Jack and had an air of grim defiance about her.

'So you heard it too?' she whispered. 'I thought it was my imagination at first.'

'I think someone is trying to get into the kitchen.'

'I'll have the bugger, whoever he is!' Ann flexed her arm. She was a big, solid woman and looked quite capable of carrying out her threat. 'You follow behind me, Lizzie. Let me have a go at him first.'

I smiled inwardly. If it hadn't been so worrying it would have been hilariously funny. I let the determined Ann go ahead of me, feeling glad that we had agreed it would be a good idea to leave some of the lamps burning until the electricity was reconnected. At least we could see where we were going.

'Be careful,' I whispered as she flung open the kitchen door. I tensed, prepared to tackle whoever was there, and then realized the kitchen had not been invaded; it was just as always. 'Oh ... there's no one here.'

We both heard the same sound as before. It was like glass smashing, outside the kitchen door. As we looked at each other, nerves jumping, there came a plaintive mewing.

'It's a cat,' I giggled as the relief swept over me. 'We put some old bottles out for the bin, didn't we? The cat must have knocked them over.'

'Well, I never.' Ann's mouth curved into a wide smile. 'Fancy that! There was me thinking we were both about to be murdered in our beds and ...' She went to the window and looked out. 'What's that?'

'Where?' I followed her to the window, peering out into the darkness. 'I can't see anything.'

'It was like a shadow. I thought I saw someone over there—in the bushes, just beyond the roses. I'm sure there was someone ...'

'I can't see a thing. It's too dark.'

'It's just my imagination playing tricks.' Ann started to chuckle as she looked round at me. 'We're a couple of right ones, we are. That's what you get for telling tales before you go to bed. Still, I'll be glad when we get the electric on again. Shadows play tricks on you. If we'd had the outside light, we could have seen it was a cat in the first place.'

'If it was a burglar, we've frightened him off,' I said. 'Look at the pair of us, Ann. Armed to the teeth. There was no hope of taking us by surprise if he had been out there—and I'm sure it was the cat. I meant to put those bottles in the rubbish but forgot.'

'Maybe it's as well you did,' Ann said. 'The breaking glass warned us. It may have been just the cat out there, but I did see something—just for a moment.'

'I'm glad it didn't happen last night,' I

admitted. 'I should have been scared if I'd been here on my own.'

'Whoever it was must have known someone was here.' Ann was thoughtful. 'We'd left enough lamps going ... a burglar should have known not to try breaking in.'

'It must have been the cat,' I said, as much to reassure myself as her. 'Why would anyone want to break in here? We don't have valuable silver or pictures like Lady Rouse.'

'No, we don't,' she agreed. 'No doubt you're right. It must have been a stray cat looking for food.'

In the morning we found broken glass and traces of blood, also the mark of a cat's paws leading away into the gardens.

'Poor little thing,' Ann said. 'It must have cut itself. I'll clear up the mess so it doesn't happen again. I like cats. If there is a stray, I shall probably feed it. I think I'll put out a saucer of milk.'

'Good idea. I'm going to pop down to the Post Office again,' I said. 'I ought to make one or two phone calls.'

'You could do some shopping while you're there,' she suggested. 'I've got a list of things we shall need here.'

I accepted the list and set off for the corner shop that doubled as a Post Office. I'd decided to telephone Richard—and perhaps Rosalind, too.

It had occurred to me during the night that there was one person I hadn't considered in my efforts to determine who had been playing nasty tricks on me. One person who had every reason in the world to be jealous and angry because I had married Richard.

Sarah Jones had shown her hostility plainly when we met—and she was a regular visitor to her aunt's kitchen. Mrs Barker had warned me of the poisonous plants in her herb garden. I had noticed something in her manner when Sarah walked in on us that day—and now I thought I understood why.

If Sarah was the culprit it all began to make sense.

And I had been wrong to blame any of the family.

My conscience had begun to prick and I felt guilty for leaving the way I had, without a word. I ought at least to have talked to Richard, to have explained that I knew he was still in love with Caroline. He probably thought I was leaving him because of what Sarah had told me about the child, but that was not so. It was simply that I considered our marriage a mistake.

Perhaps I would ring my cousin, too? Now that I was thinking clearly I was beginning to believe that I had jumped to conclusions about what I'd witnessed in Alexi's kitchen. If I talked to Caro ... asked her for the truth ... at least I would know.

The shop smelt of cheeses, fresh celery that still had the earth on it, and strong soap. That morning it was crowded with customers, all of them out for a gossip and in no hurry to be served. I had to wait for my turn and fend off the questions of curious locals who were surprised to see me there.

Twenty minutes later I left the shop with my basket full and suffering from a sense of acute frustration. I'd tried to make three phone calls and there was no reply from any of the numbers. It was still early in the morning so perhaps Caroline wasn't answering but I'd been surprised that neither Richard nor Rosalind was there.

Suddenly I stopped and stared, my heart beginning to thunder as I saw the car parked in front of the house.

Now I knew why Richard wasn't answering! He was here. Henry must have told him where I was.

I drew a shuddering breath, hoping he hadn't brought his mother with him. I could face Richard but wasn't prepared for his mother's tears and reproaches. Rosalind always managed to make me feel so guilty, though I wasn't sure why. I suspected she used her methods on many people and that they were long practised.

Richard wasn't in the car so Ann must have let him in while I was out. Oh, well, I had to get it over with! Just as well now as later: it had to be faced.

I let myself into the house and was met by an anxious Ann.

'Mr Gregory is in your room. I asked him to wait and made him a cup of tea. I hope that's all right only ...' She was clearly concerned. 'I'm afraid it's bad news.'

My mouth went dry and my legs felt as if they might buckle. 'Not my grandfather? Has something happened to him?'

Richard had heard my voice and came out into the hall; he frowned as he saw me. I noticed immediately that he had a long, red scratch on his cheek.

'It's not Henry,' he said, an odd note in his voice. 'Caroline has been attacked in her own house. They think someone must have broken in to steal her silver. She has quite a collection.'

'Caroline ... attacked?' I felt faint. I stared at him in dismay and he put his hand to his cheek defensively. I thought I saw guilt in his eyes, as if he suspected what was in my mind.

'We thought someone was trying to get in here last night,' Ann said into the rather tense silence. 'But it was only a cat ...' she faltered as she saw the look on my face. 'Excuse me, I'd better get on.'

I walked into the study. The news was so shocking that I felt ill and my knees were shaking. I walked over to the fire to warm my hands in front of the flames. Caroline hurt! But not for the silver ... no, there was more to this than a few pieces of silver.

'Who would have done such a terrible thing?' I asked at last. 'Is—is she all right? She isn't badly hurt, is she?'

I noticed that Richard wasn't wearing his ring and fancied there was guilt in his eyes. What had he done?

'She wasn't conscious when Henry rang me to tell me the news,' Richard said. 'They've taken

393

her to hospital and that's really all I know.'

'Who found her?'

'Michael. He went round to see her in the evening and she was lying there. Someone had struck her on the back of the head. If he hadn't found her when he did ...' Richard sounded upset and I looked at him hard. 'If Michael hadn't called in when he did, she would certainly have died. She may still ...'

'Who would want to kill her? I can't believe it was just for the silver, Richard.'

Something in my tone must have got to him, because he went white. 'Don't look at me like that,' he said, and touched his cheek again. 'I scratched myself with my ring—that's why I'm not wearing it.' His eyes narrowed. 'For goodness' sake! You don't think I would do that to Caroline, do you?'

He was definitely ill at ease ... guilty over something.

I shook my head. He was hiding something but I didn't think it was this. The news had genuinely shocked and upset him. Yet I sensed that something else was bothering him. He was nervous and guilty. But somehow I did not believe he would harm Caroline.

'No, I don't think that, Richard. You love her, don't you?'

He hesitated, his gaze dropping before mine. 'I have for years. I'm sorry, Liz. I thought ... I really thought I could make it work with you. I was fond of you and ... grateful, I suppose. You saved my life.'

'And you thought Henry might settle a

394

substantial sum on me when we married, didn't you?'

He turned to face me, smiling oddly. 'I see Caro has got to you. You weren't this cynical when we married.'

'I thought I was in love with you,' I said quietly. 'And I thought you loved me. You lied to me, Richard, that wasn't fair of you.'

He looked uncomfortable. 'I am fond of you, Liz. I know I'm a selfish brute sometimes but we could still make it work.'

'No, I don't think so. I am sorry I went off without telling you, Richard. I owed you that much—but it's over. I don't want to live with you anymore.'

He shrugged. 'We'll talk about it another day. I can't think straight at the moment.'

'Of course not. Nor can I. I'm too worried about Caroline to think of anything else.'

'Aren't we all?' Richard's eyes veered away from mine. I sensed something hidden—something that was making him nervous. He was frightened. Why? 'Henry told Mama you were here and she told me. I came to fetch you immediately. I presume you will want to visit Caro as soon as possible?'

He couldn't hide his concern for my cousin. But if it wasn't the attack on her that was making him nervous, what was it?

'Yes, of course,' I agreed. 'As soon as we can get there. I'll tell Ann and then we'll go, all right?'

'As you wish.' He glanced round the room, making a determined effort to appear normal.

'You've improved this. I suppose you've decided not to sell?' He pulled a face when I nodded. 'You really do have a mind of your own, don't you? Caroline told me I was in for a shock one day but I didn't believe her. She doesn't think much of me, as I expect you've guessed. Well, I wouldn't fancy sleeping in this room but you always did have nerves of steel. I expect you wish you had never dragged me out of the river, don't you?'

'Don't be silly, Richard.' I frowned at him. 'Despite everything I hope we shall be friends—and I certainly wouldn't want to see you dead.'

His laugh had a hollow ring. 'Thank you, Liz. Believe it or not, as it happens I feel the same way about you.'

We spoke very little on the way back to London. Richard seemed to be lost in his own thoughts, and I was in a state of shock. How badly was Caroline hurt? And who had attacked her? Was it an unknown intruder who had broken into the house to steal—or was there something even more sinister behind it?

I kept remembering my fall from the horse at Pentire and Caroline's conviction that someone had deliberately caused the accident. I had never been sure whether I was the intended victim or Caroline was. Now someone had knocked my cousin unconscious in her own house—the same person who had left the lilies in her kitchen?

I thought it very likely. If I hadn't been so upset because Alexi had been kissing her, I might have realized the truth earlier. Someone wanted to harm us both—someone who had access to both her house and the flat ... which meant that it was probably someone we both knew well.

I felt icy chills down my spine. Caroline had spoken of having her locks changed. Why hadn't she done it?

And who wanted to harm her? Who would want to harm us both?

I remembered the wreath of lilies outside Richard's flat and felt really afraid for the first time. Until this moment I had thought the incidents were meant more to frighten or to punish ... but something had changed. The attack on Caroline was vicious and evil. She could have died.

I had wondered if perhaps Sarah Jones had been playing malicious tricks on me but she would not have done this. She had no reason to hate Caroline. It had to be someone else ... someone who considered both Caroline and me a threat. Someone who wanted to get rid of us both.

My first thought was so terrible that I dismissed it instantly. It could not possibly be a member of the family.

Perhaps Henry had an enemy? He was a powerful man and very wealthy; such men, often made enemies. Perhaps someone was trying to destroy those he loved most? But only a malicious, evil mind could plan such a course of action.

My thoughts were so terrifying that I was

scarcely aware of time passing and when Richard pulled up in front of his flat, I looked at him in surprise.

'Why have we stopped here?'

'Surely you can come up for a drink?' he said in an irritated voice. 'You won't be able to visit Caroline for another couple of hours.'

'Then I'll find somewhere to have a cup of tea and a sandwich.' I reached for the door catch. Nothing would make me go up to the flat with him! 'Thank you for bringing me this far, Richard. I can find a cab from here.'

'Don't be ridiculous,' he said, his tone one of extreme annoyance. 'Can't we talk about this some more? Anyone would think I was a monster—that I'd beaten or raped you or something unspeakable.'

'Of course you're not a monster. I've never said that.'

Only a monster would have attacked Caroline in such a cowardly way, but it couldn't be Richard. It couldn't ... and yet there was that look of unmistakable guilt in his eyes.

'Then why must you leave me? Why can't we simply lead separate lives? Quite a few marriages I know of are like that.' He sounded desperate and there was guilt in his eyes ... guilt and fear.

What was bothering him? Perhaps I ought to have asked but something held me back. Perhaps I was afraid of the answer.

'It's not what I want,' I said, and sighed. 'There's no point to a marriage where neither partner loves the other. It's far better if we

398

both admit we made a mistake and end it now, cleanly and without bitterness—can't you see that?'

'I'm damned if I can!'

'Then we should only be wasting our time talking further.' I was calm and dignified as I opened the car door. 'Goodbye, Richard. I shall collect my things before I go down to Pentire.'

He stared at me. There was something so odd about him that for a moment I was afraid of him, then he seemed to regain control of himself

'Oh, for goodness' sake, shut the door and I'll drive you to the hospital,' he said. 'We may as well behave like reasonable adults—if only for the sake of the family. There's no point in having endless rows over it.'

I closed the door and he started the car again. He was obviously annoyed but tried not to show it as he drove me to the hospital. It would not suit Richard if Henry cut off his allowance and, even though clearly in some mental turmoil, he was sensible enough to know that it could happen if I complained too loudly of his behaviour.

He got out and opened the door for me when we arrived at the hospital, managing a smile. He had regained his composure and seemed more like the man I knew. Whatever was troubling his conscience had been conquered for the moment.

'She's in a private room in Wing C—number seven, I think. You won't mind if I don't come

399

in, will you? I can't stand the smell of hospitals and I'm not too good with illness at all. Give Caro my best wishes if she's awake and say I hope she'll soon be feeling better.'

'Yes, of course. Goodbye, and thank you for fetching me.'

I got out of the car and walked towards the hospital building. Set in its own landscaped gardens, it was a small, private nursing home where Caroline would be assured of all the attention Henry's money could provide for her, and it smelled of a soft perfume in reception rather than the clinical disinfectant I normally associated with hospitals. I quite liked the perfume. It reminded me of something but I wasn't sure what.

'Yes—may I help you?' the well-dressed, well-spoken receptionist asked as I approached the desk and hesitated. 'Have you come to see someone?'

'I'm Mrs Gregory. I should like to see Miss Caroline Caulder, if that is possible?' I said. 'Could you tell me how she is, please?'

'Let me just check my list.' The woman ran her finger down a list of names in the book lying on the antique, leather-topped desk in front of her. 'Mrs Lizzie Gregory?' I nodded. 'Yes, you are permitted to visit. You must understand that we have to be very careful. Miss Caulder suffered a violent personal attack in her own home.'

'Yes, I know. It was so dreadful—very distressing. Please can you tell me how she is today?'

400

'It is good news, Mrs Gregory. Miss Caulder regained consciousness a few hours ago. She is still a little confused and naturally feels very sore, but the doctors are confident of her full recovery. It seems that she was very lucky and no real harm was done. The wound looked much worse when she was brought in than it really was.'

'Thank goodness!' Relief flooded through me. 'I was so afraid she might have been badly hurt—that she might die even. Is it all right if I go in now?'

'Of course.' The receptionist patted her neatly bobbed hair. 'Go down the corridor to your left. It's the very last door at the end—room seven.'

'Thank you.'

Oh, thank God! Thank God that Caroline had not been as badly hurt as everyone had feared.

My eyes were moist as I followed the receptionist's instructions. My cousin wasn't going to die. All the way here I'd been dreading what I might find, now I felt weak with relief. It was a terrible thing to have happened to Caroline but it could have been so much worse.

If Michael hadn't found her when he did, or if the wound had been deeper ... it didn't bear thinking about!

I knocked softly at Caroline's door, then went in. Saree was already sitting by the bed. She turned as I entered, a finger to her lips.

'Is she asleep?'

'Just dozing, I think.'

'Should I come back later?'

'No, sit and wait. Caro was asking about you earlier.' She smiled at me. 'She is very fond of you—and you of her, I think?'

'Yes, I am.' I was mortified to remember that for a short period I had actually thought Caroline might be behind the threats and accidents. Now I knew that she was as much at risk as I—perhaps more so. 'I've been out of town. I came as soon as I could. How is she really?'

'Feeling a little sorry for herself—as she has every right to be. It was a most unpleasant experience. I came to tell her that we think Rupert may have been picked up by a French fishing vessel just off the coast of France ...' She caught herself up as she saw the look in my eyes. 'You did not know that my brother's plane had gone down in the sea? I was sure Caroline would have told you.'

'We—we haven't spoken since the night of the ball. She was upset then.' I stared at Saree. 'Was that because Rupert hadn't turned up?'

Yes, of course. It had to be! It explained so much.

'I believe they had quarrelled again,' she said. 'Caroline thought he had stayed away from the ball because of their quarrel. We none of us knew that he was missing until the next day.'

The day that I had seen Caroline in Alexi's arms! She had gone to him for help in her distress and he had naturally tried to comfort her. They were friends. Alexi would do for her what he had done for me when my father was ill—and I had been too blinded by my jealousy

402

to see it. What a fool I was! If I had not been so quick to jump to conclusions, I could have saved myself a lot of pain.

I recalled my wandering thoughts as Saree started to speak again.

'We know now that my brother agreed to do a favour for a friend. One of Bob Morrison's pilots was ill and he had to make an important delivery so Rupert offered to fly it over. He expected to be back some time that evening but must have ditched in the sea. Wreckage from the plane has been found along the French coast.'

'And you think your brother may have been picked up by a fishing boat?'

'There are some unofficial reports of a pilot being rescued but it hasn't been confirmed yet—nor do we know what sort of condition he was in.' Saree glanced at Caroline and fell silent.

'But you have hope now?'

'Yes, we have hope.'

Caroline made a little whimpering noise. Her long, silky lashes flickered and she put a hand to her head, touching the bandages before opening her eyes and looking up at us.

'Hello you two,' she said. 'I thought for a moment I'd had a bad dream—but it seems to be true, worse luck. Do I look terrible? They've cut off a great lump of my hair, haven't they?'

'You look fine,' I assured her, and bent over to kiss her cheek. 'How do you feel? That's rather more important for the moment.'

'Stupendously awful,' she said with wry humour. 'How did you get here? I thought the troops were out scouring the hills for you?'

'I went down to Norwich. I've decided to open Winspear as a boarding house. My friends are going to run it for me. I just want somewhere to go if I need to now and then—though Henry has asked me to live at Pentire with him.'

'So you're leaving Richard then?' Her brows arched as I nodded. 'Good for you. Don't let anyone change your mind. I was afraid you might think it your duty to stick with him, despite discovering that he is a rotter through and through.'

'Oh, Caroline.' I was slightly shocked by her tone. 'He's not quite that bad. He came all the way to Norwich to fetch me, because he knew I would want to visit you. That was decent of him, wasn't it?'

'He must have wanted something—else Henry pushed him into it. Come on, Lizzie! Surely you know him well enough by now? That charm is always for a reason. Or to hide something.'

'I'll go and leave you two to talk,' said Saree. 'I shall come again this evening, Caro. Is there anything special you need, my dear?'

'Michael is bringing me some more lingerie and towels and things,' Caroline said. 'But do come, Saree. You know I love to see you. And, please ...'

'If there is any more news, I shall come at once.'

'Thank you.' Caroline clung to her hand for a moment, then let go and pulled a face. 'Go on, Saree. I shall cry in a moment.'

'Until this evening, then. 'Bye, Lizzie. You

must come and visit me one day soon.'

'I should like that. Thank you.'

There was silence for a moment or two after she had gone, then Caroline stretched out her hand and I took it, holding it tightly.

'I'm glad you're here, Lizzie. I've been worried about you. And now, after what's happened to me, you must take care. It might be you next.'

A shudder ran through me at her words. I was almost certain that she was right: that we were both in danger.

'I'm so sorry you were attacked like that. Do you have any idea of who it was? Did you see or hear anything?'

She was so bitter about Richard—did she suspect him of hitting her? I was still reluctant to believe it and yet he had been hiding something.

'I'm too confused,' Caroline replied, squeezing my hand hard. She was distressed, a little frightened, and I was angry with whoever had hurt her. 'I'd been to Saree's mission and then I went home—after that it is a blank. I keep thinking there's something I ought to remember—something important—but it just won't come.'

'That's because you're trying too hard,' I said. 'Maggie says the memory plays tricks. Some facts stick and then you forget the silly, ordinary things you ought to know. I expect it will all come back when you're feeling better.'

'If my head didn't throb quite so much, I might be able to think,' Caroline said, and sighed. 'I don't know how long they intend to keep me here. It's so boring just lying here staring at the wall.'

I laughed. 'By the sound of it, you're well on the way back to normal. I doubt if they will be able to keep you here for more than a day or two.'

'Not that long if I can help it! I'm not sure I fancy going back to the flat alone, though.' She looked at me thoughtfully. 'If you're leaving Richard, why don't you stay with me for a while?'

'I've promised Grandfather I'll go down to Pentire this weekend, but afterwards I'd like to if ... well, if we both still want to.'

'I can stay with my father, of course,' she said. 'But I prefer to be on my own as a rule. I suppose I'll get over this in time.'

'It is enough to unsettle anyone,' I said. 'Last night we thought someone was trying to get into Winspear but it was only a cat knocking over some bottles we had put outside and forgotten.'

'I'm frightened,' my cousin admitted. 'I think someone wants to kill me, especially after what happened that day at Pentire. This makes me think—those shots might have been meant for me after all, but ...' She broke off as the door opened and her father poked his head round.

'How's my best girl?' He noticed me and looked relieved. 'Nice to see you, Lizzie. We've all been wondering what had happened to you.'

Michael had brought a huge bouquet of

expensive, hothouse flowers, a basket of fruit and a small suitcase.

'I'm better for seeing you, Daddy.' Caroline smiled as he came to kiss her cheek. Her eyes met mine over his head as if warning me not to mention what we had been discussing before he arrived. 'I'm being thoroughly spoilt as usual. I've had visitors all day. Saree was here before Lizzie. She thinks ... it isn't certain yet but ... Rupert may have been picked up by a fishing boat.'

'That's good, my darling.' He squeezed her hand and glanced at me. 'You girls have given us all a terrible fright.'

'Henry was cross with me,' I admitted, a little ashamed. 'As a matter of fact, I think I should go and telephone him now—so he knows where I am and doesn't start to worry again.'

'You will come back here before you leave?' Caroline asked.

'Yes, of course.' I pressed her hand and let go. 'I should let Grandfather know I'm here. We'll talk some more later.'

'Give him my love and tell him he isn't to worry over me. I'm fine. Tell him my head is made of iron—just like his.'

I laughed and went out, leaving Caroline alone with her father, but I was thoughtful as I returned to the reception area, where my request to use the telephone was graciously granted. The operator was able to get through almost immediately.

'Please go ahead, madam. Your call is through.'

'Grandfather?'

'Lizzie—where are you?'

'At the hospital. I've seen Caroline.'

'How is she?'

'She seems to be getting better. She has a headache, of course, and all this has upset her, but she's cheerful. She sent you her love. Michael is with her now.'

'What do the doctors say?'

'Just that she'll be fine.'

'Should I come up?'

'Not unless you want to. She says not to worry, her head is made of iron.'

'That's rubbish ... but like her!' Henry chuckled. 'Where are you going to stay tonight? I don't want you to be alone.'

'I'm not sure. Perhaps at Caroline's. She has invited me to stay with her.'

'No, don't go there by yourself You mustn't be alone, Lizzie. Take a room at the Savoy and put the bill on my account. I should feel safer if you were in a public place.'

'All right. I'll telephone you later and let you know exactly where I am. And I'll see you this weekend.'

'Be careful, Lizzie. I'm fond of you and don't want to hear that you've been hurt ... or worse.'

'What are you implying, Grandfather? You don't think it was an attempted robbery, do you?' I had been trying to spare him, but he already knew that something sinister was going on. 'You don't think it was an accident that Caroline was attacked ... so who was it? Could it be the same person who fired those shots that caused me to fall off Avenger? They could have been meant for Caroline. I was wearing her clothes that day.'

'I don't know who it was, Lizzie—that's what's worrying me. I know something is going on but I'm not sure who is behind it. Just be careful. I may have made enemies in business—you often do when you come up the hard way as I have. I could have stepped too hard on someone's toes and this is their way of getting back at me—through the people I love. So stay away from lonely places and keep your wits about you.'

'I shall be careful,' I promised. I sensed he wasn't telling me all he knew or suspected but his anxiety was real enough. 'Try not to worry too much—and I'm fond of you, too.'

'Bless you,' he said, and the line went dead.

I frowned as I replaced the receiver. Who would want to murder Caroline? Supposing those shots at Pentire had been meant to frighten her horse—or worse? From a distance we must have looked very much alike. Was this attack on my cousin simply the cowardly action of a burglar caught in the act or a second attempt to kill her?

Something was nagging at the back of my mind. I felt that I already had several clues—that I ought to know something important—but was unable to solve the puzzle.

'Excuse me?' A man's voice behind me made me swing round. As I saw him I gave a start of surprise. 'Aren't you Lizzie Caulder? I think we met once.'

'Yes, we did.' I studied his lean, intelligent face and felt a prickling sensation at the nape of my neck. I'd only seen Rupert Hadden once but I was almost certain it was him. I felt a surge of pleasure for my cousin's sake. This was exactly what she needed! 'You wouldn't be here to see Caroline Caulder, would you?'

'Yes, I am. How did you know?' He looked intrigued.

'I've just been talking to your sister. Lady Sara left a few minutes ago. You look very much alike, Lord Rupert—and I am so very glad that the reports of your having been picked up by a French fishing vessel were true, because I know someone who really wants to see you.'

'Obviously Saree has been busy.' A smile tugged at the corners of his mouth and I could see why my cousin had fallen so hard for this man. 'I shall enjoy getting to know you, Lizzie. Caro has spoken to me of you often.'

'We are fond of one another. I'm sure you will want to see her but you will need to be passed by the receptionist before you can visit—and I think it may be best if I go in first to prepare Caroline.'

Rupert agreed. I waited until he had been checked in by the efficient receptionist, who became very gracious when she saw his title on the list, then we walked together down the corridor to the door of Caroline's room.

'Wait here for two seconds,' I whispered. I flashed him a conspiratorial look and went in.

410

My cousin was inspecting a bunch of large, luscious black grapes but looked up as entered. 'Caro ...' I said, feeling the pleasure of being the bearer of good news bubble up inside me so that I felt like laughing and crying at the same time. 'It's wonderful news, dearest.'

'Rupert!' She went pale and clutched at her father's hand. 'He's been found—he's alive?'

'Better than that—he's here, waiting to see you.'

'Rupert ... oh, Rupert ...' Caroline's bottom lip trembled. 'Where is he? I want to see him. I want to see him ...'

I felt the emotion choking me as I saw my cousin's face when the door opened and Rupert walked in. How could I ever have imagined she was lying about loving him? Any lingering doubts I might have had died instantly. No one could doubt that she was very much in love with this man.

I watched as he moved towards the bed, taking Michael's place as the older man tactfully retreated into the background, leaving them gazing at each other in wonder.

'Caroline, my darling,' Rupert said huskily. 'When I rang Saree's house and they told me what had happened, I came straight here. Are you all right? What happened?'

'It doesn't matter now that you're here.' She held out her hands to him. He took them and bent to kiss her, his lips lingering over hers. 'Oh, Rupert. I love you so much ... so very much.'

Michael beckoned to me. I nodded and we went out together.

411

'I believe they can do without us for the time being,' he said, and looked pleased. 'It's about time that young man asked her to marry him.'

I started to cry. Michael took out his handkerchief and handed it to me. I accepted it with a choking laugh.

'How silly I am. It's just so—so wonderful. That he should walk in like that—after all that has happened.'

'After what happened the other night, it's a relief,' Michael said, looking grim. 'She can't be left alone until this is cleared up, Lizzie. I think someone tried to kill her and I believe I know ...'

He broke off as if he had suddenly remembered he was talking to Richard's wife. His look of embarrassment told me exactly what he was thinking: Michael was very transparent.

'You think it was Richard?' I saw the truth in his eyes before he averted them; his face flushed a brick red. 'But—but he loves her. He told me so himself Why would he want to kill her?'

Richard had seemed very upset when he told me about the attack on Caroline but he was an accomplished liar and I had sensed that he was very nervous ... that he was hiding something. Coldness washed over me. He could have been covering up for his crime—but why would he want to hurt Caroline?

It didn't make sense to me. I was missing something, an important part of the puzzle—but what?

'Richard loves only himself,' Michael said

412

harshly. 'I suspected that Paulinski fellow at first but he was so good over getting the ambulance and the police, so concerned for her, that I realized I was wrong. He told me he thought he had seen Richard go to the house earlier in the day, but Caroline was out at the time.'

'But why would Richard want to kill her?' I asked again.

It didn't add up so far as I was concerned—none of it followed a pattern—and I thought Michael was clutching at straws, blaming anyone who might conceivably have had the opportunity to do it without giving proper consideration to their motives.

We were outside the hospital now and the cold wind made me shiver. It was all so puzzling and unpleasant. Why would anyone want to harm Caroline?

'One less to inherit the money,' Michael said, having reached his own conclusions. 'Richard hounded her for years to marry him, wouldn't leave her alone. She told me he'd used force on her once when they quarrelled—so I paid him a visit. Told him that I would see Henry cut him off without a penny if he didn't leave her alone. He has hated me ever since, of course. I don't mind that for myself but if he hurt Caroline ... I'll kill him! If I learn for certain that it was him, I will.'

Was it all to do with the Caulder inheritance? I felt the sickness swirling inside me. If Michael was right ... it had to be Richard.

That scratch on his face. He had said he'd

done it with his own ring, but was he lying? Had Caroline tried to defend herself? Was that what she felt she ought to remember?

'Don't do anything reckless,' I begged Michael. 'I know how you must feel but you might make a terrible mistake. You can't be certain it wasn't a burglar. Just make sure that Caroline is never alone at her flat until this is all sorted out.'

'Henry doesn't want her at Pentire this weekend. He's planning something he thinks will stop once and for all whatever it is that has been going on. He says it wouldn't be safe for her to come down at the moment.'

'Then he must think it was Richard, too,' I said, feeling slightly sick. 'I suppose if Henry thinks he might be capable of ... no, no, it's too horrible. I'm sure you're wrong, Michael, both of you. Richard has his faults but I don't think ... no, he couldn't.'

'You be careful of him, too,' Michael said. 'He won't be pleased that you've walked out on him. Makes him look a bit of a fool—he might resent that.'

'Yes, I suppose he might.' I remembered how angry he had been when I wouldn't go up to the flat with him. But ...' I shook my head. It was all so impossible, so unpleasant, that I didn't want to believe any of it—but someone *had* tried to kill Caroline, and if it wasn't a thief it might have been Richard.

'Can I give you a lift?' my uncle asked. 'You've never been to the shop, have you?

Would you like to see some of our stock?'

'Very much,' I said. 'But not this afternoon. I should be grateful if you could give me a lift somewhere, though. If it's not taking you out of your way?'

Part Four

TARNISHED GOLD

Chapter 20

It was getting dark and the wind was bitterly cold, whistling through the streets, blowing so hard that I had to pull up my collar against its bite. There was a light on at the back of Alexi's house. I stood staring at it for a moment after Michael had driven away, my heart racing wildly as I gathered my courage.

I had been foolish the last time I was here, running away because Alexi had offered comfort to a friend in distress—as he would offer it to anyone who needed his help. That was all it had been, of course. I knew that now—just as I was certain of my own feelings at last. I was in love with this gentle bear of a man who was so very, very different from the handsome schemer I had married.

'What a fool I've been,' I murmured through stiff lips. 'Please forgive me. Please love me, Alexi. Please don't be angry with me for running away ... don't let it be too late.'

I walked up to the back door and knocked. A few seconds passed and then Alexi was there, his eyes warm, caressing, full of understanding as they moved over my face with searching intensity.

'I hoped you would come,' he said, and drew me inside. His arms went around me, holding me pressed close to his chest. 'My own darling

Lizzie. Never go away from me again.'

'I won't,' I promised. I laid my head against his shoulder, feeling suddenly at peace. After all the pain and the soul searching it was so easy, so right. It was good to be held like this, to know that I was loved and wanted. 'I was so foolish, Alexi. I ran away because ...'

He bent his head towards me. He was smiling tenderly and I knew that explanations were unnecessary, would never be necessary between us. Then his mouth touched mine, kissing me lightly at first but with a growing demand—a demand that awakened an answering hunger in me. A hunger so strong and fierce that it surprised me.

'Alexi ...' I breathed, my throat tight with emotion. 'I love you ... want you so very much. I've left Richard. I shall never go back to him. I want to be yours ... with you always. Make me yours, Alexi ...' I was melting against him, longing for his touch. 'Make me your own, my darling.'

'Lizzie ... my sweet Lizzie,' he said, and bent to sweep me up in his strong arms. 'I have waited a lifetime for you and I shall never let you go.'

He carried me so easily up to his room. I gathered a swift impression of simplicity—white walls, green carpet and drapes—cool and inviting, then became oblivious to my surroundings as Alexi began to kiss me again.

Everything he did was so gentle, so tender. He undressed me slowly, kissing my shoulders, the hollow at my throat, my breasts. Each touch, each caress, was almost a prayer. I felt the reverence in him and my body trembled as he worshipped at the temple of love. No one had ever wanted me this way, no one had ever loved me this much. He made me feel as if I were so precious to him that he was almost afraid to touch me. But I wanted him to touch me, I wanted him to possess me, to drive out the loneliness and the unhappiness.

I pressed closer to him, feeling the heat of his body through the soft linen of his shirt. I slipped my fingers inside, easing the buttons open one by one, my hands moving beneath to explore the satin softness of his skin and the crisp mat of dark hair on his chest, stroking the firm muscles of those wide shoulders and down the arch of his back. He trembled at my touch, his face working with emotion.

'I love you,' I whispered. 'Love you so much ...'

Soon Alexi's shirt had joined my clothes on the floor, then we were both naked, thigh to burning thigh, flesh to flesh, quivering with a raging desire that overwhelmed us both. We lay together on the bed, touching and stroking, drinking in the wonder of each other's body and the need that possessed us—the need to be closer ... to be one.

When Alexi entered me at last I opened to him with a silken wetness, welcoming the throbbing maleness within me, surrounding his heat with my moistness, my softness. We were perfectly matched, our bodies rising and falling in a sweet rhapsody of divine music until the crescendo came on a rushing tide that swept us both on to paradise and we lay content at last, gasping and whispering each other's name.

'Alexi ... Alexi.'

'Lizzie ... beloved.'

He held me hard against him. I tasted the salt of his sweat on my lips and buried my face in the prickly black hairs on his chest. Nothing had prepared me for the completeness, the feeling of absolute joy I'd felt as he possessed me. I understood now why I had felt so empty after Richard's love-making—that had been a sham, a parody of the real thing.

I knew now what it meant to be loved and I would never, never doubt again.

We made love again and again throughout the hours that followed, both hungry for the delight we found in each other.

At around eight o'clock that evening Alexi got up to make rich, dark fragrant coffee and doorstep sandwiches, which he ate with relish and I nibbled round the edges.

I telephoned my grandfather and was surprised that he didn't seem particularly shocked to hear where I was staying for the night.

'Good. You will be safe with Alexi,' he said. 'Paulinski is a good man. Bring him with you when you come down, Lizzie. I've been meaning to talk to him about a bit of business.'

'I've already asked him,' I said, and laughed. 'We're going to fetch my things tomorrow and then we'll come down on Friday. Alexi doesn't have a car. He borrows a van from a friend when he needs transport for his bronzes. We

422

might do that—or come by train.'

'Barker will fetch you from the station if you ring.'

Henry sounded a little breathless and I was suddenly anxious. Was he feeling ill? He was not a young man and the events of the past few days must have been a strain for him.

'Are you all right. Grandfather?'

'Fine. Never better. I've been anxious about you and Caroline but I'm perfectly well. Don't you worry your pretty head over me, Lizzie. Just come down soon. And give my regards to Alexi.'

'Yes, of course.'

I replaced the receiver and turned to look at Alexi. I was frowning though I didn't realize it until he smoothed the lines from my forehead with a kiss.

'What's wrong?'

'I think Henry is feeling unwell. He wouldn't admit it, of course, but I think he has a weak heart. He asked you to come at the weekend—I told you he would. You will come, won't you?'

'Where you go, I follow,' Alexi said, eyes bright and wicked. 'I hope he doesn't expect us to have separate rooms? I'm too large to go creeping about in the dark. The floorboards will creak and give us away.'

I laughed but there was the huskiness of emotion in my voice. 'Then I'll come to you,' I said. 'I refuse to pretend and I don't want to sleep alone.'

'Why sleep at all when we have something

more interesting to do?' he teased, making a grab for me.

I evaded his grasp, glancing at him provocatively over my shoulder. 'I want to see your studio,' I said, and ran out of the door, my bare feet noiseless on the carpet. 'Come and show me what you've been doing, Alexi. Tell me about your work. I want to understand everything about you—about your work, your feelings and ambitions.'

He followed, bringing one of his shirts for me to wear, wrapping it around me with firm, loving hands. The shirt swallowed me up, so I rolled back the sleeves and tied it in a knot below my hips.

'You may start a new fashion,' Alexi said, and picked up a sketch pad. He began to draw with quick, strong, fluid strokes, his gaze fixed on me intently as I flitted about the room, examining everything and darting questions at him whenever something intrigued me. 'I made a model of you but I couldn't finish it. I need to have you here, to be able to see you ...'

I was looking at various small bronzes, picking them up to examine the workmanship, holding them in my hands, stroking and experiencing the feel and symmetry of the exquisitely moulded pieces. They seemed to have a life, a sensuality, of their own and I knew that it flowed from the very essence of the man who had shaped them with his hands, giving them his own vitality, his own strength.

'Is this the horse you were working on the last time I was here?' I asked, running a finger

424

down the back of a wonderfully active rearing horse. Every muscle, every sinew, was straining with the pride and majesty of the beast, its eyes wild. nostrils flaring.

'Yes.' Alexi cast a critical eye over the piece. 'It's better than my first attempt but there were faults in the casting. I need more control—to work more closely with the founder.'

I could see nothing wrong with the model but Alexi had impossibly high standards where his work was concerned and would never be satisfied with anything less than perfection. But that was the man—the strong, passionate, caring man I'd come to love. My eyes moved over him, over the harsh features, the large hands I knew could be so gentle, the solid thighs and wide shoulders. He had the bearing and the watchful alertness of a battle-hardened soldier, and yet beneath the harshness was such a gentle soul.

'Why are some of the bronzes a different colour?'

'It's in the finishing,' he said. 'Sometimes we use different lacquers.' He got up from his stool and came to join me by the bench. 'This is a black lacquer I've been experimenting with recently. Riccio often used it but mine hasn't quite the same surface—it should look more flaked. I'm not sure why I can't get it right. I'm much better with this reddish translucent lacquer.'

'It looks almost chestnut with golden lights.'

'That's what I've been trying to achieve.' Alexi looked pleased with my comments. 'It was a technique much favoured in the workshops of

Giovanni Bologna. This model of a woman is a gilt bronze. Gilt bronzes are made by fire-gilding—a paste of powdered gold in mercury is spread on the bronze and in the firing it adheres, giving this wonderful effect. Unfortunately it is very expensive so I can't afford to do something like this very often—this one was for the Paris show.'

He explained various techniques to me, showing how sometimes a rough core of clay was built up and then finished with wax.

I listened in fascination as he talked, his face becoming animated, eyes lighting up with the passion he so obviously felt for his work.

'This method has been used for centuries and is what is called "cire-perdue", or "lost wax", but there are many hazards involved. Air bubbles, or pipes, which support and separate delicate mouldings, sometimes break or are wrongly placed, resulting in an incomplete statue. There are more modern techniques now, of course, but the older ones still give the best results in my opinion—providing they are done correctly.'

He could have been relating a love story from the timbre and resonance of his voice which sent a little thrill of pleasure winging down my spine. I thought I could have listened to him forever—this man of contrasts.

'I know nothing about your work,' I told him earnestly. 'But I want to understand. Will you teach me, Alexi?'

'If you really want to learn,' he said, reaching out and drawing me close, his hands moving down the arch of my back. 'There's a chance

I may be invited to work with a founder in Paris. It would give me an opportunity to learn from a master craftsman—to improve my skills.'

'Then we'll go to Paris,' I said, lifting my face for his kiss. I trembled as I felt the warmth of his breath on my face and anticipated the desire that was already beginning to sweep through my body. 'I shall ask Richard for a divorce and then we ...'

His mouth hushed me with a soft, sweet kiss. He bent down to gather me into his arms, carrying me through to the bedroom where he deposited me gently amongst the love-tangled sheets.

'Tomorrow is for talking,' he said with his mouth against my breasts. 'Tonight is for loving.'

But we did talk in whispers, holding each other close as the dawn came slowly, stealing in through a crack in the curtains.

'I want to take you to Italy one day,' Alexi said, his tongue tracing the inner curve of my ear; his breath tickled me, making me laugh. There are such treasures to see, such a feast of visual delight that you will want to gorge yourself. I know I can never be as good as those Italian masters were—but just to see such wonders enriches the mind. You could learn from the treasures of Rome for your jewellery designs, Lizzie.'

Alexi had the soul of a true artist, I thought, tracing the line of his square jaw with loving fingertips—the body of a Roman gladiator combined with all the fire of a Renaissance painter.

'I've always loved museums and art galleries. I don't want to own everything I see. I just want to experience them, to see the glory of a master at work.'

'You remember when we first met—at that little exhibition in Norwich with its one necklace of tarnished gold?'

'How could I forget?' I laughed up at him. 'When I trod on your foot and you looked at me with those hungry, dark eyes of yours—and I thought you were about to gobble me up?'

'I looked into your eyes and fell in love,' he murmured huskily. 'Just like that. It was a thunderbolt from Zeus—kismet. I wanted to snatch you up and run off with you, then and there.'

'I wish you had, Alexi.' For a moment my voice throbbed with pain. 'I wish so much that you had.'

He touched his mouth to mine, silencing me, easing the ache inside me.

'Don't, my darling. Never look back. It is all over. I promise you, we shall never be parted again.'

I snuggled against his chest, feeling the strength of his arms about me and my doubts fled. I was safe with Alexi. I had found my soul mate. The vague fears that hovered at the back of my mind seemed to dissolve and vanish like summer mist when the sun breaks through the clouds.

Nothing could harm me now.

428

The next morning Alexi drove me to Richard's apartment in the old van he had borrowed from his friend. 'Are you sure you don't want me to come up with you?' he asked as we shivered outside in the bitter wind. 'If Richard is there ...'

'I'm sure he isn't,' I said. 'He's usually out at this hour of the morning. I shall bring my cases down one by one and you can load them into the van. I think he would be angry if he came back and found you in his flat. We don't want to cause more trouble than we need, do we?'

'I shall be here if you need me,' Alexi promised. 'Don't look so nervous, darling. He can't harm you while I'm here. I would break his neck first.'

'Oh, Alexi.' I gave a soft, husky laugh as I remembered the way he had brought breakfast to our bed, insisting on waiting on me. We had kissed and fed each other pieces of thickly buttered toast with marmalade. Never once had I experienced such companionship with Richard, such happiness. 'I'm not frightened of Richard—but I don't want to flaunt our love in his face.'

'You always think of other people's feelings.' Alexi's smile caressed me. 'Go on then, but I shall be here if you want me.

I went up in the lift, listening to it hum and whirr noisily. I let myself into Richard's flat with my own key, thinking that I must leave it on the hall table when I'd removed my things.

There were three suitcases, which would be

429

too awkward to carry all at once, and a soft leather bag. I look them through to the hall, then went back to check that there was nothing else I'd forgotten. Hearing the front door open as I was coming back from the bedroom, I stopped and my heart missed a beat as I saw Richard.

'It seems I was just in time,' he said, a note of annoyance in his voice. 'I was told you might be at the Savoy but when I inquired they said you hadn't been there. Where did you spend the night—or can I guess? That's Paulinski down there in the street, isn't it?'

'Alexi is helping me to collect my things.'

I answered vaguely, my face turned from him. This was exactly what I had hoped to avoid. I tried to go past him and pick up the cases but he caught my wrist, his fingers digging into my flesh.

'Please let me go, Richard.'

'You're a cold bitch. How long have we been married? You've made me look like a fool—walking out on me before we've had a chance to make our marriage work. What do you think everyone will say?'

'I don't really care.'

'Well, I do, damn you!'

'I'm sorry you feel that way.'

'I'll just bet you are!'

'I didn't want to hurt you, Richard, but you lied to me. It was Caroline you wanted. You left me on our wedding night to get drunk because you couldn't bear it that I wasn't her.'

This was so painful. Even though I knew I

no longer loved Richard, it still hurt to quarrel with him like this.

'That's damned nonsense!'

'It's the truth, Richard. No matter how you try to deny it.'

'Just because I had a couple of drinks ...'

'I knew when she came down to Pentire with Alexi. I saw the jealousy in your eyes. You were different when she was there and you didn't want me when I begged you to stay with me.'

'You can't leave me, Liz—not now. Not after I've ...'

'After you've what, Richard?' I felt cold all over as I saw that strange look in his eyes. 'What have you done?'

'Nothing. Why should I have done anything?'

Something in his manner frightened me. Once again I sensed guilt and fear.

'What is the matter, Richard? You're hiding something.'

'Don't look at me like that—it's all your fault!' There was something so strange about him then—a queer, blind, obsessed expression in his eyes.

'I'm going.' I was afraid of him, afraid of that strange look in his eyes. 'I don't want to stay here ...'

'If it's the physical stuff you want, you can have it.' He suddenly slammed me against the wall, pressing his body close to mine so that I could feel the warmth of his breath on my face and smell the sharp tang of his hair oil. I turned my face aside as he tried to kiss me, avoiding

431

his greedy mouth. 'You can have it right now, you little bitch.'

'No, Richard ...' I cried as fear whipped through me. 'Stop it! Let me go. It's over. I don't love you. I don't want you anymore ...'

'Well, that's a shame because I want you.' He forced his mouth over mine. biting at my lips in a frenzy, as though he had lost all control. 'Bitch ... bitch ... bitch ...' he muttered through his teeth. 'Cheating whore ... just like Caroline ... like the rest of them ... they're all cheating whores ...' His hand pawed at my breasts and he forced his knee between my legs, pulling at my skirt as he started to inch it up over my thighs.

I dragged my head free and screamed several times. I hit out at Richard in an effort to free myself but before I could do much I saw Alexi charge through the open doorway and grab Richard from behind. Alexi gave a great roar of anger, then lifted him into the air as if he were a rag doll and threw him across the room.

Richard landed on a small occasional table which was crowded with pieces of fine china and glass. It went crashing down under his weight and the glass smashed, sending splinters everywhere.

For a moment Richard lay winded. He was stunned, too shocked, to realize what had happened to him, then he put a hand to his mouth and found blood; that seemed to bring him out of his trance and he yelled as he discovered what had caused the cut on his face.

'Damn you, Paulinski,' he cried as he rose unsteadily to his feet. 'Do you know what you've done? That figure was Derby and the bowl was Lalique. They were worth two or three hundred pounds.'

'I'll replace them,' Alexi said coldly. 'But if you ever touch Lizzie again—if you upset her in any way—I'll break your neck. Believe me, I mean it.'

Richard's mouth curved into a contemptuous sneer. 'I doubt if you could afford three hundred pounds,' he said, 'but I shall hold you to the deal. You can have her if you want her that much. She's a cold bitch anyway—not worth the half of her cousin in bed. You were a fool. You should have had Caro while you could.'

'Ignore him!' I cried as I saw the fury in Alexi's eyes. 'He's not worth it. Let's just go and leave him.'

I was terrified that Alexi would lose his temper and carry out his threat to break Richard's neck. He could do it easily if he tried.

Richard wiped blood away from the small cut on his mouth.

'You might like to know why I was trying to find you in the first place? I suppose you do care about Henry?'

We had been about to leave. I looked at him uncertainly. It was difficult to know when he was lying.

'What are you saying, Richard? Please don't try to cause more trouble.'

'I've been told that he had a heart attack late last night.'

I gasped, my own heart stopping for a second. 'Oh, no! Is ... is he dead?'

I had known Henry wasn't himself when I'd talked to him on the telephone the previous evening. I had known that he was not a well man, that I might lose him—but I hadn't expected to feel such pain, such a devastating sense of loss.

Richard was calmer now.

'There's no need to look like that, Liz. Apparently he was lucky. Barker heard his cry and got the doctor to him pretty quickly. It turned out to be mild as these things go. He's in bed, of course, and feeling under the weather—but sensible enough to know what he wants. He's asked for you, Lizzie. Wants you to go down there as soon as possible.'

'We must go at once ...'

'In that van I saw parked out front?' Richard looked disbelieving. 'You'd better let me take you. You'll get there a lot sooner.'

'I would rather walk,' I said, my face a frozen mask. 'Let's go, Alexi.'

'Oh, for goodness' sake,' Richard muttered. 'Can't we behave like civilized people over this? If you won't let me drive you down, take the damned car yourselves. I can follow in that wretched van. I suppose it will get me there sometime today.'

'It will get you there.' Alexi looked at my white face and accepted the offer. 'Richard is right about the car being quicker,' he said. 'There's no point in being too proud at a time like this.'

I nodded but couldn't speak for emotion. Henry ill—perhaps dying! I didn't feel like taking anything from Richard, but was too anxious to get to Pentire to refuse. I laid the keys to the flat on the hall table as Alexi gathered up my various bits and pieces.

'Expect me when you see me,' Richard said. 'I have something to do in town before I come down. Give my regards to Henry.'

'I'll tell him you lent us your car,' I said. 'That's what you want, isn't it?' I went past him and followed Alexi into the lift.

Chapter 21

'We shall soon be there,' Alexi comforted me as he glanced across and saw the lines of anxiety in my face. 'Richard said it was a mild attack, darling. Your grandfather is a very strong man. I'm sure he will pull through this.'

'I know he's strong but I'm frightened.' I caught a sob in my throat. 'I'm so frightened ...'

'Of course—but don't lose hope. He's too stubborn to let go of life just yet. Believe me, I know.'

'I don't want him to die, Alexi. I've only just got to know him and ... I love him.'

Alexi did his best to comfort me throughout what seemed an interminable journey but I was on thorns, my imagination running riot as I faced the possibilities.

How could I bear it if Henry died like this—before I had barely got to know him? I kept remembering my father lying in that hospital bed, and my own sense of inadequacy—my frustration at not being able to do anything to help him.

What was happening? It seemed as if something evil was hovering over my family, threatening them all.

United we stand, divided we fall.

The old adage kept running through my mind. We were a divided family. A family at war with itself.

Had that been the point of all the accidents ... all the threats? To upset the whole family ... to make Henry suffer a heart attack? Perhaps because someone was afraid he might alter his will.

Did someone want the money that badly? It all pointed to Richard. These painful thoughts went round and round in my head. Henry's money was the curse hanging over this family: the Caulder inheritance.

I was white-faced and tense when we finally drew up outside the lovely old house that afternoon. Pentire looked beautiful in the dying rays of the sun—such a beautiful place, peaceful and serene. It was hard to imagine the evil that lay simmering just beneath the surface.

'It will be all right, darling.' Alexi laid his hand on my arm as I was about to get out of the car.

'I hope so.' My voice shook from emotion

and it was all I could do to prevent the tears from spilling over. 'I do hope so.'

Mrs Barker seemed to have been expecting us. She had the door open as I rushed up the front steps. I noticed that her eyes were red from weeping and my heart stood still with fright.

'Grandfather?'

'No worse.' She held a handkerchief to her eyes. 'It was the shock that did it, Mrs Gregory. I ought never to have told him but he had to know. Forgive me ... it's all my fault.'

Henry was alive. Thank God! In my first flush of relief I did not take in Mrs Barker's meaning, but then I realized that there was something more. Why should it be her fault that he had suffered a heart attack? What had she told him that could have brought it on? I felt a clutching sensation in my stomach and knew that something terrible had happened even before my grandfather was taken ill.

'What are you talking about? What has happened?'

I was gripped by a feeling of horror as I saw the stricken look on her face, and somehow I knew even before she said those fateful words.

'It was last evening,' she said, almost choking on the words. Tears spilled over and ran down her cheeks. 'They found her, you see, in the woods. She had been strangled and her poor face was all bruised. It was him what done it, of course. The wicked creature! She ought never to have married him with that temper of his ...'

'Who do you mean?' I asked as she faltered,

437

and yet I knew. Of course I knew. I had been warned it was going to happen but I had not been able to interpret my dreams. 'Not ... Sarah?'

She nodded, covering her eyes with her handkerchief as the sobs broke from her. The story came tumbling out of her between her tears.

'It was her husband ... run off and shot himself he did after they told him she'd been found ... couldn't face the guilt of what he'd done. I warned her he was a jealous brute before she married him, but she wouldn't listen ... she never would listen ...'

'Sarah's husband?' I remembered her bruised face that morning by the village pond. 'What happened to ... where is Lily?'

'She's with her grandmother,' Mrs Barker said. 'I was going over this morning but Barker says I'm needed here with the master took bad the way he is ... and me to blame for it.' She shook her head, wiping the tears from her face. 'You'd best go up to Mr Henry, madam. I'm delaying you and the master so poorly. He wanted you to go straight up when you arrived.'

'Yes, of course.' I reached for her hand and pressed it. 'We shall talk later, Mrs Barker. It wasn't your fault. You had to tell my grandfather. And of course you must go to your sister. We'll manage here somehow. I will speak to Barker.'

I turned to Alexi. He was clearly shocked by her news but came forward as I threw him a

438

look of appeal. 'Look after her, please. She is upset.'

'Of course. You go up to your grandfather.'

I left Mrs Barker talking to Alexi, whom I knew would find the right words to comfort her in her devastating grief, and began to run upstairs, impatient to see my grandfather.

My mind was still reeling from the shocking news. Sarah Jones had been strangled by her husband—and in our woods! My terrifying dream had come true. It was a terrible, terrible thing and I knew it would cause me many restless nights of remorse; there was something nagging at me, something I needed to think about—but for the moment all that mattered was my grandfather.

Mrs Barker thought the news of the murder had brought on his heart attack. Did he know that Sarah's child was also Richard's ... did he suspect? No, of course not!

Please don't let Henry die! My lips moved in fervent prayer. So many frightening and tragic things had happened in these past weeks that I felt as if a great weight was descending on me. I was not sure I could bear it if my grandfather died.

I paused outside Henry's room, my heart thumping wildly as I prayed: 'Please. please let him be all right! He must not die. Please don't let him die.'

Taking a deep breath, I knocked very softly in case he was sleeping. 'May I come in?' I asked, peeping round fearfully. Relief flooded through me as I saw him sitting propped up against the

439

pillows. 'Grandfather ... how are you?'

His face lit up in a smile of welcome and he held out his hand to me. 'Lizzie—come and give me a kiss, girl. I wasn't expecting you until tomorrow.'

'I came as soon as I heard. How are you?' I took his hand then bent to kiss his cheek. His skin felt soft and smelled of shaving soap. As ill as he was, Henry had no intention of lowering his standards and Barker had shaved him. 'We wouldn't have been here as soon as this but Richard lent us his car.'

'Knows which side his bread is buttered, I dare say,' my grandfather muttered. 'After the way he has hurt you, I was half inclined to cut him off altogether. I've told Rosalind I'm reviewing the situation.'

Did Henry suspect ...? The thoughts crawled in my mind like stinking maggots. Was it possible that Richard had ...?

No! I must not let the suspicion take root. It was too horrible, too evil to be considered. My mind was overwrought. I wasn't thinking clearly. I must not do or say anything to make the situation worse. I had to be careful, for Henry's sake. Another shock might kill him.

'Please don't do anything against Richard, for my sake,' I begged. 'It—it wasn't all his fault. I was too young and silly to know what I was doing when I rushed into marriage.'

'We'll see,' Henry said gruffly. 'I've always felt responsible for Richard so I don't suppose I'll stop now. Besides ...' He paused as there was a hesitant tap at his door. 'Who is it?'

'It's me, Henry.' Rosalind peeped in at him, looking apprehensive. 'Michael brought me down. Wasn't that thoughtful of him? I wanted to come at once and there wasn't a train until later.'

Henry frowned and I sensed he was annoyed because she had interrupted us.

'Is Richard here?' he asked.

'I saw his car ...' Rosalind seemed surprised, slightly hurt. 'Didn't he bring you down, Lizzie dear?'

My heart sank. I felt embarrassed and awkward. I had been dreading this moment but there was no point in putting it off any longer.

'Alexi brought me down in Richard's car. He lent it to us and will come down in the van we had borrowed.'

'Why would he do that?' Rosalind was puzzled. 'I don't understand, dear. Why didn't Richard bring you himself? Surely he could have brought you himself ...'

'You know very well why he didn't,' Henry put a stop to her testily. 'I told you on the phone the other day that Lizzie was leaving Richard—and he told you himself the night she went missing. The marriage hasn't worked out so they've very sensibly decided to part rather than prolong the agony and make themselves unhappy.'

'I thought it was just a lover's tiff?' Rosalind's cold, pale eyes moved over my face with dislike. 'Marriage isn't something you abandon at the first hint of trouble. It is for life ... until death do you part.'

441

'Richard doesn't love me,' I said, finding it impossible to meet her accusing eyes. 'He ... loves someone else. He agrees that it was a mistake.'

'Nonsense,' Rosalind scolded. 'You are being a very silly girl, Lizzie. Richard is devoted to you. You owe it to him to give your marriage a chance. You can't simply walk away from it just like that.'

'No, I'm sorry, but I can't go on with it.' I was annoyed by her refusal to understand. 'I am truly sorry if this upsets you. I didn't want to hurt anyone—but I have left Richard. It is over and I shall ask him to divorce me. If he refuses, I shall go and live in France.'

'Richard will do the decent thing,' Henry said decisively. 'He'll see it's for the best when I speak to him. He can provide grounds for you to divorce him. It's easy enough to arrange and I am sure he would prefer it that way.'

'You always have to have your own way, don't you, Henry?' Rosalind's eyes were suspiciously bright as she looked at him, as though she might burst into tears. 'When my husband left me, I told Richard his father was dead because you thought it best. We've all had to dance to your tune. Well, Richard may still do so if he wishes but I've had enough of all this. You expect too much ... too much!'

When her husband left her!

Had I heard correctly? Was Richard's father still alive? Caroline had always wondered why no one would ever tell her how he had died—now, in her anger, Rosalind had revealed the truth.

442

I was still trying to take it in when she went out abruptly, slamming the door behind her. There was silence for a moment, then Henry rubbed at his chest, as if he could feel pain.

'Are you all right?'

'Confound the woman!' he muttered. 'Always was inclined to tantrums—but she's right, I have had my own way. Maybe I've been hard on her. No ...' He caught at my hand. 'Forget her. Let her go. She'll calm down when she has thought it through. I know Rosalind. We've had our arguments before this but she usually comes round in the end.' His fingers curled possessively over mine. 'Can't have you going off to France, girl. I haven't much time left. I want you here at Pentire ... where you should have been long ago.'

I sat with my grandfather for nearly an hour, talking to him, holding his hand, watching as he gradually slipped into a peaceful sleep.

Leaving him to rest, I came downstairs again. There was no sign of Alexi so I decided to pay Mrs Barker a visit.

She was sitting at the kitchen table, a pile of vegetables in front of her, staring into space. She started when she saw me, and picked up her knife and began to shred a cabbage, as if she needed to keep her hands occupied.

'Let me help,' I said. 'I'll do the sprouts, shall I?'

'I can manage, madam,' she said, then gave a watery snort and burst into tears.

'Me and Barker never had any children of our

own.' she sobbed as she mopped at her eyes. 'Sarah was like a daughter to me ... I warned her she should have told Ted the truth before she married him ... but she was always one for her own way.'

'Lily was Mr Gregory's child, you knew that, didn't you?' Mrs Barker nodded, an odd, guilty look in her eyes. 'It's all right. Sarah told me but I think I had half guessed it already. She told me that Ted found something Richard had given her for Lily. I suppose that's what made him ...' I broke off, my throat catching with emotion. 'I'm so very, very sorry.'

'Ted always had a wicked temper on him,' Mrs Barker said, 'but what I can't understand is why she was in the woods at night. Lily was forever running away when she brought her to see me and Sarah would have to go into the woods after her—but not at night.'

'Do you think she might have gone to meet someone, that her husband followed and then strangled her, perhaps because he was jealous?'

'I should think it must have been that way. But I still don't understand it. Sarah was a good girl. She told me there hadn't been anyone since her marriage ... and I believed her. It must have been Ted that killed her or he wouldn't have shot himself, would he?'

'I don't suppose we shall ever know for sure. I'm so very sorry. I know you must want to be with your sister and Lily. I'm sure I could cope for a day or so ...'

Mrs Barker blew her nose hard. 'I wouldn't dream of deserting you at a time like this, madam—but I'm grateful for the offer. I'll go over and see them in a couple of days, when things have settled.'

'I shall be living at Pentire for a while,' I said. 'Once the rest of the family go home, I shall be able to manage if you want a few days off.'

'Thank you, Mrs Gregory.' She smiled at me. 'I'm glad you've come. It's time this old house had a proper mistress again.'

'Managed to get here in time, did you?' Richard asked as he walked into the study where I was sitting an hour or so later.

'Oh, Richard.' A little gasp escaped me. 'You startled me.' He gave me an odd stare. 'Don't tell me he's dead?'

'No—he seems very tired but he's alive.'

I sensed he was in a flaming temper. 'What's the matter, Richard? Why are you looking at me like that?'

'You may well ask! I've never had a journey like it in my life. You can take that van back to London, because I'm never going to get in the damned thing again!'

'I'm sorry. Was it dreadful?'

'The radiator kept boiling up to a head of steam. Twice on the way down I had to stop and ask for water ...'

I had a sudden vision of Richard having to call at a house and ask a favour. He must have hated that! I wanted to laugh and realized I was close to hysteria. Here we were talking about a faulty radiator when a young woman had been murdered and Henry had suffered a heart attack because of it. Should I tell Richard about Sarah? Somehow I could not.

'You should have abandoned it and caught the train.'

'I would have done if I'd been anywhere near a station but I should have had to walk five miles to get there—so I sat and waited for the radiator to cool down.' He glared at me. 'Have you seen my mother?'

'She went out for a walk a few minutes ago,' Alexi told him, entering the room at that moment. He came over to me as Richard walked off without answering him. 'How is Henry now?'

'Very tired, but he seems cheerful.'

I couldn't smile for Alexi. I was remembering the previous night when he'd held me close and talked of his plans for the future ... wonderful plans for trips to Italy and France. He had been so excited about all the things he wanted to show me. Now it had all gone horribly wrong and I was dreading the moment when I would have to tell him that I could not go to Paris with him after all. He was bound to be disappointed, to accuse me of putting my grandfather first—but how could I leave Henry when he was so ill?

'You mustn't let all this upset you,' he said, giving me an understanding smile. 'I know it is terrible, that poor girl being murdered by her husband and your grandfather's illness, but ...'

'It's only that I ...'

I heard voices and jumped up, running out into the hall just as the door opened on a gust of wind and my brother came in, bringing a small flurry of leaves with him that settled in a heap on the hall carpet. His left arm was in a sling and there was a bandage round his head.

'Jack!' I cried as the room began to spin round me and I felt faint. 'What happened to you?'

I had a strong sense of foreboding, a presentiment of evil. My head was going round and round and I could hardly breathe. If Alexi had not been there to steady me, I think I should have fallen.

'Sit down, Lizzie.' he said, pressing me down on to a wooden hall chair. 'Breathe deeply. It's all right.'

'But, Jack ...' I whispered. 'Jack ...'

'No need for all that, Lizzie. I'm all right,' he said cheerfully. 'Pranged the car at Brooklands. Not to worry, though, it wasn't badly damaged. They tell me I shall be able to drive it again next week.'

'Who cares about the car?' I cried shrilly as I felt an urge to scream. 'It's you I'm bothered about. You could have been killed!'

'It's just a sprained wrist and a little cut, nothing to upset yourself over,' he assured me. 'Looks much worse than it is. How is the old boy then? I was coming down anyway but Richard left a message for me so I caught an earlier train.'

'Did the army let you go just like that?' I was beginning to recover from the shock, beginning to feel angered by his thoughtlessness. 'I'm surprised you can come and go as you please.'

'Hasn't Henry told you?' Jack looked embarrassed. 'He's bought me out. It wasn't what I expected—or maybe there are more exciting things to do now. Henry is giving me a job at the workshops so we'll both be a part of the family firm.'

'Oh, Jack,' I sighed. I had never wanted him to join the army but now I saw this sudden change of mind as a failure. Jack had failed to achieve his dream and I had failed in my marriage. What a pair we were! 'Are you sure you want to become a jeweller?'

He shrugged carelessly. 'I think it's more about learning the whole business. Seeing what aptitude I have for various aspects of the trade—probably management. It will do until I find my feet.' He glanced at Alexi. 'Where's cousin Caroline?'

'Alexi is with me,' I said. 'You may as well know at once that I've left Richard and I'm going to marry Alexi when my divorce comes through.'

Jack gave a long, low whistle. 'So that's the way the wind blows! What does Henry think about that?'

'He has accepted my decision,' I said, annoyed at his reaction. From the way he was grinning at me, he seemed to think it a huge joke. 'It's not funny, Jack.'

'I was just thinking I would rather have Alexi as my brother-in-law than Richard, that's all.'

'I thought you liked Richard? You don't have to turn against him just because my marriage didn't work out.'

I didn't know why I was reacting like this, defending Richard. Perhaps I felt guilty because of the shocking suspicions in my mind—or perhaps it was nerves. I felt so tense, on edge, as if I were waiting for another blow to fall.

Alexi looked puzzled, but I couldn't tell him what was on my mind with Jack there. I had promised to go to Paris with him, but how could I? How could I leave Henry when he was so ill?

I had left Ben and he had died; I was still feeling guilty about that. Henry was expecting me to live at Pentire now that I had left Richard and it would hurt him if I refused. But I couldn't expect Alexi to see things my way. His career might depend on his spending time in Paris and he would want me with him. It was all muddled up in my head, which was beginning to ache.

'Oh, let's join the others,' I said. 'I want a cup of tea.'

Everyone turned to look at us as we entered the drawing room and I was aware of hostility from both Richard and his mother, who was in her usual place dispensing tea from the big silver pot. The atmosphere was so strained that my stomach tightened nervously. I sensed the deep emotions beneath the surface and the tension seemed to press down on me unbearably.

It was so bad that I felt as if I couldn't breathe. Something was going to happen ... something evil. I curled my fingers, my nails digging into the palms of my hands.

I was so afraid ... so terribly afraid. There was

such hatred in this room ... such intense anger ... such evil. Or perhaps it was all in my mind? I was feeling so muddled and tense, my nerves stretched to the limit. I looked round at their faces, my suspicions making me feel ill. One of these people was a potential murderer.

Michael got up to offer me his seat, which was close to the fire.

'Ah, there you are, Lizzie,' he said, smiling at me as if he wanted to prove that he at least was on my side. 'Father has asked all of us to go up to his room after tea. Seems he's feeling a bit better and he has something to say. It was the reason he asked us all to come down this weekend and now that we're all here ...'

'Caroline isn't,' Richard objected. 'Isn't she coming?'

'Don't suppose she feels like it after that bang on the head,' Michael said, and glared at him. He still clearly felt that Richard was the number one suspect. 'I'm here to look after her interests. She's safer where she is with the Haddens.'

'You needn't look at me like that. I didn't hit her.' Richard returned his glare with interest. 'I wouldn't harm Caro.'

'We've only your word for that.'

'Please, please, don't quarrel,' I begged, feeling that I would scream if they continued to snipe at each other. 'Why would Richard have tried to kill her? She must have disturbed a thief who panicked and ...'

I was making excuses for him again. Why?

'Perhaps it was you, Michael.' Rosalind's pale eyes had an odd intensity about them. 'I heard you quarrel with her the other night at the ball. Perhaps you did it yourself because she knew too much ...'

'That's a damned lie!' Michael's fleshy face turned brick red. He looked as if he might explode at any moment. 'Anyone who believes that is a fool! I love my daughter and don't care who knows it.'

'Of course you do. Everyone knows it couldn't have been you,' I cried, unable to bear this any longer. Why couldn't they see what they were doing to themselves? Caroline had once told me the Caulders were cursed and now I believed it—it was the curse of too much money! 'I can't stand anymore of this.'

I ran from the room and was close to tears when Alexi caught up with me at the foot of the stairs.

'Lizzie,' he said. 'Lizzie, dearest.'

He drew me into his arms and I laid my head against his shoulder and shuddered, feeling close to tears again.

'Why do they have to be so awful to each other?'

'Don't let them upset you,' he said, his big hands gently stroking my hair. 'I should imagine all this anger and jealousy has been simmering beneath the surface for years.'

'It's horrible,' I said, emotion catching at my throat. 'Grandfather is so ill and all they care about is the money. It's tarnished gold, Alexi, tarnished gold.'

'It isn't just them, is it, Lizzie? Something else is upsetting you.

451

'Yes.' I raised my head to gaze up at him uncertainly. 'Grandfather wants me to live here. Oh, Alexi, how can I deny him that when he could die at any moment?'

'I don't see the problem?' He ran the tip of his finger down the line of my cheek, sending delicious little tremors through me. 'Pentire is only an hour or two away from London.'

'But much further from Paris.'

'I don't have to go. I can continue to work in London. It may be best if we don't set up home together until you get your divorce—and I can come down at weekends. You'll be able to come up to town now and then. Henry wouldn't expect you to be tied to his apron strings. He just wants you under his wing so that he can look after you.'

'You said it was important for your work that you went to Paris. You must go, Alexi. I want you to.'

'Paris isn't that far away these days.'

He ran his thumb across my mouth, making me want to melt into his arms. I wished that I could go with him now ... that I had never become a part of this family ... and yet I felt the pull of my love for Henry holding me back.

'Oh, Alexi.'

'I wouldn't expect you to desert him while he's ill, darling. Stop looking so guilty. We love each other and we're young. We have the rest of our lives.'

I nodded but didn't get a chance to tell him how frightened I was ... frightened that something evil was going to happen that would change everything ... because Michael came out into the hall with Jack, closely followed by Richard and his mother. Rosalind gave me a strangely chilling look, full of accusation and dislike. I turned away and held tight to Alexi's hand for reassurance.

'Are you coming, Lizzie?' Michael asked. 'Henry has sent to say he is ready for us. He wants us all together—the family, that is.'

Michael clearly hadn't accepted Alexi yet, even though he knew Caroline wasn't involved with him.

'Will you wait for me in Grandfather's study?' I asked, gazing up at Alexi earnestly. 'Henry has something important to say to us and I have to be there.'

'I shall go for a walk,' he said. 'I'll come to the study when I get back.' He pressed my hand. 'Don't worry, darling. It will all work out, I promise you.'

If only I could tell him! If only I could stop what was going to happen, but there was nothing I could say ... nothing that would explain this fear inside me.

It was as if we were all caught up by some strong, malevolent force that was sweeping us on to tragedy.

'I don't suppose I shall be long.'

I gave him a look of love and longing, then followed the others upstairs. Alexi had succeeded in calming me for a while but now the feeling of unease was beginning to intensify once more; I sensed the simmering resentment and anger in the others. It was hateful to hear the family quarrelling so bitterly. A family divided by greed and jealousy because of money. The Caulder inheritance ...

Was that the curse of the Caulders? Or was there more ... something hidden in the past of which I had no knowledge ... something that could arouse this deep, simmering bitterness ... a bitterness I could almost taste?

What did Henry want to say to us? He must think it important to ask us all to gather here. I suspected that it had something to do with his will and was reluctant to hear it.

Rosalind had lingered at the top of the stairs and I sensed that she was waiting for me.

'You're a sly whore,' she hissed as I approached. 'Just like your mother. She thought she was marrying into a fortune, but when I'd finished telling Henry about her, she discovered her mistake.'

I was too stunned to retaliate. There was such viciousness, such hatred, in those few words that they made me feel sick. I stood still, watching as Rosalind walked down the corridor, her back stiff with anger.

What did she mean? She had told Henry things about my mother—what things? I had always believed that Rosalind had tried to bring the family together that she had played the role of mediator not snake in the grass.

I followed the others at a distance, my reluctance making me the last to enter my grandfather's room. I was reminded of something Caroline had once said about the vultures gathering as I studied their expectant faces.

Even Jack looked excited, as though anticipating a share of Henry's vast wealth.

I wanted to run away. I didn't want anything I hadn't earned. I didn't want to be in this stuffy room with these people —and I didn't want to hear what Henry had to say.

'Come here, Lizzie. I want you next to me.'

Henry's voice had the ring of command, as though he had sensed my urgent desire to flee. I went to him reluctantly but when he smiled and held out his hand I took it, some of my tension melting away. I loved him despite my initial doubts ... despite the way my mother had been treated ... and I could not desert him now, when he was ill.

His fingers closed protectively around mine. I felt the slight tremor that went through him and understood that this was a strain for him, too. I pressed his hand, feeling protective towards him.

'I've asked you all to come because I'm concerned about certain things that have happened recently.' His fierce old eyes roved round the faces of the people gathered about his bed. 'I'm talking about Lizzie's accident and the cowardly attack on Caroline—the two people I love most in the world.'

'You don't think one of us did it?' Richard demanded angrily. 'Why should any of us want to harm them?'

'I hope none of you would,' Henry said, brows furrowing. 'Lizzie's accident may have been just that—and Caroline may have disturbed an intruder.'

455

'How did he get in?' Michael objected. 'The police did a thorough search and there was no sign of a forced entry.'

'Everyone knows Caroline leaves a spare key under that Georgian urn ... the lead one near the French windows,' Richard blurted out, and turned bright red as everyone stared at him. 'Well, she always has, it isn't a secret.'

'The family knows that,' Henry agreed, 'but I doubt if many other people do. That is why I've called this meeting. I don't know who was responsible for these unpleasant incidents but if anyone in this room imagines a death in the family will change my will, they are mistaken. No one has anything to gain from the death of someone else.'

Suddenly they were all silent and watchful. I felt Henry's fingers tighten on mine and knew that he was afraid—for those he loved. I glanced down and saw the pulse beating at his temple.

'This is too much for you,' I said. 'Can't it wait until you feel better?'

'It's all right. We may as well get it over, then I can stop worrying.' His gaze moved round the room, lingering for a moment on Michael, then Richard and Rosalind. 'You will get my half of the shop, Michael. The workshops will go to Jack. He's going to be running them in a year or so, and knowing they will be his should make it worth his while to learn the business. The money will be split between Caroline and Lizzie—apart from five thousand pounds each to Richard and Rosalind. The trust funds I set up for each of you years ago will continue to provide you all with an income. If anyone dies before I do, their share goes to charity. So none of you gets one penny more.'

So there is no point in harming those I love.

I looked at the watchful faces and knew they all understood the words Henry had left unspoken.

For a moment there was silence. Michael was the first to speak. 'That sounds fair enough to me. Jack is entitled to his share as Ben's son. I never expected anything more for myself. Thank you, Father. I'm grateful.'

'You haven't mentioned this house. Who gets Pentire?' Rosalind asked in the silence that followed Michael's statement. Her face had gone very white and her eyes had a peculiar staring look.

Henry squeezed my hand. 'I bought Caroline's London house for her and you have the cottage in Cromer, Rosalind. Richard and Michael have their own homes, which I helped them to buy—as I did your husband when he married you. Jack has living accommodation over the workshops, if he cares to use it. Pentire means more to me than all the rest.' He glanced up at me. 'I want my dearest Lizzie to have Pentire.'

'Grandfather!' I was shocked. This house was the thing he valued most. 'Surely it should go to Michael or Caroline?'

'Neither of them would want it,' he said. 'I know you will love the place as I do, and welcome the family whenever they care to visit as I always have.'

'Yes, of course, but ...'

'It's yours, my dear. I made a new will after your father died—and it is safely locked away in my solicitor's office.' His brooding gaze seemed to harden. 'If either you or Caroline were to meet with an accident, your share of the estate would go to charity. I want everyone to understand that.'

'I think you've made that very clear,' Richard said. 'I've never expected more than you've left me. If that's all you have to say, I think I shall go and change for dinner.'

He walked out of the room without another word. It was impossible to see from his expression what he felt. Rosalind followed him out. She looked stunned, as if she couldn't believe what she'd heard.

'I never expected anything more for myself,' Michael said. His satisfaction was plain to see. 'I really am most grateful. The shop will go to Caroline eventually, of course, but it means I can safeguard it for her until she settles down—though I'm hopeful that may be sooner rather than later if she marries Hadden. It is good of you to show your trust in this way, Father.'

'It is your due,' he replied. 'You've little enough to thank me for. I haven't been much of a father to you. But if I'm granted a stay of execution, I shall try to do better in future.'

Michael blinked as the easy tears sprang to his eyes. 'I've loved you,' he said in a choked voice. 'You didn't make it easy but I've always cared—and I'm in no hurry to inherit.' He

458

turned and walked hastily from the room, obviously choked by emotion and knowing full well that sentiment and tears only irritated his father.

'I suppose this means I shall have to buckle down and learn the trade?' Jack still looked stunned, as though he couldn't quite take in what had happened. 'This is very good of you, sir. I'm not quite sure what to say—except thank you, of course.'

'Just make a success of your life,' Henry said. 'I should like a little time alone with your sister now, if you don't mind?'

'What? Oh, no, of course not.'

Henry patted the bed beside him as Jack followed in the wake of the others and we were left alone.

'Sit here, my dear.' I did as he asked and he reached for my hand. 'You've brought me such joy in the past few weeks. Did you know that?'

'Oh, Grandfather.' I was choked with emotion, close to tears, but I mustn't give way to them, for his sake. 'Please don't talk like this. You're going to get well again. I don't want you to die.'

'That little performance just now wasn't about my dying.'

'Wasn't it?' I was doubtful, my eyes anxiously scanning his face. 'It sounded very much like it to me.'

He patted his chest. 'This was just a warning. I shall have to take things more easily in future but my doctor tells me I'm an old fraud. I shall probably live past a hundred.'

'I do hope so!' I croaked, and blinked hard. 'Oh, Grandfather. I don't think I could bear it if ...'

He frowned at me. 'No tears! Never could stand them. Your grandmother nearly drove me mad with them at times. That's better.' He pressed my hand as I gave a watery laugh. 'I thought it was best to let them all know where they stand—put a stop to any monkey business.'

'You don't really think that any of them ...' I felt sick again as I realized what it had all been about. 'That's horrible.'

'I don't know who has done what, and don't want to know. All I care about is you and Caroline being safe. Jack's accident was his own fault—or mine for giving a reckless young man a car like that. Should have known better, but I wanted to make up for all the years of him not having his share.'

'Don't spoil him too much, Grandfather. He's a good person but still very young—even though he would hate me to say it.'

'That's why I want him at the workshops so that we can keep an eye on him.' There was a hint of mischief in Henry's face. 'I know I'm an interfering old man but I'll never change. Got any new designs for me yet?'

'I've been working on some rings but there's nothing I'm satisfied with yet. I want to talk to Johann about the various properties and quality of rubies and emeralds. I'm learning

460

so much and I want to be a little more adventurous.'

'That's right, he'll put you straight. You can't do better than to ask his advice on stones.' Henry nodded his satisfaction. 'What about Alexi—are you going to settle with him?'

'Yes, when Richard and I are divorced ... if that can be arranged?'

'You leave him to me. I'll pay him to give you grounds, make it easier for you. He knows he isn't going to get enough to serve his expensive tastes when I die so he'll be glad of an extra few thousand in the meantime.'

'It's so sordid! I feel terrible about causing you all this trouble and upset. And just when you're unwell.'

'You're not to blame.' Henry yawned and his eyelids flickered as if they felt heavy. 'Tell Alexi to come and see me in the morning. I'm tired all of a sudden and I want to rest—but there's some business I need to settle with him. Overdue as it happens. Ought to have seen to it ages ago. Nothing to do with you, girl, so you needn't pull a face.'

'I wasn't,' I said, and kissed his cheek. 'Alexi will come and see you tomorrow. Try to sleep now, dearest. Shall I pop in later?'

'No, I'll see you in the morning. Go and find that man of yours. He will be wondering where you've got to.'

'Yes, he will,' I said, and smiled.

I walked to the door. When I looked back his eyes had already closed.

461

Chapter 22

I was thoughtful as I left Henry's room. He must suspect it was Richard who had tried to kill Caroline. What other reason could he have for calling the family together to reveal the contents of his will?

Richard was selfish and could be violent but was he a cold-blooded murderer? The sort who would strike someone down from behind ... I had my own suspicions but I was not sure and knew I must be very careful.

Outside the wind was on the rise, howling through the trees, sounding almost evil as I reached the bottom of the stairs then crossed the hall to the study. My nerves were taut and the feeling of unease had grown steadily during the day; I glanced over my shoulder, feeling that I was being watched—but I was being silly. Nothing could happen here in my grandfather's house.

I tried to dismiss the foolish fears, to think about my own problems. It seemed my life was destined to be here at Pentire for the foreseeable future. I would enjoy living in such wonderful surroundings but was going to hate parting from Alexi—and yet I knew that I had to let him go to Paris, for his own sake, for the sake of our future together. I must do it with a good heart, make it easy for him, no tears, no recriminations.

Smiling, I opened the study door and called his name. 'Alexi ...'

The room was empty. He had obviously not returned from his walk. I went over to the window and looked out. It was very dark at the moment but I thought I caught a flash of lights—like car head lamps. Someone was either coming or going.

Perhaps Richard had decided to return to London; he didn't really like it much down here and might feel it wasn't worth staying on in the circumstances—now that he knew he had nothing more to gain.

I wondered what would happen to the family now. Would it draw together, lick its wounds and become stronger? Or ...? Hearing the door open behind me, I swung round eagerly.

'Alexi ...'

The word died on my lips as I saw it was not him. Rosalind had entered the room, the smell of her sweet, cloying perfume wafting towards me ... the strong, unmistakable scents of roses and lavender.

The perfume I had smelled the day that horrible letter had disappeared from the flat. The strong perfume that had lingered in Caroline's house the day she found the lilies in her kitchen.

'Rosalind ...'

The back of my neck had begun to prickle and my chest had gone tight. I was aware of evil in the room and suddenly I knew. The clues had all been there, waiting for me to solve the puzzle. How stupid I had been not

463

to have seen it before.

Rosalind's face was very pale in the shaded light from the table lamps and the flickering flames of the fire. There was something very still and strange about her, as though she were not quite aware of what she was doing. Of course. Why hadn't I realized it sooner?

A chill trickled down my spine. 'What is it, Rosalind? If you're looking for Richard ...'

'You're the one I want.' Her voice was flat and emotionless, though beneath the surface simmered an intense emotion that I recognized as hatred. 'You won't get away with this. It should be mine. He always promised me that Pentire would be mine one day ... he *promised* me.'

I moved away from the window. I suddenly felt most peculiar and my mind became very alert, as if I were seeing with new clarity. Something was terribly wrong here. Rosalind looked and sounded so unnatural, almost as if ...

'What are you talking about?' I asked, deliberately drawing her out, playing for time. 'Why should Henry leave you Pentire when he has a son and three grandchildren?'

'Because he owes it to me.' Rosalind's eyes held an odd shine as she moved into the lamplight. 'When my husband left me, Henry made me tell Richard his father was dead. He promised he would always look after us both.'

'He has kept his promise,' I reminded her. 'You yourself told me what he had done for Richard. You both have an allowance and ...'

'A pittance!' she cried, two spots of colour in her pale cheeks. 'Five thousand pounds!' Her voice rose in shrill indignation. 'I was more of a wife to him than that sickly Selina ever could be. He loved me. I know he loved me. He owes me because of ...'

'Why does he owe it to you, Rosalind? What did you do that should make Henry so grateful to you?'

'I was his mistress.' Her eyes had taken on a blind sheen, as if she were looking back into the distant past. 'Selina wasn't a proper wife to him for years, but I was. He came to me when she turned him away from her bed.'

'And what did you do then, Rosalind?'

She laughed, a chilling, eerie sound that made me tremble inwardly.

'Shall I tell you?' she said. 'Caroline has tried to find out my secrets but I was too clever for her.'

'You have lots of secrets, don't you, Rosalind?'

'I can tell you because it doesn't matter anymore.' She laughed again, a sly, secretive look on her face. 'I nursed Selina for months when she was ill. I was fond of her, you see. I didn't want to hurt her. 'That's why I sacrificed my ...' A flash of anger came into her eyes. 'I was devoted to her and then ... she found out I was Henry's mistress. She told me to leave ... said such wicked things to me ... told me never to come back to Pentire.'

I knew what had happened next. Of course I did. I had seen it in my dreams.

'You couldn't do that, could you, Rosalind?

465

So you waited until the opportunity came and then ... you pushed her down the stairs.'

Rosalind gave another high-pitched giggle. A thin trickle of saliva ran from the side of her mouth.

'She heard me ... just at the last she saw me ... and she knew.'

'What happened then, Rosalind?'

She blinked. 'I thought he would marry me after she was dead ... but he sent me away. He gave me the cottage in Cromer ... told me it wouldn't look right if I stayed on at Pentire.'

'That wasn't fair, was it, Rosalind—not after all you had done for him? To send you away when you had done so much for him.'

'I knew you would understand,' she said, a queer smile on her lips. 'I could have been so fond of you, Lizzie dear. If only you hadn't been such a naughty girl ...'

It was all so clear to me now.

'You sent me that dead rat to punish me, didn't you, Rosalind?'

'You refused to let me help you choose your wedding clothes—then you went to stay with that bitch ... I had to punish you. You do see that, don't you?' She was almost pleading with me then, as if she needed me to understand.

'Yes, I see that,' I agreed. 'But why did you do all the other things, Rosalind?'

'Henry was getting too fond of you ... I couldn't let you take everything that should be mine ...' Suddenly the fierce hatred was back in her eyes. 'Pentire should be mine ... will be mine.' Her hand came up and I gasped

466

as I saw the gun for the first time. 'When you are dead Henry will change his mind. He won't see Pentire go to a stranger. He will remember his promise to me ... the promise he made that night when he came back from the woods.'

I had to seem calm, uncritical, encouraging. 'The night Henry came back from the woods? What happened there, Rosalind? It was something that meant a lot to you, wasn't it? Something you have never been able to forget. That's why you take the flowers, isn't it?'

'You've begun to guess, haven't you? I knew you would when you saw the flowers. That wretched child Lily! I caught her touching them once and told her she would be punished if she came to the woods again ... but then you started to walk there and I knew you would see them.'

'Who is buried there, Rosalind? Is it Richard's father?'

She hadn't heard me. She was lost in the maze of her own fevered thoughts, caught in the past.

'He left me,' she said. 'He didn't love me but it didn't matter because I had Henry. When I knew I was carrying his child I had to be careful. If Selina had known ... so I laced myself tightly ... so tightly ... and the child was born dead. I sacrificed my baby for her sake and then she ... was going to send me away. It wasn't fair. I had nowhere to go ... nowhere ...' Tears filled her eyes. I was aware of intense pain, a pain she had carried inside her for too long.

I had to break the silence. She must keep on talking.

'And so Henry buried the child for you?'

'He knew I'd sacrificed my child for her sake and promised to give me whatever I wanted ... but he has broken his promise! He is giving you Pentire and so you must die. You do see, don't you, Lizzie? I don't want to hurt you but I have to punish him ...'

There was a wildness in Rosalind's eyes now, an unbalanced, unnatural glitter that frightened me. She had gone mad! Surely she didn't believe she could get away with murder, not in this house? But she was beyond reason, all sense of balance and normality gone.

'You can't kill me here,' I said, desperately trying to sound calm. Alexi would be back soon. He would do something. 'Everyone will hear the shot. They will know you did it, Rosalind. This time you can't put the blame on Michael. I saw his car leaving just now.' It was a lie but I was so terribly afraid. I must keep Rosalind talking at all costs.

'So you've worked it all out, have you?' Her laughter was soft and sly, a horrible sound that made me feel slightly sick. 'You are so clever, Lizzie. I knew how it would be. That's why I tried to warn you not to interfere in things that did not concern you.' There were tears of self-pity in her eyes. 'I'm not a bad woman. You made me do it, Lizzie. When you were ill and everyone thought Michael had tried to poison you, I knew it would work. I didn't want to kill you then—just to make it seem as if Michael

468

had been spiteful, that he had wanted you to fall and hurt yourself. I thought Henry would cut him out of his will and leave more to you and Richard.'

'But it didn't work, did it?' I reminded her. 'Henry wasn't fooled. He won't be this time—he won't leave Pentire to you. He'll send you away, Rosalind.'

Her head jerked up and there was a wild, blind look about her. 'I would rather die than let you have Pentire—you and that new lover of yours. If you had stayed with Richard it wouldn't have mattered, because it would all have been his in time—just as I always planned.'

'Richard doesn't love me. He loves Caroline.'

'That whore! I should have hit her harder. I should have made sure she was dead.' Rosalind's hatred seemed to swell and flow out of her in a great wave. 'I shall get rid of her too ... but you first ... you first ...'

I fought against the tide of panic that threatened to overwhelm me. The house was full of people. I only had to wait and someone would come. Someone must come!

I must keep her talking, go over and over it all, again and again.

'You caused my accident and you tried to kill Caroline why, Rosalind? Why do you hate us so much?'

'Henry loved me once. He came to me when he couldn't stand being with that silly woman he married. Why should her sons and their brats inherit everything?' Now Rosalind's eyes had the fixed, glazed stare of insanity. She was lost in the maze of her own mind, her memories and the web of hatred she had spun for herself. 'It was so easy to get rid of the first one ... the one he loved most. I slipped into his study after I heard Michael say he had put the gun in Benedict's desk and ...'

'You loaded the gun, didn't you? It was you Maggie heard—and you slipped out into the garden when she started to open the door.'

The darkness gathered in my mind. Such evil! Such terrible hatred. It was difficult to hold on to my senses and not to slide into hysteria. I wanted to scream and shout but the pain had begun to intensify about my heart. It hurt so much that I could hardly breathe. Ben hadn't meant to kill himself after all. He had been trying to clean a loaded gun and it had gone off by accident ... just as Henry had said.

'I killed him.' Rosalind was gloating, filled with the confidence of the broken mind which believes itself invincible. 'They all thought it was an accident but I planned it and knew it would, happen. Benedict was never much good with guns ... always so accident-prone. I knew he would manage to make a mess of things. I killed him and now I'm going to kill you ...'

'Mama! Stop!' Richard's voice shocked us both. Neither Rosalind nor I had been aware that he had entered the study.

'Richard ...' she faltered, looking bewildered. 'What are you doing here? You shouldn't have come ...'

'You're not well, Mama. Give me the gun,'

he commanded, holding out his hand. 'Give it to me now!'

Rosalind turned to look at him. She seemed dazed, uncertain what to do next.

Richard took a few careful steps towards her and then she pointed the gun at him.

'Don't be silly, dearest,' he said, speaking in a soft persuasive tone now. 'You're having one of your funny little turns, Mama. You should go and lie down until your head is better.'

Richard must have been aware that his mother was not well. For how long had he known that her mind was beginning to crack under the strain of her grief?

Rosalind hesitated uncertainly. She looked close to tears, more pitiful than dangerous.

'Stay there, Richard. Don't make me hurt you. You're all I have since your father left me ... since he deserted me for that whore! Please don't make me hurt you.'

'My father is dead, Mama. He died years ago.'

'No, no ...' She moved her head negatively. 'Henry made me lie to you. Your father went off with another woman ... a rich, young woman. He wrote once asking to see you ... he wanted you to live with him but I didn't tell you. I couldn't let you go to him ... you must see that, Richard? You must see that I had to keep you here ... because it was all going to be yours one day. I planned it that way ...'

'My father is alive?' Richard's face drained of colour, disbelief and then anger in his eyes. He seemed not to have heard the rest of her words.

471

'You've lied to me all these years ... he wanted me ... my father wanted me ...'

I heard the pain in his voice: the pain of a young boy's loss.

'Henry made me ...' Rosalind's voice was rising to a whine of self-pity now, her hand trembling. She used her left hand to support the right but was shaking so hard that the gun wobbled. 'Don't look at me like that, Richard. It was all for you ... Henry promised to look after us. He has cheated us but I'll make him sorry. I'm going to kill her ... I have to kill her, don't you see? It's the only way to punish him for what he has done ... the suffering ... the slights ... the shame ...' Rosalind swung the gun back towards me. She was obviously about to fire, her face wild with hatred and the madness that had finally overwhelmed her.

I should have died then if Richard had not lunged at her, bringing her down. I stood watching in horror as they struggled on the floor in front of me. I knew I ought to run for help but I was numbed, frozen to the spot, unable to move or cry out. Suddenly the gun went off and Richard lay still.

'Richard!' A wail of grief broke from Rosalind. She knelt by his side, running her hands over his face in a frenzy, trying to stop the blood oozing from the wound in his chest with her fingers, sobbing wildly. She flung herself on his body, embracing him like a lover. 'Richard, don't die ... don't leave me. Please, don't leave me. It was all for you ... all for you ... You can't leave me. You can't ...' She was sobbing, tears streaming down her face. Her screams rose higher and higher as she rocked back and forth in an outpouring of grief and madness.

'Let me send for the doctor.'

Rosalind became aware of me once more as I moved. 'You!' she screamed. 'This is all your fault. I'll kill you. I'll kill you ...' She snatched at the gun but before she could reach it Alexi chopped at the back of her neck with the side of his hand and she collapsed unconscious in a heap beside Richard's body.

I had seen Alexi enter the room a split second earlier but had not dared to show my relief. Now I ran to his arms.

'Is she dead?' I asked, shuddering as I looked down at Rosalind. 'Oh, Alexi—it was terrible. She is mad ... insane.'

'Not dead. Just unconscious. I used a disabling blow—though it might have been kinder to put her out of her misery. She'll rot in an asylum for the rest of her life, as perhaps she deserves.' He knelt down beside Richard. 'She shot her own son.'

'Richard tried to save me ...'

Someone came rushing in. It was Caroline, looking pale and frightened. Her eyes widened in horror as she saw both Richard and his mother lying on the floor.

'My God!' she cried. 'I knew I was right. I made Rupert bring me down. He didn't want to but I was sure it was Rosalind who fired those shots—and I know she hit me. I remembered the scent ...'

'You remembered her perfume? I did too, just

this evening. It was her all the time, Caro. She put the lilies in your kitchen ... she did it all ... everything.'

'It came back to me quite suddenly,' my cousin said. 'I knew it had to be Rosalind who had hit me. I tried to warn you, Lizzie, but she answered the telephone when I rang Pentire earlier today. She wouldn't let me speak to anyone else. She sounded so odd that I was worried and there was no way of warning you. I've been frantic all the way down here, afraid I would be too late ...' The words came tumbling out of her in a rush. 'I thought she would try to kill you because you had left Richard.'

'She almost succeeded.' I put a hand to my mouth as the full horror of what Rosalind had done came over me and I began to shake uncontrollably. 'She was going to kill me but Richard stopped her. I don't know if she meant to hurt him. I think the gun just went off as they struggled ...'

Alexi was bending over Richard, searching for a pulse. He had kicked the gun across the room in case Rosalind came round and made a grab for it. Caroline stooped to pick it up in her gloved hand.

'You'd best put that thing somewhere safe until the police get here—and tell Barker to phone them.' Alexi summoned her back as she was about to leave. 'Wait! Get the doctor first. I think there is a faint pulse. I'll do what I can to stop the bleeding but he needs urgent medical help.'

Richard was still alive! Thank God.

I pulled up my skirt and ripped off my cotton underslip, watching as Alexi used part of it as padding and then tore the rest into strips to bind Richard tightly.

'Is he going to die?' I felt a tightness in my chest. 'He saved my life ... he saved my life, Alexi.'

Alexi finished his task and stood up. 'He will die if we can't stop the bleeding,' he said. 'I've done my best but I've seen cases like this in the war and ... we can only pray for him.'

'Poor Richard,' I whispered. 'Poor, poor Richard.'

I had suspected him of so many things and now he was close to death, because he had saved my life.

It seemed an eternity before the police finally left. Richard was already in hospital, fighting for his life, and Rosalind had been sedated and taken away to a secure sanatorium.

'She was insane,' Caroline said when the family were at last alone in Henry's study. 'Completely mad.'

A rug had been pulled over the bloodstains on the carpet but there was no shutting out what had happened.

'She must have been cracking up for ages. I'd noticed she seemed a bit odd for a while, and when I was in hospital I knew there was something I ought to remember—but I wasn't sure what it was until I caught a whiff of that strong lavender pot-pourri in the reception area. That triggered something, and then I realized

475

what it reminded me of. I remembered smelling her perfume just before she hit me.'

'She had been in the flat the day you met me outside,' I said. 'I smelled something then but didn't realize what it meant. She sent me that letter to frighten me then knew she dare not let anyone else see it—so she used her key when I was out to retrieve it.

'I wondered at the time but thought I was being unfair to her.' Caroline looked at me. 'When I realized she was trying to kill us both, I tried to warn you but Rosalind answered the phone and told me everything was all right. She insisted that Henry didn't want me to come down. I made Rupert bring me but I should have been too late if Richard hadn't ...' She stopped and shuddered. Rupert reached for her hand and she smiled at him.

As I saw the look that passed between them I knew that my cousin was happy again; she and Rupert had clearly made up their quarrel.

Henry had heard all the commotion and insisted on coming down to join us after the police left, so Alexi carried him and he was comfortably ensconced in his favourite highbacked chair with a rug over his knees.

'I suspected something,' he admitted, shaking his head sorrowfully as he looked round at his family. 'But I just couldn't believe it was her. I thought Richard might be up to something but I ought to have known—he was always inclined to be weak, to take the easy way. My fault, I suspect. We spoiled him from birth, Rosalind and me. Poor silly woman. I never dreamed she felt that way about Pentire. I can't remember ever having promised it to her. Surely I didn't? She must have deluded herself into thinking it was going to be hers.'

'Richard wasn't weak this evening,' I said, my voice tight and strained. 'He saved my life. If it hadn't been for him, Rosalind would have killed me. She was too far gone to realize she wouldn't get Pentire whatever she did.'

'I thought I had put a stop to it all this afternoon,' Henry said. 'But it seems I just pushed her over the edge.'

'It's probably just as well.' We all looked at Caroline as she spoke. 'It brought everything to a head. She might have picked us off one by one if ... well, she might. Lizzie said she heard something that night she went down to Winspear. That could have been Rosalind trying to get in and I could have died if I hadn't been found. I'm glad it's all over and finished ...' She blushed as Rupert gave her a meaningful look. 'I mean, I'm sorry about Richard but ...'

'I'm going to ring the hospital,' I said in a choked voice. 'Excuse me. I'll be back in a moment.'

Caroline followed me out into the hall a few moments later as I was replacing the receiver.

'What do they say?'

'Just that he is undergoing an operation to remove the bullet.' I choked back a sob. 'I feel so guilty, Caro. If Richard dies ...'

'Don't be an idiot,' she said. 'It wasn't your fault.'

'If I hadn't come to Pentire ...'

'She might have concentrated all her efforts on me. And she would probably have succeeded, sooner or later.'

'Oh, Caroline.'

'Richard will survive,' she said. 'Stop worrying about him, Lizzie. Just because he saved your life, he hasn't suddenly become a saint.'

'No, I don't suppose so.' I looked at her. She was glowing. 'You've got something to tell me, haven't you?'

'I wanted you to be the first to know.' She held out her left hand. 'Rupert made me take it off for a while but I wanted to show you. I'm so happy, Lizzie.'

She was wearing a magnificent ruby and diamond ring on the third finger of her left hand.

'I'm so pleased for you, Caro. It's wonderful news.'

'Rupert told me he realized that nothing else mattered when he was down in the sea. He suddenly discovered that it was very important to him that he survived—because of me. We might not be able to have children but I've told him I don't care. I told him all I wanted was to be with him ... and when he thought he might die he realized that loving each other, being together, was the only thing that really mattered.'

I kissed and hugged her.

'I'm so very, very glad for you, dearest.'

'Henry wants to talk to you alone, Lizzie. He has sent all the others off and asked me to find you.'

478

'Thank you.'

I went into the study. My grandfather was sitting alone, staring into the fire. He looked tired and very ill, his skin an odd grey colour. My heart caught with fright. All this had been too much for him. I went to kneel at his side and he looked down at me, placing his hand on my head. He was very sad.

'I didn't realize how much Rosalind had come to hate me.'

'She must have been ill in her mind for a long time.'

'Yes, a very long time. I see that now.'

'You know that she confessed to killing Selina?' He nodded and sighed heavily. 'That must have been the start of her illness—because she was ill.'

'All these years.' He shook his head as if it was almost too much for him to bear. 'When Selina died, I did wonder ... but I could never bring myself to believe it. Rosalind always seemed so devoted to her ... to the family.'

'Perhaps she was at one time,' I said to comfort him. 'I think it all began to change after she lost her baby.'

'I shouldn't have let her bury him there in the woods. It was what she wanted but it was wrong,' he said. 'I should have insisted on bringing it all out into the open then. If I had, perhaps none of this would have happened.'

'You didn't want to hurt her,' I said, and kissed his hand. 'Or Selina. You did what you thought was right at the time.'

'Rosalind was so afraid of what people would

think: she was my nephew's wife; the relationship was almost incestuous, and she was a respectable woman. It was my fault. If I hadn't ...' Henry's hand trembled in mine. 'I knew she had started taking flowers to the woods again. I thought it had stopped long ago ... but it started again just before you married Richard. I should have guessed that something was wrong with her then. To think she was capable of such evil ...'

'Rosalind's madness came on her slowly,' I said. 'She must have become bitter against Selina after the child was born dead and then, when my grandmother threatened to send her away, Rosalind pushed her down the stairs.' I gazed up at him. 'Think how that must have preyed on her mind over the years: to know that she had murdered a woman of whom she had once been fond.'

'It was my fault. All my fault. I should have seen, been more aware, but I was only concerned with building up the business, with making more and more money ... and for what? My money is tarnished gold, Lizzie. I became rich but I destroyed everything I loved ... everything that really mattered.'

'No, you mustn't say that.' I held his hand tightly. 'I love you. You made mistakes but you've paid for them, over and over again. Please don't blame yourself for what happened.'

'You're a good girl, Lizzie.' He smiled down at me. 'Grigory would definitely have approved of you, my dear.'

I sensed that Henry would have liked Grigory's approval for himself; that much of his striving had been because of his need to achieve a good life for his family, to build on what his grandfather had given him through his own suffering. Henry had tried so hard to become rich and respected, and it must seem that all his efforts, all his work, had brought nothing but pain to those he loved.

I bent to kiss his cheek, feeling my love flow out to him. He needed me more than he would ever say and I would not desert him.

'Let Alexi carry you up now, dearest,' I said. 'You need to rest.'

'Very well,' he accepted with a smile for me. Then his smile was replaced by a slight frown. 'What are you going to do about Richard, Lizzie, if he lives? He may well be an invalid for the rest of his life.'

'I know.' I squeezed his hand. 'Don't worry about it now, Grandfather. I'll ask Alexi to take you upstairs.'

I was alone in the study, standing looking out at the night and the dark shimmer of the lake, when Alexi came back from helping Henry. I turned to smile at him, trying to hide my doubts and fears.

'How is he?'

'Barker is seeing to him. He is very tired—but Henry is strong, Lizzie. He will pull through this.'

'Yes, perhaps.'

I turned away to look out at the lake once more. The moon had come out and it looked vast, dark and silvered, mysterious. I shivered

481

as I remembered what had happened out there in the woods.

Alexi was aware of my unease. 'You are worrying about Richard, aren't you?' he asked, his gaze fixed on my face.

'Yes.' I caught back a sob. 'I feel guilty. He saved my life, Alexi. If he dies ...'

'It won't be your fault. You mustn't torture yourself, Lizzie.'

He was right, of course, but I couldn't help myself.

'I just feel that I ought to have done something ... that I should have realized before it came to this. I've been blaming Richard for so many things but I should have known it was Rosalind, that she was ill. The signs were there if I had only looked.'

'No one else saw it and they all knew her much better than you. Besides, I don't believe you could have stopped it. This has been building up for years—the jealousy, the hatred and bitterness—it was all there beneath the surface, waiting to boil over.'

'Yes, I know,' I sighed as he reached out for me, taking me in his arms. 'Alexi?'

'Yes, my darling?'

'You know that I can't come to Paris with you?'

'I don't have to go.'

'Yes, you must. I want you to go.' I gazed up at him earnestly. 'It is important for your work and ...'

He stared down at me, features becoming hard and unyielding. 'This has something to do with Richard, hasn't it?'

'Yes.' I moved away from him, turning to look out of the window once more. 'He may need nursing for the rest of his life ... if he survives.'

'A nurse can be found. No, Lizzie. I won't let you do this.'

I turned and saw the anger in his face.

'I can't walk away from him now,' I said. 'You must see that? Please, you must try to understand. I meant to leave Richard but now ... I can't.'

As I saw the look in Alexi's eyes, it was as though a knife had entered my heart. He was angry with me ... bitter and angry.

'Please, you must understand,' I begged.

'No,' he said. 'No, I don't understand, Lizzie. It seems to me that you are determined to punish yourself—and that is something I cannot condone.'

He looked at me for several minutes with dark, accusing eyes then turned and walked from the room, leaving me to stare after him.

Chapter 23

'There are some letters for you in the hall, madam,' Mrs Barker smiled at me as I came downstairs that morning. Since her niece's funeral, which I had attended with her, we had become much closer, more like friends than mistress and employee. 'The post was late this morning but better late than never.'

'Yes, much better.'

She was recovering from the shock of Sarah's death, though I sometimes saw her sitting alone in her herb garden, staring at nothing, and knew she had been crying.

I picked up the bundle of letters waiting for me and took them into the study. Quite a few were to do with the business and I would discuss them with my grandfather later; Henry was spending the morning in bed, though he would come down for lunch. He was getting steadily better, but his doctor had warned me I must not let him slip back into his old ways.

'He thinks he's a young man, Mrs Gregory. You must make him take things more easily. He doesn't need to work at his age.'

Easy to say but not so easy to achieve. Henry would always want his own way and we often argued, but never in anger. There was too much love between us for that.

I slit open the first envelope, reading the letter through several times before laying it aside and going to look out of the window at my favourite view. How beautiful the lake was, how serene and peaceful in the spring sunshine.

The letter was from the nursing home and its contents had made me uneasy; it was a request from the Matron for me to come and see her before I visited Richard again.

Three months had passed since he had saved my life—three long, lonely, painful months in which he had clung to life with a surprising tenacity. I visited him at least three times every week. At first he lay in a daze and did not know me, but then, as he came out of the fever he became very dependent, clinging to my hands and begging me not to leave him.

'I need you, Lizzie,' he said over and over again, tears running down his cheeks. 'Please don't leave me ... please let me come home to you and Henry. I don't want to stay here.'

The doctors had told us that Richard would never walk again. The bullet had gone right through him, damaging his lungs and his spine. He would always be an invalid, always need constant nursing.

It was history repeating itself. I could see the way it would be when he was well enough to leave the nursing home: him in a wheelchair, becoming more and more bitter with the passing of the years, me tied to him by guilt and remorse.

'We shall take you home as soon as we can,' I had promised him on my last visit. 'I can't pretend to love you, Richard. That part of our marriage was over before. But I shall take care of you. I shall never leave you.'

It was the only thing I could say in the circumstances. How could I leave Richard now? Even if Alexi still wanted me ...

He had been three months in Paris ... three months during which I had heard nothing from him. It was as if he had walked out of my life and it was breaking my heart.

I felt as if there was a grey mist all around me, invading my mind, threatening to creep in and overwhelm me. I was alone, frightened, vulnerable. The future loomed dark and empty.

Something else hovered at the edges of my mind. Something I had tried very hard to put aside. Something I would not let myself think about, because if I did I should not be able to bear my life.

For three months I had been living in a kind of daze, moving from one moment to the next without daring to hope for more than the strength to carry on—but that morning the rooks had come back to nest and the sound of their raucous cries had somehow lifted my spirits. Somehow I would face the empty years. Somehow I would make a life for myself, Henry and Richard.

'I'm glad you came to see me, Mrs Gregory.' Matron invited me to sit in her office. 'I wanted to warn you before you saw your husband.'

'Is he worse?'

'I'm afraid his condition has taken a downward turn since you were last here. We were hopeful for a while ... he seemed to be holding his own ... but it is his lungs. I'm afraid the damage has proved too great.'

'What are you saying? Is he dying?'

'We think it is a matter of days now.'

'No ... no!' I felt overcome with guilt. I did not want Richard to die like this. 'Is there nothing anyone can do ... nothing at all?'

She looked at me with pity. She must think me such a tragic case—so young to be widowed.

'I'm afraid not. I'm so sorry, Mrs Gregory.

I wanted to warn you before you went in to see him.'

Richard was lying against a great pile of pillows, his eyes closed as if sleeping, but he opened them as I approached and smiled at me. He held his hand out to me and I took it. The flesh had wasted; it felt thin and fragile and I held it gently, afraid of causing him pain.

'Have they told you?'

'Richard ...' I looked into his eyes and realized there was no point in lying. 'I'm sorry ... so very sorry.'

'Don't be, Liz. It's probably for the best.' He spoke with difficulty, his breathing laboured.

'No.' I felt the tears begin to slide down my cheeks. 'No, Richard. If it hadn't been for you ...'

'You saved my life and I saved yours,' he said with an odd little smile. 'That was probably the only decent thing I ever did.'

'Richard ...'

'No, don't let's pretend,' he said. 'I want to be honest with you, Liz. There's something you should know about Sarah ...'

'No, Richard.' I didn't want him to tell me. I didn't want to know what had happened that day in the woods. This was the thing I had been trying to forget for the past three months ... the thing that haunted me both in my dreams and my waking thoughts. 'Please, don't.'

'I met Sarah that evening,' he said, grabbing my hand as I gave a cry and turned away. 'Please hear me out, Liz. I have to tell you. I

487

need to tell you. I was angry ... angry because she had told you about Lily. I thought it was the reason you had decided to leave me.'

I shook my head. 'No, Richard. That wouldn't have mattered if you had ever really loved me.'

'But I do love you, Liz. I thought I still wanted Caro but these past weeks ...' He stopped as if he found it difficult to breathe. I could see he was in pain.

'Don't say anymore, Richard. Just rest. It doesn't matter.'

'But it *does* matter. It's because I care about you that I want you to know, Liz. I met Sarah and we quarrelled. I hit her and she scratched my face. I hit her again and my ring flew off ... it's out there somewhere in the woods.' He took my hand, holding it so tightly that I winced. 'I killed her, Liz. I didn't mean to, please believe me. I don't know what got into me. We were shouting at each other and then my hands were round her throat and ...' He lay back against the pillows, his face white, exhausted by the effort. 'I killed her. It terrified me afterwards and I couldn't hide it from you. You knew something was wrong that day I fetched you from Winspear, didn't you?' I nodded and he closed his eyes for a moment. 'Sometimes I think I must be as crazy as my mother.'

'That was different, Richard. She was ill. You were angry. You lost your temper ...'

I felt the sickness swirling inside me. I had known there was something and yet I had tried to put it out of my mind, tried not to listen to the prompting of the little voice in my subconscious.

I looked at him. He was watching me intently. 'Why are you telling me this?'

'Because I know you,' he said. 'I know you are feeling guilty over what happened to me ... I don't want you to grieve for me, Liz. I want you to be happy ... after I've gone. I'm setting you free, Liz. I'm setting you free ... because I do love you.'

'Oh, Richard,' I said, and the tears began to roll down my cheeks. 'Oh, Richard ...'

I stood in the woods. It was cold and the light was fading. I did not know what had brought me here to this spot, but I had come and I knew that this was where they had found Sarah's poor, battered body.

Suddenly it was happening around me, just as it had that night, the night Sarah was killed. I saw her running towards me through the trees, the branches whipping into her face, tearing at her, catching her hair as they had in my dreams. I felt her fear, smelled it, tasted it on my tongue and I cried out, screaming to her to run faster.

It was too late. Richard was there beside her. He caught her and they struggled and then something flew through the air and landed in the debris on the floor of the wood.

Sarah was lying there on the ground, her dead eyes staring up at me, begging me to help her.

'I'm sorry ...' I cried. 'I'm sorry.

'You could have saved me ...'

'Please ... forgive me ...'

Suddenly she was gone and I was alone in the woods. The wind howled about me, sounding like a soul in torment

I looked down and saw Richard's ring, gleaming amongst the undergrowth. I bent down to retrieve it and it seemed to burn my hand. I gasped and let it fall to the ground ... and then I woke up with tears on my cheeks.

It was just the dream again. The dream that would torment me for so many nights to come. Now, when it was too late, I understood.

'Oh, Richard ...' I wept. 'Richard ...'

I looked for the ring that afternoon—the day after Richard's funeral—but I could not find it. I did not know the exact spot where the murder had occurred. Only in my dreams was I able to find it, to hold the ring in my hand. And perhaps that was best.

Richard's ring was lost and I did not want to find it.

I had told no one of his confession. There seemed no point in distressing Henry over something that was beginning to fade from his mind. He knew now that Richard had had a child; he had made provision for Lily—a trust fund that would see her through school—and he had told Mrs Barker she must have the child to the house whenever she wished.

I myself had given her one of Wolfie's pups. I was making friends with her, slowly but surely. I would do my best to see that she had a good life. Perhaps it wasn't enough, but what good could it do to tell her or anyone else the truth? Sarah's husband had been unfairly branded as a murderer, but he was dead and Richard's confession could not help him.

Perhaps one day, when Lily was older, I might tell her; she might be able to understand then, but not now. She knew that both her mother and father were dead. Surely that was enough for any child to cope with?

It wasn't cold in the woods that afternoon, but I had been gone some time and Henry would be waiting for me. I turned homeward, walking quickly. He would be worrying ...

As I reached the front lawn someone came out of the house and started to walk towards me. I stopped and stared. At first I could not believe it, then my heart gave a joyful leap and I began to run towards him.

'Alexi ... Alexi ...' He caught me up in his arms, holding me as if he would never let me go. 'Lizzie ... my darling ... my love.'

I gazed up at him. 'I've missed you so.'

'I wanted to come before but Henry told me he would send for me when the time was right.'

'Henry said that?'

Alexi touched my face so lovingly. 'We both knew that you had to have time—time to grieve, time to come to terms with what had happened.' He looked into my eyes. 'Is it time, Lizzie?'

'Oh, yes,' I said. 'Oh, yes, Alexi.'

Alexi held me in his arms, kissing me, holding

me as if he would never let me go. I closed my eyes, letting the waves of love and longing wash over me like a healing balm.

'I thought you would never come back.'

I looked up at him, my eyes moist with tears of happiness

'Surely not?' he said, his fingertips caressing my cheek. 'Surely you knew that I would come back and claim you? You must have known, Lizzie? You must have known that I would come ...'

'Yes,' I sighed as I surrendered to the clamouring of my own senses. 'Yes, in my heart I believed.'

And suddenly I knew it was true. Somewhere, deep down inside me, I had known he would not let me go. He was mine; I was his—and that was the way it would always be.

We were all in Henry's study. He had asked us to join him after dinner. He sat staring into the fire for a while, seemingly lost in thought, then he glanced up.

'Lizzie girl, would you oblige me by getting something from the safe?' He took a key from his waistcoat pocket. 'You know where it is. Just lift the picture down.' He nodded as I obliged. 'There's a black box and a newspaper cutting. Bring them here, will you?'

I did as he asked and he took the box, opening it to show Alexi the contents. 'Recognize it? The Paulinski necklace ... belonged to your mother.'

It was the magnificent diamond necklace he

had shown me once before!

Alexi frowned, hesitated, then looked at him. 'I think it could have been but I can't be certain. I've only seen it in her portrait—and that was years ago.'

'Your father had it made for your mother as a wedding gift. I had the pleasure of designing it for her—a beautiful woman.' Henry paused and sighed. 'Years later your father wanted it altered to fit his mistress. He brought it to me and ... it was stolen from my safe in this room.' He handed Alexi a piece of faded newspaper. 'All the details are here.'

'Yes, I know.'

'You knew?' Henry's brow furrowed.

'I once made a few inquiries. You paid my father compensation at the time.'

'A lot less than it is worth today.' Henry closed the box and held it out to Alexi. 'In fact, it was stolen by Richard's father. He was a rogue through and through. I knew but could do nothing about it—for Rosalind's sake. I managed to recover it some years later but I couldn't make the fact known—it would have created a scandal, and I cared about those things then.' He paused, rubbing his chest. 'Well, now I'm returning it to its rightful owner.'

'That's very good of you, sir, but I can't accept it.'

Henry's brows shot up. 'You know it could fetch seven, eight thousand pounds—maybe more at the right auction?'

'It does not belong to me. I could not repay the compensation you paid to my father.'

'Have I asked you to?' Henry said a little testily. 'For God's sake, Alexi, can't you take it without all this fuss? You can sell it, build a foundry and import all the craftsmen you need from wherever you like. Think, man—think what it could mean to you.'

Alexi was silent for a moment. 'I could sell it and repay you the compensation then use whatever is left.'

'It's yours, damn it,' Henry said. 'Do whatever you like, you stiff-necked fool—but don't go away again and make my girl unhappy!'

'Thank you, sir.' Alexi smiled at me, holding out his hand. 'I think I can promise you that at least.'

'Thank you, Grandfather,' I said, and kissed his cheek before I went to Alexi and took his hand. 'We are going to be married as soon as we can arrange it.'

'I should think so, too,' he said. 'If that man of yours is too proud to accept my offer, I'll give you the damned necklace as a wedding gift!'

'Alexi will sell it and the original compensation can be paid to Saree for her mission,' I said, laughing as I saw their stubborn faces. They were both proud men. Neither of them was prepared to give way. 'That should satisfy both of you.'

'Got a mind of her own, my girl,' Henry said and there was a gleam in his eye. 'I hope you know what you're taking on, my boy?'

'Oh, yes,' Alexi said with a smile for me. 'Oh, yes, sir. I know exactly what I'm doing.'

The rooks have finished nesting in the tree outside my window and their young are ready to fly. The sound of their cries drew me from my bed early this morning ... the morning of my wedding.

As I look out of my window towards the woods, the sun is shining and the shadows have gone. I am no longer afraid to be happy.

If my dreams had been clearer I might have averted at least a part of what happened—but perhaps it was meant to be. It all began long before I came to Pentire. Long before I stopped to watch the swans that sunny afternoon.

I do not believe that Richard was evil. He was weak and spoilt, but not evil. What happened in the woods was a terrible thing ... but perhaps if he had not been brought up to expect his share of the Caulder inheritance it would never have come about.

Richard saved my life. He freed me from guilt and I shall never forget him. He was my first love—a naive girl's dream. Alexi is my true love and it is a woman's love that I feel for him.

Poor Rosalind's madness came on her slowly. I think she has paid a harsh price for her wickedness and in my heart I am able to feel sympathy for her despite all the terrible things she did.

Now that the curse has been lifted from our family I believe the future holds a bright promise for all of us. Wealth can be an evil thing if used unwisely, but it can also bring good. Whenever I can, I shall use it to bring happiness to those who are less fortunate than I.

This Large Print Book for the Partially sighted, who cannot read normal print, is published under the auspices of

THE ULVERSCROFT FOUNDATION

THE ULVERSCROFT FOUNDATION

. . . we hope that you have enjoyed this Large Print Book. Please think for a moment about those people who have worse eyesight problems than you . . . and are unable to even read or enjoy Large Print, without great difficulty.

You can help them by sending a donation, large or small to:

**The Ulverscroft Foundation,
1, The Green, Bradgate Road,
Anstey, Leicestershire, LE7 7FU,
England.**
or request a copy of our brochure for more details.

The Foundation will use all your help to assist those people who are handicapped by various sight problems and need special attention.

Thank you very much for your help.